CW00833293

SCI FI
TWO BOOK
BUNDLE

Two More You Say Which Way Adventures

Secrets of Glass Mountain
&
Volcano of Fire

by:

BLAIR POLLY & DM POTTER

ISBN-13: 978-1519716743
ISBN-10: 1519716745

How This Book Works

- These stories depends on YOU.

- YOU say which way the story goes.

- What will YOU do?

At the end of each chapter, you get to make a decision. Turn to the page that matches your choice. **P62** means turn to page 62.

There are many paths to try. You can read them all over time. Right now, it's time to start the story. Good luck.

Oh, and watch out for shape shifting plants and morph rats!

Which book would you like to read first?

- Secrets of Glass Mountain. **P1**

- Volcano of Fire . **P163**

Secrets of Glass Mountain

In the beginning.

With the screech of diamonds on smooth black rock, a troop of Highland Sliders comes skidding to a stop ten yards from you and your schoolmates.

"That's what I want to do when I leave school," says Dagma. "Being a Highland Slider looks like so much fun."

Another classmate shakes his head. "Yeah, but my cousin went mining and struck it rich on his first trip out. Now he owns two hydro farms and his family live in luxury."

You look around the small settlement where you grew up. It's a beautiful place, high on the Black Slopes of Petron. Far below, past the sharp ridges and towering pinnacles, the multicolored fields of the Lowlands stretch off into the distance. At the horizon, a pink moon sits above a shimmering turquoise sea.

But the beauty isn't enough to keep you here. You could never be a farmer or a merchant. You've always dreamed of travel and adventure.

Maybe mining is the right thing to do.

You imagine heading off into the wild interior looking for diamonds and the many secrets these glass mountains contain. Imagine striking it rich!

Or do you become a slider like so many others from your family? What would happen to your home without the protection of the Highland Sliders? How would people move around the dangerous slopes from settlement to settlement without their expert guidance? And who would stop the Lowlanders from invading?

Your part in this story is about to begin.

You will leave school at the end of the week and it's time for you to choose your future.

It is time to make your first decision. Do you:

Start cadet training to become a slider? **P3**

Or

Go to mining school so you can prospect for diamonds? **P57**

You have decided to start cadet training to become a slider.

"Eyes front, cadets!" the uniformed officer yells. "If you are going to become sliders you'd better listen like your life depends on it, because believe me, it does." The officer stamps a heavy boot for effect and scans your group "You've all made it through basic training, now it's time to see if you have what it takes to become true Highland sliders."

You knew this part of cadet training was going to be tough, but this officer looks like he eats black glass for breakfast. His dome shaped skull is covered in scars and half his right ear is missing.

You squirm on the hard stone bench and give the girl next to you a weak smile. The room is full of young cadets and like you, they all look a little scared.

Your stomach feels like it is full of moon moths. You cross your fingers and hope you won't let your family down.

"Right, you lot, I want to see you all at the top of the training slope in ten minutes. Anyone who's not there when the bell goes may as well slide right over and enroll in mining school. Now let's go cadets, move it!"

You stand up and quick march out of the room with the others. You've seen the training area from below with its shadowed gullies, crevasses, and sharp ridges, but you are about to look down upon its glistening black slopes for the first time.

You are third to arrive. You check the strap leading from your tow clamp to the belt of your harness and make sure everything is connected properly. As you line up for the tow, more moths have come to join their friends fluttering in your belly.

You point your front foot forward, and engage the metal rod that locks your boots together to form a stable platform for you to slide on. Then you bend your knees in readiness for a high-speed, uphill ride.

The towpath looks slightly damp and you know the black rock will be slipperier than the smoothest ice. The towline whirls around a big, motorized wheel downhill from where you are standing before it extends up the mountainside and disappears into a purple fog. You know there is another wheel at the top that takes the cable and sends it back down the hill again, but you won't be able to see that one until you've gained some altitude.

After flipping your tow clamp over the rapidly moving cable you gradually squeeze its handles together and slowly increase the pressure. Before you know it you are accelerating. The cable hums and vibrates as it drags you uphill. Wind whistles across your visor and around your helmet. You taste the dampness of the mist.

The two cadets on the towline ahead of you stand with knees slightly bent, their front feet pointed forward, their back feet angled slightly to one side. Lock-rods hold their boots just the right distance apart for maximum control. But despite months of training on the simulator, their knees still wobble a little.

You are a little unsteady on your feet too, but you figure this is caused as much by nervous anticipation as anything. When you relax a little, you find you do better. Fighting the tow just makes your leg muscles ache. You remember what the instructors have said about letting the cable do the work. You lean back into your harness and let it take your weight. As you do, you feel your legs relax.

You feel every bump and irregularity through the soles of your boots as you slide along, allowing you to make subtle corrections of balance. You must keep alert to remain upright.

The fog thins as you gain altitude. The top wheel comes into view and you know that in the next twenty seconds or so you will have to disengage your tow clamp and slide off the path onto the staging area. A clean dismount is all a matter of timing.

There are instructors at the top of the hill ready to grade your efforts. You disengage your tow clamp, hook it over a loop on your utility belt and spread your arms slightly to stay balanced.

You shoot off the tow a bit hot, but adjust your speed by lifting the toe of your leading foot a little, dragging the spike fitted to your heel into the rocky slope. A high-pitched squeal fills the air as the diamond digs into the surface and slows you down.

When you come to a stop, you release your back foot, kick the lock-rod back into the sole of your boot and stand to attention.

"Well done, cadet," an instructor says. "You've been listening to the lectures I see."

"Thank you sir," you say, snapping off a quick salute.

With a screech, the next cadet slides in and stands beside you. Others cadets arrive at the staging area every ten seconds or so until there are three rows of ten cadets standing shoulder to shoulder.

The cadet next to you is a tall boy with clear blue eyes. "Ready for the slide of your life?" he says with confidence.

You nod to the boy. "I think so. Bit late now if I'm not."

You are as ready as you will ever be. After all, you have been training for this day for the last year with classes during the day and practice on the simulator every night. You've had guide stick training, terrain training, balance training, combat training. You've studied geometry, navigation and communications. Now it's time to put everything into practice and have your first run under real conditions.

"Right cadets, it is time to show us what you're made of," the training officer says. He takes a step forward and points to the scars on his head. "I got these on my first run when I missed a turn and ended up crashing into the lip of an overhanging ridge. If you think my head looks bad, you should have seen the helmet I was wearing. I suggest you concentrate so you don't make a similar mistake." The officer looks along the line. "First one to the bottom will be promoted to troop leader. Are you ready?"

"Yes sir!" the cadets yell in unison.

"Right, line up and get ready to slide."

Shuffling forward, you stand near the edge, ready to leap off the narrow shelf onto the much steeper slope below. You look left, then right.

You've gotten to know the strengths and weaknesses of each cadet over the months of basic training. Your strongest competition is a stocky girl named Dagma from a neighboring community. Dagma doesn't like to finish second.

Gagnon, a tall boy with short spiky hair and pale green eyes nods in your direction. "Good luck," he says.

"Luck's got nothing to do with it." Dagma snarls. "Sliding is about skill. If you're going to rely on luck you should take up mining."

You look at Gagnon, and roll your eyes. Dagma can be such a grunter at times.

"Lock boots!" the instructor orders.

You release the lock-bar from the sole of your left boot and attach it to a fitting near the instep of your right. You hear a satisfying click as it snaps into place. You now have a rigid platform to slide on.

The instructor hands each of you a guide stick. "These are worth more than you are, so don't lose them."

The guide stick is almost as tall as you are. Its shaft is made from a flexible and incredibly strong wood obtained by trading crystals with the border tribes. Mounted on one end of the shaft is a sturdy blue-diamond hook. On the stick's opposite end is a thick pad of tyranium needle crystals.

The ultra-fine tyranium crystals create friction when dragged on the ground. This friction is used to control a slider's direction and speed when moving down the slope.

You rest the pad end on the ground and immediately feel how the crystals grip the glossy black surface. It's no wonder they are only fractionally less prized than blue diamonds. Without them it would be virtually impossible to travel, harvest eggs from the red-beaked pango colonies, drill mines and reservoirs, or build sleeping and hydro growing pods.

The instructor stands tall and barks out orders. "Are you ready cadets?"

You lower your visor and work your front foot as close to the edge as possible. Gripping the guide stick tightly in both hands, you rest it on the ground behind you. Now, the slightest push will send you plunging down the hill. The other cadets crowd together, bumping shoulders, hoping to achieve the most favorable slide path down the centre of the course.

You look down the run. There are gullies and ridges, knobs and small pillars. Some parts are near vertical, others flatten out only to drop steeply when you least expect it.

The most popular line runs down the side of a steep ridge and then sweeps into a broad valley on the right hand side of the course. At the bottom of the valley it angles back towards the centre, cuts below two small pinnacles and then straightens towards the finish line. All the cadets have studied the course map and know the relative advantages and dangers of the various ways down.

The instructor raises his arm. "On my mark! Ready to drop in five, four, three, two, one…" His arm falls. "Slide!"

With a firm push you are over the edge and sliding. You squat low to create less wind resistance and tap the needle end of your stick to make subtle course corrections.

Dagma's strong push has her leading the pack, sliding smoothly to your right. The other cadets are sticking to her tail, trying to gain advantage by using her bulk as a wind shield.

Gagnon is near the front as well, sliding effortlessly, but unless Dagma makes a mistake it will be hard to pass her. It looks as though the other cadets have chosen to take the conventional and less risky route down the mountain.

You've seen the times posted on the classroom wall and know the winner of this race for the last three years has taken this route. But you also know that crowded slopes are dangerous. Each year at least one cadet has been badly injured after being bumped off course.

During your study of the map, you've seen an untried route that runs between the two small pinnacles in the centre of the main face. It's risky, but if you can turn sharply enough, you just might be able to enter the narrow chute at a point above the two small pillars, and take a straighter, faster line to the finish.

However, if you misjudge your timing, and miss the turn into the top of the chute, you could end up in a gulley of dangerous ripples. If that happens and you lose your footing, these ripples will slice you to ribbons.

You are sliding fast. If you are going to try to make the turn you will have to do it now. You've practiced this move plenty of times on the simulator, but in real life conditions, nothing is guaranteed. You look right, then left. It's now or never.

It is time to make a quick decision. Hurry! Do you:

Go for it and try to turn into the chute, despite the danger? **P9**

Or

Follow Dagma and the others and try to win the race using the normal route? **P12**

You have decided to go for the chute despite the danger.

Making sharp turns on a slope of black glass isn't easy. Luckily you've had plenty of practice on the simulator.

You stand up tall and spread your arms. Special pockets of fabric, where your arms meet your torso, catch the wind and slow you down a little. Then you swivel your hips and drop your diamond hook. A three-second drag slows you down even more. Once you've lost enough momentum, you flip your guide stick around and repeatedly stab the ground with the needle crystal end. Each time the crystals hit the surface, you move a little to your left.

Looking ahead, you try to spot the entrance of the narrow chute leading down between the two pinnacles. On the shiny black surface it's difficult to see the contours. It should be coming up about…

You spot it, but you're too far left! More jabs of your stick move you back to the right. As you stare ahead, sweat drips down your forehead into your visor. You are on the correct line now. You crouch to regain speed. Your arms and guide stick are tucked tight to your body.

Flying over the lip at the top of the chute the ground falls away and you lose contact with the slope. As you drop into the steeply angled half-pipe, you rise slightly from your crouch and hold the guide stick out in front of you, using it to help keep your balance. If you are going to win the race, you must stay on your feet.

When your boots touch the ground you drop into a tuck and streamline your body. Momentum takes you up one side of the half-pipe and then gravity brings you back to the bottom.

You are really moving now, going faster than you've ever experienced on the simulator. Wow, what a feeling! You look down the slope. It's a straight run to the bottom.

Moments later, you flash across the finish line and drop your hook. But are you the first to arrive?

"What are you smiling about cadet?" the instructor at the bottom of the course says as you screech to a stop. "You think this is supposed to be fun?"

"Yes sir!"

The instructor scowls at you.

"I mean no sir!"

You hear the sound of diamond hooks above you. When you glance up, you see Dagma in a low crouch, leading the other cadets down the hill.

You've won!

"Congratulations cadet," the instructor says, giving you a mock salute. "Seems you've just earned yourself a promotion."

You can't wait to tell your family. They will be so proud. But you also realize this is only the beginning. You've only made it through basic training. Now the real work begins.

Seconds later, the other cadets are beside you. Some have their hands on their knees panting from exertion.

"Okay cadets, line up," the instructor says. "I'm pleased you've all made it down without incident. I want you to meet your new troop leader."

The instructor waves you forward. You move off the line and come to stand by his side.

"Leaders are only as good as their troop," the instructor says to the assembled cadets. "If you don't work as a team out there on the slopes, none of you will survive a season. You all have strengths and weaknesses. The strongest of you isn't the fastest. The best in navigation isn't the best in communications. You all have a vital part to play in the Slider Corps. Our communities depend on you working together to keep them safe."

The instructor turns to you. It is time to dismiss your troop.

"Right you lot," you say. "Head back to the pod and get ready for our first patrol tomorrow morning at dawn."

As you are about to move off, the instructor places his hand on your shoulder. "Wait," he says. "We have some things to discuss."

As the other cadets enter a narrow portal cut into the black rock, you wonder what the instructor has to tell you.

Once the last cadet has disappeared he turns and gives you a serious look. "You know they look up to you," he says.

Do they really? You know Dagma doesn't. She just sees you as competition, as an obstacle to her rising through the ranks. How is she going to react to your promotion? Will she follow you when the going gets tough, or will she undermine your every move?

"Not all of them sir," you reply.

The instructor raises one eyebrow and scowls. "I know you and Dagma have had your differences, but she's got a lot of skill and determination. You'd do well to give her some respect and see if you can utilize her strengths."

"Yes sir."

"Now it's your choice, but you need to select one of the cadets to be second in charge. Do you know who you'd like?"

It is time for you to make an important decision. Do you:

Choose Dagma to be your second in charge because of her strength? **P16**

Or

Choose Gagnon as your second in charge because he is a good navigator? **P19**

You have decided to follow Dagma and the others.

You see the pinnacles ahead, but realize you are moving too fast to make the turn into the chute. You have no option but to join the other cadets in their crazy slide down the main route.

Dagma is out in the lead due to her strong start, but her size is also creating more wind resistance and you know that if you optimize your stance you can gain some ground on her.

You bend your knees a little more and twist your torso so that you are as thin to the wind as possible. Your elbows are tucked tight to your sides and your guide stick trails behind you, just a fraction off the ground, ready to hook when you need to slow down.

A cadet to your right is trying to snag Dagma's harness with his stick and pull past her, but every time he reaches forward, either the wind catches him and slows him down, or Dagma bats his stick away with her own.

The slope is faster than you'd imagined. You've picked up so much speed you wonder if you'll be able to keep your feet once you hit the more uneven terrain below.

Some of the cadets have already started dragging their hooks, trying to slow themselves down before they sweep around a banked turn and enter a section of the course known as "the jumps".

Although this part of the mountain is not as steep as the slope higher up, it has a series of rounded humps to negotiate. Hit a hump too fast and you lose your balance. Get your timing wrong and you land on the uphill slope of the next hump and twist a knee or an ankle.

Everyone is moving too fast. The first jump is coming up sooner than expected. All around you the screech of hooks is deafening as the other cadets desperately try to slow down. Even Dagma is leaning hard on her hook, trying to reduce speed, before hitting the first jump.

This is your chance.

Rather than dropping your hook, you twist your lower body so that both feet are side by side and the lock-bar between your boots is side-on to the slope, rather than the traditional stance of one foot in front of the other. You bend your knees and get ready to spring up. Now it's just a matter of timing.

Your knees are forced to your chest when you hit the front of the hump. A split second later, as you near its crest, you spring up with all your strength.

The ground falls away as you soar through the air. "Woot, woot!" you yell. "I'm flying!

While holding your guide stick at arm's length in front of your chest, you swivel your lower body back around so your front foot is pointing straight down the hill again. Then you bend your knees a little and get ready for impact.

You've done it! When you make contact with the ground, it is on the downward side of the third jump, having cleared the second one altogether. You force you legs upwards and spring off the crest of the fourth jump and land on the downward side of the last jump with a satisfying swish of boots on rock. You tuck back into your arrow stance and gain even more speed as you race to the finish.

You can't believe how fast you are moving. This is so much faster than on the simulator. The wind is howling. Wow, what a feeling!

You see the finishing flag less than a quarter of a mile ahead. A quick glance back up the hill and you know you've won. The others are well back. One cadet has fallen and is sliding on his backside trying to regain his feet. Dagma is the best of the others, with Gagnon close behind.

You flash across the finish, rise from your crouch and drop your hook, forcing it down hard onto the shiny black surface. You screech to a halt next to an instructor.

"What are you smiling about cadet?" the instructor says. "You think this is supposed to be fun?"

"Yes sir!"

The instructor scowls.

"Well it is sir!"

The instructor's eyes soften as he suppresses a grin. "If you say so, cadet."

You hear the screech of hooks behind you as the others finish. Dagma bangs the ground with her stick in frustration.

"Congratulations," the instructor says, giving you a mock salute. "It seems you've just earned yourself a promotion."

You can't wait to tell your family. They will be so proud. But you also realize this is only the beginning. You've only made it through basic training. Now the real challenge begins.

"Okay line up cadets," the instructor says.

They shuffle into line, breathing hard.

"I'm please you've all made it down without incident. I want you to meet your new troop leader."

The instructor waves you forward. You push your shoulders back and stand by his side.

"Leaders are only as good as the troops they lead," the instructor says. "If you cadets don't work as a team out there on the slopes, none of you will survive a season.

The instructor taps his guide stick on the ground. "Right, head back to your pod and get ready for your first patrol tomorrow morning at dawn."

As you are about to move off, the instructor places his hand on your shoulder. "Wait," he says. "We have a few things to discuss."

You watch as the other cadets enter a portal that has been cut into the sheer black wall and head back towards their accommodation area. You wonder what the instructor has to tell you.

Once the others have gone, the instructor turns and looks into your eyes. "They look up to you," he says.

"Not all of them, sir," you reply.

The instructor raises one eyebrow. "I know you and Dagma have had your differences, but she's got a lot of skill and determination. You'd do well to give her some respect and see if you can utilize her strengths rather than concentrating on her weaknesses."

"Yes sir."

"Now it's your choice, but you need to select one of the cadets to be second in charge. Do you know who you'd like that to be?"

It is time for you to make an important decision. Do you:

Choose Dagma to be your second in charge because of her strength and skills? **P16**

Or

Choose Gagnon as your second in charge because he is a better navigator? **P19**

You have chosen Dagma to be second in charge.

After thinking over what your instructor has said, you realize that you need to find a way to work with Dagma if your troop is going to become a cohesive unit. The sooner you can forget your differences, the better off everyone will be.

"Well?" the instructor says. "Who's it to be?"

You straighten your shoulders. "Dagma will make a good second, sir. The others will follow her without question if I am injured."

"Dagma it is then," the instructor says. "Now get back to your troop. You leave for the Pillars of Haramon at first light."

As you walk through the portal and down the corridor towards the accommodation pods, you take in the significance of what the instructor has just said. The Pillars of Haramon are an advanced base an 80-mile slide from the training ground. You've heard stories and seen pictures of these towering, fortified columns of black glass ever since you were a child. You remember the history lessons you've had about the brave miners who first discovered these diamond-packed volcanic pipes that rise nearly a thousand feet from the shining slopes below, and of the legendary sliders who have protected the outpost over the years.

These days the twin towers of rock are honeycombed with tunnels and chambers and form one of the Highland's strongest and most beautiful fortified positions. Mining still takes place deep beneath the pinnacles, but the above-ground pipes were cleaned out many years ago and now form sleeping, hydro, and defense pods.

As you walk along the corridor, you look up at the ceiling. Circular shafts have been bored to bring light down from the surface. Halfway along the first corridor a junction splits four ways. You turn right and follow the eastern access towards pod 6.

You still can't believe you're going to the Pillars of Haramon. You remember hearing stories about the battles fought against the Lowlanders who have tried to capture them and the rich source of blue diamonds they contain. But generations of Lowlanders have been repelled by the Highland Slider Corps. Many songs have been written about their bravery.

For years now the Lowlanders have been quiet, building up their forces and growing stronger. Everyone knows it is only a matter of time before they attempt another invasion. When that happens, it will be up to you, your troop, and others of the Highland Slider Corps to make sure they don't succeed.

The thought of war does not thrill you. Nobody really wins a war. Even the winning side loses people that can never be replaced. After a few more twists down the tunnels you reach Pod 6E.

The pod has curved walls with a series of notches cut into it. Each notch contains a cubicle complete with bunk and storage space for the cadet's personal effects. In the center there is a seating area with a table, large enough to accommodate the 30 person troop.

"Congratulations," Gagnon says as you enter. "That was a brave move you pulled out there."

"Lucky," Dagma says from the end of the table. "You could have been sliced and diced trying a stunt like that. Was it really worth the risk?"

You turn towards Dagma. "Luck's got nothing to do with it. It was a calculated risk I'll admit, but I've been practicing the move on the simulator."

"So who have you chosen for your second?" Dagma says. "Your friend Gagnon, I suppose."

The troop looks at you expectantly. Twenty-nine sets of eyes are upon you. This is your first act of command. Will they understand?

"I've chosen you, Dagma. You're the strongest across a range of skills. If we can work together I'm sure our troop will be the best to graduate this year. Gagnon will be our advanced scout, because he is our best navigator."

When you look around, you see heads nodding. Gagnon seems happy with his role. The tight muscles in Dagma's face have relaxed a little. You hope it is a sign of her becoming more cooperative.

"Now, hit your bunks," you say. "We leave for the Pillars of Haramon at first light."

This last statement has the troop buzzing. Whispers and comments pass between its members. They too have heard the legends.

"Dagma and Gagnon, would you please come into my cubicle. We need to plan for tomorrow."

Gagnon grabs a map from a drawer in the table and follows Dagma. Once inside, he unfolds the map and sticks it to the wall of your cubicle.

"There are two possible routes to the Pillars," Gagnon says. "Do you want fast or safe?"

After a quick look at the routes, you turn to Dagma. "What do you think?"

"If it was just us three I'd say fast," she says. "But there is always a chance of rain and with a troop of newbies I think we should go for safe. The last thing we need is an accident on our first day out."

Both options have advantages. Fast means you'll spend less time exposed to the elements, which is a good thing, but the safe route will be easier for those with less skill.

It is time for you to make your next decision. Do you:

Choose the slower, easier route to the Pillars of Haramon? **P23**

Or

Choose the fast route and spend less time on the slopes in case of rain? **P30**

You have chosen Gagnon to be second in charge.

You've decided to choose Gagnon to be your second in command because you know he won't undermine your authority. He is also the troop's best navigator which is one of the most important jobs a slider can have.

Many sliders have come to grief because of a simple mistake in navigation. Take the wrong valley and you can end up going over a bluff or into a crevasse, especially in flat light, when the ground's contours are hard to see and cracks in the surface are hidden in shadow.

Sliders navigate by triangulation. The navigator takes sightings from at least three prominent features with a handheld compass. Mountaintops, bluffs, or pinnacles work best. The navigator then transfers these bearings onto the map. Somewhere on the map, these three lines will intersect to form a triangle. Your location will be somewhere inside that triangle.

The more accurate a cadet is when they map out the compass bearings, the smaller that triangle will be. Some cadets are sloppy and always end up with large triangles, while others, like Gagnon, have tiny triangles that show a high level of accuracy.

"Well," the instructor says. "Who's it to be?"

You straighten your shoulders. "Gagnon will make a good second, sir," you say, hoping you've made the right choice. "I think even Dagma will follow his orders without question if I am injured."

"Gagnon it is then," he says. "Now get back to your troop. You leave for the Pillars of Haramon at first light."

As you walk through the portal towards the accommodation pods, you take in the significance of what the instructor has just said.

The Pillars of Haramon is an advanced lookout some eighty miles from the training ground. You've heard stories and seen pictures of these towering pinnacles ever since you were a child. You remember the history lessons you learned at school about the miners who first discovered these diamond packed volcanic pipes rising a thousand feet from the shimmering slopes below and of the legendary sliders who have protected them.

They are honeycombed with tunnels and chambers. These form one of the Highlands strongest and most unusual outposts. Mining still takes place deep underground beneath the Pillars, and many diamonds are still being uncovered, but above-ground the diamonds were cleared out years ago.

Your footsteps echo. Initially the tunnel is lit by light penetrating in from the portal by reflecting off the mirror black surface of the walls. Deeper inside, circular shafts bored into the roof, bring light down from the surface. Your unit's pod is 6-East. Halfway along the first corridor a junction splits four ways. You turn right and follow the eastern access.

You remember hearing stories about the battles fought against the Lowlanders who tried to capture the Pillars and the rich source of blue diamonds they contain. Generations of Lowlanders have been repelled by the Highland Slider Corps and many songs have been written about their bravery.

For years now the Lowlanders have been quiet, building up their forces and growing stronger. It is only a matter of time before they invade again. When that happens, it will be up to you, your troop, and others of the Highland Slider Corps to make sure they don't succeed.

Pod 6E has curved walls. A series of notches are cut into the rock. Each recess contains a bunk and a shelf for storing personal effects. In the center of the pod a table, long enough to accommodate the whole troop takes pride of place.

"Congratulations," Gagnon says as you enter. "That was a brave move you pulled out there."

"Lucky," Dagma says from the end of the table. "You could have been sliced and diced trying a stunt like that. Was it really worth the risk?"

You turn towards Dagma. "It was a calculated risk I'll admit, but

I've been practicing on the simulator more than most. The odds were in my favor."

"So who have you chosen for your second?" Dagma says. "Your friend Gagnon, I suppose."

The troop looks at you expectantly. There is a hum of voices.

"Yes, I've chosen Gagnon. You might be the strongest across a range of skills but with your attitude I'm not sure we can work together."

"But…" Dagma is stunned. It is obvious that she thought she'd win the downhill race, and now she's not even going to be second.

"But I want you to prove me wrong, so I'm going to make you advance scout. Your strength and sliding talent will give us a real advantage if we met Lowlanders. I'm sure if we work together, our troop can be the best to graduate this year."

When you look around, you see heads nodding. Gagnon seems happy with his role. Even the normally strained muscles in Dagma's face have relaxed a little. You've helped her save face by giving her an important role. Perhaps this new responsibility will make her more cooperative.

"Now, get some sleep," you say. "We leave for the Pillars of Haramon at first light."

This last statement has the troop buzzing. Whispers and comments pass between cadets. They too have heard the legends.

"Dagma, Gagnon, come into my cubicle, we need to plan for tomorrow."

Gagnon grabs a map and brings it with him. Dagma follows you and once inside, leans casually against the wall of your cubicle.

"There are two possible routes to the Pillars," Gagnon says, pointing to the map. "Do you want fast or safe? We'll be exposed for a shorter length of time if we take the quicker route."

After studying the map, you look at Dagma. "What do you think?"

"If it was just us three I'd say fast," she says. "But with 30 newbies, I think we should take the slower route. The last thing we need is an accident on our first patrol."

It is time for you to make your next important decision. Do you:

Choose the slower and easier route to the Pillars of Haramon? **P23**

Or

Choose the faster route and spend less time of the slopes in case of rain. **P30**

You have chosen the slower, easier route to the Pillars.

While the cadets sleep, you've been up studying the map. On it Gagnon has marked his suggested route to the Pillars of Haramon. For most of the trip you will traverse the upper slopes on one of the wider, main tracks. But you also want to become familiar with alternative routes in case a change of plan is required.

It's just as well you decided to take the slow route to the Pillars. Moments ago you received orders from Slider Command to take a class of mining students with you.

This seems unusual. You're only cadets yourselves. Why would your superiors give you such a responsibility? Traversing the high tracks will be dangerous enough without having to babysit a bunch of miners on your first patrol.

Even though all Highland children are given needle-boots as soon as they are old enough to toddle, and quickly become familiar with moving about on slippery ground, no sane Highlander would venture far from home without slider guides.

Escorting a group of mining students is a big job, especially when there's a possibility of rain. Even the best quality needle boots will lose over fifty percent of their grip on black glass if the surface becomes damp.

Because of their high cost, only members of the Slider Corps are issued with guide sticks, fitted with best-quality diamond hooks and premium tyranium crystals.

Mining students, traders and ordinary citizens are dependent on guides to move on even the simplest of routes between the communities, mines and hydroponic chambers dotted around the Black Slopes.

Your instructors have taught you all about guiding. They've taught you that having a plan-B is advisable. Now that your troop is escorting miners, you want a plan-C as well.

When the wake-up buzzer sounds, the peace and quiet is broken.

The cadets bound out of their bunks and dress quickly. They sort their equipment, pack their backpacks and sit at the breakfast table with a bubbling nervousness.

You feel a few moon moths fluttering in your stomach too, but you are determined to keep your nervousness in check for the sake of your troop.

Gagnon looks over your shoulder at the map. "Check, check and double check, aye?"

You see the hint of a smile on his face. He seems as calm as ever.

"I like the route you've planned," you tell him, "but it never hurts to have options."

"The higher we stay, the more options we have. There is nothing worse than being caught on low ground."

"Slider rule number one," the two of you say in unison. "Altitude is advantage."

As every slider knows, it's hard to slide when you're already at the bottom.

Gagnon points to the map. "Once we get past Mount Tyron we can follow Long Gully all the way to the Pillars. It's only a 1 in 30 gradient so it should provide a gentle ride for our passengers."

After making a few more notes, you join the other cadets. Most are eating their hydro with gusto, knowing that this will be the last fresh food they see for a while.

You help yourself to a large plate of the succulent greens and pour yourself a cup of steaming broth. When Dagma comes to sit beside you, you secretly smile. Maybe your plan to include her is working.

"A lovely day for babysitting miners," she grumps.

You can understand why Dagma isn't thrilled, but you want the trip to start on a positive note. Negativity can easily ruin morale. "I can't wait to see the Pillars," you say loudly. Around you, other members of your troop smile and nod. Your tactic worked.

Dagma shrugs and shovels another large spoonful of hydro into her mouth. She's a big unit, and it takes a bit of feeding to keep her energy levels up. Then she looks up from her plate. "Couldn't the miners use their whizzo anchor bolt launchers and zippers to make their own way?"

"No," you say. "They're only students. Besides, it's way too dangerous with overloaded sledges. None of them would make it."

Dagma grunts and shovels more hydro.

Once you've finished eating, you stand and tap your cup on the table. The rest of the cadets stop talking and look at you expectantly.

"You've all probably heard by now that we're escorting mining students today. We'll be leaving soon, so let's get this pod ready for departure. I'll see you at the bottom of the tow in fifteen minutes. Remember, we're professionals so act like it. Let's make the Slider Corps proud and the miners welcome."

The sound of scraping boots and excited voices echo off the pod's walls as cadets finish packing and tidy up their cubicles.

You put on your utility belt and adjust the strap on your backpack. Then you grab your newly acquired guide stick and make your way along the corridor back towards the portal. The walls of the corridor are as dark as your mood. Responsibility is a burden, but you know once you get used to it, it will be rewarding.

Outside the air is crisp and still. The sky is without any hint of cloud.

An instructor is waiting for you at the bottom of the first tow. Beside him stands a group of ten mining students, each with their own sledge loaded high with equipment. Once your troop has assembled, the instructor clears his throat and everyone goes silent.

"I know some of you are wondering why Slider Command has decided to give a group of cadets the responsibility of getting these mining students to the Pillars of Haramon," the instructor says as he looks out over those gathered before him. "It's certainly not something we planned on. But yesterday, one of our advanced units spotted a large number of Lowlanders camped in the northern foothills. It's estimated they outnumber the Highland Slider Corps by three to one. They also have some unusual equipment hidden under tarpaulins."

The cadet standing next to you gulps in the deathly silence.

"The Highland Slider Corps are now on high alert. All available personnel are moving into defensive positions. All leave has been cancelled and any further cadet training has been suspended."

The officer's expression is serious. "We all knew this day was coming."

The instructor sweeps his arm, indicating everyone before him. "Some of you standing here are sliders and some of you are miners, but remember first and foremost, you are Highlanders."

You look along your troop. Dagma's face is tight, her lips pressed together. One or two cadets look about ready to pee themselves.

"The Pillars of Haramon give us control of the upper slopes," the officer continues. "If the Lowlanders can't get up the mountain, they are below us and will remain vulnerable. We need your help if we are to keep the Highlands safe for our families. So, are you with me Highlanders?"

"Yes sir!" both the sliders and miners shout.

You step forward and salute the instructor. "Slider Troop 6E is ready for departure sir."

"Off you go then. Be careful, we need this equipment delivered safely."

You feel a wave of nervousness wash over you, but you are determined to do your family and the Slider Corps proud. "Yes sir," you say, straightening your back. "We'll get there or die trying sir."

"Just get there cadet. You are not allowed to die today. That is an order."

"Yes sir," you say. "No dying today, sir."

You look over your troop. "Right, three cadets per sledge, two front, and one back. Miners, double-check that your loads are secure and climb aboard."

The sliders form themselves into groups and attach their harnesses to the sledges. After checking their loads, the miners climb up and strap themselves on.

Pulling the sledges, the sliders shuffle towards the towline. The two front sliders stand opposite each other, one on either side of the humming cable. The slider at the back gets ready to act as brake if required.

The front sliders hook their tow clamps over the whirling cable and squeeze. As the clamps grip onto the cable, everyone accelerates up the hill.

You lead the last group. Dagma, because of her superior strength, is at the back of your sledge, ready to put on the brakes should your group become separated from the tow somehow.

When you reach the top of the first tow, you repeat the exercise up the next, and the next. Before you know it, the training ground is a faint speck in the distance.

At the top of the last tow, you stop briefly to enjoy the view. A range of glistening black peaks stretch off in the distance. You feel the cool wind that has blown in from the north and notice that faint wisps of cloud have appeared on the horizon.

You turn to your troop. "Right, Gagnon is our navigator, his group will take the lead. We've chosen the safest route to the Pillars of Haramon for a reason, so keep your speed down. Stay in control of your sledges at all times, and stay alert … Gagnon?"

Gagnon raises his arm and points to a tooth-shaped peak in the distance. "Our first waypoint is sixteen miles to the west, just beneath Mount Transor."

The cadets turn to look at the towering peak. Mount Transor is one of the many unclimbed mountains on Petron. Light reflects off its near-vertical face. The tops of even higher mountains can be seen through the haze further inland.

"Now that we're traversing," you tell your troop, "we'll travel with one cadet in front of the sledge to steer, and two behind for braking. I want the strongest sliders at the back and, if in doubt, slow down.

Unlike our competition yesterday, this is not a race."

As the slider troop rearrange their order and refasten their harnesses, you do the same in preparation to leading your sledge. Once everyone is ready you wave your arm. "Okay move out!"

Gagnon leads. The track is about two sledge widths wide and slants ever so slightly downhill, which lets gravity do the work of moving the heavy sledges.

The sledge's metal runners slide easily over the ground. A fine coating of diamond dust on their outside edges keep the runners tracking in a straight line.

You look at the clouds and hope they stay away. Conditions can change rapidly in the mountains. Squalls often race in after picking up moisture from the lowlands. Troops have been surprised by rapidly moving fronts before. Your hand moves over your utility belt and checks that your tether and anchor bolt gun are in their usual places. One of the first things you learned as a cadet was how to fire an anchor into the rock and tether a sledge. The troop record for this procedure is six seconds, held by Gagnon.

After checking that your boots are firmly locked together, you point your front foot down the path and push with the needle end of your guide stick. Before long you are moving at a quick, walking pace, except you're not expending any energy. Gravity is doing all the work.

Those ahead of you are making easy work of the gentle terrain and everyone is starting to relax. The miners seem to be enjoying the ride. Dagma brings up the rear.

Just as you are thinking all is well, the lead slider in the group ahead of you takes a fall and loses grip on the surface. As soon as she hits the ground, the sledge behind her slews off course and slips perilously towards the edge of the track.

There is a screech of diamond hooks as the two cadets at the rear of the sledge lean down hard on their guide sticks. But one of the front runners has veered off the path onto steeper terrain. As much as the cadets try to hold it, the weight of mining equipment is slowly pulling the sledge off the track.

"Get ready to brake, Dagma," you yell, giving a big push in an attempt get close enough to hook one of the brakemen on the sledge in front of you, in order to give them some extra stopping power. You just hope that Dagma is as strong as you think she is, and that her technique will be enough to slow the runaway sledge.

Another big push and you've caught up to the group in front. You reach out with your stick and hook on to the backpack of a cadet in front of you.

"Brake, Dagma!" you yell.

As Dagma and the other cadet drop their hooks and dig them in, you feel the straps of your harness tighten. Will this added pressure pull the guide stick from your hand? How could you lead your troop without it?

If you get tangled, both sledges could be in danger. As Dagma digs deeper, you hang on as tight as you can. Your sweaty hands are beginning to slip. You are not sure if you can hold on.

It is time to make a quick decision. Do you:

Hang on to your guide stick and try to save the runaway sledge?
P36

Or

Unhook your stick from the group in front and save your own group? **P42**

You have chosen the faster route to the Pillars of Haramon.

You're up well before the alarm buzzer to check the fast route that Gagnon has marked on the map. It is the most direct route way to the Pillars of Haramon but has some switchbacks and tricky sections to negotiate. One part you're particularly concern with is known as "Zigzag Drop".

As you pore over the map, a courier enters and hands you a bright green envelope.

The envelope contains orders to escort ten mining students to the Pillars, all the more reason to get there as quickly as possible.

The chance of rain is low, but you are convinced that moving quickly and exposing your troop and the miners to the elements for the least amount of time is the right thing to do.

Miners, traders and common people are reliant on linked transport — where sliders escort travelers on specially designed sledges — to get around the various tracks. There are many stories about unaccompanied travelers "going to the bottom".

You are thinking about the best way to organize your caravan when the silence is broken by the wake-up buzzer. Cadets bound out of their bunks and dress quickly. They sort their equipment, pack their backpacks and eat breakfast with a bubbling nervousness of quick sentences and subdued giggles.

Gagnon looks over your shoulder at the map "Fast is good, eh?

"I like the route you've planned," you tell him. "There are a few tricky sections, but we should be okay."

After making a few more notes, you join the others at the breakfast table. Most are eating like hungry morph rats, knowing it will be a while before they'll have a chance to eat something other than travel rations and the occasional cup of broth.

You fill a large plate and pour yourself some steaming broth. You're pleased when Dagma comes and sits beside you. Maybe your plan to include her is working.

"I hear we've got miners to escort," Dagma says.

"At least it will give us a chance to show off our skills."

Dagma shrugs and shovels a large spoonful of stringy hydro into her mouth. Green strands hang down to her chin. She noisily slurps them up. You turn your head in disgust.

You stand up and tap your cup on the table. The rest of the cadets stop talking and raise their eyes.

"You all probably know by now that we're escorting a group of mining students to the Pillars of Haramon. We'll be leaving soon, so let's get this pod squared away for departure. I'll see you at the bottom of the towline with your gear in fifteen minutes.

The sound of scraping boots and mumbled voices fill the pod as the cadets move to their cubicles and finish packing.

You put on your utility belt and adjust the straps of your backpack. Then you grab your guide stick. It is your prize possession. You turn it up and check the tyranium crystal pad on its foot by running your thumb over the tightly compacted ultra-fine needles. They seem in good condition. At the other end of the six-foot-long handle is a two inch hook of pure blue. This diamond is the hardest material on the planet, it will dig into anything. It will slow you down when sliding on the slopes, and also act as a weapon if required.

Happy with your equipment, you make your way out of the pod and along the corridor back to the portal. Outside you find an instructor and ten mining students. One of the mining students is laughing and joking around. His high pitched squeal rings out over the assembly.

Unfortunately, the instructor is not in a mood for jokes. "If you're finished playing around, Piver, it's time to listen up."

Suddenly, it is so quiet that you can hear the distinctive screech of a red-beaked pango miles down the valley.

The instructor clears his throat. "Yesterday one of our scouts spotted a large number of Lowlanders gathered in the northern foothills. It's estimated they outnumber the Highland Slider Corps by three to one.”

"Geebus!" you hear the funny little miner say as his face goes pale.

The instructor gives him a sharp look and continues. "The Highland Slider Corps are now on high alert. All leave has been cancelled."

Groups of miners and sliders are a buzz of conversation at this news.

The instructor holds up his hand, requesting silence. "Controlling the Pillars of Haramon gives us control of the Black Slopes. As long as we control the base and Haramon Pass at the head of Long Gully, the Lowlanders can't gain access to the pathways and reservoirs we have developed over the centuries. We need your help if we are to keep the Highlands free and safe for our families. Are you with me?"

"Yes sir!" the sliders and miners shout in unison.

You step forward and salute the instructor. "Slider Corps 6E is ready for departure sir."

"Off you go then. We need these miners and their equipment at the Pillars as quickly as possible."

A wave of nervousness floods over you, but you are determined to do your family and the Corps proud. You straighten your back. "Yes sir."

"Don't allow the Lowlanders to cut you off."

"Yes sir. We're going to take the fast route. With luck we'll avoid contact with any Lowland patrols that way."

"Luck's got nothing to do with it cadet. Just remember your training and everything will be fine."

You salute once more and then look over at your group. The miners' sledges are loaded to the max with equipment.

"Right sliders," you call out. "Two per sledge, one front and one back. The rest of you, keep an eye out for Lowlanders. Miners, climb aboard and strap in tight, this is going to be a quick trip."

As you watch, twenty cadets harness themselves up to the heavy sledges leaving ten cadets free for quick deployment should

Lowlanders be spotted along the route. A mining student jumps aboard each sledge.

"Ready to tow," the front cadet on the first sledge says.

You nod and lift your arm. "On my mark, three, two, one… go!"

The leading cadet hooks the tow clamp attached to the front of his harness, over the whirling cable and squeezes its handles. As the clamp grips the cable, the slack is taken up in the cadet's harness and the sledge begins to move up the hill.

Your group brings up the rear. Once you reach the top of the first tow, everyone repeats the exercise up the next tow, and the next. Soon the training ground is a speck far below and you can see the curvature of the planet off in the distance.

At the top of the last tow you stop briefly to enjoy the view. Peak after shining black peak stretch off into the distance.

Pleased at the lack of cloud in sight, you turn to your troops. "Right, Gagnon is our navigator. He will take the lead for now. We've chosen the quick route for a reason, so keep moving. Our first waypoint is sixteen miles to the west near Mt Tyron."

You look towards the towering peak in the distance. Light glints off its reflective face as the sun tracks around to the west.

Once everyone is ready you wave your arm. "Okay, move out!"

Gagnon, unencumbered by a sledge, shoves off with a push of his stick. The line of sledges follow.

Most of the sledges are overloaded with extra gear from Command. This equipment is needed at the Pillars to defend against the impending Lowland attack. The cadets at the back of the sledges are constantly dragging their hooks to keep them from gaining too much momentum as they make their way along the narrow track traversing the across the slope.

You feel every bump and irregularity as you slide along. Occasionally you need to correct your balance. A quick tap of your stick on the ground is usually all that is required. But you must keep alert. Things on the upper slopes can change in an instant.

When you hear a series of high-pitched screeches, you look up and see a flock of pangos heading out to feed. Their formation creates a massive V in the sky. The bird's wings barely move as they soar on the thermals created by the hot air rising from the dark, heat-absorbing slopes below

Above the pangos, Petron's smallest moon glows a faint pink. A fuzzy ring around it circumference shows that there is moisture in the upper atmosphere.

Instinctively you pat your utility belt and feel the row of anchor bolts every slider carries in case of emergency. If you are caught in a sudden downpour you'll only have seconds to fire a charge into the slope and clip yourself on. If you are too slow, you'll be swept down the slope without any chance of stopping.

You point your front foot ever so slightly downhill and push with your guide stick. It doesn't take much to get moving on the slick rock. Before long, the troop is moving along at a running pace, except you're not expending any energy. Gravity is doing all the work.

This track is steeper than the usual transport tracks. Still, everyone seems to be coping with the gradient so far. The troop is making good speed and you start to relax.

Just as you are thinking all is well, you hear a shout. The cadet leading the front sledge has fallen.

You can see the brakeman struggling to stop.

When a steering runner slips off the main track onto the steeper slope below, the front of the sledge lurches and skews sharply downhill. Its speed increases in an instant.

"Abandon sledge!" the brakeman yells. "I can't hold it!"

The fallen cadet unclips her harness and kicks herself out of the heavy sledge's path. Then she spins onto her back and digs in her heel spurs. The miner hits the quick release on his waist strap, jumps off the sledge, and rolls onto his belly, digging the tip of his pick into the slope to stop his slide.

The brakeman unclips his harness and, pressing hard on his guide stick, comes screeching to a halt.

As the runaway sledge rockets down the hill, you hear gasps from your group. Thankfully its crew, although shaken, seems to be okay. The slider who first fell is up and has made her way to the miner who is hanging onto his pick for dear life. With a *pop* an anchor bolt is fired into the rock and the miner is secured. Another cadet throws down a cable and those below clip on and start working their way back up to the track where the rest of you wait anxiously.

"Geebus!" a familiar voice exclaims. "That was close!"

You realize how right the funny little miner is. It's time to reassess things. Maybe taking the fast route with a troop of untested cadets wasn't such a good idea after all. But then the extra time you've taken after the accident means you are behind schedule.

What do you do now? It is time to make an important decision. Do you:

Slow down and put more safety precautions in place? **P64**

Or

Carry on down to the Pillars and make best speed. **P77**

You have decided to try to save the runaway sledge.

At first the strain is so great you think your arms will be pulled from their sockets. Your muscles burn, but you grit your teeth and hang on. Then after a few seconds, the pressure eases. Dagma and her fellow cadet have managed to bring the uncontrolled slide to a halt.

Once you come to a complete stop, you unhook your stick from the harness of the cadet in front of you and exhale with relief. "Are you all alright?"

The cadet who had been steering the sledge is back on her feet and looking over the pile of equipment at you. "Thanks. I've got it now."

The two cadets at the rear of the runaway sledge are red-faced and panting from exertion.

"Thanks for that," one says.

The other cadet tries to put on a brave face. "Yeah thanks. We nearly went to the bottom that time."

Everyone knows exactly what he means when he says "the bottom". The bottom is not a place people come back from … well, not often, anyway.

You shake your head and try to get the ugly thought out of your head. "Okay, let's heave this sledge back onto the track and try it again."

As the cadets get to work, you can see they are still a little shaken from their close call … and so they should be.

Once the sledge is safely up and its load secured, it's time to move off again.

"Let's take it a little slower this time," you say.

Thankfully, for the rest of the morning your group slides on without incident. Gradually your nerves settle down and you relax once more.

For lunch you stop on a small plateau which provides enough flat ground for everyone to anchor their sledges. It is the junction where the west and eastbound tracks cross.

The cadets remove their harnesses and sit on the ground. It's been a long morning. Tired legs and backs need a break. Ration packs are broken open and burners are lit to heat broth.

Gagnon informs you that the troop has traveled just over seventeen miles and lost 3000 feet of altitude.

You do a quick mental calculation. That equates to thirty feet of forward progress for every foot of lost altitude, pretty good going for a group of rookies. "At this rate we'll reach our camp well before dewfall," you say to Gagnon.

Since the accident you've been moving slower, but you know that once you get to smoother slopes your troop will be able to make up some time.

Lunch lasts half an hour. You make a few adjustments to the teams, and give Gagnon a break from leading now that you've come off the face and have reached a wide valley that is almost impossible to get lost in.

Dagma is keen to lead so you put Gagnon with her team at the rear and send Dagma forward to lead the next section.

"Just remember, Dagma, we're not all as strong as you, so keep your speed down."

Dagma gives you a curt nod and steps into the lead sledge's harness. "Don't worry, I know what I'm doing," she says. "Remember, I've done just as many hours as you have on the simulators."

You're still not sure about Dagma's attitude. She seems determined to prove to everyone how good she is despite what is best for the team. You suspect she still hasn't forgiven you for beating her in the race to become troop leader.

Before you have a chance to say "move out", Dagma is off, pushing with big strokes to get her sledge up to speed.

"Let's go," you say to the others. "Go at your own pace and don't worry if Dagma gets a bit of a lead on you. This is not a race."

The valley is nearly half a mile wide, mainly smooth and at the perfect angle for sliding. It stretches far into the distance. Steep hills crowd in on both sides. Occasionally a vertical pillar of black rock will rise up from the otherwise featureless landscape. These dormant volcanic pipes are a constant reminder of Petron's volcanic past.

The young miner on your sledge makes a comment about the possibility of blue diamonds being present in the pipes as you pass. His voice is filled with excitement and nervousness at the same time. You are happy to chat. It helps pass the time on this less demanding part of the journey, but after a while you start getting a sore throat from having to shout over the sound of the wind whistling around your visor as you whiz down the slope.

The planned stopping point for the night is a fortified tow-base near the bottom of this valley, almost ten miles away. Then tomorrow, you'll tow up to the top of a ridge where you'll find the track that will take you to Long Gully and then on to the Pillars of Haramon.

The tow-base has a maintenance crew of ten and a number of accommodation, defense and hydro pods bored into the solid rock. It will be a crowded night with the miners and their cargo, but even crowded accommodation is better than being out on the slopes after dewfall.

When you look down the valley you see that Dagma has pulled away from the rest of the troop. You shake your head and grumble under your breath. Why does she always need to prove herself like this?

You are about to send Gagnon off after her to tell her to slow down when your eyes are distracted by movement below and off to your left.

It takes a second to realize that what you've seen is a group of Lowlanders working their way up the left hand edge of the valley about half a mile away. The Lowlanders' dark uniforms are nearly invisible against the shimmering black rock.

Dagma has missed them. Unfortunately she is too far away for you to yell out a warning. You grab your scope and watch as the Lowland scouts raise their bows and prepare to fire at Dagma's group.

Luckily you've noticed the Lowlanders while you are still well above them. Your troop's camouflage is even better than the Lowlanders'. Even the sledges are almost invisible with their shiny black covers.

The Lowlanders haven't seen you. They must think that Dagma's group is travelling solo. You have the advantage.

You raise your fist with one finger extended, the signal for a silent stop. The cadets slow the sledges by turning them side on to the slope rather than dragging their noisy hooks.

"Lead cadets prepare for attack," you whisper once you've pulled to a halt.

You unhook your harness and spin your backpack around so it rests against your chest to act as a shield. Then you unlock your boots so you have a full range of movement.

"V-formation," you order. "We'll send them to the bottom before they know what's hit them."

You and nine other sliders group together, sitting on your utility belts with packs to the front. Your guide sticks are tucked tight under your arms with the hook end forward and the crystal end resting on the ground ready to steer you one way or the other in an instant.

"On my count," you say quietly. "Three, two, one, push…"

Within seconds, your formation is sliding down the slope, each cadet tucked close, protecting the cadet beside them.

"Time to increase our speed and show these Lowlanders who owns the slopes," you shout over the whistling wind.

On the front of your pack, behind a thin protective plate, is a small reservoir. You pull a lever and a fine stream of water shoots out onto the slope in front of you. After sliding through the damp patch, you feel the friction lessen and your troop accelerate like someone has fired a rocket launcher.

"Hard left, on my mark. Three, two, one, now!"

The cadets follow your order instinctively, forcing their guide sticks hard against the smooth rock and pushing your tightly-packed group to the left. You are bearing down on the Lowland scouts, sliding faster and faster.

A Lowlander looks up and sees you coming. He warns the others. They stop firing at Dagma and turn to face your group racing towards them.

"Sticks up!" you yell.

"Woot, woot!" your cadets yell.

The Lowlanders reload and fire. But your group is still accelerating and they misjudge their aim. Only one arrow strikes a member of your group and it is deflected by the cadet's armored backpack.

Your group is close now. The diamond spurs imbedded in the heel of your boots sparkle in the sunlight, ready to strike like fangs at the legs of the invaders.

When you collide with the Lowlanders, it is with such force that despite their protective armor, they fly off their feet and are propelled down the slope.

The impact has had the reverse affect on you and your cadets. It's brought you nearly to a halt.

"Hooks down!" you command.

The piercing screech of diamond digging into the black rock reminds you of the call of the wild pango as your cadets come to a stop. Their grim expressions have turned to elated smiles at having survived their first encounter with Lowlanders.

Down the valley to your right, Dagma has brought her sledge to a stop and is tending a cadet with an arrow sticking out of her leg.

The Lowlanders are off their feet and free sliding out of control. You watch their desperate attempts to stop before they run into something nasty. Then, as the terrain flattens out a little, the Lowlanders manage to bring their slide to a halt. Despite being bruised and battered they've survived, but they don't hang around. They quickly organize themselves and retreat further down the slope. Before long they are nothing but dots in the distance, scurrying home in defeat.

"Sliders one, Lowlanders nil," you say to your troop. "Well done.

Now, I suppose we'd better slide over and see if we can help Dagma."

You signal the cadets who remained with the sledges further up the hill, to proceed with caution down the slope and then stand up, lock your boots together and start pushing your way towards Dagma.

The cadet hit by the arrow is in pain, but at least the arrow missed all the major arteries, nor has it hit bone. After disinfecting the wound and wrapping a bandage around the cadet's thigh, she has no problem standing. The wounded cadet is given a couple of yellow capsules, a combination pain killer and antibiotic, and helped to her feet.

"Let's get you on one of the sledges," you say. "You'll be fine in a day or two if you take it easy."

"It's only a scratch. I can slide," she says gritting her teeth. "The pain killers should kick in soon."

You shake your head. "You may be able to slide, but for now there's no need. Just rest until we get to the tow-base."

Finding Lowlanders along your intended route was unexpected.

It also means you need to make a decision. Do you:

Carry on down the slope towards the tow-base in your current formation and make best speed? **P77**

Or

Send some advanced scouts to test the route first? **P84**

You have decided to unhook and save your own group.

You can feel the guide stick being pulled from your grasp. You know that if you don't unhook from the group ahead you will lose it, or even worse, send the sledge you are leading tumbling down the steep hillside as well.

With a twist of your wrist you free yourself from the group in front. Will they be able to stop without your help?

You aren't sure, but it's up to them now. Both of the brakemen are desperately trying to stop the runaway sledge but seem to be fighting a losing battle. The miner on the sledge is panicking and looks ready to jump.

"Stay on the sledge!" you yell. But has he heard you? If he jumps now, you know he'll end up sliding out of control. You doubt his pick will be enough to stop him from slipping all the way to the bottom. At least on the sledge he's got a chance.

Then miraculously, the lead slider regains her feet and with a desperate drive of her guide stick manages to turn the nose of her sledge side-on to the slope. The sledge is still moving fast, but without gravity trying to drag it down the mountain, the momentum is reduced. The two cadets at the back renew their efforts and gradually the sledge slows.

You exhale loudly and wipe the sweat off your forehead.

"Phew, that was close," you mumble as you slip out of your harness and slide closer to where the runaway sledge has come to a stop. They are slightly below you and off the main track, but at least they are all in one piece. The miner is white-faced and trembling.

With some ropes and extra pulling power you and your cadets manage to get the runaway sledge back onto the main track. After 30 minutes your troop is back in formation and ready once again to move off.

You've had a lucky escape. Thankfully, for the rest of the morning everyone slides on without incident.

For lunch you stop on a small patch of flat ground which provides enough space for everyone to remove their harnesses and anchor their sledges. Most of the sliders sit to give their sore legs and backs a break. Ration packs are broken open and a small burner is fired up to heat broth.

Gagnon informs you that the troop has traveled just over seventeen miles. "And we've only lost 3000 feet of altitude. That's thirty feet of forward progress for every foot of lost altitude, pretty good going for a group of rookies."

"And despite the accident, we're making good time," you say to Gagnon, acknowledging his navigational and route planning skills. "At this rate we'll reach the tow-base an hour before dewfall."

After lunch, you decide to take the lead and give Gagnon a break. There isn't much navigation to do in this section because you'll be travelling down a broad valley.

The terrain on the right-hand side of the valley is undulating but smooth. The other side is a different matter. A major fault line has created a chaotic jumble of crevasses and ridges. Not the sort of place to want to take sledges anywhere near.

"Remember to keep well to the right," you tell the cadets as you push off with your stick. "We've still got a fair way to go. Let's try to keep things unexciting."

For the first fifteen miles everything goes without a hitch, but when you see movement up on the slope to your right, you order everyone to come to a halt.

You take out your scope and focus. It is a group of fifteen Lowland scouts, climbing up towards the ridge. How did they get past the lookouts at the tow-base? How are they managing to get a grip on the steep slope? Have the Lowlanders developed some new technology that allows them to move on the slick black glass? Maybe they've found a source of needle crystals.

"Can your catapult reach that far?" you ask Dagma.

Dagma pulls out her scope and points it at the group of

Lowlanders. After making a few adjustments she lowers the instrument and looks at its dial. "It's reading just over half a mile. We'll need to get closer to have a chance of reaching them."

With the Lowlanders holding the high ground, their arrows will reach your group before your catapults can knock them off their perch. Sending your cadets any closer would be suicidal.

As you discuss the problem with Dagma, the miner riding on your sledge coughs. "Can I make a suggestion?" he says.

You nod. "As long as you do it quickly."

"I've got a cable launcher on my sledge," he says before pointing up the slope towards a small pinnacle on a rise behind you. "If we fire a line up to that outcrop, you can use my heavy-duty zipper to gain some altitude."

You think about what the miner has said. "How many cadets will it hold?"

The miner thinks a bit. "Six or seven I would think. Will that be enough?"

"It should be."

Sliders always try to attack from above. All their tactics are based on having the advantage of altitude. Trying to dislodge the Lowlanders from below will almost certainly mean the loss of some of your cadets.

After a brief discussion with Dagma you turn to the miner. "Okay, break it out. Let's get it set up before the Lowlanders realize what we're up to."

The miner removes the cover off his sledge and grabs a long tubular piece of equipment. This is attached to a sturdy tripod.

After setting the launcher up, the miner looks through a scope on the top of the firing tube and adjusts dials and levers. Then he attaches a spool of ultrafine cable to the back of a sleek projectile with fins on its tail and fits it into the back of the tube.

"Ready to fire," the miner says.

You've decide to lead the attack yourself so you grab the miner's heavy-duty zipper and attach it to the front of your harness ready to clamp onto the towline as soon as it is secure. Five other cadets link up to you, one behind the other. You look at the miner. "On my count. Three, two, one, fire!"

The miner pulls the trigger and the projectile hisses towards the pillar. The reel of cable whirls out after it.

A puff of dust erupts from the pinnacle as the projectile buries itself deep into the rock.

"Ready to zip on my mark. Three, two, one!"

You squeeze the grip on the battery-powered zipper and next thing you know you and five cadets are rocketing up the side of the valley.

As you slide, you wonder if the Lowlanders have spotted you. Surely they've heard the launcher or have seen you, despite your uniforms blending into the dark rock of the slope.

When you reach the top of the tow the zipper cuts out. The six of you look towards the Lowlanders. They are below you now, but not by much.

"Okay, get ready to traverse," you tell your cadets. "We need to get closer before they have time to get any higher. Dagma, let us know when you're within catapult range."

The other cadets follow as you push off with your stick. The swish of your boots sliding across the smooth rock sounds like compressed air escaping from a hydro growing chamber. You try to keep as high as possible as you traverse across the hillside.

It isn't long before Dagma signals a halt. "I think I can reach them from here."

She removes a Y-shaped piece of metal and strong synthetic tube from the top of her backpack along with a handful of water bullets. Each bullet is about the size of a pango egg and has a rigid shell designed to break on impact.

"Aim well above them," you say to Dagma.

Dagma slips a water bullet into the catapult's pouch and stretches the tubing back with all her strength. With a *zing* the bullet arcs off into the sky and splats on the uphill side of the Lowlanders.

The water, now released from its container, has nowhere to go but down.

You notice the first of the Lowlanders slip slightly as the first trickle runs under his feet. When Dagma's second bomb hits the slope they are all scrambling for anchor points.

Now that the Lowlanders' attentions are fully focused on staying attached to the slope, you can move closer. There is no way any of them are going to let go of their anchor points long enough to fire an arrow.

"Forward," you order.

You push off and slide closer to the Lowlanders' position. When you feel all the cadets will be able to reach the Lowlanders with their catapults, you motion them to stop.

"Load up hard shot," you say, grabbing your catapult and some lumps of stone from a side pouch of your backpack. "Let send these invaders to the bottom."

The Lowlanders are in trouble now. If they let go of their anchor points they will plummet down the hillside. If they don't, they will be pounded by hard-shot.

The Lowlanders' only choice is to rappel down on whatever cables they have and retreat with all haste. Even then it is unlikely that all of them will get away without injury. You see one of their scouts frantically untangling a cable and attaching it to an anchor point he's quickly fixed to the rock.

Just as he's about to clip on, he's knocked off his feet. He lurches for the cable as he falls, but misses it by a hand's width.

"That's one off," Dagma cries with glee. "Now let's get the rest of them!"

The cadets are all firing now. Hard shot is peppering the remaining Lowlanders. Desperately they push each other aside in their attempt to be first down the cable.

When another Lowlander slips and starts sliding towards the bottom, a cheer goes up.

Dagma fires more water bullets to keep the slope as slick as possible. The remaining cadets keep the hard shot flying. The Lowlanders are taking a beating.

Finally, the remaining Lowlanders manage to clip on and abseil down the cable at breakneck speed.

A mile or so down the valley the two Lowlanders who were knocked off have managed to stop and are regrouping. You peer through your scope and see them tending to their scrapes and bruises. Once the remaining Lowlanders have made it to the valley floor, two of them pull out their bows.

"After them," you say. "V-formation on my mark!"

Your cadets stow their catapults and unlock their boots. They reverse their backpacks, so they cover their chest and act as a shield, and point the hook end of their guide sticks to the front. The cadets sit on their utility belts in a V formation and lock arms, ready for a super-fast downhill slide.

"On my mark … three, two, one, go!" you yell.

When the Lowlanders see your flying wedge coming down the hill at them, they realize the hopelessness of their situation, drop their bows and flee.

"Hard right on my mark!"

You and your cadets push right with your sticks.

"Again!" you yell.

As one, your cadets stab the ground with the needle end of their sticks, aiming themselves at the Lowlanders.

"Line formation! Boots up!"

In seconds, what was a V-formation is a line spread across the slopes. Cadets have their sticks up like lances and their diamond studded heels raised, ready to knock the Lowlanders off the mountain.

The Lowlanders' eyes are huge. They have seen all they need to. With a yelp of panic they fling themselves down the hillside. By the time your troops hit the valley floor they are scurrying off toward their unlucky comrades further down the mountain.

"Hooks down!" you order.

You swivel your stick around and dig its hook into the slope behind you. You don't need your eyes to tell the other cadets are following suit. The screech of diamond on black glass is unmistakable.

Your cadets have all stopped within a few yards of each other.

"Well they won't be back for a while," Dagma says with a grin.

You stand and signal the cadets further up the valley to bring the sledges down. Then you look at the young Highlanders around you.

"Stop grinning, cadets! Do you think this is supposed to be fun?"

Your cadets hesitate a moment.

Then you burst out laughing. "Of course it is! Now let's give those Lowlanders a slider farewell!"

"Woot, Woot!" the cadets yell. "Woot, Woot, Woot!"

By the time your caravan is reorganized, the Lowlanders have disappeared and you have the valley to yourselves again. It's time to proceed towards your destination. You cross your fingers and hope for an uneventful afternoon.

But after sliding for less than an hour a miner, who's been looking through his scope, yells "Stop! There's something strange going on."

Once again you order the troop to a halt and pull out your scope.

Then you see what the miner is pointing at. There is an eerie light coming from a split in the side of a small rocky outcrop about 200 yards up the slope to your left.

"What's that glow?" you ask the miner. "Is it light reflecting off blue diamonds, do you think?"

At the mention of diamonds, everyone is scrabbling for their scopes.

The miner shakes his head. "I don't think so. It could be tyranium crystals, but it would have to be a pretty big deposit to glow so brightly."

Whatever it is, it isn't normal. Could it be a Lowland trap? You look up at the sky and calculate the time left before dewfall. There is just enough time to investigate, but you will be cutting it fine.

It is time to make a decision. Do you:

Go investigate what is causing the blue light? **P50**

Or

Keep going and forget about the blue light? **P54**

You have decided to go and investigate the blue light.

"Get a cable launcher set up," you tell a couple of miners. "Dagma, you and I will investigate. Gagnon, stay here with the rest of the troop."

"Shall we get our catapults ready?" Gagnon asks. "Just in case?"

"Good idea. But be ready to take off in a hurry if something happens or Dagma and I get captured."

There is a buzz of voices as you and Dagma adjust your harnesses in preparation for a quick ride up to the outcrop.

Within minutes the two of you are zipping towards the eerie glow. As you climb, you see moon moths flitting about.

"Those moths are acting strangely," Dagma says.

The higher you climb the more moths you see. They are congregating around the crack in the rock.

"Moths are always attracted to the light," you say.

Dagma shakes her head. "But look at the patterns they are forming. They're like mini tornadoes."

Dagma is right. The moths are swirling funnels of iridescent blue, the bottom tip of which points down into the crack.

The zipper cuts out when you and Dagma reach the end of the cable. You unclip and slide your way over to the hole in the rock. As usual, Dagma rushes ahead.

Never have you seen so many moon moths in one place.

"I can squeeze through," Dagma says.

Before you can say "wait" she's disappeared into the opening.

Then you hear her laughing.

Of all the cadets in your troop, Dagma is the least jovial. Normally to get her laughing, someone has to break a leg or step in pango poo.

It's hard to believe it's actually her cackling away.

At the opening, you push your head through the swarm of swirling moths and look in. As soon as you do, you realize the crack is actually the opening to a large cave that extends quite some distance into the hillside. Due to the many moon moths, it is almost as bright inside as it is outside.

You hear laughter again. This time it's above you. You look up and see Dagma and a hundred or more moon moths. They have picked her up and are swooping around the cave with her dangling in mid air. Others are fluttering around, tickling her under the chin and spraying a fine mist into her face.

Dagma is laughing and woot-wooting like she's been drinking fermented fruit broth.

"Isn't this great?" Dagma yells. "Look I'm flying!"

Dagma is flying all right. What are those moths spraying into her face?

It isn't long before you find out. You were so busy watching Dagma swooping around that you didn't feel a bunch of moths grab onto the fabric of your uniform and lift you off your feet.

When you open your mouth in surprise, moths spray a slightly sweet mist into your mouth.

Instantly you relax. It's as if flying is the most natural thing in the world.

The moon moths are taking you deeper and deeper into the cave.

"Where are we going?" you ask Dagma.

"I don't know, but I don't care. This is so much fun!"

It isn't until you hear a familiar scurrying, and the gnashing of teeth that you start to worry.

"I hear morph rats," you tell Dagma.

"Me too. Woot woot! Here ratty, ratty."

Is this the Dagma you know? What has got into her? Here ratty ratty? Is she nuts?

Then you see where the moon moths are taking you. This is their breeding chamber. Hundreds of slender transparent tubes hang from the roof of the cave. Inside each tube you can see a dozen or so moth larva. On the floor of the cave below the tubes, morph rats are piling up on top of each other in an attempt to reach the baby moths.

"I think they want us to save their babies," Dagma says. "Look!"

You turn to where Dagma is pointing and see fifty or so moon moths picking up morph rats and dropping them into a pit at one side of the cave, but more rats are entering the cave than the moths can't deal with.

"Have you got a screecher?" you ask Dagma.

She reaches for her utility belt. "Just the one."

"Let it rip," you say. "We'll just have to plug our ears."

You pull two plugs from your utility belt and stuff one in each ear, then nod to Dagma.

Even with the earplugs, the screecher is loud. But loud for you is unbearable for the morph rats. It's only seconds before they start rushing from the chamber like their lives depend on it.

As you hover above, it's like watching water run down a plughole as the rats swirl around and dive into the pit to escape the sound of the screecher. In less than a minute, all that remains is the smell of fart.

A swarm of moths flutter about your face, ticking you under the chin and around your ears. Both you and Dagma are laughing now.

"We'd better get going," you tell Dagma. Dewfall isn't far away.

Dagma gives you a big smile. "These moths will hatch out in the next day or two. It would be a pity if the rats came back and ate them all. Maybe I should stay and protect them?"

You think about what Dagma has said. It must be the mist, Dagma usually only worries about herself. A couple days with the moths would probably do her good.

"Maybe I could train them to fly me places?" Dagma says. "Wouldn't that be good for the Slider Corps?"

She's right. Trained moths would be an amazing advantage. Imagine swooping over the slippery slopes without being reliant on needle boots and guide sticks.

"Okay, come back down to the sledges and get what you need. I'm sure there are a few extra screechers around somewhere. While you're here, try to find the spot where the rats are getting in and plug up the hole. Then the moths will be okay next year."

Dagma nods enthusiastically. "I think I saw some tyranium crystals when the moths were flying me around too. I'll try to collect them and bring them down when I come back to the Pillars of Haramon."

Ten minutes later, Dagma is heading back up to the chamber, armed with four screechers and a pack full of supplies. She still has a big smile on her face, possibly from the moth mist, or maybe it's just that for the first time in her life she's actually let herself have some fun.

(some years later)

"And did Dagma get back to the Pillars of Haramon okay Grandee?"

You adjust your grandchild on your knee and ruffle their hair.

"She sure did. Not only did she come back, she brought some pet moths with her. She was always happy after that and used to tell the funniest jokes ever. She's the reason Highlanders say, "What a dag", when something's funny.

"Geebus! Really? They named a word after her?"

"They sure did. Maybe one day we'll slide over and pay her a visit."

Well done. You've reached the end of this part of the story, but have you tried all the different endings? You now have another decision to make. Do you:

Go back to the very beginning and try a different path? **P1**

Or

Go to the list of choices and read from another part of the story? **P307**

22222252222222

You have decided to continue and forget about the blue light.

As interesting as the light is, getting to the Pillars of Haramon before dewfall is more important. You can always come back when you've got more time and less responsibility.

After getting everyone lined up and ready to move out again, you have a feeling in your gut that there might be more Lowlanders about. "Dagma," you say. "It might be a good idea if you to take the lead for a while. I'd rather we have our best and strongest cadets at the front."

Dagma loves being out in front. She moves forward.

"On my mark, two, one…" Dagma yells, wasting no time in pushing off.

The only thing Dagma loves more than being in front is going fast. Everyone in the troop is fully concentrating on the sledge in front just to keep up with her breakneck pace.

It's not until you notice your shadow is in front of you, rather than on your left where it should be, that you realize Dagma, in her haste, has taken a wrong turn and led you down a side valley.

"Stop!" you yell out. "You're going the wrong way!"

You pull out a map, and spread it out on top of the sledge's cover.

Gagnon slides over to have a look too.

You point to an area on the map that is littered with crevasses. It is directly between you and your destination.

"Pango poo!" Gagnon says, "I should have been paying more attention. Now we've got to climb all the way back up to where we missed the turn, or find a way through the crevasse field."

You pull out your scope and focus on the crevasses.

"They don't look too bad," you say to Gagnon. "Maybe we should try to cut across rather than go all the way back up. We'll never make it to safety before dewfall if we do that."

"The field isn't properly mapped," Gagnon say. "But, if we take it slow…"

You look at the sun sinking towards the horizon. It's either that or camp in the open. "Let's do it," you say. "Single file, Gagnon take the lead."

For twenty minutes Gagnon leads your troop in a weaving course through the jumbled field of crevasses and ridges. At times the sledges are perfectly safe with lots of room for maneuvering, at others you're right on the edge looking straight down hundreds of feet.

It's one of these scary times, when you're squeezing between two deep fissures, with little room to spare, that you see a glint of something down in the crevasse. You give the signal to stop and carefully work your way nearer the edge.

It looks like something made of metal, but you need to get closer to see it properly.

Taking an anchor bolt, you fire into the rock and clip yourself on. Very slowly, you lean out over the edge and peer down into the yawning crack.

A first you can't quite tell what you're seeing. Then as your eyes adjust to the light, you realize you're seeing the back half of a spaceship. The front must be embedded in the rock, or missing altogether. The ships skin is covered in metallic scales that remind you of pango feathers. A series of portholes run down the ship's side. Near the rear, just in front of a large thruster, is an open portal.

You've seen drawings of ships like this in the story books your family use to read you when you were a child. But you always thought that the tales of the first Petronians arriving in spaceships were just myths.

This could be a great historical discovery.

"Grab me that cable launcher," you say to the nearest cadet. "We need to investigate this."

It doesn't take long before you've rigged up a sling so you can safely make your way across the cable to the ship.

The ship is much larger that it looks from the small portion sticking out of the rock. Rows of cryogenic sleep chambers line the walls and stretch off into the gloom.

You hear a scraping on the metal floor behind you. It's a wide-eyed Gagnon looking around.

"Wow this thing is amazing," he says.

You nod in agreement. "We'll make camp here tonight. Let's get the troop to tether the sledges and come across to the ship."

Gagnon looks around at all the empty sleep chambers. "Good idea. There's certainly no shortage of beds."

Once everyone is safely across, some of the cadets set up a burner and heat broth. Others wander around the ship gawking at all the controls and pipes and wires and other equipment.

"Geebus," Piver says. "So, all the stories are true. Petronians did come from another planet."

You look at the funny little miner and smile. "It certainly looks that way."

Piver scratches his head and wander over to a row of symbols on the wall. He stares a moment and then turns to you. "I wonder what this says and why they came all this way?"

You walk over and trace the unfamiliar symbols with your finger. *Victoria* LIFERAFT ELEVEN – PLANET EARTH 2108. "Yeah I wonder."

Congratulations, you have reached the end of this part of the story. You have made an historical discovery that could change the history of your people.

It is time to make another decision. Do you:

Go back to the very beginning and try another path? **P1**

Or

Go to the list of choices and start reading from another part of the story? **P307**

You have decided to go to mining school.

Members of your family have joined the Highland Slider Corps for generations, but you have always wanted to become a miner and go prospecting. It's not that you don't respect your family's traditions. It's just that the idea of hunting for blue diamonds fills you with excitement. Ever since your first science class at school, geology has fascinated you. You even dream of finding blue diamonds. Besides, miners get to play with all the best equipment.

Maybe you'll go prospecting around an active volcanic vent and look for tyranium needle crystals. Although risky, the rewards can be great. After all, where would the Highlanders be without crystals to provide grip on the slopes?

Maybe you'll dig for diamonds. How would a slider's guide stick work without a diamond hook for stopping? How would the communities bore tunnels in the nearly impregnable black rock to create hydroponic growing chambers and secure sleeping and defense pods?

You've always felt mining technology has been responsible for keeping the Highlands free. Sure, the Slider Corps protect the communities and keep them safe from attack by the Lowlanders, but without the blue diamonds and needle crystals, the Highland communities could never have been built in the first place. Were it not for miners, the only inhabitants of the Black Slopes would be colonies of red-beaked pangos, cave-dwelling moon moths, and feral packs of egg-eating morph rats.

For the first year at mining school, you've studied mineralogy, mine construction and planning, mechanical engineering, and safety procedures. You've learned how to operate the diamond bores needed to grind through the layers of dense black glass to get at the diamonds hidden in the rock below. You've learned about cable launchers, exploration methods, volcanism and geology as well as mathematics and mining history. Every possible technique has been drilled into you.

Soon you'll be going on your first field trip to test your newfound knowledge. On this trip you'll receive practical instruction on how to distinguish between areas that contain diamonds from those that don't, as well as learn how to get at them.

You've been packing you sledge all morning next to a boy named Piver who keeps cracking jokes. He is the only other person at mining school that comes from a slider family and because of that, the two of you have become friends.

Your sledges will carry a boring machine, lubricant, drills, blasters, rock screws, diamond picks as well as food, personal gear and other equipment.

"Where do you find a morph rat with no legs?" Piver asks you as he throws a cover over his load.

"I don't know. Where?"

"Exactly where you left it."

You shoot a look in Piver's direction and shake your head and groan. "That was so bad."

Piver chuckles anyway.

As the two of you finish securing your loads, you hear Piver giggling at something under his breath. He's a strange one, but you'd far rather be around someone who's laughing than a grump any day. And you must admit his silliness makes the time pass.

Each sledge weighs over two hundred pounds by the time it is fully packed and takes a crew of two or three sliders to maneuver it safely around the Black Slopes.

Linked transport, using slider guides, is really the only way to get around safely. Mining expeditions have tried going solo, but accidents are common and many end up crashing to the bottom. It is far safer with an escort.

Your group is heading off to the volcanic rim of Glass Mountain, an area rich in tyranium needle crystals, not far from the Pillars of Haramon.

"OK students, listen up," one of your instructors says. "You'll be leaving in an hour so make sure you've got everything on your checklist packed and tied down securely."

You look at the long list in your hand. There are so many things.

The instructor looks sternly at the group, making sure everyone is listening. "Now I have an announcement to make. Every mining expedition needs a leader so we are going to appoint one of you to be in charge of your group."

There is a hum of voices as the students speculate on who it will be.

The instructor walks over and looks you in the eyes. "Are you up for it?"

This has come as a big surprise. "I think so, sir," you reply.

"Good. You've been our top student this term so trust your instincts and work with your slider escort. I'm sure you'll do fine. The rest of you, follow your leader's instruction."

Piver comes over and slaps you on the back. "Congrats."

But the instructor hasn't finished. "Make sure you keep your picks and anchor guns close at hand. Not only is rain a possibility, there have been sightings of Lowland scouts in the last few weeks. You'll need to be ready to help your escort if required."

The thought of coming across Lowlanders while prospecting takes some of the fun out of the expedition and being the leader increases your responsibility even more.

Fifteen minutes later, a group of thirty sliders arrive. You are introduced to the lead slider and the two of you discuss the trip. You do a quick tour of the sledges and make sure each of the miners has packed properly and then return to double check your own.

Three sliders come over to your sledge. Two of them attach their harnesses to the front and one attaches to the back. The slider at the back introduces herself as Shoola. She's a strong looking girl in her late teens. You can see the muscles in her legs and arms through her close fitting uniform.

"You can climb aboard now," Shoola tells you. "We're about to head up the first tow."

You climb on top of the sledge and hook your boots under a strap, another you clip around your waist like a belt. These will keep you from falling off as the sledge is dragged up the steep towpath.

The sliders lock their boots into a stable sliding platform with a short metal bar that slides out the sole of their left boot and attaches to a notch near the instep of their right. Shoola, at the back of your sledge, will act as the team's brake.

As the front sliders get ready to clamp onto the tow, they stand with knees slightly bent. One positioned on either side of the quickly moving cable.

You look up the towline. A faint purple mist shrouds your view to the top. The low sun creates a light show as its rays reflect off the shiny, black rock.

"On my mark," the head slider calls out. "Three, two, one, go!"

The two front sliders throw their cable-clamps over the towline and squeeze down on its handle. As the clamps grip, the slack goes out of the strap running between the clamp and the sliders' harnesses. There is a short jerk, and the sledge starts moving.

The acceleration up the slope is exhilarating. You feel your abdominal muscles tighten in an attempt to keep yourself sitting upright. When you look back down the hillside, past Shoola, you see the other sledges racing up the towpath behind you.

"Yippee!" you yell. "What a ride!"

Up and up you climb until you enter the mist. The view disappears and the temperature drops. You reach for your flask and take a few gulps of hot broth. You secure the flask and grab a couple hard-boiled pango eggs to munch on. Turning around, you show an egg to Shoola. She nods and rubs her stomach. Tossing an egg in her direction, she deftly catches it one handed while easily keeping her balance and takes a bite.

Finally, your group emerges from the mist and you see a large motorized wheel whirling the cable around its belly and sending it back down the mountain.

The two sliders at the front of your sledge prepare to release their tow clamps and dismount. Shoola gets her guide stick into position, ready to drag its diamond hook to slow you all down.

You come to a screeching stop on a flat platform cut into the side of the mountain. Before the next group arrives, your group uses their sticks to push the sledge along a short path towards the bottom of the next tow.

While you wait for the sliders to clamp on to the next cable, you look around at the scenery. Now that you are above the mist the air is clear. You can see a long way. To the west and east, a towering range of mountains extend as far as you can see. To the north a braided river delta protrudes into a turquoise sea. On the flatlands, crops create a patchwork of green, yellow, orange and red, and wisps of smoke from cooking fires drift on the light breeze. Behind you, to the south, the slope keeps rising up towards the jagged skyline.

You are brought back to the present when you hear a slider start the countdown as they get ready to head up the next tow. Moments later you're off in a blur, rocketing higher up the mountain.

After repeating this process three times on three different tows, the training center has disappeared far below.

From the top of the last tow, your group turns to the west and takes a narrow path along the ridge. This will lead you to a slightly wider traverse path across an exposed face into the head of the next valley.

Once in this new valley, it should be a simple slide down to the next series of tows some seventeen miles away.

As you slide along, you dream of diamonds, sparkling, blue and translucent. You wonder if you'll be a success or if you'll go broke and end up back in your home community growing hydro. After all, if diamonds were that easy to find, everyone would be out looking.

By the time you reach the next tow, your backside is sore from sitting on the sledge. You are looking forward to getting off, stretching your legs, and having some food.

Off to your left, on the far side of the valley, is a sheer cliff dotted with bore holes. Specks of light flicker and flit about in the various openings.

You point. "Look, moon moths!"

"Wow, there must be a lot of them for us to see them from way over here." Shoola says.

You pull out your scope and take a closer look, but even through the high-power lens you can't make out much detail being so far away. It's at night that the moon moths really shine. Their wings absorb sunlight and then at night their wings give off a shimmering blue glow.

Miners often capture moon moths and put them in little cages to use as a light source when their battery supplies run low. But you hate the idea of caging these beautiful creatures. It seems cruel somehow.

"Meal break," the lead slider says as the sledges pull up at the bottom of the next tow. "We leave in half an hour, so get some broth in you while you have a chance."

"And don't forget to tether your sledges," you say to the other miners, as you unbuckle yourself, climb down, and hook on to an anchor. "This ground may look flat but the slightest slope and anything not securely tethered will be off and away before you can say "Woosho."

Once you're happy with your tether, you test out your needle boots. Unlike the sliders who are used to moving around the slopes, and have diamond spurs permanently fitted to their heels, your boots have far less grip so you need to be careful.

You eat some dried hydro and drink a cup of broth, and then start doing a few squats to stretch out your tight muscles.

Piver comes over and starts stretching next to you. As you exercise, you watch the humming cable disappear up the slope.

"This one looks even steeper than the last," you say.

Piver gives an excited jiggle. "I was talking to one of the sliders. He reckoned it's the longest tow in all of Petron. One thousand nine hundred vertical feet gained in less than fifteen minutes. Nearly a one in one gradient, no platforms, just straight up!" Piver's enthusiasm is contagious.

"Wow, that is steep," you say.

"See you at the top," Piver says. "It's all downhill from there."

You give him a thumbs-up and then start checking the straps on your sledge just in case something's come loose during the morning's run.

As you finish cinching the last belt, the lead slider clears his throat. "OK, everyone, mount up. We've still got some miles to cover before dark."

Just as you are about to climb onto your sledge a voice yells out.

"Take cover! Lowlanders!"

You and Piver duck down behind your sledges just as a small group of Lowlanders carrying a white flag come into view.

Off to your right the lead slider is forming his troop into an attacking formation.

Piver looks at you. "They're carrying a white flag. Why are the sliders getting ready to attack? As leader, aren't you going to say something?"

It is time to make a quick decision. Do you:

Encourage the sliders to attack the Lowlanders? **P106**

Or

Yell out for the sliders not to attack so you can find out what the Lowlanders have to say? **P113**

You have decided to put extra safety precautions in place.

Hindsight is a wonderful thing, but anyone can look back. Sliders are supposed to plan ahead so accidents don't happen in the first place. You should have known that one cadet on the back of a heavy sledge wouldn't be enough to control its speed.

Dagma stays silent, but by the scowl on her face you can tell she has a poor opinion of your leadership. Not that you can blame her.

"New formation," you say. "Two cadets at the back of each sledge. We need more braking power."

Why didn't you do this from the beginning? If you had, you wouldn't have lost a full sledge of valuable supplies.

"I take full responsibility," you say. "But we can't let this get in the way of completing our mission."

Dagma can't help herself. "So we're going to go slow now are we? How is getting caught in the rain going to help our safety record?"

"Better to arrive a bit late than not at all," you say. "Besides, there's no sign of rain at the moment."

"At the moment…" Dagma mumbles while kicking her sledge with the toe of her boot.

Yes, choosing the fast route was a mistake. But learning from your mistakes is how one gains experience. You're not too proud to admit you were wrong and change your methods.

"Everyone is going to have to keep an eye out for Lowlanders now that we're all harnessed up," you tell the cadets. "It's a setback, but we have to keep positive."

Dagma starts to comment. "Knowing our luck we'll…"

"Enough, Dagma!" you snap.

Dagma looks at the ground and grinds her teeth, but she stays quiet.

You look back to the other cadets. "Get ready to move out. We need to keep going if we're going to make the Pillars of Haramon by dewfall."

Even the bright and usually cheerful Gagnon looks a little shaken.

"Gagnon, you'd better stay out in front. We can't afford to have our navigator in harness."

Gagnon nods.

"In fact, why don't you extend out a bit. Signal with your guide stick if you hit a tricky section, then the rest of us will be ready for it."

You tell the miner whose sledge was lost to climb aboard yours then give the signal to slide. "Remember, eyes front and hooks ready."

Gagnon takes off down the track. The rest of the group follows. The other miners sit nervously, eyes wide, watching the track, but helpless to do anything.

You know that before long you will come to the most technical part of the journey, a series of steep switchbacks, known as Zigzag Drop.

The new combinations are working well. At least now, if one of the lead sliders slip, there are two others to stop the sledge and allow their fallen comrade time to regain their feet.

As you crest the broad ridge that leads onto the steep face of Mt Transor, and the start of Zigzag Drop, you call a brief halt.

The slope in front of you is dark and foreboding. Its black surface gives it the appearance of being smooth … if only that were the case.

A well worn track, cut into the rock, and used by Highlanders over the centuries, runs like a ribbon back and forth down the hill. You can't believe how narrow it looks from the top.

On a plateau far below, a jumble of sharp ridges and crevasses, the results of a backwash of superheated black glass when the mountains were first formed, look dangerous enough to weaken the knees of even the most experienced Highland slider.

Going over the edge here would be fatal.

"Cadets, let's take this real easy," you say. "Scrape the mountainside with your loads if need be, the further you are from the edge the better. If a single runner goes over here, you'll be heading towards the bottom before you have time to correct. Believe me, if there was ever a time you don't want to be free sliding, this is it."

You are about to wave your arm for everyone to move out when you remember the wise words of one of your instructors. He spoke of leading by example. Now might be a time to do just that.

After unclipping your harness, you move forward, past the other sledges, until you reach the first in line. You put your hand on the front cadet's shoulder. "I'll take the lead sledge down. You go and take my spot at the rear."

The cadet breathes a sigh of relief and wastes no time unclipping his harness.

You connect to the steering runners on the front sledge and wave your arm. "Okay, let's move. Steady as we go. Cadets at the back, keep your hooks down. I don't want to be moving at anything more than walking pace until we get to the bottom."

You can feel the sledge wanting to take off, but whenever the speed builds, you turn the runners inward and let the overhanging bundle of mining equipment scrape the slope. This, and the heavy braking from the cadets at the rear, seems to be keeping the load under control … so far anyway.

The screech of diamond hooks on rock sounds like a flock of angry pangos fighting for scraps.

Before long you've traversed across the width of the face. The first switchback is coming up. You lift the toe of your front boot and dig a heel spur into the rock. The front of the sledge presses against your backside. You can hear hooks digging deep behind you as the sledge slows even more.

Just before you reach the apex of the turn, you stab the needle end of your guide stick into the slope and kick both heels, pushing firmly to your left. The nose of the sledge responds, its runners grip, and the cumbersome load slowly swings around the hairpin. Once safely past the corner you realize you've been holding your breath and suck gulps of fresh cool air.

"One down and thirteen to go," you mumble to no one in

particular.

The second turn has been cut deeper into the rock leaving a knee-high barrier between you and the edge, but as soon as you are around the corner, the edge and the void beyond reappear. One hundred feet down the steep face, you see the track coming back the other way.

Sweat trickles down your forehead. A quick glance over your shoulder reveals the clenched jaws and wide eyes of the cadets behind you. You try to control your breathing. In through your nose and out through your mouth, slow and easy.

You were hoping the switchbacks would get easier as you went along, but that isn't the case. If anything they get harder. Your nerves jangle even more as you approach each new switchback. Your knees tremble. Some of the tremors are a result of the physical strain of sliding downhill, of holding back the weight of the sledge, but mostly your knees tremble in fear.

An instructor once told you that bravery isn't about not being afraid, it's about doing something despite your fear. Now that you're half way down the face … brave or not you've got no option but to continue.

When you finally round the last switchback you breathe a sigh of relief and raise your arm, signaling everyone to stop. "Once we get around these crevasses we'll have a proper break."

After a brief rest, Gagnon leads off once more. Ten minutes later you come to a halt on a flattish area beyond the crevasse field.

You give the order for the miners to tether their sledges. "Well done everyone. Let's break out the hydro and light the burners. I don't know about you, but I could do with a cup of hot broth."

Gagnon and Dagma fill their cups and come to sit beside you as you drink.

"I'm pleased that's over," you say. "That was tough."

Gagnon smiles. Color has returned to his face. "Now it's just the run down Long Gully and we'll be at the Pillars."

"We should go back to one brakeman per sledge," Dagma says. "If we're going to run across Lowlanders, Long Gully is where it's most likely to happen. Having all the cadets in harness will make us too slow to react. We should send a scouting party ahead of the main group as a precaution."

Gagnon shakes his head. "The sledges are too heavy. Why don't we double-sledge? With two sledges linked together we could get by with three cadets at the back. That way we can move fast but still have 50 percent extra braking power when we need it."

Dagma's head is nodding in agreement. "And we'll still have some spare cadets to scout ahead for trouble," she says.

You like Gagnon's idea. "Sounds like a good compromise. You're the strongest Dagma, would you like to choose another three cadets and lead the advanced team?"

Dagma seems surprised at your display of confidence. "What should we do if we come across Lowlanders?"

"Assess their numbers. If there's only a couple, try to capture them. That way Command can question them once we reach the Pillars of Haramon. If there are more than two, wait for the rest of us to arrive. No point in taking unnecessary chances."

Dagma calls out the names of the cadets she wants for her advanced team.

"Don't get too far in front, Dagma. Remember our goal is getting everyone to the Pillars in one piece. Let's not make any more mistakes, okay?"

Dagma gives you a funny look. "Have I made any mistakes today?"

She's right … you're the one who's made mistakes. A good leader has to trust their team members. You'll never gain her respect if you don't trust her.

"No, and that's why you're in charge of the scouting party. You're one of the best scouts we've got."

Dagma stands a little taller with the compliment. The hint of a smile crosses her face for the first time today.

"Okay everyone, listen up. Dagma and her team are going to scout

out front. Let's get these sledges reorganized. We've got to get to the Pillars before dewfall, and that means we need to get moving. Gagnon you act as guide for the rear group."

"Let's go," Dagma says, turning to her scouts.

Within a few minutes, Dagma's group are little more than charcoal dots on a black landscape.

The rest of the cadets are quick to reconfigure the sledges into pairs, a short cable linking them, one behind the other. One cadet clips on to the front of the front sledge and three cadets clip on to the back of the second sledge.

Long Gully is a slightly twisted half-pipe a quarter of a mile wide and sixty miles long. The idea is for the sledges to swoop back and forth down the valley in big sweeping S-turns using the natural contours of the gully to change direction and keep the sledges from gaining too much speed.

This part of the trip, assuming no Lowlanders are spotted, should be high-speed fun with little risk.

But things in the Highlands, are rarely simple, and never without an element of danger. To the south clouds are forming, pushing their way up the mountains from the interior. As the warm air rises, much of the moisture it contains fall as rain on the southern side of the divide but, unknown to you, some of the rain has crept over to the north and has begun to fall on the slopes high above you.

The first hint of danger is a trickle of water streaking the black rock on the far side of Long Gully. The water reflects silver in the afternoon light and is only a few yards wide, but there is no way you could run sledges through it without losing control.

Luckily one side of Long Gully is slightly lower than the other. By sticking to the high side your group can continue to travel. But, depending on how much rain falls on the upper slopes, you know this harmless looking trickle could spread and become a deadly torrent in a short space of time. Once that happens, wherever you are, you'll have no option but to find a place to anchor yourself and ride it out until it's safe to move off again.

You wonder if Dagma and her scouts have seen the danger. If so, they should have stopped by now, but there is no sign of them. Where could they be?

You signal the troop to a halt. "We need to find a safe place to anchor," you say raising your arm and pointing towards the rapidly widening stream. "That water is spreading."

The other cadets are chattering nervously between themselves.

Gagnon slides over to your position. "According to the map, there are some abandoned mine shafts about a mile down the valley. If we keep left we should be able to make it to them before the water spreads to this side."

There is no time to wait. You must make up your mind quickly.

"Everyone follow Gagnon. We need to get to shelter right now," you order.

Gagnon pushes off and does a series of shallow turns, keeping to the left-hand side of the valley. The rest of you follow. The water is spreading as new rivulets form. The water isn't that deep, but it doesn't have to be deep to be dangerous on the Black Slopes of Petron.

"There they are!" a cadet yells out. "I see the portals!"

Gagnon has seen them too. With a stab of his stick, he pushes towards a pair of narrow entrances cut into the slope of the half-pipe.

Some old scaffolding, once used by miners prospecting for tyranium needle crystals, is bolted onto the rock nearby, but there is no sign of current habitation.

"Hurry!" you shout to Gagnon. The water is nearly here."

Gagnon points his front foot at the portal and pushes harder with his stick. You look behind and see that new streams are forming across the slope. It is going to be a close call.

When Gagnon disappears into the hillside, you breathe a sigh of relief. The rest of you are right behind him. As long as there are no surprises in the tunnel, your troop will be fine.

"Tether your sledges everyone, we could be in for a long wait."

Once you've secured your sledge, you have time to look around. When you look up, it's like looking at the night sky. Moon moths have taken over. After admiring their beauty, you turn to look back outside.

The clouds have rolled in from higher up the mountain. Now, misty rain is falling and the far side of the gully has disappeared altogether. Water rushes downhill, following the contours of the ground. Small rivulets join together to form torrents.

Where is Dagma? Are she and her group of cadets still out in this weather?

They must have anchored themselves to the hill somewhere further down. If they haven't found shelter somewhere, they will be in for an unpleasant night out in the open.

Then you hear a hollow sounding voice echoing from further along the tunnel.

"What kept you?" It's Dagma and her scouts. "Didn't you see the water coming?"

Typical of Dagma to boast.

"You did have a head start remember. I thought I told you not to get too far in front."

"We've been investigating," Dagma says, changing the subject. "There's a side tunnel that runs downhill. It could lead towards the Pillars. Maybe we should go that way?"

Gagnon pulls out his map. "It's an old tunnel that comes out a mile above the Pillars, but it's miles long and over a hundred years old. Who knows what condition it's in."

"I think we should try it out," Dagma says. "Otherwise we're stuck here doing nothing until the slopes dry. Boring!"

You're not a big fan of sitting around either. It would be great to get closer to the Pillars. Then your troop won't have so far to go once the rain lets up. Command did say the equipment was urgent.

But old tunnels can deteriorate over time, and they get colonized by morph rats. How do you know if it is safe? You also know that earthquakes still rumble from time to time as the molten core tries to force its way to the surface.

It is time to make a decision. Do you:

Try to get closer to the Pillars by going down the tunnel? **P73**

Or

Stay put and wait for the slopes to dry before proceeding to the Pillars? **P75**

You have decided to go down the tunnel.

Moon moths light your way down the tunnel for the first mile or so, but as you and your troop get further into the tunnel, the moon moths become less frequent.

Before long you are forced to strap on headlamps so you can see where you're going. Slender veins of tyranium crystals streak through the black rock and make patterns along the walls as you slide.

Gagnon is back in the lead, with Dagma and her scouts close behind. The rest of your troop is sliding in formation behind them. In parts of the tunnel the slope is steep, requiring the dragging of hooks. Screeches fill your ears as they echo down the tunnel.

At first, you don't notice the trickle of water as it creeps down the tunnel behind you.

With every drop the rock you are sliding on becomes slicker. You need to put in an anchor bolt, and quickly. But to do that, you need to be stopped. All you can do at the moment is lean down on your hook and hope the ground levels out.

The rear sledges, caught by the water, are sliding faster than those in front. You hear a yell behind you. With moisture underfoot, nobody can slow down. You hear the sound of sledges colliding. Another cadet yells as she is knocked from her feet.

Will Gagnon and Dagma realize what is going on in time and be able to put in an anchor to stop the rest of you from sliding uncontrolled to the bottom of the tunnel in a jumble of bodies and equipment?

"Emergency anchors!" you yell at the top of your voice.

But it is too late. Water is rushing down the tunnel.

The sledge behind you smacks into your back and knocks you off your feet. You've made a huge mistake. Now your entire troop is heading towards the bottom of the tunnel in an uncontrolled slide.

Unfortunately, this part of your story is over. It was a poor decision to take your group down the old tunnel without checking it first. If you had, you would have discovered the tunnel had been damaged by earthquakes and that water would leak into it from the surface.

With luck some of your cadet might survive the pile-up at the bottom, but for you this part of your story has come to an end. Would you choose differently next time?

It is now time for you to make another decision. Do you:

Go back to the beginning of the story and try another path? **P1**

Or

Go back to your last decision and make another choice? **P75**

Wait for the slopes to dry rather than go down the tunnel.

"We may as well light a burner and have some broth," you say to the cadets. "Who knows how long it will be before we can head out."

The others waste no time in getting a makeshift kitchen organized. A thin boy with blond hair comes to where you are sitting and hands you a steaming cup.

"Thanks," you say, leaning back against your pack and looking up as you sip. Hundreds of glowing moon moths hang from the ceiling

After finishing your broth you close your eyes and try to sleep.

The rain continues for the rest of the afternoon and most of the night. When you wake up and look outside it is just getting light. As the temperature rises, and the sun sneaks over the ridge, vapor rises from the black rock.

Thankfully, the sky is clear with no further sign of cloud.

"Okay everyone, the slopes are drying fast. We should be able to move out in less than an hour. Get some food into you and then get these sledges turned around and ready to go."

Everyone is keen to get moving again, especially Dagma, who helps light the burner and gives the other cadets a hand passing out broth and dried hydro.

"There might be a few damp patches on the slope, so let's hook up with two brakes per sledge," you say. "We don't want any accidents so close to the Pillars."

"But what about scouts?" Dagma says, disappointed to be back in harness.

You shake your head. "I doubt any Lowlanders will be left on the slope after that downpour. Better we play it safe."

Dagma shrugs and finds a spot at the back on one of the sledges.

When you feel the slopes have dried enough, you turn to Gagnon. "Shall we get out of here?"

The morning air is cool and clear, but already you can feel the warmth of the rock beneath you. Whatever dust was in the air has been washed away by the rain. You can see so far it's amazing.

The braided river delta far below sparkles like a diamond necklace. The ocean and horizon beyond seem closer somehow. Twenty miles further down Long Gully, you can just see the tops of the Pillars of Haramon poking above the surrounding terrain.

Gagnon pushes off and leads the group on a swooping path that takes you up one side of the valley and then across to the other.

You smile as you slide, the wind in your face, whipping at your hair. This is what you like best about being a Highland slider. It's the feeling you get as you race down a mountainside, the whole world spread out before you. It's being part of a group that will do anything to keep you safe and knowing you will do the same in return. It's the way a slider can use gravity to move with grace and speed with so little effort. It's the closest thing to soaring you've ever felt.

Before you know it, your troop is screeching to a stop outside the main portal of the northernmost pillar.

An officer is there to greet you. "Well done, cadets," he says. "Welcome to the Pillars of Haramon."

Congratulations, you have made it to the Pillars of Haramon. You've brought much needed supplies and equipment that will help keep your communities safe from the Lowlanders. This part of your mission is complete. But have you tried all the different paths the story can take? Have you gone mining? Fought off morph rats? Discovered the moon moths' secret?

It is time to make another decision. Do you:

Go back to the beginning of the story and try another path? **P1**

Or

Go to the list of choices and start reading from another part of the story? **P307**

You have decided to make best speed.

"Keep an extra sharp lookout everyone," you say before giving the order to move out.

You look over your shoulder. Back up the valley, clouds are beginning to boil over the upper slopes from the south. Scouting ahead takes time. Getting down the slope quickly makes more sense. At the tow base you will find shelter from both the elements and any Lowlanders that might be lurking.

The base you're heading towards is built deep within the rock face. Its defensive positions overlook the slopes, making approach from below by any attacking force difficult.

You've seen pictures of Tow-Base 9's defenses in the cadet training manuals. Once the sun's rays shine into the valley, the base is almost unassailable. Mounted in strategic positions are a number of dish-shaped lenses that can focus the burning rays of the sun onto any intruder foolish enough to attack. Like a magnifying glass, this concentrated beam will fry anything it touches faster than pango egg on a burner's plate.

After dewfall in the early evening and until the slopes dry the next day, moisture makes movement almost impossible for the Lowlanders, who lack high quality needle crystals, and the other hardware needed to traverse the slope in anything but the best possible conditions.

The tow's rotating wheel is protected by huge blocks of black glass on its three exposed sides, leaving only a narrow slit, on the uphill side, open to allow the towline an unobstructed run up the towpath to the ridge above.

The Highland Slider Corps have placed this base with precision. Any attack would have to be late enough in the day for the dew to have evaporated, but be staged prior to the sun shining into the valley when the Highlanders can focus their burning disks, a window of less than an hour each day.

As you slide, you wonder what the Lowlanders had been planning.

You suspect they were trying to circle around and get above the base. That way they could mount a surprise attack from above. It's just as well your troop showed up. Lowlanders in control of the tow would have been a disaster for the Slider Corps.

Now is not the time to think about your success, you tell yourself. You need to keep your mind on your current task. But with the amazing views off to the north, it's hard to focus. You try to imagine the awesome forces that formed this place — the rumbling earthquakes, and massive lava flows. Despite the seriousness of the situation, you can't help but smile. After all, your love of nature was the main reason you became a slider.

As you travel down, you notice the terrain on both sides of the valley is getting steeper. On one part of the slope, a number of slender volcanic columns thrust up from the slope to tower above the surrounding terrain. You can tell that these pinnacles have been here a long time because wind and rain have eroded them. Fissures and holes are dotted about their pitted surface.

In these cracks and crannies, hundreds of wild pangos have made their nests. You can see the bird's light grey bodies and shiny red beaks contrasting the dark rock as they crowd together, screeching and squabbling for the limited nesting spaces. At the base of one of the columns is a crude shelter used by egg hunters during the laying season.

During the breeding season female pangos sit on their eggs while the males fly many miles to the lowlands where they fill up with grain and fish before making the return journey to empty their gullets to feed the sitting females.

Once the clutch of pango eggs hatch, both parents make the journey each day, bringing back food for their babies until the young are able to fly and hunt for themselves.

Your attention is distracted from the pango colony by Gagnon waving and pointing down the slope to the right. It's Tow-Base 9. You can see the sun glinting off the tow's cable as it runs up the hillside.

You lower your guide stick and turn the sledge you are leading a little more to the right. A hand signal tells the cadets on the back to get ready to drag their hooks. Within minutes, your group is pulling up at the tow-base.

Some crew members have spotted you coming down the valley and have opened a portal. Pushing right once more, you allow the last of your momentum to carry the sledge neatly through the opening and into the parking bay bored deep into the rock.

Two members of the tow-base's crew are there to greet you.

Once your cadets are inside, a door glides shut with barely a sound. Thin slits in the outer wall provide just enough light for you to see a three-way junction about ten paces further on.

In typical Slider Corps fashion, single letters indicate where each tunnel goes. A indicates accommodation, H for hydro chambers, and D for the base's defensive positions. The Slider Corps have always been ones for simplicity.

"Okay everyone get your harnesses off and await instructions." You turn to the tow's crew and salute. "Troop 6-E reporting as instructed."

"Nice to see you made it, cadets," the older of the two crew members says. "We've had reports of Lowlanders in the valley."

As you tell them about your trip, one walks to a series of small holes bored in the smooth black wall. She shouts into one of them and then listens closely for the reply. You've heard about these communication pipes, but this is the first time you've seen them.

"Your troop is in accommodation pod 2," the crew member says. "I'll call ahead and let them know you're coming."

You are impressed with the base's method of communication. These holes must lead all over the base.

"Let's get you lot settled. Your gear can stay where it is."

You and your team follow the tunnel marked "A" deeper into the hillside. Holes bored in the roof provide just enough light to see where you are going. Although long and dingy, the corridor eventually leads to pod 2. The pod is circular and has sleeping notches cut into the wall like those at the slider training base. But unlike the training base, the notches here are stacked three-high and there is not much extra space to store personal stuff. Not that you expected luxuries at an advanced base like this one.

The crew member waiting to assist your group to settle in is surprising in more ways than one. Firstly, she is taller than any of your group and secondly her flame-red hair makes you look twice. It has to be the brightest hair you've ever seen.

When Gagnon sees her, he can't help staring.

"Is there anything else I can get you?" the redhead asks.

You shake your head. "I think we can find our way around. This pod is laid out similar to our last one."

"I hear the Lowlanders are gathering," she says. "Sometimes they dip their arrows in pango poo you know. Boy, does that cause infection."

"Thankfully we carry antibiotics for that," you say.

"Just as well. Now, if you'll excuse me, I'd better get back to work."

Just as she is leaving, another crew member comes in with a trolley loaded with hydro and broth. The cadets and mining students are starving and descend on the cart like a pack of scavengers.

Just as you're finishing the last of your broth, a slightly distorted voice echoes through a communication hole in the wall.

"Cadet Leader 6-E, please report to Defense One."

You're not exactly sure where Defense One is, but you know it will be down the "D" corridor somewhere.

When the message is repeated, you figure it must be urgent and waste no time in leaving the sleeping pod. When you reach the junction you turn into the D corridor. Not far along, the tunnel splits into four. Each is marked with a number. You take the first and start up a narrow set of steps cut into the pure black rock.

The staircase spirals around in a tight circle. You start counting each step as you go without even realizing it.

Defense One has a curved window of black glass, ground so thin it is almost clear. "Nice view," you say to a pair of officers sitting around a small table in the middle of the pod.

The window overlooks the entire valley. Wisps of smoke rise from the foothills far below where the Lowlanders have made their camp.

"It will be until I see those 20,000 Lowlanders marching up the valley," an officer says.

You gulp when you hear the number.

The officer does not look happy. "We've heard they've got some new machine that moves up the slope by drilling holes that allow a rotating sprocket on the front to grip the slope. Our scouts have seen them from a distance but that's about all we know. The machine our scouts saw was towing a hundred Lowlanders at a time. The Lowlanders must have found a new source of diamonds somewhere."

You start to say something, but then stop. This is a time to listen to those with more experience.

The officer has worry lines across his forehead. "We'll need more information if we're to send these machines to the bottom."

"So what is Troop 6-E to do, sir?"

"Tomorrow morning you will continue on to the Pillars of Haramon, as planned. If you see one of these machines along the way, your orders are to stop, watch, and in the event you spot a weakness, attack. We can't let the Lowlanders get above us. All our defensive positions are based on them coming at us from below. If one of these machines transports enough of their men up onto one of our main trails we could be in real trouble. Think your troop is up for that?"

You swallow hard. "Of course sir!"

"Okay. Best you get back to your cadets and get a good night's sleep. Tomorrow could be a long day."

That night you dream of shiny black pillars, and all the possible ways tomorrow might go. When the wake-up buzzer goes off, you bounce to your feet, keen to get going.

After a quick meal and toilet stop, you lead your troop back to the sledges and sort out the teams. This tow is steeper and longer than the others you've been on and there are no stops on the way up. It's just one long run to the ridgeline.

You check your harness and get ready to clamp on. The cable is a blur as it whirls up the slope. "On my mark…"

As your clamp grips, you and your sledge start moving up the slope. You've been warned by the base's crew that the offloading platform at the top is narrow. Hopefully everyone will be alert. The last thing you want is for a team to overshoot the ridge and go plummeting down the other side.

The intensive cadet training has paid off and everyone arrives at the top in one piece. An officer is waiting.

"Now keep your eyes open," he says. "Remember, we know almost nothing about this new machine, so obtaining information is vital. Don't risk yourselves unless you see a weakness you can exploit. Good luck."

You salute and order your troop move off along the ridge. This narrow track will lead you to a traverse that runs towards the top of Long Gully. Then it's down Long Gully to the Pillars of Haramon, some fifty-two miles from where you are standing.

Once again Gagnon takes the lead. Everyone handles the traverse track well, but when you turn into Long Gully proper, you spot something you've not seen before.

A series of angled holes have been bored into the rock. As you inspect the holes you can just imagine how a machine, fitted with a large rotating sprocket, could move up and down these holes without any problem. Each tooth on a sprocket would have a corresponding hole for it to lock in to. The machine could climb as fast as the wheel could rotate and a drill could drill.

You fit your guide stick into one of the holes and the toe of your boot in another and take a step up. At least you and your cadets can use this track to gain altitude as well.

But that doesn't change the disturbing fact that one of these Lowland machines is above you. This is exactly what the officer at the tow base was afraid of. Should you follow the track and try to gain vital information? Or is the equipment you're transporting more important? You can see merit in both courses of action.

It is time to make one of the most important decisions of your command. Do you:

Go up the mountain and scout out the Lowlanders' new machine? **P93**

Or

Take the vital equipment to the Pillars of Haramon? **P102**

Send some advanced scouts to test the route first.

Sending advanced scouts to check the route makes sense. Advanced scouts will enable you to see any Lowlanders that may have infiltrated the area before they see you, and more importantly, while you are still above them. Altitude is a critical advantage when on the Black Slopes of Petron.

Rather than sending Dagma out, you choose to lead a small group yourself. Now that you know Lowlanders are daring to come up the mountains, you want to be in a position to make quick decisions.

"Gagnon, come with me. Dagma, you hang back with the others and wait for my signal."

Dagma frowns. You can tell she hates being left at the rear. "So we all need babysitting now do we?" she mumbles.

It annoys you that Dagma isn't a team player. Why does she have to make snide comments under her breath? What good will that do the troop?

"Shut it, Dagma," you say. "One more word and I'll put you on report."

"You wouldn't."

"Just try me!"

Dagma, so often the dominant personality in the troop, isn't used to being told what to do. Her mouth begins to open, but no words come out. Instead, she looks down at her feet in silence.

The other cadets snicker.

"Right, Gagnon, let's get going. The rest of you wait for my signal before sliding down to our position."

You relock your boots, put your front foot forward and push off with you guide stick. Gagnon follows. The soft hiss of boots on rock is all you can hear.

You aim towards the far right-hand side of the gully where you'll get a clear view down the slope. Once there you sweep left in a gentle arc towards the center again.

It's amazing how quickly you progress down the slope. Within a few minutes the cadets look like toys in the distance.

You drag your hook and come to a stop. Then you pull out your scope and look down the slope.

"All clear," you say to Gagnon.

You know Dagma will be impatiently studying you through her scope. You wave an arm and signal her and the other cadets to slide down and join you.

At first, the vibration under you feet is barely noticeable. You attribute your slight loss of balance to a gust of wind. But when the second tremor shakes you off your feet, you realize it's an earthquake.

You pull the anchor gun from your belt and fire a bolt into the rock. Both you and Gagnon clip on as quickly as possible. There may be more to come.

As suspected, the first jolts were pre-shocks to the main event.

A low rumbling is approaching, getting louder and louder as it does so. When the wave of energy reaches the surface a huge crack appears in the slope above you, ripping the gulley in half from one side to the other and creating a gaping crevasse between you and the cadets sliding down the slope towards you.

The shaking goes on for over a minute. The crack widens. How deep it goes is hard to tell from your position, but you have no doubt it will be deep enough to severely injure, if not kill, anyone falling into it.

You get your scope out of its pouch and focus on the cadets above. Some have fallen. There is nothing you can do apart from shout a warning and hope they manage to stop in time.

Another aftershock hits you, nearly as big at the first jolt. The dots above are getting bigger. You hear screeching. When the shaking stops and you manage to focus your scope again, you see that many cadets are still off their feet desperately trying to get up.

Standard procedure in these situations is to turn your sledge side-on to the slope to stop its downward momentum, but to do that, the cadet steering the sledge needs to be in control. That is impossible when you are on your backside free sliding down the hill. Sledges are skewed. One sledge is on its side dragging its crew down the hill behind it.

Before long, those above are close enough for you to pick out individual faces. Dagma is nearest. Her large frame stands out from the crowd. She is still on her feet with her hook hard down. Her sledge has nearly stopped. For once Dagma rushing off in front is an advantage. Thankfully the others sliding behind her are still much further up the slope.

You hear the pop of an anchor gun as Dagma fires a bolt into the rock. In a flash her sledge is tethered and she is looking back over her shoulder figuring out how to stop the others.

A couple of the sledges are slowing due to good work by their crew, but two are out of control and gaining speed. They are now within a quarter of a mile of the yawning chasm angling across the slope below them.

Another rumble passes up from below. The edge of the huge crevasse cracks and sends sharks of black glass plummeting down into it.

Your eyes are riveted on the drama above. You hear another two pops in quick succession, as more cadets manage to anchor their sledges.

Dagma quickly shrugs off her harness and slides across the slope, pulling a cable behind her. She crosses the path of the two out of control sledges sliding down towards her. Once she's gone far enough she fires another anchor bolt into the ground and wraps the cable around it.

"She's trying to snag the runners of those two runaway sledges," you say to Gagnon.

"Will it be strong enough?" Gagnon asks.

"We'll know in a couple of seconds." You cross your fingers and hope Dagma's plan works.

When the runners of the first sledge slide under the cable you can see the line begin to stretch. The sledge's momentum slows, but in the process the sledge skews sideways.

Dagma fires another anchor bolt into the slope and wraps the excess cable around it.

The cable seems to be holding, but the sledge is now side-on to the slope and starting to tip over.

"It's going to roll!" Gagnon yells.

Just as the sledge reaches tipping point, the second sledge hits the cable.

The extra stretch its impact provides drops the first sledge back onto its runners long enough for the cadets harnessed up to it to get their own anchors in.

Thankfully the second sledge is going slower than the first. Its runner slides under the cable and it comes to an abrupt, but satisfying halt.

"Wow that was close," you say.

"You're telling me," Gagnon says. "But what now?"

You look up at the tangle of sledges and their shaken passengers. A huge crack lies between you and the rest of your troop. To your right the crack runs slightly downhill, across the slope and all the way to the cliffs beyond.

To your left the crevasse runs to the far side and up the opposite slope for nearly fifty yards terminating in a steep bluff. There is no detour around the crevasse that way. You have no option but to find a way across.

You and Gagnon start working your way back up the slope towards the newly formed crevasse. Dagma has clipped on to a line and is abseiling down to check out the obstacle from above.

The crevasse is deep. The gap between you and your troop is about five yards.

"What now?" Dagma yells out across the void.

That is a very good question. You could sling a cable and get your cadets across the gap, but the heavy and cumbersome sledges are a different proposition altogether.

You would fail in your mission if you left all this valuable equipment on the slope when it is so desperately needed at the Pillars of Haramon.

One of the miners has abseiled down to where Dagma is standing.

She secures herself and then looks at you across the empty space. "Can I make a suggestion?" the miner says.

"Sure," you say, happy to have some ideas come your way.

"If we put a series of anchor bolts on both sides of the crevasse, we can use mineshaft props to build a makeshift bridge."

"Would it hold the weight of a sledge?"

"No problem," the miner says.

You look at Gagnon. He nods.

"Okay," you say. "Let's do it."

It takes about an hour for the miners to get the metal bridge bolted together. It looks like a big ladder made from pipe. Then you've got the tricky job of maneuvering the bridge across the crevasse and anchoring it securely to both sides.

Once it's secure, the runners of a sledge should be able to slide across the ladder without falling through the gaps … in theory at least.

Each sledge has a steering lever that can be controlled from onboard so the crew can climb aboard and ride across. The sledges speed can be slowed by a cable attached to a belay point on the uphill side.

The first trip across the bridge is a nervous affair.

"Geebus that's a long way down!" Piver says once the sledge he's riding is safely across.

Once all the sledges have crossed, a miner comes over to you. "I'm pretty sure I saw a vein of diamonds in that crevasse as I was crossing."

"Really? You've got good eyes."

"Light reflects differently off diamonds. It's just a matter of knowing what to look out for."

You look at the miner and wonder if he knows what he is talking about. But then if anyone is to know about diamonds, it makes sense that it would be a miner. Why would he make this up? In fact, why would he tell you about the diamonds all? He could just come back at some time in the future and keep them all for himself.

"So why are you telling me?"

"You sliders saved my life. I was on that sledge heading for the crevasse."

Of course, one of the sledges Dagma saved.

The miner continues. "I think we should take some samples and stake a claim. We can all share it. Imagine how rich we'll be."

He has a point. Finding a vein of blue diamond would be big news and big profits. Few of the cadets come from wealthy families. Nobody joins the Slider Corps for the money.

"Can we do that?" you ask.

The miner shows you a sparkling row of teeth. "Yep. We sure can. I'll get my climbing gear and some survey pegs, okay?"

"Sounds like a plan," you say, eager to find out if what the miner says about the diamonds is true.

It only takes ten minutes to rig up a harness so the miner can safely abseil down into the crevasse. Attached to his belt are a hand pick, collection bag, impact drill, and pry rod.

"Dewfall isn't that far away," you tell the miner before he goes over the edge. "You've got fifteen minutes to get what you need. After that, we're pulling you up."

The miner nods, leans out over the void and walks backwards down the sheer wall of stone, letting out cable as he goes. When he gets to the layer he spotted earlier he stops and starts chipping away.

You lie on your belly and look over the edge. "Are they diamonds?"

"Sure are. Number 1s by the looks of them," he yells back.

Number 1s are top grade, used for making the hooks on guide sticks and drills for boring holes in the tough black glass.

After a few more minutes you yell down again. "Okay time's up. We need to get going."

Half a dozen cadets start hauling on the cable. Before long, the miner and his collection bag are back on the surface.

"Have a look," the miner says.

You hold out your hand and he pours a number of sparkling blue stones into your palm.

"They don't look much in their raw state," he says. "But once they've been polished, you'll barely be able to look at them without some sort of eye protection."

You are lost for words. They are beautiful, alive with light, glowing softly in your hand.

"Wow," you finally get out.

It takes some discipline to take your eyes away from the mesmerizing sight, but you know you need to get your troop down to the tow-base ... and soon. Dewfall is fast approaching.

"Are you just going to leave the ladder here?" Dagma asks.

"Yes," you say. "If we need to get back across in a hurry, it will come in handy."

Dagma grunts and attaches her harness to the back of a sledge.

"Oh and well done Dagma, you did a great job saving those runaway sledges. I'm going to recommend you for an award when we get to the Pillars of Haramon. You deserve one."

The others overhear your comments and congratulate her too. For the first time during the trip, you see her smile.

You give Dagma her moment in the sun, but when you look back up the slope you can see wispy clouds forming near the tops. "Okay, let's get moving. We've still got a few miles to go and it's starting to look like rain."

The aftershocks have stopped. After sliding for another hour or so without incident, Gagnon yells and points down the slope to the right. It's your destination.

As the last of the sun reflects off the oiled cable from Tow-Base 9, you lower your guide stick and turn your sledge a little more to the right. Then you signal the cadets at the back to begin dragging their hooks.

Someone has spotted you coming down the valley and has opened a portal. Pushing right once more, you allow your remaining momentum to ease the sledge neatly through the entry and into the parking bay bored into the rock. The others are right behind you.

Two members of the tow-base's crew are there to greet you. They guide the troop to its sleeping pod where a meal has been prepared.

The next morning your troops make their way up a long tow, along the ridge and then into the head of Long Gully. Sixty miles down this picturesque valley are the Pillars of Haramon and your final destination.

You imagine turning up with your troop, a bag of number 1s and a $1/40^{th}$ share in what could be one of the biggest finds of diamonds in recent times.

The miner who spotted the vein of diamonds in the crevasse has transferred to your sledge, and he's been giving you a crash course in prospecting and mine management while you travel.

It's amazing how finding diamonds has sparked an interest you never realized you had.

By mid afternoon the next day, your troop is pulling up outside one of the Pillars.

An officer greets you with a salute and directs you and your cadets to their accommodation pod. The miners get busy unpacking the much needed equipment for improving defensive positions and creating more magnifying disks to fight off invasion.

You climb up a narrow set of stairs to the top observation pod where you are debriefed by Command. While you are there you register the mining claim you've pegged out on behalf of your cadets and the student miners.

"Looks like everyone's hit the jackpot," the officer says. "Once tax is taken out, you should be left with a tidy profit."

You think about the officer's words and realize you *have* hit the jackpot. You're doing something you love. The profit you make from your share of the diamonds means you can help your family out, and you're standing a thousand feet above one of the most beautiful landscapes on the planet. What's not to like about that?

From high up in the observation pod you can see a patchwork of fields on the Lowlands below. Bright purples, greens, pinks and oranges create a mosaic of color across the flats towards the delta where braided rivers shimmer like necklaces as they meander back and forth. Beyond the delta, the ocean stretches off into the horizon.

You've heard stories about the ocean and wonder what it's like to swim in so much water. You wonder what it's like to be a Lowlander, to walk around on flat ground, where there isn't any danger of slipping and sliding to the bottom. Then you look back towards the towering Black Slopes of home and you realize you're happy where you are. Like generations before you, you are a Highlander, and proud of it.

Congratulations, you have reached the end of this part of your story. You have made it successfully to the Pillars of Haramon with your precious cargo and you have a share in a diamond mine. Well done!

But have you followed all the possible story lines? Have you gone mining, found tunnels, heard the cry of the wild pango, been attacked by morph rats? Discovered the secrets of the moon moth?

It's time for another decision. Do you.

Go back to the beginning of the story and try another path? **P1**

Or

Go to the list of choices and start reading from another part of the story? **P307**

You have decided to go scout out the new Lowland machine.

The track is nothing more than a series of fist-sized holes drilled into the slope. It runs straight up the mountain. Each hole is a perfect fit for the toe of your boot so it should be no problem following the track uphill.

The sledges are another matter. There is no way you can take them with you. Nor do you want to leave them unattended where another Lowland patrol might find them.

You'll have to split your troop up. But how many cadets should you leave behind to guard the sledges? Maybe rather than having them wait, you should send the sledges on down to the Pillars of Haramon with the mining students while a smaller group chases this machine.

You decide that three heads are better than one when it comes to making decisions.

"Dagma, Gagnon, we need to talk."

The two cadets unclip from their sledges and slide over.

You look once more at the track running up the hill. Then you take your glove off and stick your hand in one of the holes. The rock is still slightly warm from the friction of being drilled. The machine can't be too far away.

"What do you think? Should we split up and get the miners down to the Pillars while the rest of us check this out?"

Gagnon's gaze follows the track up the slope. He shakes his head. "Weirdest thing I've ever seen. It must be quite a contraption to be able to cut into the rock like this."

"Let's go up and get them," Dagma growls. "I'm not afraid of Lowlanders and their stupid machine!"

Once again Dagma is overflowing with raw emotion. Is it clouding her judgment? You wonder if she will ever realize that being afraid is okay. Real bravery is about doing what you must, despite your fear, not rushing at things like a demented morph rat.

You wish you had more time to consider things, but the time is passing. Your troop must get to the Pillars of Haramon before dewfall makes the slopes impossible to travel.

"I'm thinking most of our group should keep sliding down the valley towards the Pillars. A small scouting party will be less visible from above. If we can find out what the Lowlanders are up to, we might even come up with a plan to stop them."

Gagnon nods. "Sounds like a good idea. You have to walk softly to catch a pango."

"What?" Dagma snarls at Gagnon. "Why are you talking about pangos?"

Gagnon shakes his head and shrugs.

You turn to Dagma. "He means we need to move slowly and cautiously."

"Well why didn't he just say that?"

You ponder things a moment. "I agree with Gagnon. If we're going to get any useful information there's no point in rushing blindly up the hill just to get captured and end our days picking grain on some Lowland penal farm."

Your mind is whirling with options. Do you want Dagma on this expedition or should you send her down to the Pillars with the miners? What if she loses control and does something stupid?

"Okay. Listen up everyone," you say, "I'm sending the majority of you on to the Pillars of Haramon. Gagnon you'll be in charge."

Most of the miners seem relieved to be heading towards safety. You have little doubt the level headed Gagnon will get them there in one piece.

"Dagma, myself and two other cadets, will scout up the hill and try to find out what the Lowlanders are up to. If they spot us, we'll free slide back down as quickly as possible and catch up with you." At least with Dagma by your side, you can keep an eye on her. "Gagnon get going. We want this equipment as far from the Lowlanders as we can get it."

After picking two of your fittest cadets, you prepare to start the chase. "I hope you all feel like climbing," you say to your small group, "because it's all uphill from here."

Over your shoulder you hear Gagnon give the order for the sledges to move out.

You look at your three cadets. "We'll take turns leading. One will climb then the others can zip up to conserve their strength. That way we won't have to stop for breaks. It's the only way we'll have any chance of catching up with this machine of theirs. I'll go first. Get ready to move."

Without waiting for comments from the others you grab a cable and climb rapidly up the line of holes provided by the Lowland machine. After a hundred quick steps, you stop and belay the others who clip their battery-powered zippers onto the light-weight cable. The tiny, but powerful rotor whirls and the cadets are quickly dragged up the hill.

"Dagma, you climb next," you say.

She takes hold of the cable and repeats the procedure, sprinting up the hill like it's a race. When Dagma reaches the end of the cable and has a secure belay in place, you and the other two cadets clip on and zip up to her.

By taking turns doing the hard uphill slog, it isn't long before the four of you have made considerable progress up the mountainside. When you reach the highest point on the ridge, the machine's tracks turn west.

You pull out your scope. In the distance you see the Lowland machine steaming along. A mechanism mounted on an extendable arm in front of the machine is drilling the track holes with quick precision. Behind the drill is a big sprocket with pointed teeth that fit neatly into the pre-drilled holes. As this sprocket rotates, it pulls the machine along the smooth rock on its long metal runners.

The machine has armored sides with viewing holes along its length and there is some sort of spring loaded mechanism on top and piles of cable. These must be the nets you've heard about.

Sitting on top of the machine are Lowlanders.

The machine is also towing a cable with at least thirty more Lowland troopers clipped on to it. How many Lowlanders are inside the machine is anyone's guess.

You and the other cadets lie on the ground and study the scene before you.

"Where do you think they're going?" Dagma asks.

You pull a map from a pouch in your utility belt and spread it out on the ground before you. "They must be heading toward the Haramon Reservoir," you say. "All the settlements north and west of here, not to mention the base at the Pillars, rely on that water."

"Do you think they are going to poison it?" Dagma asks.

"I don't know. But we need to find out."

Protecting the Haramon Reservoir has never been a priority. Lowlanders have never been able to get this high up the mountain before, so security is minimal.

"What are we going to do?" Dagma asks.

"We're going to think of a way stop to them," you say. You turn to the cadets crouched behind you. "I need you two to slide back down and let those at the Pillars of Haramon know what is going on, just in case Dagma and I get captured or injured. Can you do that?"

"Yes," they say in unison.

"Well get going. It's important that they know that their water supply might be compromised, so be safe and get there in one piece."

You would have liked to have kept one of the two cadets with you, but you know that traveling in a pair is always safer than going solo. The two cadets waste no time in locking their boots together and sliding off down the slope. You and Dagma resume your study of the Lowland machine through your scopes.

After a few minutes you put your scope down. "Any ideas, Dagma?"

"There are so many of them," she says. "We might be able to handle a few, but…"

For the first time Dagma's voice seems a little shaky. You lift your scope again, hoping you'll see something that Dagma has missed.

The machine is making steady progress along the ridge towards the next valley where the reservoir is located. As you follow the ridgeline with your scope, you notice there is one point where it narrows to little more than the width of the machine. A plan begins to form in your mind.

"How much do you reckon that machine weighs, Dagma?"

"I don't know. A ton and a half at least … plus the weight of the crew and those riding on top."

"So that's maybe four thousand pounds altogether. What do the thirty Lowlanders being towed behind it weigh?"

As you wait for Dagma's answer you do some calculations in your head. Thirty times an average weight of 150 pounds per Lowlander is 4500 pounds, a little more that the weight of the machine, its crew and passengers.

"If we can somehow push the troopers being towed over the edge just as the machine reaches that pinch-point on the ridge, do you think their combined weight will be enough to pull the machine over?"

Dagma considers what you've said a moment and then grins. "It's worth a crack. Once the first few are knocked off, it might start a chain reaction that takes them all."

"Stealth and timing will be everything. If they hear us coming, we'll be pin cushions before we even get close."

"You'd better follow me then," Dagma says with a grin. "I'll make a good shield."

As crazy as her comment sounds, it actually makes good sense. At least with Dagma in front, if you're spotted the mission still has a chance of success.

"You're crazy, Dagma. Brave, but crazy."

Once again you look through your scope and calculate the distance the machine has to travel to the narrowest part of the ridge. Then you estimate how far it is from your current position to the Lowlanders being towed.

At the current rate of progress the machine will be in position in about one and a half minutes. That gives you less than a minute to come up with a better plan or change your mind.

You look at Dagma. "We've got to decide now. Are you sure you want to do this?"

An evil grin crosses Dagma's face as she reverses her pack so that it protects her chest. "Does a morph rat stink? Let's send these pango-headed fools to the bottom."

You were afraid she'd say that. You've already started counting down in your head. After one last look through the scope you pack it away and get ready for the slide of your life.

"Tuck in behind, hands on my waist," Dagma says. "Let's go in low, fast and quiet."

"You have the lead, cadet," you say unhooking your boots and crouching down behind Dagma's bulk.

Dagma places her guide stick on the ground ready for a big push. "On my mark, three, two, one…"

Both of you push off as hard as you can and tuck into a low crouch. Only subtle adjustments are needed to keep you heading down the ridge towards the Lowlanders.

The wind is cool against the skin on your face as you peer over Dagma's shoulder. With every second, you gain speed.

When you are forty yards away, a Lowlander riding on top of the machine spots you and raises the alarm, but it is too late to save the last Lowlander from being slammed over the edge and down the steep slope. Before the next trooper has time to brace, he too is plucked off the ridge. The first two jerk the next one off his feet and over the edge, then another, and another.

You and Dagma drag your hooks to a stop and watch the perfect chain reaction unfold.

Now it's only a question of whether their combined weight will be enough to dislodge the machine.

You hold your breath as the last of the towed Lowlanders goes over. The weight on the rope has pulled the machine's rear end off line. Its rear runners are inching closer and closer to the edge.

Just as the machine starts to topple, the troops on top shift their weight to the opposite side from where the troopers have gone over. The machine teeters on the brink.

With a squeak, the back door of the machine flies open. You expect to see more troopers jumping out and attempt to stabilize the machine, but those fleeing the machine are too small to be troopers.

"The machine's full of children," you yell out to Dagma.

This is not at all what you expected. What are the Lowlanders doing with a bunch of children way up here?

"We've made a mistake Dagma. We've got to help."

Before you have time to stop her, Dagma has pushed off and is sliding towards the machine. She pulls a light-weight cable from her belt and forms it into a loop.

As she nears the back of the machine she throws the cable over a bracket and then turns and plummets over the opposite side of the ridge to where the Lowland troopers have fallen.

Seconds later you hear the familiar pop of an anchor gun.

The machine's runners edge closer to the sheer drop. Voices of struggling Lowlanders call out from below. You hold your breath as the cable Dagma has hooked onto the machine stretches tight.

You understand what she's done and why and slide down to help. You throw another cable around a handrail along the side of the machine and shoot a bolt into the rock.

Lowland children mill about wondering what to do. The machine has stabilized, but any false step could send one these youngsters down the steep face on either side of the ridge.

The right-hand side of the machine is almost at the edge, but at least the machine isn't moving now due to the anchors you and Dagma have put in on the other side.

Then you see Dagma's head appear above the ridgeline as she

climbs back up the cable. When she reaches flat ground she flops down and heaves a huge sigh.

"Phew, that was exciting," she says, wiping the sweat off her forehead.

As you move towards Dagma, the adult Lowlanders work frantically to get their machine stabilized. A few Lowlanders look in your direction, but you are no longer a threat. Besides they are too busy securing the machine and keeping the children safe to worry about you.

"Should we take off?" Dagma whispers, her inherent distrust of Lowlanders coming to the surface once more.

"I want to find out why they have children up here. Something strange is going on. But if you want to make a run for it, feel free."

Dagma shrugs and stays where she is. "Best we stick together, don't you think?"

A few minutes later a Lowlander comes over to where the two of you are sitting. "I suppose you want to know what's going on," he says.

"We thought you were going to poison our water supply," you say as you stand to face him. "But then we saw the children and realized we'd jumped to conclusions."

"Understandable I suppose," the Lowlander says. "We've not had the best of relationships with you Highlanders over recent years."

"So why are you up here?" Dagma asks. "We nearly sent you all to the bottom."

"We're refugees from the delta. We escaped by stealing one of the Lowland army's new machines. We found some old uniforms to put on to keep warm. We're not used to the chilly mountain air."

You look around and notice that many of the Lowlanders are women. Normally Lowland troops are male. Then you see the patched elbows and frayed cuffs.

This ragtag bunch is made up of family units. It's not a troop of fighters at all.

"The Lowlanders are trying to force our men to fight. But we have no quarrel with the Highlanders. We are all the same blood after all. We just want a peaceful life, shelter, food and happiness for our children."

"Sounds fair enough, but where do you plan to go?" you ask.

"We are going to resettle on the far side of the mountains. We hear there are good pastures in the interior."

You nod. "Yes, I've heard that too. Still, that's quite a dangerous slide, especially with children and without trained people to escort you."

"What other choice do we have?"

You can understand his position. Lowlanders that refuse to fight are put into penal farms and used as forced labor. Nobody in their right mind would want that as a life.

"I have an idea," you say to the man.

The Lowlander seems interested. "I'm willing to listen if you can suggest something that will keep my family safe."

"We Highlanders are in much the same position as your family. We just want a peaceful life without interference from the Lowland Council. But unless we can come up with a way to defeat these new machines of theirs, we will have no option but to cave in to their demands."

"They are formidable machines," the Lowlander says. "They move uphill very fast and fling nets to entangle anyone who gets too close. Your Slider Corps will struggle to defeat them."

This is exactly what you were thinking.

"What if I guaranteed you safe passage and a slider escort down the mountain to the interior, in exchange for this machine? Both of us would gain. Yes?"

You can see the Lowlander thinking. His eyes close a little and his head bobs up and down. You hope he goes for the deal. For Slider Command, having one of these new machines to study would be a great advantage in the conflict that is sure to come.

A few seconds later he looks you in the eye. "You are very clever for one so young."

You smile at his compliment but remain silent.

"I like this plan of yours," he continues. "A strong Highland force will act as a buffer between our settlement and the Lowlanders. We would be able to trade too, our crops for your minerals and hydro."

"It sounds like we're in agreement then?" you say.

"Yes, I think we are," the man says.

"Okay, I think the first thing to do is to get your people settled. You can stay at the reservoir while I go back and organize some sledges and sliders to take you and your people down the mountain. There is a small base by the reservoir that has a spare accommodation pod. It might be crowded but at least you'll be safe."

The Lowlander nods his understanding.

"Some of your men can help us get this machine down to the Pillars of Haramon. Then within a few days, I'll send enough sliders and sledges back to get you all safely down the other side."

You hold out your hand to the Lowlander. "It will be nice to have some Lowland friends for a change."

"I agree," the Lowlander says. "We all bleed green, do we not?"

"Indeed we do," you say, "greener than the yolk of a pango's egg."

Congratulations, you have reached the end of this part of the story. You successfully obtained a Lowland machine for Slider Command to study, and made allies of a group of Lowlanders that will enrich your community. Well done! But have you tried all the possible paths yet? Have you gone mining or found of the secret of the moon moths?

It is time to make another decision. Do you:

Go back to the beginning of the story and try another path? **P1**

Or

Go to the list of choices and start reading from another part of the story? **P307**

Take the equipment to the Pillars, don't follow the machine.

You have decided to carry on to rather than go investigate the track the Lowland machine has made.

The officer told you that if you came across the machine you were to investigate, but this isn't the machine, it is just the machine's track. Why risk your troop? You can't take the sledges up the mountain, and for you to follow the track you'd have to split your troop into two sections which would only make each group weaker.

After unclipping your harness, you take out your scope and scan the upper slopes for any sign of the Lowlanders, but the track disappears over a ridge and there is no sign of the machine.

"Are we going after them?" Dagma asks. "We've got to do something."

"But how far up are they? They could be miles ahead. And if their machine climbs as quickly as we think, how do we know we'll even be able to catch them?"

Gagnon has heard your discussion and has pushed his way back to your position. "We can't let them get above us. Advantage comes with altitude, you know that. They could slide right down on us."

You bang your stick on the ground. "Our job is to get this mining equipment to the Pillars, not go chasing machines. I've made my decision."

Dagma looks at Gagnon and shakes her head. You hear the hiss of air as she inhales through her teeth.

"You're making a mistake," Gagnon says. "Please reconsider."

You glance up the slope once more. Maybe by rotating climbers, and using zippers to drag you up the mountain you could catch the machine, but you hesitate. What if you waste precious time climbing up and the real danger is coming from below? How are you to know?

"Let's take a vote," Gagnon says.

"Yeah." Dagma looks at the other cadets in the hope that a stare will make them agree with her.

"This is not a democracy," you say. "I'm in charge and my decisions are final."

The cadets don't seem happy with your last statement — Highland communities value consensus above all else. Having their opinion ignored is a pet hate of all Highlanders.

"Yes, let's vote." You hear a few other cadets say.

"Seems the others want a say in this too," Dagma grunts.

"No. Get ready to move off."

Before you manage to clip on, Dagma sees her chance. With a sweep of her stick, she knocks you off your feet. Then she pushes you down the slopes with all her strength.

Before you know it you are free sliding down the hill, gaining speed as you go.

You try to regain your feet where you might have some control, but the ground is uneven and whenever you try to stand, a bump in the ground knocks you flat once more.

Spinning around you sit up with your feet out in front of you. Leaning down on your hook you try to slow your speed, but before you can come to a complete stop you hit a steeper patch and take off again. Further ahead you see a series of knife-edged ridges. If you hit one of those it will cut you to ribbons.

You have two choices. Try to stop, or use your stick to steer and avoid the danger below.

You dig in your heel spurs and jab your stick, pushing yourself further into the centre of the gully away from the dangers on its left. You are moving too fast for your equipment to slow you down. None the less, you lean down hard on your hook. After the steep patch the ground levels out and you manage to stop, but by then the rest of your troop is well out of sight.

Being isolated on the slope is not a good thing. You've got no one to belay you, no one to help with the climbing. You're limited in what you can do.

In this situation you've got little option but to carefully traverse back and forth across the slope and try to get down to the Pillars of Haramon without breaking your neck.

What a disaster. Your first patrol and your cadets have rebelled, pushed you down the hill, and left you on your own, just because you didn't listen to them.

As you sit and ponder what to do, you remember what the officer said when you first started this trip, "you all have a vital part to play in the Slider Corps, and you need to listen to each other."

But you didn't listen. You thought you knew better. Your ego made you lose the respect of your troop. You didn't work as a team.

You hang your head as you traverse back and forth across the slope on your way down. What will you say when you arrive alone? How will you explain?

You can only hope that you get another chance some day to make up for your mistake. That you get a chance to regain respect and become a valued member of the Highland Slider Corps.

This part of your story is over. Unfortunately you failed in your mission to get your troop to the Pillars of Haramon. However, you do have another chance. You can go back and try another path. Next time, listen to your fellow cadets.

It is time to make a decision. Do you want to:

Go to the beginning of the story and try another path? **P1**

Or

Go to the list of choices and start reading from another part of the story? **P307**

Encourage the sliders to attack the Lowlanders.

You've heard stories about Lowland treachery all your life. You've never actually met a Lowlander, but you believe what your family says.

"Miners, grab your picks and rope up," you yell to your team. "Get ready to fight."

As the sliders form themselves into a V-formation, ready to do a high-speed downhill attack, you and your fellow miners fit a light-weight cable drum to an anchor point in the rock ready to belay down and help. Once the cable is reeled out, each miner clips on to the line.

"We'll wait until the sliders attack, then we can reinforce where required," you tell the others.

The sliders are nearly ready to go. They sit on their utility belts with their feet forward, guide sticks tucked under their arms ready to steer. The Lowlanders know the effectiveness of this tactic and are retreating downhill around a small headland.

"On my mark!" the lead slider yells. "Three, two, one, go!"

You are amazed at how quickly the sliders gain speed as they rocket down the hillside. Each has their guide sticks pointing to the front ready to strike and their diamond studded boots up and ready to kick.

The sliders use the needle end of their guide sticks to make a sweeping turn to the right. Within moments they too will be out of view.

"We need to move further down the valley so we can see what's going on," you say to your group.

You push the release button on your zipper and slide down the cable past the protruding ridge to a point where you can see the sliders pursuing the retreating Lowlanders. The other miners follow your example.

Then you see a machine crawl out of a natural depression in the slope. It's an unusual contraption and surprisingly quick. It races up the valley towards the fleeing Lowlanders. When it reaches the retreating men, the machine stops and the Lowlanders climb in through a door in its armored side. Faces peer out tiny viewing holes along its side.

Mounted on the front of the machine is a high-speed drill which pecks holes in the ground. Behind the drill is a huge sprocket with pointed teeth. The turning sprocket is powered by a chain that runs to a gear at the back where a vent releases steam and the thumping sound of an engine can be heard coming from within. As the sprocket turns, its teeth fit perfectly into the holes made by the drill, and pull it rapidly up the slope.

"I don't like this," you say to Piver. "What *is* that thing?"

For the first time ever, Piver looks serious. His cheeky grin is gone and his face is slack. "I don't know, but I doubt it's here to make our lives any easier."

The sliders have seen the machine too. They are doing their best to stop before they get too close. The high-pitched screech of dragging hooks echoes around the valley.

But the Lowlanders have planned their ambush well. The sliders are out in the open and have nowhere to hide. The machine blocks their downhill path.

With a *twang*, a series of spring-loaded catapults, mounted on top of the machine, fling nets towards the now motionless sliders and because of their tight formation, the nets entangle many at once.

"This is not going well," Piver says

"We've got to go and help, but what can we do?" you say.

Before you and Piver have time to discuss the matter further, an amplified voice booms up the valley.

"Surrender now and you will be spared. This is your one and only warning."

Piver and the other miners look at you for instructions, their young faces showing their concern at the situation.

You never have liked ultimatums. "Quick, back to the sledges!" you yell. "Get aboard and cut them loose, we'll have to take our chances free sliding down the mountain."

Despite the look of fear on their faces, the other miners are quick to follow your lead. They zip back up the cable and rush to their respective sledges. Anchor lines are released and they jump aboard.

"Keep as high as you can, and head for the far side of the valley. We need to get out of here before the Lowlanders net us."

Each sledge has a simple steering system. Normally it is controlled by a slider at the front, but it can also be operated by a lever mounted on the side that is linked to the front runners. The diamond dust on the sledge's runners will give you some control, but any grip is reduced the faster you go.

"See those steep cliffs on the opposite side of the valley?" You say. "Aim for those. We can use the slope below them to bank our turn and direct us back down the valley below the Lowlanders."

"Are you sure this is a good idea?" Piver asks. "It's going to be a pretty wild ride."

"Fancy life on a Lowland prison farm?" you reply.

Piver shakes his head.

"I didn't think so."

Having reeled in the sliders, the Lowland machine is grinding up the hill again. White steam belches and gears clunk.

"Let's go, we're running out of time!" You wave your arm for the other miners to follow and push off.

Your needle boots give you a little grip as you give the sledge a big shove and leap aboard. Before you know it you are gliding across the slope.

You lie on your stomach and grab the steering lever with your right hand while holding tightly onto a strap with your left. Your sledge cuts across the slope above the Lowlanders' machine and rockets towards the far cliffs.

The sledges runners click and clatter as they skitter across tiny ridges in the glassy black rock.

You hear the twang of nets being fired and the dull thud as they hit the slope behind you. A high-pitched whine starts.

The speed of the free-running sledge is exhilarating and scary at the same time. You look back and see that the last sledge in your group has been snagged by a net and is being reeled in like a big fish. A day that had held such promise is quickly turning into a nightmare. Now there are only nine of you.

Normally, speed on the slopes is your enemy. Today however, it is your only chance to escape. How the Lowlanders got past the fortified Pillars of Haramon without being detected, you're not sure. What you do know is getting down the valley to the fortified base is your best chance. You certainly can't hang around on the slopes with this many Lowlanders around.

Your sledge slows as it begins to climb the slope on the far side of the valley. The cliffs are close now.

You pull the lever hard back to turn right and use the natural contour of the hill to bank your turn. The sledge swings around and you head back towards the opposite side of the valley at an angle that will take you well below the Lowlanders' position.

The valley has become a gigantic half-pipe as the sledges race down toward the Pillars. You swoop from one side to the other, using the natural banking to help you change direction and control your speed. A cool breeze whistles around your visor.

The machine is obviously better going uphill than down, because you've left it and the Lowlanders far behind.

After just over an hour of high-speed and at time crazy, on-the-edge sledging, you see two towering black columns rising from the valley floor. A distance that would have taken you and your slider escort a whole day to cover has been completed in hardly any time at all.

The massive Pillars of Haramon rise straight up from the valley floor for over a thousand feet. They glisten in the afternoon light. At 100 yards wide, and perfectly smooth, apart from the numerous tunnels that pockmark their surface, the Pillars are one of the natural wonders of Petron.

Between the two monoliths are strung a number of sturdy cables with gondolas hanging beneath them so people and equipment can travel from one pillar to the other. Magnifying disks sit in some of the tunnel openings ready for use in case of attack.

A colony of pangos has made its home near the top of one of the pillars. These tasty but rather stupid birds provide a plentiful supply of fresh eggs and protein for the fort's occupants.

Although you can't see them from down below, you also know that some of the old mining tunnels are now used as hydro growing chambers and sleep pods for the three hundred or so Highlanders that make this isolated outpost their home.

As you steer onto the loading platform near the base of one of the pillars, a strong safety net catches your sledge and brings it to a halt. The rest of your group soon slides in to join you.

"Welcome to the Pillars of Haramon," says an officer that has come out of a portal to join you. "Where is your escort?"

After describing how your escort was captured by the Lowland machine and detailing your wild ride down the valley, the officer gets your group to park their sledges in a large chamber where cable drums, drills, grinders and other tools are stored.

"You must be exhausted after your ordeal," the office says, "but I'll need you to report this new information to Command right away. This is a serious development."

After your troop is directed to a visitor's pod where they can eat and rest, you follow the officer through a narrow portal and up a series of steps cut into the smooth black rock. Moon moths hang from the ceiling, lighting the way.

You crane your neck up so you can look at them as you walk.

"We encourage them to breed here. Saves us a lot of effort lighting all the tunnels," the officer says when he sees you studying the bright-winged creatures. "The Pillars have one of the biggest moth colonies on Petron."

You've never seen so many moon moth this close before. You are amazed by how their iridescent wings glow softly in the dark.

"They're beautiful," you say. "I'm surprised they aren't disturbed by your movement through the tunnels."

"Occasionally they'll get spooked and fly off all at once, but that's rare. I think they realize we mean them no harm."

Your leg muscles start to burn as you climb. Your breath is coming in gasps by the time you enter the command pod.

There are six officers in the pod. All but one gives you a quick once-over and then turn back to their work. The other comes over and directs you into a side chamber.

After repeating what you told the first officer about the capture of your escort and the Lowland machine, the officer leans towards you. "So you've seen it. Do you think we can defeat this machine?"

You haven't really had much time to think about it. You and your fellow miners have been far too busy trying to stay alive on your crazy slide down the valley to have time to think about defeating the Lowland machine.

"Well?" the officer says.

"I … I'm not sure, sir. I'm a miner, not a slider."

"But you and your troop learned about engineering and mechanics in mining school. What is your honest opinion?"

You remember how easily the machine captured the sliders. How the drill on its front-end cut a track in the tough black rock allowing it to move quickly up the slope and how the machine's armor plating protected the Lowlanders within.

But then you remember the openings along the machine's side that allowed those within to see out, it's slower speed when moving downhill, and its reliance on an engine. You try to imagine how you would go about attacking such a contraption.

"Well…" You close your eyes and try to picture the machine. "If we can jam the drive gears the machine won't be able to move uphill," you say. "But can your sliders get close enough without being captured in their nets?"

The officer thinks hard for a moment and then nods slightly "Would you be willing to come with us? Sliders aren't trained mechanics. We aren't used to dealing with machinery. If you could come and tell us what we need to do to disable this thing, we'll find a way to get close enough somehow."

You want to help but you've not been trained for this sort of thing. You're a miner, not a tactician … or a fighter for that matter. You know about drills and crystals and props and shafts. Maybe talking peace is the answer?

It seems to you that there are two possible solutions. Fight or talk.

There is a chance the Highlanders might be able to send the Lowland machine crashing back down the mountain. But do you want to be responsible if your plan doesn't work and it results in injury and death? Maybe talking peace with the Lowlanders is the best idea. Everyone loses something when it comes to war, even the victor.

It is time to make a decision. Do you:

Tell the office you think they should talk peace with the Lowlanders? **P116**

Or

Volunteer to go with the sliders and attack the Lowland machine? **P118**

You have decided to yell out for the slider not to attack.

You stand up and move towards the head slider. "Hang on a minute! Aren't you going to find out what they want?"

The head slider looks at you and scowls. "They're Lowlanders. You expect me to trust them?"

"Do you see them carrying any weapons?" you say.

Squinting into the glare, the slider looks down at the Lowlanders again. He grumbles something under his breath, and then turns back to you. "Well I suppose we could hear what they have to say. But any tricky business and my troop will send them straight to the bottom!"

Piver gets up from behind his sledge and comes to stand beside you. He turns and whispers, "I'll come with you. Two heads are better than one, even if they are pango heads."

"You're crazy Piver, but I like your logic."

You take a step towards the head slider. "Piver and I will speak to them. I think it's better if your troop stays here. They'll feel less threatened that way."

The Lowlanders have stopped. They look up at you, their white flag fluttering.

"Well if you want to risk your lives, who am I to stop you?" the slider says.

You wonder if you really are risking your life. Maybe the head slider is right. Even though the Lowlanders are waving a white flag, have they really come in peace?

"Looks like the j—job is ours," Piver says nervously. "Do you want to do the talking or should I?"

"When we want to make them laugh, I'll let you know. In the mean time let me do the talking, okay?"

"We'd better throw down a line and go see what they want then." Piver takes a light-weight cable from his utility belt and ties one end onto an anchor bolt. Once it's attached, you both clip on and start working your way down the slope towards the Lowlanders.

When you and Piver are about five paces from the group you stop.

A couple of the Lowlanders look a little nervous. Not surprising considering there are thirty armed and highly trained sliders, arranged in attack formation, just waiting for an excuse to send them to the bottom.

"What are you doing way up here?" you ask, trying to keep your voice from wavering. "You're a long way from home, don't you think?"

One of the Lowlanders takes a step forward and pulls out a small tablet. He unfolds its protective cover and starts to read. "I come as a representative of the Lowland Council. My council wishes to meet with your Highland leaders to see if we can find a way to end the bloodshed that has plagued our two peoples for so many years. In exchange for peace, all the Lowland Council requires is a small act of good faith on behalf of the Highlanders."

"Act of good faith?"

"A small tax, to cover the cost of administration, health and education," he continues. You will gain many benefits from becoming part of the Federation of Lowland States."

"What do you consider small?"

"A mere ten percent of any minerals mined from the Black Slopes. A very reasonable request, don't you think? You pay nearly that much to the border traders already in commission, not to mention what it must cost you to defend the Highlands."

You shrug. His proposal doesn't sound unreasonable. Some education you already get, but there are only limited health facilities in the Highlands. You look briefly at Piver, shrug, and then turn back to the Lowland leader. "I'm happy to pass your message on to my superiors. How do we contact you with our answer?"

"We have troops gathered in the foothills below the Pillars of Haramon. Tell your leaders to send an envoy to us there with your answer no later than the last day of the full moon. If we don't hear from you by then…"

You wait for him to finish his sentence but he remains silent.

"Then what?" you ask.

"Let's just say if I were in your position, I'd do my best to persuade my leaders to do as we suggest. Believe me when I say your Highland sliders are no match for our recently developed technology. The Highland communities can either choose to be a small part of our federation or we will send you all to the bottom. It's your choice."

With that, the Lowlanders turn and move off down the hill.

You press the trigger on the handle of your zipper, its battery whirs and pulls you up the cable where the others have been waiting.

The head slider shuffles over. "Well, what did they say?"

You give him the main points of the discussion.

"Those ... those Lowland scum," the lead slider says. "We should send them back to their leaders in pieces. How dare they demand such a thing!"

"Wait," Piver says. "The Highland Council should be the ones to decide."

You nod your head. "Piver's right. It's not our place to start a war. Besides, their offer could be of some benefit."

The head slider is almost growling in disgust. "I think we should attack while we have the numerical advantage. Then there will be less Lowlanders to fight later. But seeing you miners are paying for our escort to the Pillars…"

You understand the slider's position. Hatred of Lowlanders runs deep in the Slider Corps, but you also know that war is a costly exercise, even for the winner.

The situation is tense. It is time for you to make a decision. Do you:

Join the sliders and attack the Lowlanders? **P106**

Or

Carry on to the Pillars with the Lowlanders' message? **P149**

Tell the officer you think they should talk peace.

"Look," you say to the slider officer, "I don't know how to disable the Lowlanders' machine. What if my ideas fail? Surely talking peace is a better option, especially when the opposition has a technological advantage."

The officer sneers at you like you're a pango dropping he needs to scrape off his boot. "If you won't help, I'm sure one of the other miners will come up with a plan."

"But…"

The officer's face is turning red. "Sliders do not surrender. We attack!" he yells. "I should have known better than to ask a miner for help."

You can't understand the officer's reaction. When did you say anything about surrender? Talking and compromising isn't surrender, it's saving lives. "Wait, I didn't say surrender…"

But the officer isn't listening. He has stomped away and is talking with a stern-faced officer on the far side of the pod. You can tell you'd be wasting your breath trying to reason with him anymore. He stopped listening the moment you said "peace".

After being ignored for a few minutes, you realize you may as well head back to the other miners. Besides, you're not a slider, and therefore not under slider control. You and your fellow miners can make up your own minds about the situation.

When you re-enter the pod, the miners look at you expectantly.

"What's going on?" one of them says.

"Yeah," says Piver. "Has war been declared?"

"It's certainly looking that way," you say. "These sliders aren't keen on talking."

"What should we do?" Piver asks.

"We need to make a decision. We either help Slider Command or leave the Pillars and make our way back up the mountain to home. If there is going to be an invasion I know where I want to be and that's with my family."

You look at the worried faces all around you.

"But how will we get home?" one of the miners says.

Piver is looking increasingly agitated, but he stands by your side.

You glance around, trying to gauge the mood of the others. "We can leave the mining equipment here and make our way back home by using the tows and the safe routes."

Miners are shaking their heads and mumbling under their breath. Most come from a long line of mining families. The idea of striking out across the slopes without a slider escort is unthinkable. They are far less informed about travel on the slopes. Understandably it frightens them.

You may not be a trained slider, but you've heard slider stories and discussions on tactics and tricks for maneuvering on black glass ever since you were a baby. Mining school taught you a few trick about getting around as well. With a bit of gear from your sledge, you're confident you can get back home without an escort.

From the body language, and mumblings of the miners, you can tell they want to stay where they are, safe under the protection of the base commander here at the Pillars of Haramon.

But you're not sure about that man. He seems a little too eager to fight. You were always taught to think for yourself rather than blindly follow orders that don't seem right. On the other hand, you can't deny that travelling the slopes can be dangerous, and you don't like the idea of leaving your classmates behind.

It is time to choose. Do you:

Help Slider Command disable the Lowland machine? **P118**

Or

Leave the Pillars and strike out for home on your own? **P127**

Volunteer to go with the sliders and attack the machine.

You can't bring yourself to leave your comrades, so helping Slider Command seems your only option. The Lowlanders and their strange machine will create havoc amongst the Highland communities if something isn't done quickly. You'll most likely end up fighting anyway, so you may as well do it before the Lowlanders are any higher up the mountain.

Your family would be disappointed if they found out you hadn't volunteered. If things go wrong, at least you would have tried to make a difference. You let your fellow miners know what you intend and go back to the stairs and start climbing.

"The miners will help," you tell the officer in the command pod. "We all have mechanical knowledge, but only myself and Piver come from slider families and know how to move safely around the slopes. The others should stay here to help fortify the Pillars."

"That makes sense," the office says with a curt nod. "The last thing I want is a bunch of miners slowing us down." The officer holds out his hand. "Welcome to the mission. Glad you've decided to come along."

As you shake the officer's hand, you wonder if you've made the right decision. You've been on a few trips around the Highlands with your family and they've taught you a few basics about travelling around the slopes, but your experience is limited. You might know more than the other miners in your group, but compared to these sliders, you're only a beginner.

"Go get your equipment. Make sure you and Piver are at the main portal in twenty minutes," the officer says. "Pack as light as you can. We'll be moving fast."

You start back down the steps towards the accommodation pod, but before you get far, a faint voice echoes down the staircase. You stop to listen.

"You really think two miners are going to make any difference?

They're not much more than kids."

"What other option do we have?" the officer says. "Their mechanical knowledge is our last hope. How many people did we lose trying to stop that machine from skirting around our defenses?"

The unfamiliar voice does not reply.

The conversation fades as it moves to another part of the command pod and all you can hear are mumbles.

Maybe the outspoken Highlander was right. Maybe you won't be much use stopping the machine. All that you know is that you have to try.

When you get back to the others, you pull Piver aside and tell him the plan.

"We're going with the sliders?" Piver says. "Geebus! Thanks for asking me!"

You give Piver a little grin. "The sliders seemed a bit glum. I thought you could cheer them up a little."

"Funny ha ha," Piver says. "I doubt there will be much to joke about when we're all free sliding towards the bottom."

The two of you head down to your sledges.

"I think tangling their machine in cables somehow, is our only chance to stop it," you say to Piver as you work. "It shouldn't take much to jam up all those gears and chains."

"Assuming they don't net us before we get close enough."

Piver is right. Your slider escort didn't do too well. Why should this lot fare any better?

Between the two of you, you sort out what you need from the sledges. It isn't much because you have to carry whatever you take. You pack a launcher with some spare charges, an impact drill, and an assortment of hand tools, cables, zippers and clips.

Piver grabs a spool of high-temp cutting cord as well. "I've always wanted to use this stuff!" he says. "I hear it cuts through rock at over a foot a second."

"Just don't drop it. I've also heard it's not that stable."

You hear movement behind you as a troop of sliders make their way down one of the tunnels towards the portal. The sliders tower over you and the even smaller Piver. Their uniforms show off their muscular legs and arms. Each has a pack on their backs and a utility belt around their waists.

The officer from earlier is among them. "You miners ready?"

You swallow and nod.

He throws you each a pair of diamond spurs. "Better put these on. Should keep you from slipping."

The diamonds on the spurs are tiny, but each is cut in such a way that a sharp point digs into the rock every time you dig in your heel.

Once strapped onto your boots, you try them out. The grip they provide is remarkable. Then to your amazement he hands you a guide stick.

"You'll need one of these too," the office says. "Look after it, they're expensive to replace."

You look at the stick in your hand. "Wow, thanks. I never thought I'd get to use one of these."

"Pretty hard to travel with the Highland Slider Corps without one," the office says. "Just remember it's a lot more sensitive than the cheap commercial models so don't over correct on your turns."

Without further ceremony, the officer pulls a lever just inside the portal and a section of the wall rolls back to reveal a steeply angled tunnel disappearing down into the ground.

One of the Highland sliders sits on the ground next to the hole and lowers his feet into it. Then without warning he pushes off and disappears with a *whoosh*.

"Where's he going?" you ask the officer.

"This shaft takes us below ground to a secret chamber," the officer says. "When the miners first started excavating here at the Pillars of Haramon, they had to figure out a way to get rid of all the excess rock. To solve the problem, they drilled a tunnel from under the Pillars, up through the hillside to the ridge above. Inside this tunnel, they built a high-speed conveyor that took the rubble up and dumped it into the valley on the other side where it slid down the hill and into a crevasse."

"Sounds like a lot of work," you say.

"It was, but the rich pickings made it all worthwhile. Fifty years ago, when the main mining operation ceased, the Slider Corps began using the conveyor as a lift to get troops up the mountain where we have the advantage of altitude over any invaders. Sure beats climbing or using tows. Besides, a conventional tow would be vulnerable to attack. This one is totally hidden."

"Why haven't I heard about this?" you ask the officer.

"It's ultra-top-secret."

"Great." Piver said with a grin. "Now that we know their secret, they'll have to kill us."

The officer looks down at Piver, shakes his head and chuckles. "Only if the Lowlanders don't get you first."

The two of you watch slider after slider drop feet first into the tunnel. When it is your turn you sit on the ground and scoot nervously towards the edge. All you can see is the first fifteen feet of smooth black rock angling steeply down into the darkness. You hesitate…

"Happy landing," the officer says pushing you towards the edge with the toe of his boot. "Don't forget to bend your knees."

"Wait I'm not… Whoa!" You feel your stomach lurch for a second or so, but then the tunnel gently angles you down into the core of the mountain. It feels strange sliding in complete darkness. The turns and twist are so frequent, at times it's hard to tell up from down.

When a faint light reflects off the stone in the distance, you know you'd better relax and get ready for impact. With a *swish* you pop out of the tunnel into a wide chamber. Moon moths cluster together on the ceiling, giving you enough light to see sliders standing around waiting for the rest of you to arrive.

You skid across the floor and come to rest in a fine net stretched across the chamber. Strong hands pull you to your feet.

"Wow, that was strange," you say. "Sliding in the darkness is really disorientating."

"You get used to it," a slider says.

You hear a delighted squeal as Piver pops out of the tunnel. "Geebus that was fun! Forget this mining lark. I want to be a slider!"

Piver throws his head back and laughs with his mouth open so wide you could drop a pango egg down his throat without even touching the sides. You've never seen him so animated.

"Pleased you enjoyed it," the officer says. "Now will you stop giggling like an idiot and get ready to move out."

Piver snaps his mouth shut, turns bright red and adjusts his pack.

While you sort your gear, the officer walks across the chamber towards a wide belt whirring up another tunnel. Every ten feet or so, a metal lip runs across the width of the belt. These barriers would have stopped the crushed rock from sliding back down the belt as it travelled to the surface for disposal.

"This next part is tricky," the office says. "You've got to time your jump so you end up on a flat part of the conveyor. Those metal shutters are hard and the belt is moving at pace so be careful. If you keep low and lean forward, you'll be fine."

You watch the sliders time their jump as you move towards the front of the line. The large drum that is rotating the belt beneath your feet makes the floor of the chamber vibrate.

"I'll count you in," the officer says.

You move to the edge of the conveyor and prepare to jump.

"On my mark. Three, two, one, now."

You hit the belt and immediately drop to all fours. The belt is really moving. Before long you are in total darkness once again.

"Don't worry," the slider behind you says. "Getting off is the easy part."

When you get to the top you see why. The belt dives around another drum, and deposits you into a narrow chute that slopes down towards a drop-off some twenty yards away. All you can see at the end of the chute is … nothing!

"Whoa!" you yell, as you scrabble for something to hold on to. But there is nothing but smooth black glass.

You only see the ultra-fine netting strung up across the chute, as it brings you to a sudden stop a yard from the edge of the cliff.

"Phew." You say as you regain your feet. "You should warn people about that. I thought I was heading to the bottom."

You see the sliders trying to suppress their laughter. It's obviously a trick they play on everyone who takes the conveyor for the first time.

When you hear a squeal of abject terror behind you, you know Piver has arrived.

"Geebus!" Piver says as he wobbles over to join you. "I nearly pooped myself."

A few of the sliders hear Piver's comments and laugh.

"Tell me about it!" you say to Piver. "Seems you're not the only comedian on this trip."

The officer taps his guide stick on the ground. "Okay, listen up people. We've got an important mission to accomplish. We need to figure out how to stop this new weapon the Lowlanders have developed. We've brought two miners with us for their mechanical expertise. Look after them. We need them in one piece."

"I like being in one piece," Piver whispers.

You tap him in the shin with the toe of your boot. "Shush."

The officer continues. "We're going to traverse along this ridge as far as we can. Hopefully the Lowlanders are still in the valley. Once we find them, we'll assess the situation and then decide what to do."

"You miners will be linked to a slider front and back. If you feel yourself beginning to fall, yell out immediately so my men have time to put in an emergency belay. Got it?"

The two of you nod. This is all beginning to sound rather serious.

"Parts of this ridge have been overrun by morph rats, so watch out for burrows," the officer says. "We don't want anyone breaking a leg."

"Just what we need, morph rats," Piver says. "Those things give me the creeps."

You're not a big fan of morph rats either. They eat everything in their path and they leave burrows in the most unexpected places. You also hate the sticky slime that covers their hairless bodies, and the sucking sound their feet make as they move around the slopes.

You've heard they're edible, but by the time all the slime and stench is boiled off them, and their tough hide is removed, the small amount of stringy meat you'd get seems hardly worth the effort.

The officer is speaking again. "… okay, let's get our boots locked and get ready to move out. We need to take advantage of what light we have left."

Everyone clips their boots together and shuffles into a line. The officer is out front and will lead the troop himself.

"On my count. Three, two, one…"

He pushes off and starts traversing across the slope along a narrow path worn into its surface.

The path runs ever so slightly downhill, but because the ridge is high above the valley floor, you are still able to travel up towards its head. By the time you reach the valley floor, your group is already three or four miles above the Pillars.

"We'll have to use zip lines from here," the office says.

You pull your scope from your pocket and scan the upper slopes. Everything is dark and in shadow. There is no sign of the Lowlanders or their machine.

The officer turns to you and Piver. "Can you fire an anchor bolt into that pinnacle up there?" He points up the slope to where an old volcanic pipe rises out of the slope near the ridgeline. "We could zip up and continue traversing that way. Save our legs for when we find the Lowlanders."

You waste no time in setting up the launcher. Climbing has never been your strong point.

When the launcher is ready to go, Piver sets off the charge. The anchor bolt streaks off towards its target, and the fine cable whirls off the drum beside you. With a cloud of dust, the bolt smacks into the rock at the base of the pinnacle.

"Nice shot," the officer says. "Okay. Let's get up there and get sliding."

Once you're on the ridge, having gained some valuable altitude, you pull out your scope again. The machine is hard to spot in the shadows of the upper slope, but its tiny puffs of steam give its position away.

"I see them," you say. "They're at twenty-eight degrees, south by southeast."

The officer pulls out his scope and checks the coordinates. "Good spotting. Looks like they're getting their camp sorted before dewfall. We need to get above them if we're to have any chance of sending them to the bottom."

You go back to your scope and watch the Lowlanders' preparations. You can just barely make out the track their machine has made as it drilled its way up the hillside. The Lowlanders have anchored it on a semi-flat spur near a side gully.

Some of the Lowlanders are rigging up covers in case it rains, while others are tending cooking pots.

You can see Lowland guards stationed on the upper side of the machine. If an attack is to come, they know the Highlanders are most likely to strike from above.

Meanwhile the sliders are talking about climbing around the Lowlanders so they can attack from above in typical slider style. This makes you think.

You zoom in on the track and see the regular series of holes the machine has drilled into the slope. This track runs all the way up the valley like a staircase.

If the Lowlanders are expecting an attack from above, why not use the track made by their own machine to climb up and attack at night after dewfall when the Lowlanders least expect it?

But what happens if the Lowlanders spot you coming? You will be below them and they will have the advantage of altitude. Your suggestion could be responsible for a terrible defeat.

It is time to make a decision. Do you?
Suggest an attack from below? **P138**
Or
Stay quiet and let the sliders plan an attack from above? **P143**

You have decided to leave the Pillars and strike out for home.

You put your hands on your hips and look at the other miners. "Well I don't know about you lot, but I'm not going to get involved in a war without at least trying to find a peaceful solution. If you want to follow some blood-crazed slider, be my guest!"

As you start packing up your gear, everyone mills about not knowing what to do.

"In fact, you probably should stay here," you say, as you shoulder your pack. "I don't need a bunch of inexperienced miners slowing me down."

You leave the pod and head towards the sledges to get the extra gear you'll need to make the long trip back to your home community.

After untying the cover on your sledge you grab a spool of light-weight cable, an extra zipper, some anchors and a cable launcher and stow them in your pack along with some travel rations and broth. Then you sit to strap on the pair of diamond spurs your family gave you as a going away present. "In case you ever need grip in a hurry," they'd said.

Just as you are tightening the last strap, you hear footsteps coming down the corridor. It's Piver.

"Didn't think I'd let you go on your own did you?"

You give him a big smile and slap him affectionately on the back. "I was hoping you'd decide to come," you say as he starts packing. "It's a lot safer moving around the slopes with two. That's for sure."

After ten minutes or so, you've both got everything sorted. Then Piver starts strapping on some spurs.

"I see you got a going away present too," you say.

"Slider parents are like that," Piver says. "Just as well, eh?"

"Yup, just as well."

"Should we tell the sliders we're leaving?" Piver asks.

"Don't worry, they'll see us. Let's just hope that crazy slider in charge doesn't go completely mental and try to fry us with one of their big magnifying lens."

Piver's eyes widen. "Would he do that?"

"Don't worry, it will only hurt for a minute,"

Piver's face goes white.

"Got you!"

Piver exhales with a rush of air. "That wasn't funny."

You chuckle and lift your pack onto your shoulders and tighten the waist strap. "Shall we start climbing?"

Without looking at Piver, you head towards the portal. You're pleased when you hear the distinctive click of diamond spurs behind you.

It's just as well you've studied this area. There are a number of routes you can take, but because dewfall isn't that far away, you and Piver will need to find a safe place to camp for the night within a couple hours.

"Let's launch a cable up to the ridge and gain some altitude," you tell Piver. "We need to get sliding if we're to make any distance."

The two of you put a charge in the launcher's tube and fire a light cable up to a rocky outcrop on the hillside above you. There is a puff of black dust as the anchor bolt buries itself into the rock.

"Up we go," you say as you clip your zipper onto the cable. "See you at the top."

The charge in the zipper is good for three thousand vertical feet. After that, you'll have to do your climbing the hard way.

Once the two of you reach the top, you look back at the Pillars below. "Beautiful, aren't they?"

Piver is deep in thought and doesn't reply.

Far below, low cloud is banking up against the foothills. The Borderlands are disappearing into the mist, which make the Black Slopes look like an island set in a violent sea of purple foam and crashing waves.

Over the next two hours, you and Piver make good distance by zipping up and then traversing. You are pleased you paid attention in navigation class when the entrance of an abandoned mine appears right where you calculated it would be.

"Looks like we've got shelter for the night," Piver says.

"As long as the morph rats haven't taken over." The thought of the slimy creatures gives you the shivers.

"Should I toss a screecher in?" Piver asks "That'll flush them out."

"Good thinking, but I didn't bring any."

"Just as well I did then." Piver unclips a round object from his belt and pushes a button on one end. A high-pitched ear-splitting screech starts to blast out.

"Quick toss it!" you yell, clamping your hands to the side of your head.

Piver throws the sphere into the opening of the mine shaft and steps to one side. You do the same. If there are morph rats in the hole, it won't be long before they scurry out.

As the two of you stand with your backs to the stone wall on either side of the shaft's entrance, you hear the screecher rolling further down the tunnel.

At first the clicking is faint, but before long its volume increases. Morph rats are coming. Within a minute it sounds like a thousand pebbles are bouncing along the tunnel towards you. The first morph rat scuttles past and throws itself out of the opening and slurps and slimes its way down the slope. More follow in a slithering mass of hairless bodies.

The rats don't notice the two of you in their headlong rush to get away from the brain piercing sound that is amplified by their extremely good sense of hearing and the hollowness of the tunnel. It smells like the tunnel has farted as the rats pass.

"Geebus that's horrible!" Piver says holding his nose.

You look over at him and can't help but laugh at his expression. "You should have stood on the upwind side of the opening."

'Piver clutches his throat and screws up his face, playing it up for all he's worth. By the time the last morph rat has disappeared, the two of you are on your hands and knees laughing.

You give the stench a moment to clear and then enter the tunnel, careful to walk on the high side of the tunnel, away from the puddles of slime left behind by the departing rats.

While you set up a small burner to heat some broth, Piver rummages in his pack for some hydro bars. Once camp is sorted you sit down around the burner and eat.

Piver takes a sip of broth and then looks up. "So what are you going to do when you get home?"

"I'm not really sure. Try to talk the communities into making peace with the Lowlanders I think. It's time we try to work things out between us. Surely we have more in common than differences. Who benefits from war?"

Piver takes another sip and nods his head. "Makes sense."

Then you hear the sound of footsteps at the mine's opening. Who could that be?

You and Piver look up from your food.

"Hello traitors!" a gruff voice says. "We thought you might stay here for the night."

You recognize one of the men from the command pod. It's the slider the officer was talking to after you told him you thought they should talk peace with the Lowlanders.

"What are you doing here?" you ask. "And what do you mean, traitors?"

"You didn't think Slider Command was going to let you walk away did you? Stupid miners!"

You don't like the sound of this. What is he inferring? Are they going to take you back to the Pillars?

"Yeah, stupid miners," the other slider says. "Time you had an accident and went for a slide."

The two sliders look at you and Piver. It sounds like they're planning to throw you down the slope.

"But it's after dewfall." you say. "We'll go all the way to the bottom."

"Not our problem," the officer says. "We've been listening to your conversation and know you're off to spread discontent amongst the communities. That doesn't suit Slider Command."

"Peace doesn't suit Slider Command?" you ask the officer. "Are you afraid you'll lose all your power and influence?"

"So naïve," the officer grunts.

The two sliders turn and have a brief conversation. While they do, you catch Piver's eye and nod towards the slime trail running down one side of the tunnel where the morph rats ran out. It's a slippery mess, but it might be your only chance.

"Time for a slide all right," you say to the men as you snag your pack and launch yourself, belly first, onto the trail of slime heading down into the depths of the tunnel.

You hear a grunt as Piver hits the slope behind you.

You spin around onto your back and place your feet below you, hoping they will protect you if you run into anything unexpected.

"Whoaaaa!" you hear Piver say behind you. "Where does this go?"

His voice sounds frightened, and so he should be. But at least this way, you are sure the sliders won't follow you.

"Stay loose and get ready for a sudden stop," you yell back to Piver. "If I remember the map correctly, there's a side tunnel coming up that leads to an exit further down."

Your speed is increasing as you slide through the darkness. The slime smells of rat and feels both sticky and slippery at the same time.

"I feel I'm sliding through liquid fart," Piver yells. "Death might be better than this!"

No way are you opening your mouth to reply.

Your momentum is slowed as you splash into the pool of slime at the bottom of the tunnel. Before you know it, you are sitting waist-deep in the awful stuff.

Faint moonlight reaches you from a tunnel opening to your right.

"Ewwww!" Piver say, lifting his arms above the slimy mess. "This stuff is worse than pango poo!"

"Better than going to the bottom though don't you think?"

"Only just," Piver says as he stands up and struggles out of the sticky muck.

The two of you use your hands to sweep the slime off your torso and legs. Thankfully your uniforms are made from a tightly woven water repellant fabric that comes clean relatively easily.

"I don't hear anything from above," Piver says, tilting his head. "What now?"

"Don't worry, I have a plan."

"I hope it's better than diving into a stinking pool of slime," Piver says.

"If only it were that simple," you say with a smile. "Did your family ever tell you the story of the back-to-back slide made by two slider cadets when the Black Slopes were first being settled?"

"They got caught in a storm, didn't they?"

"That's right. They had no option but to abandon their camp after six days and take their chances free sliding. They sat on their packs and linked arms back to back. Then, using only spurs to steer, they took off down the mountain."

"I remember," Piver said. "But…"

"Remember how the rear cadet dragged his spurs like an anchor to slow them down, and the front cadet used his to steer?"

"So that's your plan? A suicide slide back to the Pillars?"

"Not to the Pillars, to the Lowlands!"

"All the way to the bottom? Geebus, are you crazy?" Piver's eyes search your face. "You're serious, aren't you?"

"We have to talk to the Lowlanders and get them to hold off any invasion until we have time to speak to the elders in the communities. We need to end the conflict once and for all."

You can see Piver's mind working. He shakes his head and mumbles something under his breath. Then he looks up at you and smiles. "You always said I was crazy. Now it looks like I get a chance to prove you right."

You slap Piver on the back. "Good. Now try to get some sleep. We'll take off at first light."

The next morning, after a quick bite, you move over to the exit and pull a map out of the pouch on your belt. Unfolding it, you lay the map out on the floor in the dim light and study the contours of the terrain you will be sliding over.

"It will be plain sliding until we reach the Pillars. If we stay in the shadow, on the left of Long Gully, we should slip right past without anyone noticing."

"But not too far left," Piver says, jabbing his finger at the map. "Or we'll end up in the crevasse field."

You nod in agreement. "It's the ridges below the Pillars that scare me." You point out an area of rough ground that looks extremely dangerous.

"The words slice and dice come to mind," Piver says. "I've seen pictures of what happens to people who hit riffle ridges at speed. It's not pretty."

Your finger traces a narrow valley that branches off Long Gulley just below the Pillars. "That's why we need to take this route. It's the only safe way to the bottom."

Piver's eyebrows crease as he studies the map. "You think we'll find it sliding at speed?"

"We'd better."

The two of you sit at the tunnel's exit, your feet dangling over the edge. You realize there is every chance that this could be the last sunrise you ever see. For some reason, as the sun peeks over the mountains in the distances, this thought makes the scene even more beautiful.

When the light reaches the slopes below you, you turn to Piver. "We'd better get going."

Piver nods and follows your lead by creating a seat from his backpack. He tightens the arm straps around his legs to hold it firmly in place.

It may not be much, but at least the packs will give you some protection from the friction and bumps as the two of you slide down the hillside.

"Now make sure you keep even pressure on both of your spurs unless I yell left or right. If I do, just drag that spur until I say release. Got it?"

Piver gulps. "I think so."

After some final adjustment to your straps, you both scoot towards the edge. With Piver's back against yours, the two of you lock your arms together and stretch out your legs testing the bite of your spurs.

"Ready Piver?"

"It's all downhill from here," he replies, giving a shove that sends you both over the edge and onto the steep slope below.

Before you know it, you are moving with pace towards the valley floor. Piver's heels screech like a pair of demented pangos behind you, sending a shiver down your spine. A quarter mile down the valley you make a sweeping turn. Up to your right, you see the two sliders standing on the ridge. They are shaking their heads.

"Yippee!" Piver yells at the top of his voice. "Try to catch us now, morph heads!"

You admire Piver's spirit, but you also know the sliders have no intention of following. Why would they? They think you're sliding to the bottom, and not in a good way. And maybe they're right. They certainly will be if you miss the entrance to the side valley you hope to take.

"Left!" you yell when you see a small crevasse in the slope below you. "Left!"

The screech of Piver's spur increases as he digs it in. You kick your right boot into the slope at the same time, shunting the two of you further to the left. You skid past the crack with barely a yard to spare.

"Whoa, that was close," Piver says looking back up the slope.

"Release!"

Piver goes back to dragging both heels equally.

You see the Pillars looming up in the distance. "Left!" you yell again. "Pillars coming up. "

Surely guards at the Pillars will hear your spurs as you slide past. Thankfully the sun isn't high enough for Slider Command to be able to use their burning lens yet. Otherwise the two of you would be toast.

Despite Piver dragging his spurs for all he's worth, the remaining dampness on the glassy black rock means you are sliding fast. The speed makes you wonder if you'll have enough control to enter the narrow valley.

"Hard left!" you yell. "I see the entrance!"

Both of you use your heels desperately trying to move left on the slope. You stab your right heel down in repeated motions. With each kick you move a yard to the left.

"Harder!" you yell to Piver.

You kick your heel into the slope, bang, bang, bang as fast as you can. Then you're in.

"Release!" You let out a breath. "Phew, that was scary."

"Imagine what it's like when you're sliding backwards." Piver says, with a slight tremor in his voice.

The sun is up over the ridge now and is starting to reach the valley floor. Within a few miles, your progress slows a little as you hit drier slopes. You feel your control growing.

"I think we're actually going to make it," you say with relief.

The slopes begin to flatten out and within another ten minutes you are barely moving.

"I can see the Lowland camp," you tell Piver.

"Let's just hope they're as pleased to see us as we are to see them."

You dig your heels in and slide to a stop just as the last of the black rock disappears under a slope covered in pale green moss. The two of you stand and stretch your backs and shoulders.

As you stretch, you look around. It seems strange to see so much flat land in front of you. "It's so lush," you say.

Piver studies the scene. "Yeah … weird isn't it. But it's pretty in a funny sort of way."

You can't help but agree. You adjust your pack and look towards the Lowlanders' camp. "I suppose we'd better go talk to them."

"Can I do the greeting?" Piver asks. "I've got a phrase in mind that I've always wanted the opportunity to use."

"Oh yeah? And what's that?"

"Take me to your leader," Piver says with a chuckle.

You shake your head. "You really are nuts you know."

"For once I'm pleased to say I'm not the only one."

As the two of you walk towards the Lowland camp, you wonder if you'll be okay. Will the Lowlanders be friendly?

You're apprehension doesn't last long. Before you get to the cluster of Lowland huts a group of children run out to greet you. As they crowd around, one holds out a crackle berry, the legendary fruit of the Lowlands.

You've heard stories about this celebrated fruit. You've even seen a picture of it in one of your school books. But no one from the Highlands has seen one up close, let alone tasted one, for over 300 years since the fighting began.

While you're thinking about this offering, Piver snatches the crackle berry and sinks his teeth into its succulent blue flesh.

You watch and wait, wondering if he'll like it.

As Piver chews, and without even realizing it, he rises up onto his toes and does a little jiggle with his hips. Then he sinks back down, wipes his lips with the back of his hand and says, "Geebus! That's the best thing I've ever tasted!"

Congratulations, you made it down the mountain in one piece and are about to start talks that might bring about peace between the Highlanders and the Lowlanders. Well done!

But have you tried all the different paths the story takes? You can always go to the list of choices and see if there are paths you've missed.

You now have one more decision to make. Do you:

Go back to the beginning of the story and try another path? **P1**

Or

Go to the list of choices and start reading from another part of the story? **P307**

You have decided to suggest an attack from below.

You put down your scope and take a step towards the officer. "I think we might have a better chance if we sneak up from below."

The officer gives you a funny look. "What? Are you mad?"

You know your suggestion goes against every slider principle. All your life you've heard about the advantage of altitude, but maybe new times need new solutions.

"Look," you say, pointing towards the series of holes running up the valley. "The Lowlanders have provided us with a staircase that leads right to their camp. We can climb at night after dewfall. They'll never expect us."

You can see the cogs in the officer's mind working. His brow scrunches together and he scratches the side of his face. He pulls out his scope and looks again at the track. Then he calls one of his men over and has a chat.

After a moment, he turns back to you. "Okay so let's say we go along with your pango-brained scheme. What do we do once we're in the camp?"

"We mount a winch further down the mountain. Once we get to the Lowlanders' camp, we hook a cable onto their machine, cut its anchors, and winch the thing off the mountain. Once the machine is dislodged from its track, it will only have one way to go."

"Can you guarantee your equipment can pull that machine out of its track?"

You nod. "We can if you and your sliders can keep the Lowlanders off our back long enough."

Piver nods his agreement. "That machine will go all the way to the bottom and believe me, it won't be in very good order once it gets there."

"May our ancestors have mercy on us," the officer says. "If this fails, we'll go down in history as the sliders who attacked from below. I hope you're prepared to become a laughing stock."

"Or heroes," you say.

With the decision made to climb the machine's track after dark, your group moves to a safe spot to wait for dewfall. Then once it's dark, the long climb up to the Lowlanders' camp can begin.

The spot the sliders have chosen to wait is tucked into a shallow depression about a mile below the Lowlanders' camp. With all the shadow in the valley, the dark colors of your uniforms will blend in with the slope.

Everyone moves carefully. Noises travel a long way in the still evening air and you don't want to alert the Lowlanders of your presence. Only the distant screech of pangos and the sound of activity in the Lowland camp break the silence.

The waiting sliders are all clipped onto a strong cable. Some eat dried hydro while they await the order to climb.

About an hour after dark the officer whispers for everyone to prepare to move out. It will be a slow climb due to the need for quiet and the dampness of the rock. Anything that can clunk or clang is secured into pockets. Your pack is heavy and awkward.

"Move out," the officer signals with his hand.

You slot your toes and fists into the holes bored by the machine and take a step up. Shifting you hands to the next set of holes, you repeat the motion until you and the sliders have established a rhythm. The weight of your gear wants to pull you back so you make sure to keep your weight forward on the steep slope.

When your group is about 100 yards below the Lowland camp, you and Piver use a couple of expansion bolts to lock the winch into the track holes. Piver attaches a heavy-duty cable to the winch's drum and hands the spool to one of the sliders to carry the rest of the way up.

Leaving Piver below, you and the sliders start to climb again. It will be your responsibility to connect the cable to the Lowland machine in such a way that it does not snap when the winch is activated. The sliders will cut the machine's tethers and keep the Lowlanders busy.

Despite the cold night, sweat drips from your forehead. You're not used to this sort of exercise.

The leading sliders have reached the camp. You can see their shadowy figures moving around just below the machine. Through a series of hand signals, you are instructed to move forward. A slider hands you the end of the cable and you start looking for the best possible place to attach it to the machine.

It's important that the cable twists the machine sideway so it dislodges the sprocket from the holes in the track. If it only pulls straight down, the winch may not have enough power.

You look at the sides of the machine, but they are smooth. There is no obvious protrusion for the cable to hook on to. Then you see a bracket that forms part of the catapult mechanism. It looks a perfect place to attach the cable, but it's above your reach along the top edge of the machine.

You signal the slider beside you and point to the bracket. He nods, understanding your problem. Interlacing his fingers he creates a place to put your foot and hoists you up so that you can hook the shackle onto the bracket.

You've just finished securing the shackle when there is a shout from the camp.

The Lowland guards have spotted someone and raised the alarm.

"Down the cable!" you yell to the Highlanders.

The Highlander lowers you to the ground and the two of you clip on to the cable.

"Quickly."

Going down is a lot easier than going up. All you have to do is pull a trigger on your zipper and you slide freely down the cable. Release the trigger and the zipper clamps onto the cable and brings you to a halt.

Before you know it you and the Highlanders are back beside Piver.

"Now, Piver. Let's rip that scab off the mountain!"

Piver wastes no time in throwing the winch into gear. It splutters and coughs, then starts to wind the excess cable around the drum. By the time all the slack cable is wound up the drum is spinning at quite a good speed.

You hold your breath. Will it be strong enough to jerk the machine off the hillside?

When the last of the slack has been taken up, the cable rises off the ground and starts to stretch.

Any moment now.

"I don't know if it's going to be strong enough," Piver says as the winch groans in protest.

Then you hear yelling from up the mountainside. Lowlanders are shouting warnings to their comrades. All their gear is on the machine. They'll be stranded if they lose it.

Suddenly the cable goes slack and you hear a scraping noise from above.

"It's off," you yell. "Cut the cable!"

Piver grabs a pair of cutters from his belt and bears down on the cable. With a *ping* it separates from the drum.

The scraping is getting louder.

"Geebus, I hope it doesn't take us out on its way past," Piver squeaks, nervously.

So do you, but there is nothing you can do about that now.

Whoosh! The machine slides by before you even see it coming.

"Whoa that was close," Piver says.

Piver's teeth sparkle in the dark.

"Well done, miners. I'm proud of you," the officer says. "That's one machine that won't be roaming the Highlands any time soon."

You must admit you're a little proud of yourself too. Sliders will sing songs of this encounter for many years to come. You and Piver have etched a place in slider history, even though you're only miners.

"Okay troops, the sun will be up in less than an hour. Let's get out of here."

"What will happen to the Lowlanders?" you ask.

"We'll send some sliders for them in a day or two. They'll be very happy to surrender after a couple of cold nights on the slopes.

The climb back down is easier. With a series of belays, you and the sliders make your way down to the Pillars. By the time you are standing outside the main portal, the sun is climbing over the ridge.

It's another beautiful day on the Black Slopes.

"Hey," Piver says. "Where do you find a group of Lowlanders when they've lost one of their fancy machines?"

It's a bit early in the morning for jokes, but you're in a good mood. "I don't know. Where?"

"Exactly where you left them!"

Congratulations, you and Piver have saved the day. Later that month you were both awarded the Highland Medal of Bravery and made honorary members of the Slider Corps. The sliders even let you keep your guide sticks.

But have you followed all the possible paths this book has to offer? Have you encountered morph rats? Found the secret of the moon moths?

It's time for you to make another decision. Do you:

Go back to the beginning of the story and try another path? **P1**

Or

Go to the list of choices and start reading from another part of the story? **P307**

Stay quiet and let the sliders plan their attack from above.

You are hesitant to tell the sliders how to do their job, even though you think that sneaking up from below might be the right thing to do.

The slider officer has gathered his troop together to discuss strategy. You move a little closer so you can hear what they are saying.

"We'll have to wait until morning," the officer says. "Trying to get above the Lowlanders at night would be too dangerous with a couple miners in tow."

You watch the Lowlanders through your scope as you listen in on the sliders' conversation.

"But if we wait till morning, we may never catch them in time," another slider grumps.

You think a moment. "Wait, I have an idea."

"And what might that be?" the officer growls, angry at having his thinking interrupted.

"What if Piver and I climbed up the machine's track to the Lowland camp, while you and your troop go up and around? If you distract the Lowlanders from above, it will give us time to hook a cable onto to their machine and pull them off."

"You think you two can handle that on your own?" the officer asks, a little surprised.

"Climbing the track will be easy. The holes will give us all the hand and footholds we need. The winch we need to pull them off is heavy, but we won't have as far to go as you sliders so we can take a few breaks during the climb."

The officer looks at his team. Many of the sliders are nodding their heads.

"Okay, that's the plan then. You two will have one hour after dewfall to get your equipment in place. When we attack, you'll need to move right away. There is always a chance the Lowlanders will retreat behind their machine. If that happens they will see you for sure."

"Just go easy on them for the first few minutes of your attack.

That's all it will take for me to hook a cable on that steaming contraption of theirs," you say. "After that, you can do whatever you like."

Everyone seems happy with the strategy. The Highland sliders adjust their gear and get a few extra anchor bolts out of their packs.

"Good luck," the office says. "Remember, exactly one hour after dewfall."

You wave as the sliders head off. It will be hard climb time for them. Still, that is what they've trained for.

Unlike the sliders who are climbing the long way around, you and Piver waste no time getting ready to take a gentle slide across the valley to the point where you will intersect the track made by the Lowland machine.

The winch is broken down into two parts, with Piver taking the drum of heavy cable while you take the motor and mounting.

The valley is in shadow. Dewfall is less than an hour away by the time the two of you point your boots slightly downhill and get ready to push off towards the other side of the valley.

"Let's keep as quiet as we can," you say to Piver. "We don't want the Lowlanders to know we're below them.

Piver grins. "Not wrong there. It could get tricky if they start throwing rocks."

With a grim determination, the two of you start your slide. The wind in your face is cooler now that the sun has disappeared behind the ridge. Everywhere you look it is a duller shade of black now that there is no light reflecting off the surface of the slope. Were it not for the flickering lights of the Lowlanders' camp, you would never have known they were there.

You are almost upon the track when you see the series of holes running along the slope. "Here it is," you say to Piver. "Let's get an anchor in and a sling rigged before dewfall. Once it's fully dark, we can start climbing."

You and Piver only get half an hour's rest before the light is gone completely. The night is still, and the only sounds are the odd rattle and voices from the Lowland camp.

"Steady as we go," you say to Piver. "This rock is slipperier than the slime on a morph rat's back."

Standing with your toes jammed into holes, the two of you tighten your packs and rope yourselves together.

"Only one of us moves at a time," you say. "A brief tug on the rope will signal that I'm ready for you to move up."

Piver chuckles nervously, jams his guide stick firmly into a hole and braces himself, ready to hang on should you fall. "Well you'd better get going then," he says.

You sling your stick over your shoulder, stretch forward, and place a fist in each hole. Once your hands are secure you take a few steps. You repeat this process until you're fifteen or so yards further up the slope before jamming your stick in a hole to belay Piver. Giving the cable a light tug, you signal him to climb up to join you.

The two of you repeat this procedure until you are only twenty yards at most below the Lowland camp.

"Quiet," you whisper.

Setting up the winch in absolute silence, in the dark, is even trickier than you thought it would be. Luckily there aren't many moving parts, and most of the assembly can be done by feel. Attaching the winch firmly to the slope with expansion bolts is the hardest part. Thankfully the holes in the track save you from having to drill your own. By the time the job is finished, both you and Piver are sweating.

"When the sliders attack, I'm going to drag that cable up the last few yards and shackle it onto their machine as fast as I can," you say.

Piver smiles. "Then I start the winch and drag the morph-heads off," Piver whispers, his teeth gleaming in the dark.

"Exactly," you say. "Just make sure you give me time to get out of the way before you turn it on. Oh and don't forget to cut the cable once they're off. Otherwise it will swing the machine in your direction and…"

"Squish, splat. I get it."

You tap Piver on the arm and throw the cable over your shoulder. "I'm going to get a little closer," you whisper. "The sliders" attack should start any moment now."

With your belly close to the ground, you slowly work your way up the track until you are lying only yards away from the platform where the Lowlanders are camped. You are so close to the camp, you can hear the Lowlanders farting around their burners as they eat their beans and mash.

All is black around you until a slice of moon pokes its head above the western ridge of a mountain in the distance. You're please to have a little more light, but hope the diversion the sliders are going to create happens soon, otherwise you might get spotted.

When you look down the mountain you can just make out Piver's silhouette against the slope. Moonlight reflects off his teeth, and you wish for once the plucky fellow would stop smiling.

Time moves slowly. Your heart pounds. Thump, thump — thump, thump — thump, thump. It sounds so loud. "Hurry up," you whisper. "They're going to hear me."

When you hear a yell from above, you are relieved. Within a few moments the entire hillside is alive. Moon shadows stretch across the mountain as the Lowlanders respond to the Highland attack.

You stand in a half crouch and move up the track. Before you know it you are on flattish ground and reaching to steady yourself against the rear of the machine. You need to move forward so you can attach the cable at the front where the winch will have a chance of pulling the machine's sprocket wheel out of its holes and send it tumbling down the mountainside.

The Lowland voices seem further away. The sliders must be drawing them up the slope, as they pretend to retreat.

You work your way forward, feeling for protrusions to grip on to as you go. Then you see a bracket sticking out of the side of the machine near its front left corner. It is a perfect place to attach the cable.

The shackle only takes a moment to attach. Once done, you clip on to the cable and start back down towards Piver, sliding fast. The sound of fighting above is getting closer. The Highlanders must be on the charge again.

You know that if your plan doesn't work, the sliders will fight to the death to defeat this machine.

"Winch!" you yell out to Piver. "Quickly!"

You hear the familiar whine of the motor as it takes up the slack in the cable. The winch strains at its mountings. There is a torturous scrape of metal on stone from above as the machine's front end is dragged around side-on to the slope.

Then the cable goes slack.

"It's off." you say to Piver. "Quick, cut the cable."

Piver grabs a pair of cutters from his belt and bears down on the cable. With a *ping* it separates from the drum.

The scraping and clanking is getting closer.

"I hope it doesn't take us out on its way past," Piver squeaks.

So do you, but there is nothing you can do about that now.

Whoosh! A dark shadow skids by within feet of where you and Piver are standing.

"Geebus! That was close," Piver says.

The fighting rages on for another ten minutes or so, but without their machine the Lowlanders are no match for the Highland Slider Corps. A couple of times you hear someone yell as they plummet down the slope past you in the darkness. You can't tell if they are Highlanders or Lowlanders. Regardless, mothers will weep and families will grieve.

Suddenly, it's like someone's turned off a switch and everything goes silent.

"I wonder who won?" Piver says.

It doesn't take long for you to find out.

"Hey, you miners still alive down there?" a familiar voice calls out.

"Yes." Piver replies.

The two of you climb up the path to the small plateau where the sliders have the Lowlanders sitting in a group with their hands tied together.

This is the first time you've seen Lowlanders up close. They look remarkably like members of your own family.

"Well done, you two," the officer says. "As soon as their machine was off, they gave up reasonably easily."

"So what now?" you ask.

"We'll wait until morning and then take them down to the Pillars. They'll get to go home again once their relatives have paid the ransom."

You're pleased that the Lowlanders won't be locked up forever. They don't look much older than you.

"Oh and by the way," the officer says to you and Piver. "I'm going to recommend that you and funny boy here are made honorary sliders."

"Geebus!" Piver says. "Real sliders?"

"Yes," the officer says, "real Highland sliders. Assuming you don't trip and go to the bottom on the way home that is."

For once, your grin is as wide as Piver's. Your family will be so pleased. Now you can follow your dream to be a miner, while being a slider too.

Congratulation, you have finished this part of the story. But have you tried all the different paths?

Have you found the moon moth's secret chamber and fought the morph rats? Have you explored the old mine shaft and discovered the reservoir?

It is time for you to make another decision. Do you:

Go back to the beginning of the story and try another path? **P1**

Or

Go to the list of choices and start reading from another part of the story? **P307**

Carry on to the Pillars with the Lowlanders' message.

You are pleased the sliders have left the decision up to you and are ready to continue on to the Pillars of Haramon with the Lowlanders' message. To start a war without the Highland Council discussing the matter would be irresponsible and put many lives at risk.

What if the Lowlanders really do have some new technology that would make fighting them pointless? Maybe joining their federation would bring benefits to your community. Whichever the case, the Highland Council will have to decide which course of action to take.

"Well if we're not fighting, we'd better get sliding," the head slider says. "We've still got a lot of rock to cover if we're going to get to the Pillars before dewfall."

You tell the miners to check their loads and climb aboard their sledges.

"Any objection if we take the fast route to the Pillars?" the slider officer asks. "I'm assuming this message is urgent."

"Do what you need to, as long as we get there in one piece," you say.

The officer reorganizes his troop for fast travel, one slider steering and two braking on each sledge.

You cinch your waist strap tight and get ready for a speedy ride.

"This should be fun," Piver yells over to you. "I've always wanted to be on a sledge with a bunch of crazy sliders going at top speed down the mountainside. NOT!"

You know how he feels, but you also know that the council will need time to discuss the Lowlanders' offer. The more time they have, the better decision they are likely to make.

"On my mark!" the officer yells.

And with a jerk of the sledge you're off.

The fast route zigzags down a steep face then cuts across a ridge into Long Gully. Further down Long Gully are the Pillars of Haramon, one of the Highland's most secure outposts.

As your slider escorts guide you down the mountain track, you look around at the scenery. Far below is a wonderful mosaic of color. To the west, dark brooding mountains march off into the haze.

"Here comes the tricky part," Shoola calls as your sledge screeches around a hairpin bend.

You look off to the side of your sledge and see only air.

"Geebus that's steep!" you hear Piver shout from the sledge behind you.

He's not wrong. You swallow hard and hold on a little tighter. Looking down makes you feel a little queasy. You look out over the ranges and pretend you're on a simulator. Only unlike the simulators at mining school, this one has a stiff breeze blowing in your face and the screech of sliders straining on their hooks to slow the sledge down for the corners.

When your group finally gets to the bottom, you breathe a sigh of relief. Once they've skirted a small crevasse field, the sliders turn the sledges onto a small plateau and stop.

"You have ten minutes," the leader says.

While most of the sliders sit to rest their legs, the miners are off their sledges a quickly as possible to attach tethers and then stretch. Hydro bars are unwrapped as some have a quick snack.

The bone rattling ride down the mountain has made you need to pee, so you move away from the group and duck behind a small rocky outcrop about twenty yards from the main group.

Just as you start to loosen your uniform, you hear the slurping feet and gnashing teeth of morph rats. Apart from an unexpected cloud burst, this is the most dreaded sound in all the Highlands.

"Morph rats!" you yell, forgetting all about your need to pee.

You look up the slope and can't believe you eyes. There must be a thousand of the horrible creatures, and they are heading in your direction. Their slimy bodies are a light green and the suckers on their feet slurp with every step they take on the slippery black rock.

As they get closer, the clattering of their teeth gets louder. These teeth can strip a full-grown pango to nothing but bone in less than a minute.

Feral packs eat anything in their path. Thankfully, their sense of smell and eyesight are really bad. You can fight them or hide from them.

You need to make a decision quickly. Do you:

Climb up on top of the rocky outcrop and hope the morph rats go around you? **P152**

Or

Run back over to the others and fight the morph rats as a group? **P154**

You have decided to climb on top of the rocky outcrop.

You're not sure that you have time to get to the others before the morph rats are upon you, so you start climbing up the rock. With a bit of luck, the pack of morph rats will stream around you and continue blindly on down the slope.

Their slurping footsteps are getting closer, their teeth chattering like pebbles tumbling down the mountainside.

"Sliders! Uphill V formation now! Miners, get in behind!" you hear a slider yell.

From your vantage point on the rock, you see the sliders bunch together, each has turned their pack around to the front to protect their chest. Their guide sticks, with diamond hooks to the front, are tucked firmly under their armpits, while both hands hold firmly onto the shaft.

The miners are behind the sliders' formation, hand picks up and at the ready.

The pack of morph rats move like a writhing wave of teeth and slime down the hillside.

When the wave hits, those at the point of the V-formation will sweep the rats to the side using their sticks.

"Try to flip the rats onto their backs so they lose their grip on the slope," the head slider says. "That way, by the time they regain their feet they'll be too far down the mountain to be of any danger."

The clicking and slurping sends a chill down your spine. One slip and everyone is rat food.

You don't have your pick with you. You left it leaning against your sledge when you headed for the rock. That was a big mistake.

Without your pick, all you can do is hope the rats go around the rock rather than over it. If any rats do decide to climb towards your position you just hope you'll be able to kick them away.

You watch with a morbid fascination as the wave of slimy flesh and pointed teeth surges towards your rock. Anyone that ends up in this seething mass of animals won't last long.

The sliders stand with sticks at the ready.

All you can do is watch and wait.

When the mass of rat flesh reaches your position, the sheer weight of rats behind the front of the wave, pushes rats up the rock you are standing on. The first few you manage to kick off, but before long your boots are covered in slime and standing on the rock is becoming more difficult.

You chance a quick glance at the others and see that the sliders' technique is working. The wave of rats is parting around the sliders and miners on the slope.

You feel teeth dig into your shin and try to kick the rats at your feet away, but slime is all over your rock now. You try another kick, but lose your balance. You are falling into the swarm.

Unfortunately this part of your adventure is over. You made the mistake of thinking you could escape the morph rats by climbing the rock. You should have gone back and joined forces with the others. There is always safety in numbers when it comes to fighting off morph rats.

It is now time for you to make another decision. Do you:

Go back to the beginning of the story and try another path? **P1**

Or

Go back to your last choice and make a different decision. **P154**

Run back to the others and fight the morph rats as a group.

"Sliders, uphill-V-formation, quickly! You miners tuck in behind," the head slider yells.

You move as fast as you can to where the sliders are forming into a defensive position to take on the advancing wave of morph rats. The rat's slurping footsteps are getting closer. Their teeth clatter and click as they move.

The sliders bunch together. Each has turned their pack around to protect their chest from the rat's razor-sharp teeth, should one of them break through. Their guide sticks, with diamond hooks pointing to the front, are tucked under their armpits. They clutch the shaft firmly in both hands. Grim determination is set in their eyes.

You and the other miners squeeze in behind the sliders' formation, hand picks at the ready.

The pack of morph rats moves like a writhing wave of teeth and slime down the hillside towards you. It isn't a pretty sight, and smells even worse. When the wave of rats reaches the V-formation, the sliders at the front furiously sweep the rats to each side using their sticks like brooms. The sliders near the rear of the group then try to flip the rats onto their backs so they lose their grip on the slope and slide too far down the mountain to be of any danger.

"Geebus, look at them!" Piver shivers in disgust, his pick at the ready. "Ugliest creatures alive, I reckon."

Snap, click, snap go thousands of teeth.

"Ugh, I can smell their breath from here," Piver says. "It's like rotten eggs."

The sliders are struggling to sweep aside the writhing mass as it slurps past.

"Yeow!" a miner yelps as a morph rat chomps onto his leg. He swings his pick knocking the rat out and then kicks the hideous creature down the slope. "That hurt!"

And then, as suddenly as they came, the rats have passed, slithering further down the slope in search of plump pangos.

"Well done sliders," the officer says. "Never get isolated by morph rats, if you do, you're better off free sliding. Being swarmed by morph rats is not the way you want to go, believe me."

You see Piver close his eyes and shudder. Sometimes his overactive imagination leads to funny situations, at other times it can be a curse.

"You okay Piver?" you ask. He looks a little pale.

"Yeah, it's just that…" He shakes his head. "Never mind, I don't want to think about it."

"Right, load up," the head slider says. "We've got to get to the Pillars before dewfall."

Remembering you needed to pee, you rush back over behind the rock and relieve yourself. The rock is covered in rat slime. If you'd stayed there you wouldn't have survived.

After everyone is ready your little caravan sets off again, moving at top speed towards the Pillars of Haramon.

"Cute little critters those rats, eh?" Shoola says as she slides down the mountain behind you.

"Yeah right," you say. "Ever eaten one?"

"Just once. My troop was trapped high up the mountain in a storm. All we could do for six days was anchor ourselves on the mountain and hang on. By the time it was safe to move around, we hadn't eaten in three days."

"Three days?"

"We were just about to slide off, when a small pack of rats came by. Let's just say it was messy. By the time we'd skinned a couple, there was slime everywhere. I can still smell it in my uniform some days."

You can't imagine not eating for three days. But even then, you don't know if you'd ever get hungry enough to eat a morph rat. "Yuck. Sounds horrible."

Shoola smiles. "Let's just say I've taken dumps that smelled better and leave it at that."

You laugh and look out over the valley. The sun is getting low in the sky. Soon it will disappear behind the ridge and the temperature will drop six or seven degrees. An hour after that, dewfall will start. You just hope you've arrived at the Pillars by then.

About forty minutes later, you see two towering monoliths rising high above the valley floor in the distance. The black stone pillars are the most beautiful sight you have ever seen. Smooth and shining, they dwarf everything around them. Sunshine still illuminates their tops.

You want to make some comment to Shoola about how amazing they look, but your mouth is hanging open in awe and any words you come up with seem inadequate.

"Not far now," she says.

Within ten minutes your caravan is outside one of the Pillar's main portals. A door slides open at its base and the sliders maneuver the sledges inside a cavern hollowed out of the solid rock.

With a hiss of air, the massive doors close again and you unbuckle your straps.

"Welcome to the Pillars of Haramon," a crew member says. "Cutting it a bit fine for dewfall weren't you?"

The head slider steps forward. "Considering we ran into Lowlanders and a huge swarm of morph rats, I think we've done well just to make it here in one piece."

You and the other miners mumble your agreement.

"I need to get a message to the Highland Council," you say. "The Lowlanders have given us an ultimatum."

"You'd better go up to the command pod and tell the officer in charge. Ultimatums are above my pay grade."

The crew member points you towards a spiral staircase cut into the rock. "They're on the top floor."

"You mean I've got to climb a thousand feet to the top of the Pillars?" This is not what you had in mind.

"No, silly. There's a cable-lift two flights up."

You breathe a sigh of relief and start up the first flight. You wonder how big each flight is and start counting. The first flight is 39 steps. By the time you reach the landing you are sweating. "I must do more exercise," you tell yourself.

At the top of the second flight, you come to a place where a vertical shaft has been bored into the rock. A motorized cable runs up the tunnel. Every five seconds or so, a sturdy platform appears. You watch as a slider steps onto a platform and is whisked up the tunnel. Now it's just a matter of timing your step. After counting and watching for a minute, you feel you've got it worked out and prepare to step aboard.

"Five, four, three, two, one, step," you count.

For a split second you think you've made a mistake, but then you feel something solid beneath your feet. Your knees bend slightly and you are plunged into darkness as you rise up the shaft.

"But how do I get off?" you mumble to yourself. "I should have asked someone."

Your hand tightens around the cable. You can feel it vibrating as you climb. Every fifty feet or so, you move past an opening and can see out of the shaft into what must have been mine workings many years ago. Now they are just empty chambers, with ventilation holes overlooking the valley below.

You hear voices from above. The top can't be far away. Light is starting to penetrate down the shaft from above and the sound of a drum whirling the cable back down is getting louder.

An opening appears. You jump.

Your landing in the command pod isn't graceful, but at least you've made it. You hear chuckling and see three slider officers looking at you.

"Welcome miner," one of the men says. "You have a message for us I believe."

"Yes, for the Highland Council."

"Well spit it out."

You look at the slider officer. "Are you on the council?"

The officer looks down at the three cut diamonds pinned to his chest. "See those stars?"

You nod.

"Know what they mean?"

You shake your head.

"It means I'm chief of the Highland Council. Don't they teach that at mining school these days?"

"Sorry, no," you say, a little embarrassed.

"Well come on. What's the message?"

You give him the message about joining the Lowland Federation. You tell him about the offer of education and healthcare … and the tax. You also tell him about the Lowlanders' threat, and how the one you spoke to seemed extremely confident in their new technology.

The council chief's face takes on a stony appearance as he considers what you've said. "Our spies have seen these machines. But I can't imagine the members of the council agreeing to the Lowlanders' terms. Highlanders have been fiercely independent for generations and we don't take kindly to threats."

"But what about the healthcare, education and other benefits they offer?" you ask. "Aren't they worth considering?"

"We have education."

"Not a very good education it seems."

The chief scowls at you. "I'm not sure I like your tone."

"Why can't we talk peace?" you say. "Do we have to keep this hatred going just out of pride?" You look up into the chief's brooding face. "How many will die in this war? All of us?"

The chief isn't used to people standing up to him. He stomps his foot and snarls like he's about to bite his tongue off and spit it at you. "How dare you!"

You take a step back as spittle flies in your direction. The man is grinding his teeth and growling like a wild animal. "Sliders never surrender!"

"And in my family we never enter a fight unless we know we can win!"

This makes the chief pause. He harrumphs and walks to the far side of the pod and looks out the window at the shadowed slopes below. It seems an age before he turns around and faces you.

"Do you really think we could lose everything?"

"I don't know," you say. "But even if there is the slightest chance of that happening, is it worth the risk? And if by some stroke of luck we do come out on top, how many of your friends will die in the process?"

Once again the chief's face turns to stone. You can almost see him thinking. "You're pretty plucky for a miner," he says a minute or so later.

"I come from generations of sliders, remember."

Finally you get a little smile from the chief. "Okay, get back to your pod. I'll speak to the council and see what they say."

When you arrive back at the accommodation pod, the others are eating. You grab some broth and take it over to sit with Piver and Shoola.

"So what's up?" Piver asks.

You fill them in on your meeting with the council chief.

"You think they'll talk peace?" Piver asks. "It would be the first time in three generations."

"I don't know. I just hope that the council can see the bigger picture. Life is tough enough on the slopes without having to fight all the time."

"I have a cousin who is a Lowlander," Shoola says.

"Really?" Piver asks. "How did that happen?"

"He just slid off one day and disappeared. Seems he'd met a girl from one of the border tribes during a trade meeting and fell in love."

Piver's eyes grew wide. "And he never came back?"

"He did some years later. Tried to tell everyone that the Lowlanders were just like us, but the people in the communities wouldn't listen."

"So what happened?" you ask.

"He had no choice but to go back down the mountain. It broke his family's heart."

The three of you sit in silence for a while, sipping your broth, lost in your own thoughts.

"Just like us?" Piver finally said.

Shoola nodded.

Piver looked confused. "Then why are we fighting them?"

Shoola shrugged her shoulders. "I think it's been so long, everyone has forgotten why we started."

Later, you think about what Shoola has said as you fall asleep on your bunk.

The next morning you are awoken by someone shaking your shoulder.

"What?"

"Come with me," a slider says. "Chief wants a word."

You get up and dress quickly. The slider leads you towards the cable-lift.

When the two of you reach the command pod there are twelve people sitting around a large table.

The chief waves you to a seat near one end. "Please sit."

You wonder what is going on. Everyone is looking at you.

The chief clears his throat. "This is the young miner I told you about."

Eleven faces swivel towards you.

The chief looks in your direction. "We've sent a delegation to talk peace with the Lowlanders. They left at first light this morning."

You can't help but think they've done the right thing.

An older woman stands up and walks towards your seat. She places her withered hands on your shoulders. "I am an old woman, but I know a clever mind and a good heart when I see one."

You look up into her clear green eyes.

"I want you to take my seat on the council young miner. We need new blood. Blood untarnished by years of conflict."

Is she really talking about you joining the council? Surely not. What experience do you have?

"But…"

"Quiet," the old woman says. "It's time the council heard the truth. And you, young as you are, are the first person to give it to them."

"If the Highlands are to prosper, we need to stop putting so many of our resources into fighting the Lowlanders. Joining The Federation of Lowland States might be just the opportunity we are looking for."

Heads around the table are nodding in agreement.

"So do you accept the appointment?" the chief says to you.

"I … I'm a bit…"

"Surprised?" the chief says

"Geebus!" you say, using Piver's favorite exclamation. "Now there's the understatement of the century."

A light chuckle runs around the table.

"So what do you say?" the old woman asks. "Will you help us steer the Highlands towards peace?"

You think for a moment and search the faces before you.

"Well ?" the chief says. "Are you up to the job?"

You think about your family and how proud they would be if you were to become a member of the council. How their disappointment at you deciding to become a miner would wash away like pango droppings in a heavy rain. "Of course I'm up for it. I'm a Highlander."

Congratulations, this part of your story is over. You successfully helped start the peace process on your planet and became a member of the Highland Council, a great honor to you and your family. Well done! But have you followed all the possible paths yet? Have you gone to slider school? Gone down into a scary cave? Been caught in a storm?

It is now time to make another decision. Do you:

Go back to the beginning of the story and try a different path? **P1**

Or

Go to the list of choices and start reading from another part of the story? **P307**

Volcano of Fire

The Pillars of Haramon

You sit at a long table in the command pod atop one of the twin Pillars of Haramon. The room is filled with the hum of voices. A small robotic bird, unseen by those in the room, hovers in one corner.

The man at the head of the table has three blue-diamond stars pinned to his chest, indicating his rank as chief of the council. Next to him sits a visiting Lowland general, his face as hard as the rock walls of the command pod. Around the table, other important figures from both the Highlands and the Lowlands sit nervously.

Being the newest member of the Highland Council, you have yet to earn your first star, but you have big plans to make your mark.

"Quiet please," the chief says. "We've got important matters to discuss."

The chief's scars are visible, even from your seat at the opposite end of the table. These scars are proof of the many battles and expeditions he has taken part in over his long career and are proof of the dangers of living in the Highlands where the rock under your feet is the slipperiest material imaginable. Black glass.

"Supplies of tyranium crystals have run desperately low," the chief says. "Without tyranium, workers can't move safely around the slopes and that means no progress on the trade routes being built between the Lowlands and the Highlands. If our truce is to last, trade is critical."

As you listen to the chief talk, you stare out of the large windows that overlook the slopes below. Further down Long Gully, the second pillar rises from the smooth black slope. A colony of red-beaked pangos squabble with each other for nesting spaces in the cracks near its summit.

To the south are the patchwork fields of the Lowlands, the blue ribbons of the river delta and the turquoise sea. Petron's smallest moon has just risen, pale pink in the morning light, just above the horizon.

"We need to mount an expedition to locate a new source of crystals, and soon," the chief says. "Led by someone we trust."

He turns and looks in your direction. "Someone who knows how to slide on black glass and has the ability to lead a team. Someone with a knowledge of mining and brave enough to take chances when necessary. Are you up for it?" the chief asks, catching you off guard.

"Me?" Sure you've been a troop leader in the Slider Corps and spent a little time in mining school, but leading an expedition into new territory? That's quite a responsibility.

The Lowland general stands, rests his hairy knuckles on the table before him, and leans towards your end of the table. "We need someone who is respected by both the Lowlanders and the Highlanders. Someone both sides trust to ensure an equal share of any discoveries."

"That's right," the chief says. "It was you who helped start the peace process. You are the logical choice."

Your part in this story is about to begin. You are being asked to undertake a dangerous mission, one that is important to your community. But are you really qualified? You are young. Surely others would be more suitable. Maybe you should suggest someone more experienced lead the expedition, then you could go back home and live a safe life growing hydro or hunting pangos.

It is time to make your first decision. Do you:

Agree to lead the mission? **P165**

Or

Suggest someone else lead the mission? **P170**

You have agreed to lead the mission.

"I'm happy enough to lead an expedition if I can choose the people I take with me," you say to the council.

"The Lowlands will need representation on this mission too," the Lowland general says. "I will send you six of my best troopers and you can choose which members of the Slider Corps and which miners to take. How does that sound?"

You look around the table at all the expectant faces, the chief's especially. "Okay," you say. "How soon do we leave?"

There is a look of relief on the chief's face. "As soon as we can gather the required personnel and equipment. The mission is to Mount Kakona."

"Mount Kakona?" you say, hoping you've misheard. "That's an active volcano, isn't it?"

The chief nods. "The biggest. But volcanoes are where the crystals are. Give me a list of the Highlanders you want to take along as soon as possible and I'll send out the orders."

After the meeting breaks up, you stay behind to make a list of names. Top of the list is Gagnon the navigator. Then Dagma for muscle, Piver for his mining experience and good humor, Shoola for her skill with a mountain sledge and Drexel for his climbing skills. You will make up the sixth member of the group. You only hope the Lowlander troops will be able to keep up.

You hand the list to the chief. "I'm going to go to the equipment bay and start sorting out the sledges."

The chief smiles. "I'm pleased you're so eager to get on with the job." He glances down at the list. "I'll have everyone assemble in two days. If the weather is okay, you can leave that morning."

Two days will come around before you know it and you've got lots to do. "Piver and Gagnon are here at the Pillars, chief, I'll go tell them myself if that's okay. We can start planning right away."

The chief gives you a salute, "Off you go and remember, have a plan B. Even good plans can go wrong on the Black Slopes."

As you make your way to the cable lift, you wonder what you've got yourself into. When you reach level 8 you leap off and head down a corridor.

You find the little engineer fiddling with a piece of equipment on the workbench in front of him when you enter his pod.

"What's that?" you ask. "Some new invention?"

"Well hullo to you too," he says.

After you've bumped elbows in greeting, Piver grins, picks up the contraption and slots his fingers through its grip. Then he clips a strap around his wrist, points the tube end at the ceiling and pulls a trigger.

With a sharp hiss a tiny anchor bolt shoots up and embeds itself in the smooth rock overhead. Then, with the whirl of a battery pack, Piver is lifted off the ground and reeled up a fine cable towards the ceiling.

"Weeeeeeeee…" Piver says as he rises higher and higher.

You look up. "What are you doing?"

Piver thumbs the release and comes zipping back down. "It's a pocket launcher. It's only got twenty feet of cable, but it'll be great for exploring the roofs of caves or creating a quick anchor if you're caught in the rain on a slippery slope. Here, have a look."

He hands you the launcher. "It's nice and light, I'll give you that."

Piver smiles. "The battery pack is built into the handle."

"How many lifts before you need to recharge?"

"Twenty or so. Unless you're a heavyweight hydro-gobbler like Dagma."

"Could you make a dozen of these in a couple days?" you ask.

"Sure, they're not complicated," Piver says. "Why?"

"Because we're going to Mount Kakona."

Piver lets out a high pitched giggle.

"Why are you laughing?" you ask.

"You're joking aren't you?" Piver's eyes search your face. When he doesn't see you smiling they go wide, the whites showing all around his dark green pupils. "Geebus! You're serious!"

"We're going on a mining expedition. Command needs tyranium crystals in a hurry and they think Mount Kakona is where we'll find them."

"But that area's never been explored … and it's active."

"A good reason to get in, harvest some crystals and get out as quickly as possible."

"Geebus, I hope you know what you're doing."

So do you, but you don't tell Piver that. "At least the old troop will be together again. I'm off to tell Gagnon now."

"Wait, before you go," Piver says. "Why does a red-beaked pango lift up one leg while it's sleeping?"

You know this is going to be bad, but you play along. "I don't know, Piver. Why?"

"Because if it lifts up both legs, it falls over!" Piver laughs like he's the one who made up the old joke.

Your eyes roll. "I see your material hasn't improved." You shake your head and chuckle. "Bye, Piver. Get onto those launchers. We leave for Mount Kakona in two days."

Piver's giggling follows you down the corridor. He may be a nutty little fellow, but you know from previous experience he's far braver than others realize, and smarter too.

You come to a set of steps cut into the rock wall. Two flights down you find Gagnon exactly where you expected him to be, in the map room, studying.

"What is it with you and this place? You must have all of Petron memorized by now."

Gagnon looks up and smiles. "A good navigator needs to know his way around. Let me guess, we're off to Mount Kakona."

"How the heck do you know that? It's only just been decided by council."

"I was asked by the chief a week ago if I thought it was possible to navigate a route to Kakona's southern vents. I'm guessing they're after tyranium?"

"I'm impressed, Gagnon. I always knew you were clever. And yes, tyranium needle crystals, seems there's a desperate shortage."

"So are you leading the expedition or just recruiting?"

"Leading. We set off in two days." You lean over his shoulder. "How's the route looking?"

"Like a steaming bucket of pango poo, but I've got an idea."

"A good one I hope."

Gagnon smiles. "Could we take a medium sized driller along? I know they're heavy, and it would mean we'd be able to carry fewer supplies, but we could save five days travel and a lot of risk by tunneling through the Tyron Cliffs."

"Through the cliffs?"

"See here," he says, pointing to a long line marked on the map. "These cliffs are pretty risky to climb and even trickier to get around. Crevasse fields below and overhanging buttresses above. But, I've spotted a section where the cliffs are only 30 yards thick. About ten hours drilling I figure."

You know from geography class that this wall of shimmering black rock, pushed up by a series of big quakes thousands of years ago, is over 100 miles long. Those who have seen them say they are one of Petron's natural wonders. But they are also a big headache for anyone wanting to travel west and are the main reason the Kakona volcanic field hasn't been explored.

You think hard about what Gagnon has said. "Is that our best option?"

"The shortest distance between two points is a straight line," Gagnon says. "It's either that or a five day detour with the sledges across some incredibly dangerous country."

You stare at the map a while longer. "If we're loaded with crystals on the way back I suppose a tunnel would make good sense. We can ditch the mining gear too. Plus we'll have Lowlanders with us. Not sure they're up to a big climb."

But a medium sized driller will reduce the amount of food and other equipment you'll be able to take on the journey. And what if the driller breaks down before you get through? Either option has its risks.

It is time to make a decision Do you:

Take the drilling machine along? **P173**

Or

Take more food and equipment and leave the drill behind? **P181**

Suggest someone with more experience leads the expedition.

"I appreciate your confidence in me," you say. "But surely there is someone more qualified?"

The chief gives you a stern look. "Leadership isn't always about experience. It's also about attitude and having troopers that will follow you even when things get tough. In the past you've shown you can think fast and improvise when necessary. Valuable skills for a Slider Corps leader."

"And we trust you," the Lowland general adds. "You've spent time getting to know us and I believe you'll look after our interests fairly."

Heads are nodding all around the table.

You think hard for a reason to back out, but can't find one. Everyone is depending on you. And a trip to the interior will be exciting. You thump the table and nod. "Okay. I'll do it. Where are we going?"

"Ah, that's the tricky part," the chief says. "We want you to go to Crater Canyon."

"Crater Canyon? I always thought Crater Canyon was a myth. Are you telling me it actually exists?"

"Members of the council have always thought the canyon was a myth too, until a miner turned up raving about a huge vein of tyranium he'd found. Problem is, the miner seemed a bit unstable. He talked of huge snakes, robot hummingbirds, metallic spiders and strange people living near the hull of a huge, metal, bird-like craft."

"So why don't you get this miner to lead you back to where he found the crystals?"

The chief shakes his head. "We would ... but he's gone missing."

"Missing?"

"Yes, just disappeared in the night. One witness claimed a flying disk picked him up and carried him away. Trackers tried to follow his scent up the mountain, but it faded to nothing after a hundred yards where they found small traces of an unidentified dust and burn marks on the rock. The whole thing was most unusual."

You scratch your head and think. "But if the miner was crazy, how do you know he found tyranium?"

The chief reaches down under the table and brings out a lump of rock. "Because he had this with him. Analysis shows it to be ninety-five percent pure. Our best mines only ever produced eighty percent."

The chief puts some papers on the table. "He also left these hand-drawn maps."

You walk around the table to have a look.

The chief points to a spot on the map. "We think this is Mount Transor, but it's unclear. The rest of the map looks like it covers an area on the other side of the main range."

"But the interior is totally unexplored," you say, wondering what you've got yourself into. "And if the miner was mentally unstable…"

The Lowland general clears his throat. "Just because the miner's kooky doesn't mean everything he said was wrong. I mean tiny metal birds and huge snakes sound a bit unlikely, but look at that rock. Have you ever seen such tightly bunched crystals?"

You have to admit you haven't. "They seem much finer than usual too."

The chief rubs his hand lightly over the specimen. "You could just about walk up wet rock if you had these on the soles of your boots. Imagine if we found the main source and what a difference it would make to our ability to move around the slopes. Imagine not worrying about sliding to the bottom every time there's a light shower, or in the evenings after dewfall?"

The chief's eyes are gleaming with excitement. He makes a good point. This quality of needle crystals would change life on the Black Slopes forever. And you've got a chance to be part of history.

"When do we leave?" you say with a smile, accepting the challenge. "I've always wondered what the interior is like."

"Great," the chief says. "I knew you'd come around. The only thing left to decide is if you take a big well-equipped group, or one that's smaller and faster."

It is time for you to make a decision. Do you:

Go for a big well equipped group? **P187**

Or

Go for a smaller yet faster group? **P195**

Take the driller and attempt to drill through the Tyron Cliffs.

"Geebus this thing is heavy," Piver says as he swings one end of the drill onto the sledge. "I hope this works. Otherwise we'll be humping this along for nothing."

Piver's right. It is a risk. But you trust Gagnon's ability to pinpoint the exact spot to drill. If he's more than ten yards off in either direction, or gets the angle wrong you'll be drilling for two days rather than ten hours, and two days drilling without a replacement bit is one and a half days too many.

"Just make sure you load everything we'll need for twelve hours drilling and leave the tactics up to Gagnon," you say as you help Piver with the other end of the bulky machine. "When has he let us down before?"

The two of you go back to loading up the second sledge with boxes of dried hydro and premixed containers of broth. Then you add a burner for cooking, fuel, extra harnesses, anchor guns, spare cable and plenty of battery powered zippers.

There will be no tows or formed paths on the other side of the Tyron Cliffs. All climbing will be done with portable tow launchers and zip lines and the sliding will be slow and difficult. When the batteries run out, you'll have to climb like Highlanders did in the old days, with leg power, skill and determination.

The next two days go in a flurry of work and organization. When departure day arrives, you are frantically checking lists of equipment and stores.

The chief has come down to introduce you to the Lowland members of the expedition. "This is Trodie, he's the ranking Lowland officer and their best climber," the chief says. "All the Lowlanders have had cross country experience so they should be well matched to your troop."

The chief gives you a wink as he says this. He knows no Lowlanders can match the Slider Corp for traveling on the Black

Slopes, but he doesn't want to embarrass Trodie in front of his troop.

Trodie is a head taller than you and stocky in build. The guide stick he's carrying looks awkward in his hand. The two of you bump elbows and then turn back to the chief.

"Trodie is to be second in command. I suggest you work together to make this expedition a success. Forget that some of you are Lowlanders and others are Highlanders. Just remember you are all Petronians and treat each other with respect."

The chief salutes and then heads back down the corridor towards the lift.

"Okay everyone," you say. "Let's get our harnesses on and these sledges hooked up. We've got one big tow to the top ridge and then a long slide to the end of the Western Track. After that we leave the tracks behind."

Your troop wastes no time in hooking up to the sledges. Dagma and Shoola take their customary places at the rear where they will act as brakes. Gagnon and Drexel hook their harnesses to the steering runners at the front.

Gagnon looks at Drexel. "Just as well we replaced the diamond grit on our runners last week eh? I suspect we'll need every bit of grip we can get."

Drexel pats the anchor gun hanging on his utility belt. "Quick draw's my specialty. I don't plan on going to the bottom this trip."

You turn to Trodie. "Put a Lowlander on the back of each sledge to help with the breaking. You and I will lead. Everyone else can ride on the sledges for now. We'll reorganize things once we get to the Tyron Cliffs."

Within minutes your group is ready to hook on to the 3000 foot tow that will take you up to the high ridge overlooking the Pillars of Haramon.

The high-tensile cable hums as it runs up the slick towpath. Those who are sliding swivel the lock bar out of their front boot and clip it into a fitting on the instep of their back boot to form a stable sliding platform.

Rows of tiny diamonds on their soles give the sliders some steering ability and a diamond spur on the heel of their back boot provides some stopping power. The sliders push forward with the needle end of their guide sticks and get ready to clamp onto the tow.

"On my mark," you yell. "Three, two, one…"

With knees bent, you swing your clamp over the cable and press down hard. As the clamp grips the cable you start moving up the towpath. Leaning back into your harness you concentrate on keeping your balance. You can't think of a worse way to start an expedition than to have its leader slip and fall over on the first tow.

Gagnon and Dagma's sledge is right behind you, while Drexel and Shoola's brings up the rear.

As you look back down the towline, the Lowlanders seem to be coping with the challenge of the towpath so far. You just hope they've got some traversing skills too. Sliding on formed paths is one thing, but free sliding in unknown terrain is another matter altogether.

When you reach the top of the tow, you release your clamp and slide along the offloading platform. The screech of diamonds sound across the ridge as everyone comes to a stop.

You love the feel of a guide stick in your hand. It's almost an extension of your arms. A blue diamond hook is mounted at one end for stopping and a thick pad of tyranium needle crystals are fixed to the other for steering and pushing. A guide stick and glide boots are the two items of equipment that no member of the Highland Slider Corps can do without.

The Pillars of Haramon are now far below. Light bounces off their reflective surfaces making them glisten, dark and foreboding, in the soft morning light.

To the west is the volcanic plateau. The air up this high is clean and cool. Nearly a hundred miles in the distance the black cone of Mount Kakona towers above the mountains around it. This is going to be a tricky expedition. Kakona's western vents are halfway up the mountain's flank. But climbing Mount Kakona is the least of your worries. First you have to get to its base.

"So what do you think Gagnon? Are we going to make it there and back before our food runs out?"

Gagnon has a look of quiet confidence. "My calculations say we can. If not we'll just have to eat wild pangos."

Trodie and Piver slide over to where you and Gagnon are talking. Trodie is mumbling under his breath.

"Sorry what's that?" you ask.

"I'm just trying to convince myself I'm not dreaming. I've looked up at these mountains all my life and now that I'm here amongst them. I feel so small."

You know how Trodie feels. Every time you come up here you feel the same.

Trodie points towards Mount Kakona. "Is that it? The one we're going to?"

Piver shakes his head. "Nah, Mount Kakona's much bigger than that, you can't even see it from here."

Trodie's jaw drops, "Wha…?"

"Ha! Got ya!" Piver says erupting into hysterical giggling. "How could a mountain get any bigger than that monster?"

"Hey, Piver, I thought I told you not to tease the Lowlanders," you say, trying not to smile.

Trodie grins. "I just hope you know how to take a joke too, funny man. Phew, you had me worried there."

"I'd still be worried if I was you," Gagnon says. "Climbing the volcano might be the easy part. We've got to get there first, then there's the small matter of Mount Kakona being active."

"I hear that hot rock is hard on the boots," Piver say looking at Trodie. "Melts right through the soles in minutes."

Trodie's mouth drops again.

Then Piver starts laughing again. "Geebus, you Lowlanders are gullible, if the rock's hot, you go around it."

You give Piver a sharp look. "Stop it, Piver!"

"You'll keep my little friend," Trodie says, wagging his finger and smiling. "You'll keep."

"We'd better get moving if we're going to make it to the Tyron Cliffs by dewfall," you say. "Gagnon, what's our first traverse like?"

Gagnon explains the route he's planned. "The Western Track's narrow but at least it's a track. It's 40 miles and three zips up to the head of Black Gully."

Dagma is acting as brake on the heaviest sledge with the drilling machine. Shoola has the lighter supply sledge. You notice both the girls are munching on hydro bars to keep their energy levels up.

"Eyes open and knees bent," you tell everyone. "We don't want any accidents today. Dagma let me know if you need extra help with that sledge. No playing the hero."

With that, you and Trodie lead the troop off the platform and onto the grade 2 track. The first traverse takes you due west towards the head of Black Gully. Every ten miles or so, you'll need to launch a cable and zip up to gain more altitude. This will enable you to keep traversing along the well-worn track notched into the side of the mountainside.

Then, once you've reached Black Gully, it's a twenty-mile slide down to the drill site on the spectacular Tyron Cliffs.

With your guide stick tucked under your arm and both hands firmly on its shaft, you point your front foot downhill and push off. As you slide, you hear the faint swish of Trodie's boots gliding across the rock behind you.

It's times like this that you enjoy being a slider the most, the wind rushing past your visor, the soft hiss of boots on black glass. The view out to the sea and the smell of the mountains make you feel alive.

After the first ten-mile traverse, the cable launcher is set up and Drexel fires an anchor bolt into the ridge high above. Once you've all zipped up to the next section of track, you lead off on another traverse further west.

A range of sharp peaks runs from east to west. Your group runs parallel to them. A few wisps of cloud can be seen beyond their peaks to the south, but thankfully none have crossed the divide onto your side of the range. Rain is the one danger all Highlanders fear. It can turn an easily traversable slope into an ultra-slick nightmare in seconds. Even eighty percent tyranium crystals won't hold on a slope of more than ten degrees on wet rock.

After a long and tiring slide, you and your troop reach the top of Black Gully. You call a halt on a small patch of level ground and look down the narrow chute. It's easy to see why it got its name. Black Gully is a natural half-pipe with curved wave-like overhangs on both sides. Because it runs north to south, very little natural light gets down into its depths, making the gully almost look like a tunnel at certain times of the day. Deep shadows hide the gully's many irregularities and make it a far trickier place to slide than it looks.

"Don't let this innocent looking place catch you out," you say to the group. "Black Gully's known for its sudden dips and ripples so keep your hooks at the ready and your knees bent. It's also an area where WAVs are known to roll, so stay alert."

"I forgot you had those up here." Trodie says nervously, looking up towards the peaks above.

You nod. "They start life up here. Wild pango's eat the seeds of the Wandering Adamus Vines, or WAVs as we call them and then poop them out near their breeding colonies. Some of the seeds sprout in the nutrients that collect under the pango colonies and as the WAVs grow they become these big ugly 100 pound balls of thorns. Eventually they get too heavy for their tiny roots to hold them on the slope and they roll off downhill."

"I know," Trodie says. "They come bouncing down the mountain at high speed until they reach the Lowlands. We have villagers injured by them every summer in the high pastures."

"I bet that hurts," Piver says.

"You're not wrong there," Trodie say. "I suppose you sliders get a few injuries too."

You nod. "They come from nowhere sometimes. The only warning is a dry rustling sound. Best just to lay flat and hope they roll over you without leaving too many thorns behind. If you try to run, they can knock you right off the mountain."

"I know a girl who got prickled good n' proper," Piver says. "You should have seen her afterwards. What a mess."

Trodie looks worried. "I've heard rumors these plants can think. Any truth in that?"

You shrug. "I've heard that too. An old man in my community said he saw a WAV change into the shape of an animal and run on four legs. But he was a bit happy on moth mist at the time so he was probably dreaming. The main thing is to get through Black Gully as quickly as possible and, if you do see a WAV coming, hit the deck, grit your teeth and cross your fingers."

You gesture for the group to move out and lead them down into Black Gully on a safe route that uses the natural contours of the half pipe to slow you down as you swoop from one side to the other.

"Whoopee!" Piver yells from the top on one of the sledge. "Go faster you slowpokes!"

Some of the Lowlanders aren't so happy riding on the weaving sledges. One in particular is suffering from motion sickness.

"Maybe a raw pango egg would help settle your stomach," Piver tells him.

"Eurghhh!" the Lowlander says, losing his lunch.

"Piver, stop it!" you say over your shoulder. "I told you to play nice."

"Geebus did you see that?" Piver says. "That looked nasty!"

With an empty stomach, the young Lowlander feels better within minutes. As your group exits Black Gully, you come onto a plateau and see the Tyron Cliffs spread before you. Immediately all thoughts, except those of utter amazement, are forgotten.

'Holy moly,' someone behind you says.

'Geebus!' Piver squeaks. "Look at 'em."

The cliffs rise vertically, shimmering black and almost translucent. You are so lost in their beauty that you almost forget you're in charge of the expedition.

"Tether your sledges," you say. "Remember everything slips on black glass, even on the slightest of slopes. If you don't want to lose it, tie it down."

The sun is low. You have about an hour before dewfall when the slopes will become treacherous. You could set up the driller ready for an early start in the morning, or you could set up camp and leave the driller for the morning.

It would be nice to start drilling early, the more time you save the longer your supplies will last, but you also know everyone is tired from the days travel and setting it up will mean more work.

It is time to make a decision. Do you:

Set the drill up ready for the morning? **P200**

Or

Set up camp first in case the weather turns? **P203**

You have decided to take more food and leave the driller.

"I'd rather go around the cliffs," you say to Gagnon. "We might starve to death if we take a two hundred pound drill rather than food with us. And what if the thing breaks down? What then?"

"But—?"

"Look, if we can find a way around the Tyron Cliffs. A track can be built and others will be able to follow. That will open up a whole new area."

"But it's never been done before. And going around is quite a distance."

You shrug. "There has to be a first time. Besides, who knows what interesting discoveries we'll make along the way."

Gagnon isn't all that happy, but then you are the expedition leader and the decisions are yours to make.

The next two days go in a flurry of work and organization. When departure day arrives you are frantically checking lists of equipment and stores.

The chief has come down to introduce you to the Lowland members of the expedition. "This is Trodie, he's the ranking Lowland officer and their best climber."

The chief gives you a wink as he says this. He knows full well no Lowlanders can match the Slider Corp for traveling on the Black Slopes, but he doesn't want to embarrass Trodie in front of his troop. Trodie is a head taller than you and stocky in build.

"Carry on." The chief salutes and then heads back down the corridor towards the lift.

"Okay everyone," you say. "Let's get our harnesses on and these sledges hooked up. We've got one big tow to the top ridge and then a long slide to the end of the Western Track. After that we leave the tracks behind."

Your troop wastes no time in hooking up to the sledges. Dagma and Shoola take their customary places at the rear where they will act as brakes. Gagnon and Drexel hook their harnesses to the steering runners at the front.

You turn to Trodie. "Your team can ride on the sledges for now. You and I will lead."

Within minutes your group is ready to clamp on to the 3000-foot-long tow that will take you up to the high ridge overlooking the Pillars of Haramon.

The high-tensile cable vibrates as it runs up the slick towpath. Those who are sliding swivel the lock bar out of their front boot and clip it into a fitting on the instep of their back boot to form a stable sliding platform.

Rows of tiny diamonds on the soles of their boots give sliders some steering ability, and diamond spurs on their heels provides some stopping power. The sliders push forward with the needle end of their guide sticks and get ready to clamp onto the tow.

"On my mark," you yell. "Three, two, one…"

With knees bent, you swing your clamp over the cable and press down hard. As the clamp bites onto the cable, you are dragged up the towpath. You lean back into your harness and concentrate on keeping your balance.

Gagnon and Dagma's sledge is right behind you, while Drexel and Shoola's sledge brings up the rear.

When you reach the top of the tow, you release your clamp and slide along the offloading platform. The screech of diamonds sound across the ridge as everyone comes to a stop.

The guide stick in your hand is almost an extension of your arm. A blue diamond hook is mounted at one end for stopping and a thick pad of tyranium needle crystals are fixed to the other for steering and pushing.

To the east are the volcanoes.

"Quite a sight, eh, Gagnon?"

Gagnon nods. "I'm looking forward to the view from up there, back towards home. Should be even better."

You smile at his confidence. "Especially with a sledge load of tyranium."

Trodie and Piver slide over to where you and Gagnon are talking.

Trodie points towards the east, where one mountain towers over the others. "That must be Kakona."

"That's it. Hope you brought your climbing legs along," you say.

"Does the volcano normally glitter like that?" Trodie says.

You are about to answer, when you see a disk-shaped light near Kakona's summit. "What is that?"

Piver pulls out his scope and trains it on the glint in the distance. "It's moving whatever it is."

As the rest of you look on. The light moves off towards the interior.

"Could be a meteorite," Piver says.

"Moving a bit slow for one of those, isn't it?" Gagnon asks. "And since when do they glow silver?"

When the light disappears behind the range of mountains, everyone is left shaking their heads.

"Or it could have been some strange atmospheric condition, or reflected lights from over the horizon," Piver says.

"Lights from the interior you mean?" you say. "Where it's uninhabited?"

Piver shrugs. "Anything's possible."

"Lowlanders have seen lights in the sky before," Trodie says. "Some say it's visitors from another planet."

You look at Trodie. "Those are just stories in the *Book of Myths* aren't they?"

Piver giggles nervously. "Let's hope so."

"Anyway, it's gone now so let's get moving," you say.

Gagnon explains the route he's planned. "The Western Track's narrow but at least it's a track. We've got a long traverse and we'll need to zip up a few times before we get to the head of Black Gully."

Dagma and Shoola look keen to get going and are stomping their feet in an effort to keep their leg muscles warm.

"Eyes open and knees bent," you say. "We have a long way to slide."

With that, you and Trodie lead the troop off the platform and onto the grade-two track. The first traverse takes you due west towards the head of Black Gully. With every yard forward, you lose a little altitude. Every ten miles or so, you need to launch a cable and zip up to gain more height to enable you to keep traversing.

Then, once you've reached Black Gully, it's a twenty-mile slide down to the spectacular Tyron Cliffs.

With your guide stick tucked under your arm and both hands firmly on its shaft, you point your front foot slightly downhill and push off. You hear the faint swish of Trodie's boots sliding across the rock behind you.

"Whoopee!" Piver yells. "Giddy up you guys, I want to see these cliffs everyone keeps talking about."

After the first ten mile traverse, the cable launcher is set up and an anchor bolt is fired into the ridge high above. Once you've all zipped up to the next section of track, you lead off on another traverse further west.

The Black Slopes run from east to west in a series of peaks. Your group runs parallel to them. A few wisps of faint purple mist can be seen beyond their peaks, but thankfully none have crossed the divide onto your side of the range. Rain on slippery black rock is the last thing you need.

After a long slide, you and your troop reach the top of Black Gully. You call a halt on a small patch of level ground and look down the narrow passage. It's easy to see how Black Gully got its name. The gully is a natural half-pipe of rock with curved wave-like overhangs on both sides. These overhangs thin out as they rise, leaving crests of black glass you can almost see through.

"It's beautiful," Trodie says.

"Don't let this innocent looking place catch you out," you say.

"Black Gully's known for its sudden dips and ripples so keep your hook at the ready and your knees bent."

"I was born with my hook ready," Dagma says, eager to go. "Now let's tame this beast!"

The route down Black Gully is a series of sweeping S-turns that uses the natural contours of the half pipe to slow the sledges down.

"Whoopee!" Piver yells from the top on one of them. "Let's have a race!"

"Race!" Dagma yells over the wind. "I love going fast."

Shoola picks up speed. "Woot, woot!"

The sledges whizz up one side and down the other, back and forth, up and down. Occasionally, a sudden dip has the sledges airborne for a moment.

"That's more like it!" Piver yells. "Woot! Woot! Go sliders!"

Time passes quickly when you're having fun and it isn't long before you come out of Black Gully and back into open country. It's then that you see the Tyron Cliffs towering before you for the first time. All thoughts, except those of utter amazement, are forgotten.

"Geebus!" Piver squeaks. "Now that was worth waiting for."

The cliffs rise vertically, shimmering black and semi-translucent. Another two hundred yards and your group comes to a stop at the foot of the cliffs.

Standing stock still, not a member of the group is able to take their eyes off them. You are so lost in their beauty that you almost forget you're in charge.

"Tether your sledges," you say. "I don't want to lose any gear."

The sun is low. It's only an hour before dewfall when dampness makes the slopes treacherous. "Get the burners set up, and sling your hammocks," you tell the crew. "We'll make camp here tonight."

Then finally, after a hot cup of broth, you climb into your hammock and take the weight off your feet. In minutes you sink into a deep sleep.

When you wake the next morning, the sky is clear and a light easterly is blowing. As you sit around a burner having your morning broth, Gagnon comes and sits beside you.

"So are we going uphill or downhill to try and find a way around this thing?" Gagnon asks. "I'll need to start planning a route."

"Any advantage in one over the other?" you ask.

Gagnon pulls a map out of his pocket and rests it on his knee. "The downhill terrain looks a lot easier, but we'll have to climb back up. Uphill, looks a lot tougher, but we'll gain some altitude and end up a little closer to Kakona. All in all, it's fifty-fifty I'd say."

Gagnon hasn't really helped. Fifty-fifty is just that, a coin toss. You are a little worried about the Lowlanders handling the rougher terrain if you go up, but then will they handle a long climb back up if you go down?

It is time to trust your gut. Do you:

Go up and around the Tyron Cliffs?**P274**

Or

Go down and around the Tryon Cliffs? **P281**

You have decided to go for a big well-equipped expedition.

You can't believe you've just agreed to lead an expedition to Crater Canyon.

"I think an expedition of this importance requires a big, well equipped troop," you say, studying the chief's reaction to your decision. "We'll have to cut steps, and use zip lines once we leave the Highland tracks behind. And in the event that there are unexpected dangers in the interior, we'll need quite a few sliders for protection."

"My thoughts exactly," the chief says. "Two sledges rather than one, six per sledge. One slider steering, two braking, and three riding onboard, all fully loaded with launchers, zip lines, portable tows, burners and supplies for a month."

"We'll need one of the Lowlander's step cutting machines too," you say looking over at the general. "I hear you've made them small enough to be sledge mounted. Is that true?"

"Err … um, news travels fast." The Lowland general is a little surprised at your knowledge of their new step cutting technology, but after a moment's hesitation he puffs out his chest. "As you know, our original machines were big, steam powered things. Unfortunately, they were slow and cumbersome and vulnerable to attack. As you Highlanders discovered when you sent a couple to the bottom during the conflicts a few years ago. Since the truce we've learned much and have made many improvements. Our new cutters can be carried by sledge or even short distances by a strong person should the need arise."

"General," you say. "One of those new cutters and someone who knows how to operate it would be a huge help on this mission."

The general chats to one of his advisors and then nods. "I'll get one sent up right away. My eldest son, Villum, can come with you to operate it."

You're not so sure you want the general's son along on the expedition. Will he expect special treatment? And what happens if he is harmed in some way. Could his injury put the fragile truce with the Lowlanders in jeopardy? You are about to suggest the general's son train one of your miners to operate the step cutter when the chief buts in.

"Good idea, General. Your son can be second in charge."

Your mouth is left hanging open as you look questioningly at the chief. Why has he made this decision without consulting you, the expedition leader?

After the meeting has finished, you pull the chief aside. "What was that all about, chief? The general's son? Second in charge? Are you sure that's a good idea?"

"Look," the chief says. "We need to keep the Lowlanders happy. If they feel ignored on this expedition they might decide to mount one of their own. These new step cutters give them the ability to move around the mountains as never before. And as every member of the Slider Corp knows, mobility is power when it comes to controlling the Black Slopes."

"Okay but—"

"Listen," the chief says, cutting you off. "While you're away, I need you to get your most trusted engineer to learn all there is to know about these machines. Our diamond drillers do the job but they are too darn slow and can overheat. We need to discover what it is about their machine that gives it the ability to do the job so quickly. Do you understand?"

You still don't like the idea, but you don't really have much choice. "Okay, Chief."

The chief walks to a window and looks down Long Gully to the Lowlands below. "There have been some disturbing rumors from the Borderlands about the Lowlanders stockpiling weapons," he whispers. "We need this technology and we need it now. If the truce fails and we end up having to protect the Highlands from invasion we're going to struggle without it."

By the look on the chief's face he's worried. The communities of the Black Slopes rely on him and the council to make the best decision for all of the Highlands. If he's worried about the Lowlanders breaking the truce, you are too.

"Okay Chief, I'll get Piver onto it as soon as we depart. He's far brighter than anyone realizes and one of the best engineers around. People tend to underestimate him. If anyone can work out how these Lowland cutters work, it's him."

The chief pulls a star out of his pocket and pins it onto your tunic. "Just in case anyone forgets who's in charge. Remember, I'm relying on you."

You look down at the star and try to keep your smile to a minimum. "Thanks, Chief."

"Now," the chief says, brushing a spot of dust off your jacket. "I'd better get back to playing host. You go get your troop organized. You leave in two days."

After leaving the command pod your first task is to find the little engineer.

"Piver," you say once you locate him in one of the workshops. "I want you to organize the equipment we'll need for the journey while I concentrate on logistics and communications."

"It's a wonder you can concentrate on anything with that rock sparkling in your face," Piver smirks, indicating the diamond on your tunic."

"I bet you're not laughing so much when we head off for Crater Canyon."

"Geebus!" Piver says, with a gulp "Crater Canyon? I thought that place was a myth."

You explain about the lump of tyranium the chief showed you and tell him about the slightly mad miner's vanishing act.

Piver grins. "So that's a definite maybe then."

"Yep," you say enjoying Piver's little joke. "A definite maybe if ever I saw one."

"I'd better get to work then," Piver says, turning back to his workbench. "I've just finished a new prototype launcher. This trip will be the perfect place to test it."

The next two days are a blur of packing and organization. When departure day arrives, it feels like you've been at it non-stop for weeks.

Two sledges and their personnel are assembled at the bottom of the first tow.

As the high-tensile cable hums up the towpath the sliders hook up their harnesses. Being inexperienced at traversing the tricky mountain paths, the Lowland general's son, Villum, and his assistant will ride aboard the second sledge carrying their step cutting machine, as will Piver.

The ride to the top of the first tow goes without a hitch. From there your plan is to go west, following the Western Track as far as you can. After the track peters out, all you'll have are the rough maps made by the kooky miner to follow.

At the first meal break, you and Gagnon, the expedition's navigator, sit beside one another with hot cups of broth.

"I've been comparing the miner's maps with some of our own." Gagnon says. "Thankfully he's marked a few landmarks we already know about. At least they should give us a reference point."

"Well if anyone is going to be able to decipher them, it's you, Gagnon."

"The bad news is that we've got to get over Tyron Pass."

"Yikes," you say. "That's a big climb."

"And it'll be a long slide down the other side too," Gagnon says before draining the last of his broth. "Let's just hope it's not too steep. Not much is known about that area."

The next two days are spent sliding west, launching cables, zipping up and then sliding west once more in a series of long, slow traverses.

On the first day of the expedition, the towering Mount Tyron never seemed to get any closer, but now that you're nearer, every step you take makes the mountain loom ever closer.

Villum spends much of his time napping on Dagma's sledge, atop his treasured step cutting machine. It's only when your troop reaches a steep pitch, where there's nothing to launch a anchor bolt into, that you're forced to wake him and ask him to fire up the step cutter.

"Again, already?" Villum moans. "All this climbing's giving me a headache."

You roll your eyes at Piver and then turn to the general's son. "Come on, the quicker we cut the steps the sooner you can get back to your nap."

You remind yourself to give the chief a kick in the bum when you get back to the Pillars. What a pillock he's saddled you with. He should have known better than to take a highborn Lowlander on an expedition like this.

Thankfully the step cutting machine works a lot harder than Villum. Once set up and started, the machine's front-mounted cutting bit drills an oval hole in the hard black rock, then ratchets forwards and does it again, all at walking pace.

It's hard work climbing the steps, finding an anchor point, then winching the sledges up afterwards, but your troop soon finds a rhythm and the work goes smoothly. Everyone works hard, except Villum, who expects to walk up without having to carry anything, and then complains that he's tired.

Dagma's at the end of her patience when she pulls you aside. "Permission to send this bleating LoLa to the bottom."

"If he wasn't the general's son, I'd be tempted to say permission granted. Unfortunately this particular LoLa needs to get back to the Pillars in one piece."

Dagma grunts under her breath and gets back to work. Piver hears her grumbling and wanders over.

You take a couple of paces towards them so you can eavesdrop. You know Piver and suspect he's up to mischief.

"Hey Dagma," Piver says. "What's soft and lazy and smells like pango poo?"

"Smells like pango poo? How the heck should I know?" Dagma

grumps.

Piver nods to where Villum is sitting against a small pinnacle rising from the surrounding slope. Above his head roost a dozen or so red-beaked pangos.

Dagma looks confused.

"Try this riddle then," Piver says. "What bird poops like crazy whenever they're frightened?"

Dagma looks at Villum, then at the birds above him and smiles at Piver. "You're not as stupid as you look funny man."

"And what scares a pango?" Piver asks Dagma.

"Absolutely everything!" the two Highlanders say in unison before exploding with peals of laughter.

You chuckle under your breath. At least Piver's made Dagma stop grumbling for a moment.

Dagma pulls out her slingshot and drops a small stone in its pouch. With a quick pull, she sends the stone whizzing towards the roosting birds.

"Erk! Erk!" the birds squawk, pooping as they fly off.

Villum screams in horror as a fishy mess comes splattering down all over him, then he jumps to his feet, unsure of whether to wipe the stinky stuff off with his hand or not.

Piver and Dagma watch Villum's discomfort and hoot with laughter. You turn your back and smirk, trying your best not to let Villum see that you're laughing at him as well.

Eventually, when he manages to stop himself from giggling, Piver slides over and tosses Villum a piece of cloth. "Here use this. It'll take the worst of it off."

Dagma shoulders another load of equipment and starts up the most recently cut steps with an extra bounce in her step.

"Okay everyone," you say to your troop. "One more pitch and we're at the pass. It's all downhill from there. Now I know you're tired, but keep going. We need to find a safe place to camp on the other side before dewfall."

As you climb you can't help thinking of all the possible dangers you'll face in the interior. You also wonder how accurate the miner's maps are. Will there be a safe way down to Crater Canyon and this newly discovered vein of tyranium? Will any of the wild claims made by the miner be true? Will there be snakes or mechanical creatures?

From the pass a whole new world spread before you. The other side, near the top, is bare rock, just like what you've been climbing. But further down the mountain, the interior is lush and green. In the distance, an emerald lake shimmers in the last of the afternoon sun.

"Not quite so steep this side," Gagnon says with relief looking through his scope. "I see a couple of possible ways down."

You pull out your own scope and take a look. "Anything look familiar from the miner's maps?"

"One thing," Gagnon says, raising his arm and pointing towards a hill to the west of the lake. "See that volcano? According to the miner, Crater Canyon's near the base of a volcano. That could be it."

Gagnon looks west and shields his eyes from the sun as it dips near the horizon. "We've only got an hour to find somewhere to camp. We'd better get going."

"Harness up, Sliders," you say. "Single file, two brakes per sledge. And keep your speed down and hooks at the ready. Gagnon's sledge will take the lead."

You hear the screech of diamond studs and guide sticks as the sliders move into position.

"So," you say, looking at Gagnon. "Which way do you recommend?"

"I see two options," Gagnon says, pointing down the slope to his right. "There's a natural watercourse just over there. Seeing there's been no rain recently it's empty at the moment and should be passable for sledges. Or, we can go slightly west and zigzag down that broad ridge.

You sum up the two options. "Technically, the ridge will be harder, but we'll get a better view of the surrounding territory and any possible dangers," you say.

What should you do? Both options have merit.

It is time to make a decision. Do you:

Go down the watercourse? **P207**

Or

Zigzag down the broad ridge? **P212**

You have decided to go for a smaller yet faster group.

"I like the idea of a small, fast group, with one sledge and extra muscle for the climbing."

The chief slaps you on the shoulder. "Good choice. Less crew to worry about and a reduced time on the slopes."

"We'll definitely need some extra leg power," you say. "Getting up to the pass isn't going to be easy."

As the chief and the other representatives get back to their discussions, you excuse yourself and get to work. If you're leaving in two days, there's planning to do.

First you'll need to contact Piver. His engineering and mining skills will be essential if this expedition is to be a success. You'll also want Gagnon as navigator, Dagma and Shoola for their muscle and sliding skills, and Drexel for climbing.

The Lowland general also wants you to take his representatives Trodie, and Villum the general's son, along. Bringing the total crew to eight members. Eight is a couple more than a single sledge would normally accommodate, but if you all carry backpacks with the extra gear you'll need for a long journey, it shouldn't be a problem.

After speaking to Piver in his workshop on level four, you find Gagnon, in the map room, further down on level two.

You and Gagnon bump elbows in greeting.

"Feel like a trip?" you ask.

Gagnon smiles, "Crater Canyon by any chance?"

"How did you know that?"

"The chief was asking me questions about it the other day. I figured something was in the wind."

Gagnon always surprises you. He misses very little and is an expert at reading people. "So is Crater Canyon real?" you ask him. "And if so, can we find it?"

Gagnon sits down at the map table again. You see he's been comparing a hand-drawn map with one drawn up by the Slider Corps.

"Is that the miner's map the chief was talking about?"

"It's a copy the chief gave me," Gagnon says. "From what I can tell, this mysterious miner was in the interior alright." Gagnon points to a spot on the map. "But I don't think this is to the west like everyone else thinks. I think this is much further east."

"East? Through the wild lands? I've heard rumors of strange creatures to the east."

"We can't let a few rumors stop us. And has anyone brought back proof of these monsters?"

You shake your head.

"Anyone can make up stories," Gagnon continues. "But without proof, why should we believe them?"

"Okay, I see your point. So what are you suggesting?"

"Rather than going up and over the mountains, I think we should slide fast and traverse around the eastern end of the Black Slopes. It may be a lot longer, but we'll be covering ground quickly and relatively safely. Besides, who knows what we'll find along the way."

After discussing the pros and cons, you decide to go along with Gagnon's idea and leave him to plan the route east while you go back to the accommodation pod to look for the others.

Shoola and Dagma are in the canteen stuffing their faces with hydro and broth. They are grunting between bites and arguing about who's the best brake on a sledge.

"I hate to break up your little party," you say, sitting down beside the two sliders. "But I've got a job for you."

Dagma slurps, then turns to face you. She looks interested. "Oh yeah?"

"You two might be able to settle who's best once and for all on this trip."

News of a trip is one of the few things that will take a hungry slider's mind off food. By the time you've explained what you need, you have their full attention.

Two days later, the sledge is loaded and all the organizing has come together. The chief watches from the command pod as you get ready to catch the first tow up to the ridge high above the Pillars.

The tow path is ultra-slick from particularly heavy dew so you get Gagnon and Drexel to attach their harnesses to the front of the sledge, while Dagma and Shoola to connect to the back.

As the front sliders clamp on to the whirling cable, the sledge starts to move up the slippery black rock. The sliders on the front make subtle adjustments to the steering runners to keep the sledge traveling in a straight line while those on the back get ready to drop their hooks should the sledge come adrift from the tow.

After offloading at the top, rather than turning left like so many other expeditions you've been on, you turn east and wonder what adventures this wild uncharted territory will bring.

"Well, this should be interesting," you say to the others. "Eastward ho on my mark. Three … two … one … slide!"

And with that, your group points their feet slightly downhill and traverses off across the slope. You are in the lead acting as scout. Then come the four sliders controlling the sledge. Riding on top of the sledge are Piver and the two Lowlanders, Trodie and Villum.

The rock on this part of the mountain is crevasse free so you make good time. On occasion you pass small pillars, the result of some long past eruption. Pangos have made these their nesting place, well above the marauding packs of morph rats that eat everything in their path.

Under these pillars, growing from seeds carried up from the Lowlands by the pangos, are wild adamas vines, or WAV's as the Highlanders call them. These plants grow into tightly packed balls of thorns. But eventually, these thorny plants get too heavy for their shallow roots and they go rolling off down the mountain, bowling over and skewering anything in their path.

The first day goes by without any problems. About an hour before dewfall, you find a reasonably flat section of ground and make camp. As you're warming yourself around the burner, enjoying a well earned meal, Gagnon tells you that the troop has covered nearly sixty miles.

"That's got to be a record," he says.

You look towards home, now a fair distance away, and watch the sun dip behind Mt Transor. The sky is bright orange and red, but the sunset only lasts a brief moment. Once it's dark, you climb into your hammock and drift off to sleep, dreaming of black slopes and home.

At dawn you wake to clear skies. After a quick breakfast, everyone gets back into harness ready for the day's slide. Trodie, complaining of a sore bum from riding on the sledge the previous day, decides to slide. Piver does the same. Only Villum opts to ride.

As you slide off across the slope, Piver tucks himself into your slipstream and gives you a rundown on the two Lowlanders.

"Trodie's straight up," Piver says. "But that Villum, what a stupid LoLa he is. Just complains about everything."

You've heard similar comments from others, but it's not like you could leave the general's son behind. He's one of the appointed Lowland representatives and you're stuck with him.

"Be patient, Piver. He's out of his comfort zone up here. He'll settle in."

"Or fall off the sledge while he's sleeping and go to the bottom."

"Piver! Enough of that talk. He's our responsibility. Play nice."

"Righto," the little engineer says. "Just don't ask me to like him."

Gagnon's travel plan is going well. When you stop for lunch on the second day he says the expedition's made another 32 miles. After eating, you climb up the slope a little ways to scope out the next run. As you focus on the black rock to the east, you see a bright, metallic disk sitting on the slope about a mile away.

You're not sure if you believe your eyes. "Hey, Gagnon! Come up here a moment."

"I see it!" Gagnon says. "It looks just like those pictures in the *Book of Myths*."

"Yeah. In those stories about the people from space."

"According to the *Book of Myths*," Gagnon says. "these disks were how our ancestors arrived on Petron. But they're supposed to be stories, not reality."

"Until now," you say.

"So what do we do?"

"That, my friend, is a very good question."

It is time to make a decision. What do you do? Do you.

Go check out the spaceship? **P287**

Or

Stay and observe the spaceship from a distance? **P291**

You have decided to set the drill up ready for the morning.

You've got a limited food supply and a long way to go. Your troop may be tired but every bit of time you save means you'll have a better chance of reaching your goal.

"Let's get the driller set up now so we can start first thing," you say.

As Piver and a couple of the others start untying the various parts of the drill from the sledge, Gagnon gives the sky a nervous glance and slides over to you.

"You sure you don't want to set up camp first? If it rains higher up, we won't get much warning. I'd feel a lot happier if we had some extra anchors in and some tarps up."

You shake your head. "No we need to take a few chances if we're going to succeed in this mission. Now go and show them where to drill and leave the rest up to me."

Gagnon shrugs, "Okay, but I don't like it."

Gagnon slides over to where Piver is assembling the drill, pulls out his compass and start taking sightings. Then he plots the exact position where the machine is to be mounted on the slippery black rock. Lengths of pipe are stacked nearby so they can be added to the drill shaft as it bores deeper into the cliff.

Piver and one of the Lowlanders carry over the heavy diamond bit and Piver attaches it to the front of the drilling machine.

"Hope this bit doesn't shatter," Piver says. "The machine will be as useless as a blind pango hunter if it does."

You know how Piver feels. If only the bits weren't so heavy you'd have brought a spare. Unfortunately, no matter how you did the loading calculations, there was no way to carry everything you required and an extra bit.

Piver is busy running pulleys and cables that will drive the driller when rain clouds appear over the ridge behind you. Moments later the first raindrops appear.

This is the worst possible scenario for a troop out on the Black

Slopes. Rain is a Highlanders enemy and even with the first few drops you can feel your boot's grip on the smooth black rock starting to go.

"Emergency Anchors! Now!" you yell as you pull the anchor gun from your belt and fire a bolt into the rock at your feet. "Quick! Clip on!"

Full on rain is falling now. Unfortunately some of the others aren't so quick to secure themselves.

To your right, Drexel and Piver have anchored themselves to the now treacherous slope, but some of the Lowlanders aren't so lucky.

When water starts pouring down Black Gully and onto the plateau, the sledges are in danger of being washed away by the flash flood and you wish you'd got your troop to secure themselves better before worrying about the drill.

Then there is a yell from Piver and you see the supply sledge straining on its single tether. Piver is trying to get across the slope to put an extra anchor in, but he's having problems staying attached to the mountain himself.

A screaming Lowlander goes sliding past, heading for the bottom. Moments later, another trooper is dislodged and lost to the mountain.

With a tortured screech of metal, the supply sledge's anchor bolt is straining. Then with a *ping*, the bolt snaps and the sledge is skidding down the mountain with most of your supplies.

"Geebus!" Piver yells as he struggles to hang on to Shoola, who's slipped down onto him from above. "So much for dinner tonight."

As the water rises, the drilling machine is hit by the torrent and off it slides. The machine misses Trodie by a foot. Trodie is white and shaking, clinging for dear life onto his tether. Thankfully, by sheer strength and determination, Dagma and Drexel have managed to keep the other sledge on the mountain, but only because it's nearly empty.

Then as quickly as it started, the rain stops and the excess water runs away.

Gagnon puts in an extra anchor and then rappels down to your position. "Well, that went well," he says, shaking his head and cursing under his breath.

You look around at the chaos and realize your expedition is over. Why didn't you secure the camp and put in extra anchors for the sledges before you tried to set up the drill? Why didn't you listen to Gagnon? You remember a lecture you had at slider school about the difference between speed and haste.

Haste has cost you two members of your expedition and any self respect you once had. Now you have no option but to struggle back to the Pillars of Haramon with your tail between your legs and beg forgiveness for your lack of judgment.

"Watch out WAVs!" Piver yells.

You whip your head around and look up the slope, but you see no WAV's. "What are you going on about, Piver!" you yell in anger.

"Sorry," Piver says, kicking the ground. "I didn't mean to scare you. I was just trying to show everyone that things could be worse."

And Piver is absolutely right … but only just.

I'm sorry but this part of your story is over. You've made a bad decision and have lost all your equipment and food and you have to go back to the Pillars of Haramon.

However you still have a decision to make. All is not lost. Do you:

Go back to the beginning and start over? **P163**

Or

Go back to your last choice and choose to set up camp? **P203**

You have decided to set up camp in case the weather turns.

"Let's get camp set up. I saw a hint of clouds earlier, no point in taking any chances," you say. "We need shelter, food and rest."

There are smiles amongst the Highlanders and Lowlanders alike. Everyone's had a long slide and they're hungry. Even those who've ridden on the sledges need to stretch their tired backs and legs.

Piver takes charge of setting up camp. "Tether the sledges with at least three bolts each and put some bolts into the cliff," he says. "Then we can swing some hammocks between the two in case it rains."

After helping to rig up a secure camp the burners are set up in the lee of one of the sledges to get broth heating.

Trodie hands you an energy bar from his home village in the Lowlands. "It's made from crackleberries. Tried them?"

You've tasted crackleberries once before. The thought of the sweet fruit has your mouth watering before you even bite into it. "Yummo," you sigh as a burst of flavor fills your mouth. "Oh, that's soooo good."

Trodie smiles. "It's funny, you Highlanders like crackleberries as much as we Lowlanders love roast pango. I think trade is going to be brisk between us."

"Ummm," you say smacking your lips and licking your fingers. "I'm all for that."

"Here Trodie," you say. "Try one of my snacks, it's from my uncle's hydro pod, he binds the different fungi together with bird fat. If you like roast pango you'll love these."

Before long everyone is sitting around the burners sipping broth and exchanging treats. Dagma has a greasy smile on her face and Piver is jiggling happily as he eats handfuls of dried berries.

You look along the towering cliff as it stretches off into the distance. You can't imagine the force it would have taken to lift such a massive block of rock.

Trodie seems to read your mind. "Feeling small?"

You nod. "Smaller than small really."

"I wonder how many thousands of years ago it all happened," Trodie says. "Imagine being here to witness it."

You turn towards Trodie. "My teachers at school say the Tyron Cliffs were formed long before our species arrived on this planet."

Trodie is about to reply when you hear a distinct rustling sound from above. And it's getting closer!

"WAVs!" you yell. "Hit the deck!" Grasping your safety line you throw yourself onto the smooth rock behind one of the sledges.

Trodie lands beside you just as a huge ball of thorns slams onto the spot where he was sitting. There is a shower of dust as the rogue WAV bounces off downhill.

"Phew," you say. "That was close." You pick up one of the thorns left behind by the WAV and examine it. The thorn is an inch and a half long with a barbed point of bright green. You would have expected the thorn to have been brown and dried but this one is different from any you've seen before. "The tip is still alive," you say, holding it up for Trodie to see. "Look it's moving."

The tip of the thorn is wiggling around as if it's trying to escape. In no time at all, the thorn sprouts a small tendril near its base which wraps itself around your finger. At the end of the tendril, another smaller thorn sprouts.

"Do you believe this?" Trodie asks. "How is it growing so fast?"

"I don't know," you say. "It's not normal for something to grow right in front of your eyes. Even the fastest growing fungi take overnight to grow."

Trodie nods. "Yes, something's very strange."

You have a thought and look over at Trodie. "Imagine if my uncle could cross breed this fast growing plant with edible hydro. Food could grow twice as big in half the time."

"Maybe you should take the plant back with you and get your uncle to run some trials."

You're about to agree with Trodie when the plant whips its tendril back and then springs forward stabbing your finger and burying its newly grown thorn deep into the flesh of your finger. A drop of green blood runs down your finger and puddles in your palm.

"Ouch! That little beastie just stabbed me!" You pluck the thorn from your finger and suck on the wound.

"It's growing another tendril," Trodie says, his eyes wide. "And a new thorn!"

Trodie's right. The plant is growing like crazy and is already waving a second thorn about in a threatening manner.

"Yikes," you say, flinging the plant down the slope where it turns itself into a small ball and rolls off. "It's like it could tell I was going to take it with me and attacked! I don't care how fast it grows, I don't want my food crossed with that!"

You and Trodie look around to make sure there aren't any more thorns lying on the ground around the camp

Trodie smiles. "At least crackleberries don't bite."

The first drops of rain come not long after you and the others have climbed into your hammocks. You're thankful you decided to make camp first rather than set up the drill.

Within five minutes, the wind is howling and the rain is pounding down. Anything not tethered is swept down the mountain. Your sliders lose nothing. They know to clip equipment to their anchored sledges, even when the weather looks good.

The Lowlanders aren't so fortunate. A couple of their supply containers get washed away, much to Trodie's dismay. You remind yourself to keep an eye out for wild pango colonies. You'll need to replace the lost food.

It isn't long before the patter of rain on the waterproof cover above you and the slight swaying of the hammock lulls you to sleep.

By the time you wake up, the sun is creeping over the ridge to the east and the slopes around you are steaming as the remaining moisture evaporates. Within half an hour of the sun hitting the slope, the heat-absorbing rock is dry and burners are warming broth.

Piver is already on the job and has a couple of the Lowlanders carrying equipment to the spot Gagnon has designated for the big drill. The machine is clamped onto metal track bolted onto the slope. A circular shaped blue-diamond drill bit is mounted onto the machine's front spindle while gears and pulleys are attached to the drive unit at the rear. Lengths of pipe to extend the drill's shaft as it bores into the rock are stacked nearby.

Drexel, the expedition's expert climber, brings you a cup of broth and watches the engineers set up ready for drilling. "I bet I could climb this wall in less time than it takes to drill a hole through thirty yards of black glass," he tells you.

With raised eyebrows you look at Drexel. "Really? You're awfully confident." You're surprised at this claim from Drexel. Normally he's not one to brag. "What makes you think that?"

"I was checking out Piver's new hand-held launcher," he says. "Using those and some climbing studs I could free climb it in about four hours I reckon."

You look up at the sheer wall of black glass and then back at a grinning Drexel. "You're crazy. The cliff is straight up."

"At least give me a go. What happens if the drill breaks down halfway through and we've wasted the best part of a day."

Drexel has a point. After losing some of the Lowlander's supplies in the rain, speed is even more critical than before. Maybe Drexel climbing the cliff is your plan B. But then what happens if Drexel falls and you don't have your best climber when it comes time to scale Mount Kakona?

Both options have their risks and rewards.

It is time to make a decision. Do you:

Allow Drexel to climb the Tyron Cliffs? **P243**

Or

Trust Piver to drill through the cliffs? **P251**

You have decided to go down the watercourse.

"Let's go down the watercourse," you tell Gagnon. "Water always finds the easiest route down a mountain. We may as well follow its trail and do the same."

Gagnon nods his approval and moves out, his sledge tracking along behind him. Two burly sliders have hooked their harnesses to the back of Gagnon's sledge and have their diamond hooks at the ready.

The watercourse is smooth but narrow. This means many zigzagging turns are required to keep the sledges from gaining too much speed as you descend. None the less, Gagnon is an expert guide and it isn't long before a couple of side streams join up and the watercourse becomes wider and more easily negotiated.

You reach the bush line forty-five minutes later. Trees and other strange plants begin to crowd the banks of the watercourse. After an hour, the dried up watercourse is a ribbon of black glass running through a forest of green, the likes of which you've never seen before.

When you see a suitable spot, you signal a halt. "Let's make camp here," you say, pointing to a level patch of moss-covered ground above the watercourse. "There's no black glass so we won't have to watch our step."

Getting off the black glass of the watercourse is a relief. You can't remember the last time you could walk about without worrying if your feet would slide out from under you. To have something so soft underfoot feels like a dream. Normally moss is for eating or used on sleeping platforms. Only the wealthy can afford to buy moss from the Borderlands traders and have it carried into the Highlands.

The sliders anchor the sledges to the bank and start unloading supplies into the clearing. Some of the troopers set up burners while others rig up some basic protection against any rain that might come your way.

When all that is done, you sit around the warmth of a burner and enjoy some steamed fungi, shredded hydro and a cup of hot broth.

The sky looks like it's on fire, as the colors of sunset spreads across it.

The jungle is noisier than you expected and many sounds are unfamiliar. Unlike the Lowlanders, you've been brought up on the Black Slopes where the only sounds are the flit of phosphorescent moon moths, or the call of wild pangos. Trees are an alien species to you. Black rock is what you know. Rock and tunnels bored into the mountainside that your communities use for their hydro farms, accommodation pods, schools and markets.

Piver comes and sits beside you. "Geebus it's different down here."

"Tell me about it," you say. "All this greenery makes me nervous.'

"I know what you mean," Piver says, looking left then right then left again. "Am I being paranoid or is the jungle getting closer?"

You look around. A few of the plant's leaves are quivering slightly, but that is most likely from the slight breeze. In the half-light of late afternoon it's hard to tell exactly where the jungle begins.

"Everything looks okay to—" You stop midsentence when one of the plants on the edge of the clearing reshapes itself into a ball and rolls slowly towards you. "What the…?"

"Geebus!" Piver jumps up. "What is that thing?"

Others around you turn their heads and watch as the ball stops about two yards short of where you are sitting and starts changing shape again.

Then suddenly Piver is doing a nervous jig, hopping from foot to foot in excitement. "Am I going nuts or did that plant just changed itself into a chair?"

You are about to tell Piver to stand back when he rushes over and plonks himself down. "Wow comfy!" he says as the chair adjusts to fit his body shape. "All it needs is a footstool."

There is a collective 'oooohhhh' as the front part of the bush reforms into a footrest.

Another ball of green rolls up, this one reforms into a long couch. Two troopers rush over and sit down. Then another ball comes, and another.

Before long your whole troop is lounging in comfort, laughing and drinking broth.

You wonder if this is such a good idea. If these plants are reforming into things at the request of your sliders, it means they are thinking. What's to say they will remain friendly? What if someone scares or annoys one of these remarkable creatures.

Still, the plants seem harmless … eager to please even.

You squat next to one of the green balls. "Can you hear me?"

The ball of green turns into an animal shape, small, four legs, a tail that wags. It jumps up on your lap and a small tendril tickles your face.

"Stop it," you giggle, pulling your face back.

The animal sits back on its haunches and lifts both front legs. It turns its head from side to side, as if it's looking at you, or waiting for a command.

"Can you reform into anything?" you ask the creature.

The animals shakes its head.

"But you understand what I'm saying?"

The animal nods and leaps up to tickle your face again.

"We are looking for tyranium crystal. Do you know what those are?"

The animal shakes its head and turns into a chair. You smile and take a seat. As soon as you're comfortable, vines wrap around your wrists and ankles.

"What are you doing?" you ask the plant. "Dagma! Piver!" you yell unable to move your limbs. When you turn your head you see that everyone is tied up. The plants have captured your entire expedition.

"We mean you no harm," you plead. "Why are you doing this?"

A large half man half plant walks out of the jungle. "I see you've met my pets."

You pull as hard as you can, but as you do, the vines around your wrists squeeze tighter. You look up at the strange man-plant. "Why are you doing this? We mean you know harm."

"Invaders always say that. Then the next thing you know they are chopping down the trees and digging up the ground."

"But we're just looking for tyranium needle crystal," you say. "We're happy to trade for them."

More plants close in on your group. Some of them block off your retreat and form a wall of interlaced branches that surrounds you like a cage.

The man-plant reforms into a larger animal, with a single horn in the middle of its forehead and long fangs. "We don't need your trinkets," the beast growls. "We get what we need from the soil and the rain and each other. History tells us this is all we need."

"History?" you ask. "What history is that and why didn't I learn about it in school?"

"It is the history of the planet our ancestors came from, that your ancestors came from," the beast says. "The desire for more and more ruined that planet."

"But you're—you're not... Petronian. You're half—"

"—plant. Yes. Some DNA splicing was done on the long journey it took us to get here from our home planet, your home planet. We are now the best of both species."

You wonder if this creature is related to those thorny tumbleweeds that grow on your side of the mountains. "So are all the plants on Petron related?"

"More than you'll ever realize."

This is all very fascinating, but you wonder why he's giving you so much information. Unless he knows you'll never have a chance to...

"Get some sleep," the man-plant says. "We move to our settlement by the lake in the morning. We can talk more once we're there." And with that, the creature steps back and transforms into part of the cage that now completely surrounds you.

The plants release your arms and legs. You stand rubbing your wrists and stretch while looking at the impenetrable wall around you. Others do the same. You need to talk to Gagnon and Piver about this development and make some sort of plan. But how do you do this without these creatures hearing you?

As the last of the light goes, the plants go still.

As you make your way towards where Piver is standing, Dagma grabs your sleeve.

"I have moth mist," she says sheepishly.

You raise a finger to your lips and shake your head slightly. You instantly understand what Dagma is suggesting. You also know she is risking severe disciplinary action for bringing a prohibited substance along on the expedition.

Moth mist, is a potent chemical compound collected from the moon moths that inhabit the Highlands. When inhaled, the mist gives one an intense feeling of tranquility. Some sliders use it to help them sleep.

"It we spray the plants we might be able to escape while they're dreaming," Dagma says.

You're unsure. Reactions to chemicals are never guaranteed and plants and animals have different nervous systems. What if the mist has the opposite reaction to plants as it has to people and makes them agitated?

It is time to make a decision. Do you:

Spray the plants with moth mist and try to escape?**P217**

Or

Wait until tomorrow and see what happens? **P219**

You have decided to go west and zigzag down the broad ridge.

"I like the idea of being able to see what's coming," you say. "Let's take the ridge. It's good sliding rock all the way to the valley floor, and we won't need to offload the sledges and carry our supplies through the jungle like we would if the streambed is blocked."

Gagnon takes another look at the ridge through his scope. "I agree. It's going to be technical at the top but it gets wider and easier further down. The jungle's growing right to the rock's edge, but that shouldn't create any problems."

Your troop is quick to reorganize from climbing mode to sliding mode. Dagma takes the brake position at the back of the first sledge. Once everyone is ready Gagnon leads offs.

It's a short traverse to the top of the ridge. Then, in a series of tight S-turns, your little caravan weaves it way down the narrow band of rock. About forty minutes and 2000 feet of altitude later, you see a level area off to the right with an enormous overhang that will give your group some protection from the elements.

You signal a halt. "Let's camp over there for the night," you tell the group. "It never hurts to have some natural protection from the rain."

The exhausted group is quick to agree. They break out the windbreaks and sling their hammocks between the sledges and the rock wall. Others set up burners and get some broth heating.

Villum sits and watches as the others set up the camp.

"Where are some roosting pangos when you need them," Piver says in passing.

You smile. "Just go make friends with him. Remember, your job is to learn everything about that step cutting machine."

Piver does as he's told while other sliders distribute hot broth and dehydrated fungi.

You look at the landscape below. Towards the volcano's crater, as the last of the light glistens off its shimmering black slopes, you wonder if it's cloud, steam or smoke that you see. Then you notice a red glow along the volcano's southern flank.

"Hey Gagnon," you say. "Come have a look at this."

Gagnon slides over and pulls out his scope. "An active vent by the looks of it. Could make things tricky if there's poison gas about."

"How will we know?" you asks.

"It's not easy. Hydrogen sulfide is heavier than air and can flow down the mountainside like an invisible wave. You don't know it's there until you take your last deadly breath."

"Just what we need."

"There is a solution though," Gagnon says. "If we can catch a few pango and keep them in cages, they can warn us of the presence of poisonous gas."

You remember hearing about this technique but you're not sure you remember the details. "Is it because the pangos are more sensitive than we are?"

Gagnon nods. "Yip. The pangos fall over at about three parts per million. We can take about 30 before we pass out."

"So, as soon as a pango hits the bottom of the cage, we get sliding."

"And quickly," Gagnon says. "We won't have much time."

You ponder what Gagnon's said as you sip your broth. Where are you going to find wild pango on this side of the divide? And how are you going to catch them even if you do?

"Hey Dagma," you say pulling her away from her meal of hydro. "You didn't happen to see any pangos this side of the pass did you?"

You know Dagma hunts pango with other members of her family when she's not transporting people around the Black Slopes as part of the Slider Corps. You also know she's got a keen eye for the Highland delicacy.

Dagma ponders a moment. "I heard a small group nesting on a pinnacle about 500 feet further up and out to the east."

"Do you think you could catch them?"

"If I had a net launcher I could but…"

"Piver's got a new handheld cable launcher. Maybe he could adapt it?"

Dagma smiles. "Yeah he mentioned that. I'll go find out."

Dagma's back a few minutes later with good news. "He's going to work on it tonight. I'll climb back up at first light and see if they're still there. How many do you want?"

"Just a couple should do," you say. "Any extras you can cook up."

"Yummo," Dagma says, licking her lips. "I love pango."

After a restless night dreaming of volcanoes, dawn breaks clear and warm. As the camp starts to wake, you see the silhouette of Dagma climbing back up the ridge She carries a cage made of fine mesh stretched over a lightweight frame. It will be an hour at least before she returns so you get together with Gagnon and start planning your route to the volcano.

In his role as chief spy and information gatherer, Piver has taken on the role of servant to Villum and takes him some broth and a bowl of hydro. You can hear Piver flattering Villum about his expert operation of the step cutter.

Villum strokes his own ego by telling Piver about the machine's construction and operation. "What makes my machine so good," Villum says, puffing out his chest, "is the hammer mechanism built into its base. It gives the drill extra punch when penetrating the rock."

"Oh how interesting," Piver says, grinning at the bragging Lowlander. "You are so clever, Villum. Tell me more."

Meanwhile, after studying the terrain further, you and Gagnon decide to follow the ridge all the way to the valley floor and then unpack what vital equipment you'll need to mine the tyranium and transport it by foot to the base of the volcano.

"Let's just hope we can find this canyon," you say. "Otherwise we'll have to climb the volcano and look around the vents higher up."

"Not a pleasant thought," Gagnon says. "That's like climbing an explosion waiting to happen."

Gagnon's comment sends a shiver down your spine. He's not wrong. Everywhere you look around Petron you see evidence of its violent and explosive past.

You are about to send a search party out for Dagma when you hear a 'woot woot' from above. As she nears, you see she's managed to net four pango.

"Two for you," Dagma says with a smile. "And two for me. Nom, nom."

"Well done. Now let's harness up and get ready to move," you say. "We've got a fair bit of rock to cover today."

Once again Gagnon and his sledge take the lead. The going gets easier with every foot of altitude you lose. But then strange holes begin to appear in the surface and Gagnon is forced to take evasive action.

You signal a halt and get everyone to tether their sledges. "These holes don't look natural," you say. "Far too regular to be lava tubes formed during an eruption."

"Hey Piver," you say, "get over here and tell me what you think."

After a bit of fiddling about, Piver attaches a cable to a sledge and lowers himself to the edge of one of the holes. "Looks like it's been made by machine," Piver says. "I see drill marks and it goes down at a nice uniform angle. I wonder where they lead?"

"Could they have been made by people living on this side of the mountain range?" you ask.

"Either that or aliens," Piver says with a grin.

So what are the odds? you think. Did someone come from a distant part of the universe just to drill holes in the side of a mountain and then disappear, or were they made by someone living here?

"I think we need to double our lookout," you say to the troop. "The odds tell me someone's living on this side of the mountain."

"Maybe we should investigate and see where they lead," Villum says.

"Great idea LoLa!" Dagma says in a sarcastic tone. "You go first. I'll give you a hand over the edge."

Villum pretends to tighten his boots, ignoring Dagma's comment.

You look at Piver. "Is it possible they're transport tunnels or perform some other function?”

“It’s possible they go all the way through the planet and end up on the other side of the ocean in a land of twinkling stars and purple monsters, but I somehow doubt it. More likely they’ve been drilled by the locals looking for something. Water collectors maybe? Impressive technology if that’s the case.”

Piver doesn’t seem too sure. You like the idea of them being transport tunnels to a settlement further down the mountain, but perhaps Piver’s right.

It is time to make a decision. Do you:

Send someone down the hole to investigate? P224

Or

Carry on down the ridge? P232

Spray the plants with moth mist and try to escape.

"Dagma," you whisper. "How much mist have you got? Do you think there's enough to spray all the plants?"

Dagma's face goes red. "I've got quite a bit. It's the only way I can get to sleep these days." From a pocket in her tunic, she pulls out a bottle, three quarters full of a bright blue liquid and hands it to you.

"We can't slide in the dark so we'll have to make a break at first light," you say, tucking the bottle of mist into your pocket. "In the mean time, let's tell the others what's happening, but do it quietly. We can't let our captors to find out what we're planning."

Dagma nods and moves off to spread the word. You do the same.

It isn't long before everyone is in on the plan and settles down to catch a few hours sleep and wait for first light.

Your internal clock wakes you as Petron's largest moon rises above the horizon. You can tell from its angle that sunrise is not far away. Secreting the bottle of moth mist in your sleeve, you get up and walk to the wall of plants.

The plunger on the bottle shoots a fine mist out of its nozzle and coats the nearest leaf. You make your way around the wall of green giving it a burst every few feet. Then you step back and wait.

Nothing happen for the first few minutes, but then there's a slight slumping of the rigid framework the plants have formed around you. Within five minutes the vines are unraveling like crazy and slipping to the ground.

You walk to the wall and force your hands between some of the branches and push them apart. They feel rubbery, like they've lost all their strength.

"I think they're asleep," you say to the troop. "Let's get loaded and get out of here."

Things go well until the first ray of sunlight comes over the ridge. As soon as it hits the leaves, the plants spring back to life. Some of them start weaving around your legs and arms. One wraps itself around your neck.

Before you can do anything, everyone is trussed up and unable to move.

When you look around you see the man-plant again. He is angry and has formed his bulk into a large tooth-filled mouth. A strong tendril wraps around one of your troopers, lifts him off the ground and tosses him into the gaping maw.

Moments later the plant burps and spits out a pile of bones.

"Yum, tasty," the huge mouth says. "I was going to take you back to our community and see if we could come to some peaceful arrangement, but you have proven yourselves untrustworthy. Looks like you'll have to be breakfast instead."

And with that the tendril tightens around your neck and your vision goes black.

I'm sorry, but this part of your story is over. You decided to drug your captors and try to escape. That made them angry and they've eaten you for breakfast. Burp!

However all is not lost. You still have three possible choices. Do you:

Go back to your last decision and choose to wait until morning rather than spraying moth mist on the plants? **P219**

Or

Go back to the beginning of the story and try another path? **P1**

Or

Go to the list of choices and start reading from another part of the story? **P308**

You have decided to wait and see what happens tomorrow.

You decide it's not worth the risk of trying to drug the plants. They might change into something dangerous and then the whole expedition would be in danger.

"Let's try talking first," you tell Dagma. "If we can get them to trust us, who knows what benefits that could bring. You call Piver, Gagnon and Villum over and tell them your decision."

"Okay," Dagma says, turning to go to her sleeping position.

"Wait," you say, putting your hand out. "Aren't you forgetting something?"

Dagma shrugs, delves into her pocket and comes out with a bottle of bright blue liquid.

You stretch your hand out a little more and Dagma reluctantly puts the bottle into your hand.

"You can breathe in all the mist you like in your own time Dagma, but when you're on patrol, and others are counting on you, it's just not on. Now, get back to the others and try to get some sleep. Tomorrow I want you bright and ready."

If the situation were different, you would have punished Dagma and have her standing guard duty all night, but you suspect losing her mist is enough and you want her fresh in the morning.

Villum isn't happy. "I'd rather escape. I don't trust these—these animals."

"Tough," you say. "I'm in charge so be smart and keep your mouth shut. Diplomacy is the key right now."

The next morning as the sun rises over the ridge, your troopers start stirring. You can hear the rustling of leaves as the plants reform themselves into balls in preparation for the trip to the lake.

The man-plant is back in the form of a person and steps forward to talk to you. "If you try to run, or harm any of my pets you will be caught and eaten. But if you are trustworthy I will guarantee your safety."

You gulp and nod your head. "Okay, we'll play nice."

"Good. I suggest you climb aboard your sledges. My pets will escort you through the jungle."

You're not sure what the man-plant has in mind, but you instruct your sliders to climb aboard.

Villum has other ideas. He marches up to the man-plant and puts his hands on his hips. "I demand some respect here," he says to the plant. "My father is a general and if you don't—"

Faster than you can imagine, the plant turns into a snake and wraps its body around Villum's body and starts squeezing. "How about a hug? Would you like one of those you arrogant fool?"

Villum grunts, his eyes bulging. When he's about as blue as the moth mist you confiscated from Dagma, the plant releases him and reforms back into the shape of a person.

"Care to climb aboard now young general's son? Or would you like another hug?"

Villum, still gasping for air, wastes no time in climbing aboard the nearest sledge.

You're amazed by the power of these creatures, but also impressed at how quickly they've put the demanding Villum in his place. They might become quite an ally after all.

Once everyone is aboard a sledge the plants reform around them, lift them off the ground and roll away down the watercourse towards the lake. The plants are much faster downhill than traveling by sledge would have been. Before much more than an hour has passed, your convoy is rolling up to a strange structure with metallic feathers covering its surface.

Beyond this structure is a beautiful lake.

The plants put down your sledges and the next thing you know, tiny metal birds are flitting around you, probing with their tiny beaks and looking at your with their telescopic eyes.

"These must be some of the robots that crazy old miner was talking about," you tell Piver who is staring, fascinated by the creatures. "Or maybe I should say, the not so crazy miner, as it turns out."

A circular door in the side of the structure opens and a number of people come out. They look at you like you're some sort of curiosity.

"Welcome to New Londinium," the oldest woman of the group says. "I see you've met Eva and her little friends."

You climb down off your sledge and smile in greeting. "We come in friendship seeking trade with your people."

The woman smiles. "I doubt you've much to offer that we don't have already."

You are thankful that Villum has learned his lesson and sits quietly. Piver is curious. He jumps down and comes to stand beside you.

"You sure about that?" Piver says, holding up a cold leg of deep fried pango.

"What is that?" the woman asks.

"Here, taste." Piver steps forward and passes the woman the pango leg.

The woman sniffs and then tastes a tiny bit, weary of some trick.

"Geebus, lady, just bite right in. It's the tastiest thing in the whole world. … apart from crackleberries maybe."

The woman's next bite is a little larger. As she chews, her eyes brighten. She smiles at Piver. "What is this delicious morsel? Such flavor, so—so succulent!"

Piver smiles back and does a little jig. "Pango, pango, pango, pango … Leg of pango is my favorite. It's the taste that makes me happy. Pango, pango, pango pang," he sings.

"And you can get more of this?" the woman asks.

"Much as you'd like," Piver says. "My dad's a pango hunter. The eggs are pretty good too."

You clear your throat and look at the woman. "We just need a few tyranium crystals in exchange. It's a win-win don't you think?"

The woman takes another bite of pango and then licks her fingers. "You've got a deal … on one condition."

You nod. "Sure if we can. What is it?"

"We have lots of tyranium, but we need to cement our new relationship with a wedding. My eldest daughter is of marriageable age and needs a husband. After an unusual run of girl children, we've very few men left in our community."

This is not what you expected. "Well sure, I guess. Who did you have in mind?"

The woman turns and waves her daughter forward. "I think it is for her to decide, don't you?"

"Sure, I suppose," you say.

"Geebus," Piver whispers. "She's beautiful."

"She is also our genetic engineering specialist," the woman says.

The tyranium trade is vital to your communities. If a marriage will seal the deal then that's what you'll do. "Okay," you say. "As long as whoever your daughter selects agrees as well. It's only fair."

"Agreed." The woman turns to her daughter. "What do you think darling? See anyone you like?"

"I could give your daughter a good life," Villum says, stepping forward. He give the girl a quick once over, smiling at what he sees. "I'm the son of a general and have many servants. I could give your daughter a life of luxury."

The girls looks at Villum. "But what work do you do? What knowledge do you have?"

Villum is a bit dumbstruck at her question. "But I have riches, and farmlands, and—"

The girl smiles and reaches out her arm. The arm turns into a long slim tendril and wraps itself around Piver's hand. "But I like this one," the girl says. "He's funny, and clever and smells of pango."

Piver smiles. As he steps forward he does a happy little jiggle. "Me? Really? Geebus! I'd be honored."

Congratulations you have finished this part of the story. You have found not only a new source of tyranium crystals essential to your communities, but you found another tribe living on Petron. But have you tried all the different paths this story has?

It is time to make another decision. Do you:

Go back to the beginning and try another path? **P163**

Or

Go to the list of choices and start reading from another part of the story? **P308**

Send someone down the hole to investigate.

"I think we should investigate. These holes could give us a clue to the people living on this side of the range."

"Or get us killed," Piver says a little nervously. "I volunteer to stay here."

"I'll go," Dagma says. "Anything if it means we don't have to lug our gear through the jungle."

You clip a zip line onto a sledge and carefully lower yourself to the edge of the hole. When you look down into it you see tiny dots of light attached to the smooth rock. "Moon moths have taken up residence," you say. "How much cable have we got, Piver?"

"A mile maybe, if we join it all together. You're not serious about going down there?"

"If moon moths are living here, how dangerous can it be?"

"Moon moths are insects, how smart do you think they are?" Piver asks.

The little engineer has a point. Moon moths aren't the cleverest of creatures, but then again, you've never see them nest in areas of danger so you have trust their instincts.

You look at Piver. "Get out the cable and a winch. I'm going in."

"Geebus! You're crazy." Piver shakes his head and zips back up to the sledge. He sets about rigging up a winch, splicing some cables together and feeding it onto the drum. About fifteen minutes later he tosses you a line.

"Here you go. What signal are you going to use when you want us to pull you back up? A blood-curdling scream?"

You give him a stern look. "Not funny, Piver."

Piver hands you one of his new hand held launchers. "Okay, fire this when you've had enough. I've detached the tether so we'll see the line when it comes shooting out of the hole."

"You sure you don't want me to go?" Dagma says.

You shake your head. "I'll be fine."

Piver stands by the winch and releases the break. "Right you're in control. Good luck."

After double checking that the cable is properly attached to your harness, you lean back, let out some cable, and step into space. With your feet apart for balance, you start the long slide down the tunnel.

At first there is light radiating from the luminescent wings of the moon moths to give you an idea of the dimensions of the tunnel, but it isn't long before you've left them behind and are sliding in total darkness. It's an eerie feeling and you find yourself unable to tell how fast you're going apart from the hum of the cable running though the clip on your harness.

Then you see a strange glow below you … and it's getting brighter.

You slow the release of cable and proceed with more caution. When the tunnel widens out, you find yourself in an old lava tube filled with enormous crystals. The pale blue light they emit gives the tunnel an eerie glow and just enough light for you to see the extent of the crystal field. Some crystal are bigger than tree trunks and it's hard to believe you're not dreaming.

Using the diamond studs on the heels your boots, you work your way over to a flat section where you can stand up and loop a length of cable around one of the smaller crystals.

You can't believe the size and number of crystals down here. There's no tyranium needle crystals unfortunately, but these diamonds more than make up for their absence.

Then further into the old lave tube, you see the teeth of what you suspect is a drilling tool of some sort, lying to one side. It's similar to the drills that the Highlanders use for boring accommodation pods and hydro growing chambers but this one is huge and has red teeth made from a material you've not seen before. Whoever developed this monster has technology that far surpasses what the Highlanders or Lowlanders have. And that makes you a little nervous.

After another look around, you pull Piver's handheld launcher out of your utility belt, aim it up the tunnel and pull the trigger.

With a hiss of compressed air, the bolt shoots up trailing twenty yards of filament behind it. Now it's just a matter of waiting to be winched to the surface.

When Piver sees the bolt shoot into the sky, he flips the switch on the winch. "Okay everyone, here we go."

The winch starts to turn and slowly the cable wraps around the drum.

You and the eight-foot-long crystal slowly rise up the tunnel. Soon you're seeing pinpoints of light from the moon moths again and then, as you near the surface, a disk of sunlight appears.

When you and the crystal emerge from the top of the hole, everyone looks on in amazement.

"Geebus!" Piver says. "What is that thing?"

Gagnon slides over for a closer look. "I think it's the largest blue diamond ever discovered."

"Wrong," you say, not quite believing what you're about to say. "There are others down there that are ten times bigger!"

Gagnon's eyes pop. "How is that even possible?"

"I don't know but it's true. And … there's a huge drill bit down there too, so…"

"We're not alone," Gagnon says.

"No. And they may not like us finding their mine."

This gives everyone something to consider. A few on the expedition have lost their smiles and are looking around as if they're expecting an attack at any moment.

You are still marveling at your discovery when you see an unusual metallic bird hovering nearby. Then you hear the sound of metal scraping on rock and see a metal spider skittering across the rock towards you. The spider's body is round and has a number of cogs on it. Its eight legs are equipped with miniature drills on their tips that help it attach itself to the slippery rock as it moves.

"Looks like that miner wasn't so nutty after all," you say to the others. "Look! Spiderbot."

Then you hear a voice coming from the spider. "Attention, newcomers. Please do not fear."

Piver's jaw drops. "Is that—is that thing talking to us?"

You look at the spider and then at the bird. Then you realize the bird is made of metal too and has delicate silver feathers. Its eyes are made of clear glass and they rotate and move in and out as the bird stares at you.

You take a step towards the spider. "Can you hear me?"

"Yes, newcomers, we can hear you."

"Geebus!" Piver says, peering down at the robot. "This is incredible."

"We mean you no harm," the voice coming from the spider says. "Do not fear."

Silently your sliders have moved into a defensive formation around the spider. Their guide sticks and slingshots at the ready.

"Easy," you say to your troop. "Let's hear the machine out."

The spider skitters a little closer. "Follow the spiderbot and it will bring you safely to us. Leave the diamond crystal, you will be permitted to take it with you when you return to your people."

You move closer to Gagnon. "What do you think?" you whisper. "They sound friendly enough."

"Looks like their technology's superior to ours. We'd better do as they say."

You look at the spiderbot and then the metallic bird. "Okay, we will follow as you ask. We come in peace and are only in search of minerals."

Without another word, the spider scurries over to the edge of the ridge where the smooth black rock meets the softer soil and foliage of the jungle. "Please tether your sledges and then come this way," it says. "We have a means of transportation over here."

Directing your troops to do as the spider says, you follow the spiderbot to where a metal snake, fifteen yards long and eight feet round, sits waiting. The snake is made from flexible segments and has a drill bit, similar to the one you saw underground, attached to its front end. A hatch on the side of the snake opens revealing rows of seats inside.

"Please climb aboard," the spider says.

"Wow," Piver says. "I want one of these!"

You're not surprised that Piver finds this new contraption fascinating. It is a marvel of engineering. Inside the snake, behind the rows of seats is the drive unit. In the front, behind a row of instruments, sits a humanoid shaped robot with funny looking goggles on. Then you realize the goggles are like the hummingbots eyes and are probably relaying what the robot is seeing to a control post somewhere else.

Typically, Piver, in his enthusiasm, is first aboard. You and the other sliders follow. Villum's knees are shaking as he climbs aboard and takes a seat near the back. Then a whirring sound starts and the door closes, locking you and your group inside.

The snake slithers off downhill for a short distance and then dives into a hole. Everything around you goes dark except for the blinking lights of the instrument panel at the front of the snake.

You turn to Gagnon sitting in the next seat. "I hope this isn't a mistake."

Gagnon's skin is a little pale. "You're not the only one."

The underground journey takes less than an hour. When the snake resurfaces and the door reopens, there are a number of buildings built around a much larger structure the likes of which you've never seen. This large structure is bird-shaped and covered in beautiful metallic feathers, similar to those that cover the smaller hummingbot, only larger.

A crowd of people are going about their normal business. Some of them ride on small contraptions that float just off the ground. Others ride on strange beasts that look to be half plant and half animal. The people look like members of your own community only a little greener, thinner and with less muscular legs.

"Please disembark," the spiderbot says as it skitters out.

"What is that thing?" Piver says, pointing to the large structure covered in metal feathers. "I'm sure I've seen a picture of something similar in the *Book of Myths*."

"I've seen it too," Gagnon says. "It's the part of the myth about how our ancestors arrived on this planet. '...*and they arrived in a giant bird that travelled between the stars,*' it says if I remember correctly."

"Between the stars?" you ask. "You mean from beyond our sun and moons?"

Gagnon smiles. "So the story goes. Looks like the myths are true after all."

"But how would it be possible to travel such distances?" you ask.

"Just because we don't understand how such things happen doesn't mean that it can't. There are many things we will never know."

"But that doesn't mean every crazy idea is possible either," you say, trying to get your head around all this new information."

"But there's lots of things to discover," Piver says. "I learn new stuff every day. That's what makes life so much fun."

As you ponder what your friends have said, a circular door on the side of the structure opens and a ramp lowers to the ground. A group of people, both men and women, old and young, come walking down the ramp towards you.

"Welcome newcomers," a slender, older woman says. "My name is Margaret, Chief Council of Settlement Three."

Margaret reminds you a little of your mother. Her skin is translucent and her face serene. She has laughter lines around her eyes and her expression is open. Most reassuring of all, none of the people carry weapons.

You tuck your guide stick under your arm, take a step forward and bow. "Greetings. I am the leader of our expedition. We come in peace seeking tyranium and blue diamond to help build our settlements on the far side of the mountains."

"Yes, we know. Our hummingbots have been watching your

journey ever since you left the Pillars of Haramon," Margaret says. "We have been most pleased that the Highlanders and Lowlanders have found peace. We would never have allowed you over the pass if you were still in conflict."

Your instincts tell you that these are good people and your tight shoulders begin to relax. You place a hand on your chest below the single diamond pinned there. "I am tasked with finding a new source of tyranium. Is it possible that we could sit down and talk about opening up trade between our people? I'm sure that we have things that would be of benefit to your people too."

"There is one thing we lack on this side of the mountains. Our supply of protein is limited. Unlike yours, our terrain is not very suitable for pangos to breed, so the colonies on this side of the mountains are small. We lack the high pinnacles the birds favor and are reliant on what we can grow in the soil, weak as it is. The snake you rode here is used for terraforming and mining. It turns rock into soil, but the nutrients this soil contains are few."

Dagma steps forward and holds up a cage with four pango in it. "Here are some birds I netted early this morning, before we broke camp. Please take them as a gift."

"Four pangos are a rare treat this side of the mountains. Thank you," the woman says.

"Highlanders catch thousands of pangos each season," you say. "I'm sure we can spare some in exchange for minerals. We could also allow you to mine the rock under the pango colonies with your snake. The phosphate there is the perfect nutrient for growing plants."

Margaret waves you into the structure. "Come, we have much to discuss. In the meantime, take a look around our ship. After all it contains much of your history too."

"Our history?" you ask.

"Yes. The book you call the *Book of Myths* is history not fable. We come from common stock that left our home planet many years ago. During the trip our DNA was improved by crossbreeding it with plants. Our home planet was far richer in oxygen than Petron."

Margaret sees that you are doubtful. She smiles and holds out her hand. You can see the blood vessels through her fine translucent skin. "Do we not all bleed green?"

You have to admit that if her people came from the stars, and you and she are the same, then maybe your people did too. But how did your history get lost over the years?

As if reading your mind Margaret smiles. "We've kept the pass over the mountains closed for generations, waiting for your people to tire of fighting. Much of your historic relics and books were lost during endless conflict. When we found out about the truce and felt it might last, we sent a scout, disguised as a miner, over to your people knowing that you would come for the minerals. Now perhaps we can join together and make Petron better than Earth ever was."

"Earth?" you say. "That's where we originated?"

"Yes, Earth. In the Milky Way Galaxy."

"Geebus!" Piver says. "What a funny name for a planet."

Congratulations, this part of your story has ended. You've led a successful mission to the far side of the mountains and established friendly contact with the people there. The future looks bright.

But have you followed all the paths this story takes?

It is time to make another decision. Do you:

Go back to the beginning of the story and try another path? **P163**

Or

Go to the list of choices and start reading from another part of the story? **P308**

You have decided to carry on down the ridge.

"Let's keep going," you say. "If we have time we can check out these holes on the way back."

Gagnon moves off with his sledge, keeping an extra close eye out for more holes.

As your group loses altitude the ridge keeps broadening out. The stumpy shrubs of the upper mountain are left behind and the jungle gets thicker and taller and closer to the rock you're sliding on. In places, branches overhand the ridge. Some trees tower so high you can't see their tops, while other have a host of smaller plants living in the crooks of their branches.

You're glad the rocky ridge is here. It forms a broad highway running through the dense jungle. It would have been hard trying to find your way through this near impenetrable tangle of vines and creepers.

"I smell fart," Gagnon says as he brings his sledge to a halt.

"It's probably gas from the volcano," Piver says.

"The pangos are still alive so it can't be deadly," Dagma says, holding up the cage with the four birds in it.

A few of the sliders are laughing and blaming each other for the stink. One has her hand at her throat and is doing a good impression of someone choking to death. As Gagnon continues on, the smell gets stronger and stronger until a few expedition members pull the front of their uniforms up over their noses.

"Geebus!" Piver says. "This smells worse than a morph rat hole!"

He's right. You've come across a few rat holes in your day but this stench beats that by a mile. Thankfully, your senses adjust quickly and after another half hour down the ridge you hardly notice it.

Then you hear a loud screech of diamond hooks as Gagnon and his sledge come to an emergency stop.

"Wow, look at that," he calls out.

After your sledge has stopped, you slide forward to Gagnon's position. Below you is a chasm so deep and so beautiful it's hard to believe it's real.

"It must be a half a mile deep," you say.

The multicolored layers of rock change from the darkest black to a pale blue as they go down deeper into the canyon. At the bottom, small craters bubble with magma.

"This has got to be Crater Canyon," Gagnon says.

"That looks like crystal bearing rock near the bottom," Piver says, scanning the canyon through his scope, . "That band of light blue rock is a dead giveaway. Getting to it might be a problem though."

"How much cable have we got?" you ask Piver. "Enough to get us down that far?"

"Sure," Piver says. "We've got lots of cable, but that's not the problem, it's getting the crystals back up again that I'm worried about. Any idea how much half a mile of quarter inch cable weighs?"

"Five feet per pound?" you guess, trying to remember what you learned in slider school.

"Pretty close," Piver says. "So half a mile of cable weighs in at 250 pounds, plus whatever it's attached to. Our winches are only rated to 300 so by the time you add a basket and crystals, they'll be overloaded and burn out."

You rest your guide stick on the ground and look at Piver. "So what do we do?"

"Now that's where an engineer comes in handy," he says. "We'll winch in two stages. We need to lower a team down halfway where they'll construct a platform. From there we can mount another winch that will reach the bottom. That way the cable weight is only 125 pounds max."

You see what the little engineer is getting at. "And we do the reverse on the way back out?"

"No stink on you," he says with a grin. "Apart from that whiff of volcano I smell."

You look up to the sky to make sure there is no sign of rain. Rain would make the ground too slippery to work, even for a slider wearing diamond studded boots. Satisfied the weather will hold, you get Piver and the other engineers to work.

They unload equipment from the sledges and start constructing a sturdy framework complete with brackets so they can bolt it to the canyon wall. Another engineer sets up a winch and bolts it to solid rock.

"Double check your safety lines. I don't want any accidents," you tell your crew.

It's an hour before the newly constructed platform is eased over the edge and two engineers, their belts loaded with equipment climb aboard. Piver takes control of the top winch while another engineer acts as spotter.

You hear the hum of the motor as the winch lowers the platform and the two engineers down the smooth canyon wall. When the desired level is reached, Piver puts on the brake and the engineers start drilling holes in the cliff face and begin attaching the platform with sturdy anchor bolts.

Once the platform is secured to the canyon wall, another winch is lowered. This winch is then mounted onto the platform. Only then can the miners lower themselves to the canyon floor and start looking for the rare crystals you've come so far to find.

After relaying two more miners down the cliff, Piver comes over to you. "I thought I'd go down and have a look."

"Is that a good idea?" you ask. "What if we have problems with the winch?"

"Drexel can look after things up here," Piver says. "Why don't you leave Gagnon in charge and come down too? You've got to admit it's an amazing place. Don't you want to have a look?"

Piver is right. Crater Canyon is an amazing place and Gagnon is a responsible second in command. When are you likely to pass this way again?

But do you want to be so far from the rest of your troop, especially in unknown territory? What if something unexpected happens?

It is time to make a decision. Do you:

Go with Piver into the canyon? **P236**

Or

Stay at the top of the canyon? **P239**

You have decided to go with Piver into the canyon.

"Why not?" you say to Piver. "I'd love to have a closer look."

Piver does an excited hop and rubs his hands together. "Okay, I'll tell Drexel to get ready to drop us down. Grab whatever you need and meet me at the edge."

After sorting out a few supplies you slide to the edge and wait for Piver. A moment later he arrives with one end of a cable.

"Here you go, clip on and get ready to lose your breakfast. It's going to be a scary ride."

You clip your harness onto the cable and lean back testing your weight. Piver does the same.

"Okay now we just have to walk backwards off the cliff and try not to poop ourselves," Piver says with a cheeky grin. "You ready?"

You take a deep breath. "Let's do it."

Piver waves his arm at Drexel and soon you feel movement in the cable. When you reach the edge you lean back and step over the edge.

"Keep your waist bent and your feet against the rock wall so you don't swing about," Piver says. "And try to enjoy the view."

You have to admit the view is spectacular. The canyon extends for miles in both directions. Internal forces have ripped the ground apart exposing layer upon layer of rock. Far to the east the canyon is filled with a pink mist that has settled near its bottom.

"Okay feet down," Piver says. "Platform coming up."

Once safely on the platform you re-clip your harness to the cable attached to the platform winch. A young miner smiles and lowers you and Piver down the next section.

Ten minutes later you are standing at the bottom of Crater Canyon.

"Geebus," Piver says. "It's hot down here."

The little engineer is right. You can feel the sweat trickling down the back of your uniform.

Off to your left a couple of the miners have stripped down to their vests in an attempt to stay cool while they drill away at the band of tyranium crystal in the canyon wall. A mound of crystal bearing rock is piled up to one side.

"Looks like rich pickings," you say. "As long as one of these vents don't blow."

Piver looks over at the nearest bubbling pool of magma. "Don't worry, if it erupts you'll never feel a thing."

"That's what I'm afraid of."

Despite the canyon floor being hot and dangerous, it is also a place of great beauty. Everywhere you look the rock is sparkling with crystals of some sort. The miners are laughing as they work, amazed at the size and length of the needle crystals they're finding. But a rumble beneath your feet reminds you how dangerous this place is.

"Let's start getting some of this rock back up. We don't want to be down here any longer than we have to," you say to the miners.

"A least the pangos are still kicking," Piver says pointing to a cage near the miners. "No gas at least."

You give Piver a thumbs up. "So far so good."

As the miners load rock into a basket and start winching it back up to the canyon rim, you look around at the different strata of rock. One layer is made of tiny hexagonal crystal that look like diamonds. You move closer and touch the crystals with your fingers.

"Hey Piver, are these blue diamonds?"

Piver slides over and has a look. "Sure looks like it."

Another layer of rock is a solid band, translucent like glass and two feet thick. The rock is so clear you can see right into it and …

That is when you see a pair of eyes looking back at you.

"Piver this rock is looking back at me!"

Piver laughs. "Geebus, that's your reflection silly!"

As you look at the rock, Piver giggles like a madman. Then he calls to the other miners. "Hey, guess what? The rock is looking back!"

You can feel your face redden. But how were you to know? You look again. This time the rock blinks. But you didn't blink. Then you see teeth, large and gleaming. A shimmering crystal claw reaches towards you from inside the rock.

You try to run, but one of the claws snags your uniform. You are trapped.

The rock feels liquid as you are pulled into it. You try to yell out but it's too late. As you are absorbed into the cliff face you suddenly feel peaceful. Like you are part of everything around you.

Don't worry, the stranger's voice inside your head says. *You are one of us now.*

You see Piver from inside the rock and try to shout a warning, but your mouth won't open. Then the magma in the nearest crater rises up and begins to overflow. The miners are running, but the magma is rising too fast. You close your eyes and let the warmth sweep over you.

Unfortunately, this part of your story is over. You've been swallowed by a strange silica based life force very different to your own. However you can always try another path, maybe you'll have better luck.

It is time to make one of three choices. Do you:

Go back to the beginning of the story and try another path? **P163**

Or

Go back to your last decision and stay at the top of the canyon? **P239**

Or

Go to the list of choices and start reading from another part of the story? **P308**

You have decided to stay at the top of the canyon.

"I think I'd better stay up here," you tell Piver. "I don't want too many people down there at once."

Piver looks disappointed but he's never one to stay low for long. "Well I'd better start lifting some of the crystals out of the canyon then. Looks like it's going to be a fair bit."

You train your scope on the miners working below and see they've dug quite a pile of tyranium already.

"And we don't want to be out here after dewfall," you say.

As Piver goes off to help with the winching, you speak to Gagnon who has been standing guard with some of the other sliders. "Any signs of life?" you ask.

"Nothing so far. Still I get a feeling I'm being watched."

You look around at the foliage crowding the rocky ridge. Are those plants closer than they were before? "Let's not be greedy, eh?" you say to Gagnon. "Once we've got a decent load we'll start zipping back up to where we camped last night. No point pushing our luck."

Gagnon agrees. "I'll get Villum and the others to start cutting steps and get a few zip lines strung up to save us time later."

"Good thinking," you say. "Assuming you can wake Villum up, the lazy sod."

"Oh I'll wake him up easily enough," Gagnon says, pulling out his anchor bolt gun. "Nothing like a big bang to get a Lowlander's attention."

The next couple of hours are spent hoisting crystals out of the canyon and packing the sledges. The miners are in good spirits and quite pleased with their haul.

"We'll leave the platform behind for next time," Piver says. "I'm sure with these results the council will want to send another expedition back here."

Just as your troop is about to move off, there is a low rumble from underground. "Anchors in!" you yell.

The lead slider of each sledge pulls his anchor gun out of his belt and fires a bolt into the rock. With a quick loop a tether is tied around the anchor bolts securing the sledges to the slippery rock. As the rumbling gets stronger, even the diamond dust on the sledge's runners doesn't prevent the sledges from slipping sideways down the hill to the limit of their tethers. Below, you can hear parts of the canyon wall crumbling away and crashing like glass to the canyon floor.

You know you've got to move fast when you smell fart and look over to see that the pangos are lying on the bottom of Dagma's cage. A pale pink mist is rising up over the lip of the canyon.

"Gas!" you yell. Thankfully after one last shake the rumbling stops. "Get moving, everyone, or we'll suffocate!"

Tethers are released and zip lines attached to the cables run up the hill earlier. The powerful zippers pull the sledges at a steady walking pace up the slick black rock of the ridge and before long you leave the stench of gas behind.

"Geebus," Piver says. "Just as well we weren't still in the canyon."

The little engineer is right. If you hadn't been satisfied with a modest load of crystals, some of your team would still have been on the canyon floor beneath the layer of deadly gas. The thought of losing so many of your troop gives you shivers.

You sigh and look back up the mountain. It's a long climb back to Tyron Pass. With the extra weight on the sledges, climbing is slow. Villum, well aware of how close everyone was to getting caught by the cloud of gas finally seems to have some energy and is running his step cutter at full power.

Piver helps him, becoming more and more familiar with the machine's operation.

As winches hum, and zip lines buzz, the sledges are pulled higher and higher up the ridge.

But even with everyone working at full pace, you soon realize you're not going to make it to your previous camp before dewfall.

"Keep an eye out for somewhere to stop," you say to Gagnon.

"Everyone's exhausted and it's getting late."

Ten minutes later Gagnon calls a halt. He tethers his sledge and slides over to the edge of the ridge where the shiny black rock meets a tangle of vines and trees. "I saw a strange reflection in the foliage. I'm going to check it out."

You wait as Gagnon disappears into the bush. When he doesn't reappear after a couple of minutes you signal Dagma and Shoola, to go over and investigate.

Just as they reach the bush line Gagnon reappears. "Come look at this," he calls out. "You're not going to believe your eyes."

As you detach your harness and slide over towards Gagnon, Piver arrives at your side.

"Come with me," Gagnon says turning a walking back between the shrubbery.

Curious, you and the others follow as he leads you out onto a spur looking down the valley to the east. Way off in the distance, nestled at the bottom of the mountain is a small settlement.

"So there are people living this side of the mountains," Piver says.

"Looks like it," you say. "But what caused the reflection you saw, Gagnon?"

Gagnon points to a small bird hovering above you. Its body is covered in fine metallic feathers. The bird's wings flap so fast you can barely see them moving and its eyes rotates in and out like the magnifying lens on your scope.

"Geebus," Piver says. "It's a robot and it's watching us. It must come from whoever is living in that community down there."

You look at the hummingbot and wonder if it can hear you. Maybe you should relay a message to the little bird's owner. Let them know that you come in peace and that they have nothing to fear.

"Come on let's get going," you say. "As much as I'd like to stay, we need to find a place to camp before dewfall."

You leave the sight of the distant settlement behind and carry on up the ridge. Half an hour before dewfall Gagnon spots a flattish area just west of the ridge and you and your sliders make camp.

The next morning, after another three hours climbing, your troop finally reaches Tyron Pass and stands looking over the Black Slopes towards home.

Then you notice the hummingbot is back. This time is has something in its beak. As the little bird nears, you see it's a delicate flower, tiny and perfect. The bird drops the flower in your palm and then flutters back a few yards away to watch your reaction.

You take the tiny flower between your thumb and forefinger and bring it to your nose. Its scent is the most intoxicating thing you've ever smelled. You look up at the bird and smile. "Thank you," you say, not knowing if the bird can hear you or not. "Please tell your owner we will come back soon to talk trade."

The bird tweets twice, does a quick loop the loop and flies off.

You turn to Gagnon. "I think it understood, don't you?"

"Yip," Gagnon says. "Looks like we'll be back this way sooner than we thought."

You pass the flower to Gagnon who takes a whiff. Then he passes it to Piver.

Piver lifts the flower to his nose and without even realizing it, rises up onto his toes as he inhales the heady scent. "Geebus!" he says. "That's the best smell ever!"

Congratulations this part of your story is over. You've had a successful mission, retrieved a load of crystals, and found a friendly new civilization on the far side of the mountains. Well done. But have you followed all the paths this book has to offer? Have you been to Mount Kakona or fought off the morph rats?

It is time to make another decision. Do you:

Go back to the beginning of the story and try another path? **P163**
Or

Go to the list of choices and start reading from another part of the story? **P308**

You have decided to allow Drexel to climb the Tryon Cliffs.

You have every faith in Piver's skill as an engineer, but it never hurts to have a plan B.

After glancing up at the towering cliffs, you look back at Drexel. "Are you sure about this? Who will lead the climbing team on Mount Kakona if you fall?"

"I'm not planning on falling," Drexel says. "Besides, I'll put in anchors every twenty feet or so."

You rub the back of your neck as you think. "What about someone to help in case you get into trouble? Sliders usually work as a team."

"All I need is someone here at the bottom to send up more line and bolts," Drexel says. "I'll be fine doing the climbing. Once I get to the top, I can haul up a winch and hoist everyone up."

"Okay," you say. "And if the drilling goes as planned we can meet you on the other side."

Drexel smiles. "Deal."

Drexel wastes no time in getting the gear he needs for his attempt to be the first person to scale the Tyron Cliffs.

Meanwhile, Piver has the drill in position and four of the strongest expedition members ready to start the physical task of turning the drill. Each of the four pushers sits in a line with their feet stretched out before them. Their feet rest on footpads linked to the shaft through a series of pulleys. With each push of their feet, belts from the pulleys rotate the shaft. With four people pushing and the gearing of the pulleys, the shaft rotates fast.

Linked to the end of the shaft is the diamond drill bit which claws its way into the rock with every turn. The rubble is hauled back out of the hole by others using a small conveyor belt that sends the debris sliding off into a crevasse further down the slope.

Dagma sits in the lead seat nearest the cliff. She'll be the one the other pushers try to keep up with.

Dagma counts, "One, two, three, four," as she pushes, one foot after the other.

As one pusher tires, another takes their place. Highlanders take great pride in being able to outlast their fellow sliders. And now that Lowlanders are here, the competition will be hard fought and the tunnel will be drilled in record time.

In between counts, Dagma rallies the other pushers and munches on hydro bars to keep her energy levels up. After an hour, the first changeover happens. One of the Lowlanders is exhausted in the thin mountain air. Another quickly slots into his place to keep the drill turning.

"How's it going Piver?" you yell over the grinding of the drill. "Are we going to make it through before the bit gets too dull?"

Piver nods. "Only three more hours I reckon. The bit should last eight."

"That's good news," you say. "Three hours is quicker than I expected."

You step back from the cliff face and look up to where Drexel is making steady progress up the cliff. He's put in half a dozen anchor bolts so far and is about to put in another. Then, once the new bolt is secured, he attaches his harness to it and starts climbing again.

Drexel's climbing technique is impressive. His legs are powerful and he uses them to great effect by kicking his toe studs into the glossy black rock and then pushing his body upwards. In each hand he holds a sturdy pick of high-quality needle crystals. These give him grip wherever he finds a flaw in the rock, however tiny. Then once he's made ten yards or so, he puts in another bolt to protect his position in case of a fall.

Trodie watches Drexel climb. "He's good. You sliders certainly know your stuff up here."

You smile at Trodie's compliment. "It's what we've trained all our lives for."

"I look forward to giving you a tour of the Lowlands sometime," Trodie says. "Have you ever ridden on the water? We have floating gardens you know and boats for catching fish. Fish aren't as tasty as pangos, but when smoked over newly cut crackleberry branches they're not too bad."

"Water and the Highlands are usually a bad mix," you say. "Up here whole troops can be sent to the bottom by a sudden storm."

Trodie nods his understanding. "But in the Lowlands we don't have black glass. The soil is soft and easy to walk on. You must come down and try it some time."

After promising to do just that, you go over and see how Gagnon is getting on.

He looks up as you approach. "I've checked my calculations. The target looks good."

"Excellent," you say. "Drexel's doing well too."

"I need some exercise," Gagnon says, giving you a sideways glance. "Fancy a race on the foot pads?"

You look over towards the drilling machine and notice that a couple of the pushers are tiring. "Okay you're on. Loser has to empty the latrine bucket."

Emptying the latrine bucket is the worst job while on expedition, but it has to be done. You've always respected leaders who were prepared to do the smelly jobs alongside those of lower rank. Respect in the Highlands is earned and not given without good reason.

Gagnon gives you a confidant laugh. "You asked for it!"

The two of you slide over to the drill and tap the two exhausted pushers on the shoulder.

"Time for a rest," you say. "Go have some broth."

Dagma is still pushing after three hours. She's slowing down a little, but even so her pace is hard to keep up with. You and Gagnon fall into step. Left. Right. Left. Right. One, two, three, four.

"Come on push!" Dagma yells down the line. "Outlast me and I'll empty the stink bucket!"

Shoola has just completed a break so she taps another weary slider on the shoulder and rejoins the race. "I'm in too."

Suddenly the race takes on a new urgency. The first one who stops, empties the bucket. One of the other sliders gets out a broth pot and starts keeping rhythm by clanging it with his harness buckle. Others gather around to watch and to cheer for their favorite.

Meanwhile at the cliff face, Piver is pumping a mixture of diamond dust and water onto the drill bit to keep it cool and others struggle to keep up with shifting the rubble out of the hole. With the race on, the drill bit is rotating at twice its normal rate and the tunnel is getting longer and longer by the minute.

After two hours your legs start to cramp. Sweat pours down your back. Dagma and Shoola grit their teeth and push like crazy, each determined to outdo the other. Gagnon's face is flushed and he is breathing heavy. You're sure that any minute now, he'll throw his hands up in defeat and you'll have won.

"Stop!" Piver yells, throwing a lever that disengages the drive shaft. "We're through!"

Suddenly the resistance on the footpads is gone. You lean back and gasp for breath.

Gagnon wipes his forehead and looks over at you. "Lucky we had to stop. I just about had you there."

"Yeah right! Is that why your face looks redder than a pango's beak?"

"Come on everyone," Piver says, ignoring the banter. "Help me pull this drill out."

The drive is disconnected and the drilling machine is dragged back through the perfectly round hole in the cliff.

You slap Piver on the back. "Good work my friend. I suppose we can tell Drexel to come back down now."

"Let's nip through and have a look at what's on the other side first," Piver says. "It might be impassable for all we know."

Piver's making good sense. The terrain on the far side of the tunnel needs to be negotiated by sledges. If that's not possible you'll have to rethink everything.

You wave your arm. "Come on Gagnon, Piver and I are going to see where your tunnel has come out."

You grab your guide stick, put on your headlamp and push your way over to the tunnel entrance. The tunnel walls are almost smooth with only a faint trace of the drill's rotation etched into the surface. A small circle of light, like a moon in the night sky, burns bright at the far end of the blackness.

"Righto, follow me," you say to Piver and Gagnon. "Let's see what we've got."

You step into the tunnel and clip your boots together. Your legs feel like jelly after all the pushing, but as soon as you crouch into the familiar slider's stance and shove off with your stick, you feel the power return to your muscles.

As you slide, the roof of the tunnel is only inches above your head. With its floor being level there is no danger of going too fast and losing control, but about halfway in, when your headlamp picks up a change in the rock's color, you drag your hook and screech to a halt.

"Look here," you say, pointing to a spot on the tunnel's wall. "This rock is more blue than black. It looks similar to tyranium but…"

Piver has the most mining experience. He shines his headlamp onto the lighter section of rock and pulls a small pick from his utility belt. With a short chopping motion, he digs the tip of his pick into the pale rock. "It's hard alright, but not hard enough."

"Worth mining?" you ask.

Piver shakes his head. "The crystals haven't formed enough to be of any use on black glass. Give it another thousand tons of pressure and a million or so years."

You shrug. "That's a shame, it would have saved us a long slide." Then with a big push, you glide the last 15 yards to the end of the tunnel.

The terrain beyond the tunnel is reasonably level, but frequent earthquakes have caused the rock to split, creating long crevasses in the otherwise smooth surface. Still, it looks passable. If the cracks had been running across the slope, then going any further would be impossible. At least these crevasses are running in the same directions as you want to travel and there is flat rock between them.

Off in the distance, rising in a perfect cone, is Mount Kakona. Around the volcano's peak hovers a ring of cloud. A red river of lava runs down its left flank.

"Look, the mountain's creating its own weather," you tell Piver and Gagnon as they come to stand beside you. "The only clouds in sight are around Kakona's summit."

You learned a bit about volcanoes while in Slider School and know that the rain that falls on a volcano's warm upper slopes doesn't take long to evaporate. Then it condenses into clouds again, creating a continuous cycle.

Piver looks up at Kakona's peak. "How are we meant to climb that?"

"Carefully," you say giving the engineer a wink. "Very, very carefully."

Gagnon has his scope out looking for a course through the tricky terrain ahead of you. "At least most of the crevasses are running north south," he says. "As long as we only have to bridge one or two of them, we might get there."

"Why don't you start marking a trail?" you say. "We'll go back and get the others."

Gagnon nods. "Good idea. If we're going to reach the base of Mount Kakona today we're going to have to make good time."

With that Gagnon pulls out his chalk bag and covers the crystal end of his guide stick in bright red powder. Now, whenever Gagnon pushes with his stick, he'll leave a mark for the sledges to follow.

You slap Gagnon on the arm. "Be careful. We'll catch up as quickly as we can."

With that you and Piver push your way back through the tunnel. When you emerge at the other end your troop is waiting anxiously to hear what you've found and Drexel is near the top of the cliff.

You gather everyone together. "The bad news is that there are crevasses between us and the volcano, but the good news is the cracks run north to south so we can slide in between them and will only have to build bridges when two crevasses merge. Gagnon's off scouting a trail so let's get loaded up and move out. We've got a long slide this afternoon."

A hum of excitement buzzes around your troop as gear is strapped down and the sliders connect their harnesses to the sledges. The drill is left behind to reduce weight. With Gagnon out scouting, you decide to take the front harness on the lead sledge yourself. Once everyone is ready you give a big push with your stick and maneuver the sledge into the tunnel.

The diameter of the tunnel is only just big enough to take a sledge. Those riding on top have to duck down so their heads don't scrape the roof. When you emerge on the far side, members of the expedition gasp at the sheer beauty of the volcano in the distance.

As if on cue, Mount Kakona belches out a blast of steam and you feel a slight tremor run through the rock beneath your feet.

"Geebus!" Piver says. "This is going to be interesting."

You smile at the little engineer. "Interesting is putting it mildly."

"Woot! Woot!" Drexel calls from high on the slope behind you. Now he's got a steep slide to get down to your position.

But with skills taught in Slider School, Drexel has no problem. He swoops down the rock in a series of tight S-turns, shifting his weight from one side to the other, his knees bent and guide stick tucked tight under his arm, applying drag as required. The screech of his diamond hook echoes across the landscape and the distinctive swish of his boots cutting turns in the black glass slope is music to your Highland ears.

Drexel skids to a stop beside you. "I see you got through okay."

You nod. "And you've become the first to scale the Tyron Cliffs. Well done."

Drexel gives you a big grin. "I'll have to give some of the credit to

Piver for designing his hand-held launcher. I would have struggled on the last bit without it."

As Drexel goes to thank Piver, you take out your scope and look for Gagnon. The red trail leads between two huge crevasses and then disappears behind a narrow pressure ridge.

"Let's move out," you say, waving your arm. "Keep your hooks at the ready and watch out for the unexpected."

"Woot, woot!" the sliders yell.

You give a big shove with your stick and feel the sledge start to move. Once you gain some momentum, it's easy to keep the heavy sledge moving on the incredibly slippery rock. Every ten yards or so you pass a red mark.

For almost an hour you follow Gagnon's trail, the red marks getting fainter as you go. Then, after coming around a small pinnacle, you see him silhouetted against the sky. He's come to a stop on a narrow triangle of rock where the two crevasses merge into one.

You slide up to his position. "Bridge building time, eh?"

Gagnon nods. "But which side do we take? Left or right?"

You look up at Kakona. Taking the left side of the crevasse will give you a more direct path to the mountain's base, but it also means you'll end up on the side of the volcano where the lava is flowing. If you take the right-hand side of the crevasse, the route looks longer, but you'll be further away from any potential eruption. Or will you?

It is time to make a decision. Do you:

Go left towards the lava? **P256**

Or

Take the right hand side away from the lava? **P258**

You have decided to trust that Piver can drill through the cliffs.

"Sorry Drexel, I'm going to stick with our original plan."

"But—"

You shake your head. "Look, if you want to help, I suggest you use your leg muscles and help power the drill. Piver's looking for volunteers in case you haven't heard."

Drexel looks downcast, but then brightens up. "If the drill breaks can I have a go?"

You shrug. "Sure."

By the time Drexel gets to the drilling machine, the seats for the pushers that will power the drill are already full and a line has formed of those wanting to take their turn as others become weary. As always, competition to be the one who keeps peddling longest is enthusiastic. Dagma and Shoola are already giving each other a hard time and the drilling hasn't even started yet.

Once Piver has all the pulleys connected, he engages the drill and the pusher start pressing the footpads down — left, then right, then left again, one after the other. As the pushers work the pedals, the shaft rotates and turns the drill bit which grinds into the black glass of the Tyron Cliffs.

Those who aren't pushing, or standing in line, are doing other jobs around the site. A fine slurry of water and diamond dust needs to be directed onto the drill bit to keep it cool, and the debris from the drilling needs to be directed downhill towards a crevasse for disposal.

The drilling goes on for hours. Sliders and Lowlanders alike take a turn on the footpads. Some push for an hour, others exhausted themselves by trying to go too fast and are swapped out quickly. Dagma, her legs pumping in a steady rhythm goes on and on tirelessly. Her years acting as break on Highland sledges have been a good training ground for this activity.

You are about to nod off when you hear a commotion near the drill site. When you look up Piver is waving his arms.

You jump down from the sledge and slide over. "What's going on, Piver?" you ask.

The little engineer looks worried. "We've hit a pocket of something, we need to pull the drill out and see what's going on."

You watch on anxiously as Piver and his team slowly withdraw the long shaft from the hole in the cliff. Then finally, as the bit itself appears, Piver checks that the diamond teeth are okay and then straps on a headlamp.

"I'm going in," Piver says, taking a step into the hole. Then he giggles. "If I'm not back in a week send out a search party."

"Nah," you say joining in the joke. "We'll just plug the hole and move on."

But as Piver slides off into the darkness you realize you're holding your breath. You move closer to the opening and stick your head inside. Off in the distance you can see the reflection of Piver's lamp. Then you hear a faint yelp and the light disappears.

"Piver? Stop fooling around!" you yell.

Nothing.

"Piver! Turn your light back on. That's an order!"

Still nothing.

You turn to the others. "Something's happened to Piver. Sliders ready!"

"Can I help?" asks Trodie.

"Just keep an eye on the sledges," you say. "And pass me another cable. Sliders never leave one of their own on the slopes regardless of the danger."

You, Dagma and Gagnon clip on to a cable and slide forward into the tunnel, your guide sticks pointing forward in a defensive position. Drexel and Shoola feed out cable. The Lowland contingent stand watching, not knowing what to do in this unfamiliar environment.

"What's happened?" Dagma asks. "Crevasse?"

You shrug. "I don't know but we're about to find out."

The tunnel is dark, even with your headlamp on. The black rock doesn't reflect much light and your eyes take a while to adjust. As your pupils dilate and your vision comes into focus, Piver is nowhere to be seen.

"Where's he gone?" you mutter. "This is impossi—"

Then you hear a faint echo. You slide cautiously forward then feel yourself falling. "Brake!" you yell.

There is a screeching of hooks from above and your harness jerks tight. Next thing you know you are swinging in space at the end of the cable.

"I meant to warn you about that," Piver says.

You look down and see Piver crouched on the ground about ten feet below you.

"You okay?"

"Keep your knees bent and relax," Piver says with a smile. "Slider rule number one when falling into an unknown void."

"You just made that up!" you say, relieved your friend is alright. "Where the heck are we?"

"In a massive lava tube by the looks of it," Piver says. "They can run for miles. Our tunnel must have clipped the top of it."

Above your head you hear the sound of anchor bolts going in. Then, a moment later, Dagma zips down a cable and comes to a halt beside you. "I see you found our little friend."

"And more," you say. "Piver's fallen into a lava tube. The perfect place to find tyranium crystals."

"Hey, lower me down a bit more," you yell to the sliders above. "I want to check this place out."

When you've got both feet back onto solid ground you unclip your harness and shine your light down the tube in each direction. "This thing is huge!" you say.

Dagma hands you the chemical light she's brought down with her. "Here take this. It's a million moth power. Should brighten things up a bit."

You take the chemical-light and flip the switch. A beam of light six inches wide stabs into the darkness, spreading out as it goes. Twenty yards away, the walls are flecked with pinpoints of reflected light.

"Those sparkles look like gold or copper," Piver says. "If that's the case, tyranium won't be far away."

The three of you move cautiously down the tube, scanning the walls as you go. Then you see them, needle crystals, hanging from the ceiling about twenty yards away, a vast row them stretching as far as you can see.

"Tyranium!" Piver says. "Squillions of it!"

"Grazillions," Dagma says, with a chuckle.

"Pazillions," you say, making up your own word for the massive cluster of crystals and joining in the fun. "That, my friends, is an impressive amount of rock."

Piver slides forward for a closer look. "Geebus, you're not wrong there. Looks like it's good quality too."

You turn off the chemical light and point your headlamp up at the ceiling. With all the crystals reflecting, it's like looking at the night sky only brighter. Everyone is speechless.

After a minute you break the silence. "We'd better get back and tell the others what we've found," you say.

Once you're clipped on to the cable again, the sliders up top pull you back to the surface.

The expedition members are buzzing with excitement after hearing what you've discovered. Only once or twice in a generation is such a rich deposit found. This one will break records, of that you have no doubt. Although the majority of the minerals will go to the council, there is always a small proportion that goes to the expedition members that make the discovery. A small piece of a very, very large pie, is still a lot of pie.

The next few days are spent rigging pulleys and bringing the mined crystals to the surface. Once the sledges are loaded to capacity, your group starts back.

Trekking back with heavy sledges takes time and effort, but slow and safe is better than losing a sledge so close to success.

Three days later, from near the top of Long Gully, you see a familiar sight. "Look, the Pillars of Haramon!"

The glimmering pinnacles shimmer in early afternoon sun, reflecting beams of light around the valley. In the distance the Lowlands, with their patchwork fields of crops stretches off to the turquoise sea on the horizon. A line of towering black peaks runs off to the east like the spine of some ancient monster.

Trodie comes to a screeching halt beside you and looks down at his homeland beyond the pillars. "Hard to believe anything could be so beautiful, isn't it?"

"Does it make you feel small?" you ask.

"Smaller than small," he says with a smile. "And luckier than you'll ever know."

Congratulations, this part of your story is over. You've led a successful expedition, discovered a new source of tyranium crystals, and made new friends. However, have you followed all the paths the story takes?

It is time to make a decision. Do you:

Go back to the beginning of the story? **P163**

Or

Go to the list of choices and start reading from somewhere else in the story? **P308**

You have decided to take the left hand side of the crevasse.

"Let's go left," you say.

"What about the lava?" Gagnon asks. "Aren't you worried about that river of molten rock?"

You laugh. "I'm not planning on swimming in it. Besides, the whole reason we're here is tyranium crystals and if they're going to be found without having to dig for them, we'll need to look around the active vents or find an old lava tube."

Gagnon smiles. "Just be careful. Get too hot and Dagma might think you're a roasted pango and take a bite out of your leg."

"I heard that!" Dagma says with a big toothy grin. "Watch it or you'll be the one I roast over the lava flow."

Gagnon snorts. "For someone who can get lost in their sleeping hammock, you'd be lucky to find a lava flow before it snuck up on you and melted your boots. There's more than one reason they put you on the back of the sledge you know."

Shoola and a couple of the other sliders laugh along with Gagnon. Dagma takes the ribbing well though, she's been right through Slider School with Gagnon and their banter is always good humored.

After the laughter subsides and with the decision made about which direction to go, Piver and the other sliders get to work unloading the pipes, brackets and bolts needed to construct the makeshift bridge.

The other sliders are quick to follow Piver's instructions, so it isn't long before the ladder-bridge is maneuvered across the crevasse and anchored in position. Then the sledges are pushed across.

"Geebus! That's a long way down," Piver says from halfway across. "Don't look down unless you want to fill your pants."

Once everyone is safely on the other side, the bridge is broken down and reloaded onto the sledges.

"Good work everyone," you say. "Let's get moving. We've got a lot of rock to cover before we can make camp."

Gagnon takes off in the lead again, but it isn't long before you wonder if you've made a major mistake. The strip of rock you're sliding on is getting narrower and narrower the further you go and the crevasses on each side are getting wider and deeper. At some points, there is barely enough rock for the sledge's runners to grip on to.

When the terrain begins to slope downhill, sliding on the narrow strip of rock gets really tricky. The screech of hooks from Dagma and Shoola, acting as brakes, is constant as they try to keep the speed under control. Rumblings under foot as the mountain spews more lava adds to the tension.

The next time two crevasses merge you build your bridge so you can head further west, away from the lava, and more importantly, away from the continual earthquakes shaking the ground under your feet. The last thing you want is for one of your sledges to be jolted off course and tumble into a crevasse.

Nerves are on edge as you spend the afternoon sliding, building bridges and watching the volcano erupt. As you get closer the mountain looms larger and steeper and becomes way more dangerous looking. Every few minutes a new burst of smoke and steam shoots skyward, peppering the area with grit and tiny pebbles.

About an hour before dewfall you finally break free of the crevasse field and slide out onto a smooth plateau of rock. The plateau is reasonably flat. Along one side is an old lava flow rising sixty or seventy feet above the surrounding terrain. Some of the cave openings in the old flow look interesting. Rocks as small as your fist and as large as a sledge litter the plateau around you.

Your troop is tired and needs rest before they try to scale Mount Kakona tomorrow in search of tyranium crystals. It is time to make a decision. Do you:

Make camp on the plateau? **P265**

Or

Go check out the caves? **P268**

Take the right hand side and go away from the lava.

You point to the northeast. "Once we're across the crevasse, let's go away from the lava. It'll be safer."

Piver looks at you and chuckles.

"What are you laughing about?" you ask him.

"You said 'safer'. That's like saying jumping off a 100 foot cliff is safer than jumping off a 200 foot cliff. If this baby blows, we're in the bucket whichever way we go."

"I disagree," Gagnon pipes in. "The eastern side's upwind of the volcano. Less chance of getting gassed if that monster belches out hydrogen sulfide."

"Yeah, Piver," you say. "I'm saving you from death by volcano fart so stop complaining."

"Me complain? Never! Besides, I've got no sense of smell. If the worst happens I'll just lay down and go to sleep forever while all of you are on your knees gagging and ralphing your guts out."

A cold shiver runs up your spine. "Thanks for that thought. Remind me to leave you at home next time."

Piver cocks a leg and lets off an explosive fart. "What? And miss out on my sweet music?"

"Holy moly, Piver!" you say pinching your nose. "That smells worse than the south end of a northbound pango. You're on the last sledge from now on, stinky pants."

Piver giggles and slides off to organize the equipment he and the other engineers will need to build a bridge across the crevasse.

About an hour later, once the sledges and members of the expedition are over the chasm, your group slides off towards the volcano. Maybe you'll get lucky and discover an old lava tube full of tyranium crystals on this less active side of the volcano. If not, you'll have to risk investigating further west. Then it will be a matter of avoiding the lava as well as rocks and gas volcanoes tend to eject at random.

Another hour and your group finally clears the crevasse field. Here, nearer the base of the mountain, the cracks in the ground have been filled in with lava from recent eruptions and is almost back to it normal smoothness. Only the odd slump in the surface remains to show where the massive crevasses once were.

One of these slumps still has some water in it from the last rain. It's only two feet deep, but it gives everyone a chance to fill their containers and drink their fill.

The only other irregularities in the smooth landscape is the occasional pressure ridge, where massive plates of rock have been forced together, tilting one plates upwards as the other plate dives beneath it. These ridges give you an awesome respect for the power of nature. They also expose a different strata of rock and are of immense interest to the miners.

Most of these ridges you can work your way around, but as the ground starts to rise in its sweep towards the mountain's summit, a particularly large pressure ridge blocks your path. This plate of hardened lava, nearly 30 feet thick, has been push up and over until it's overhanging.

Gagnon pulls out his scope and starts looking for a way around the obstruction but the ridge runs for quite some distance in each direction. "Might have to winch ourselves over."

You call Drexel over. "How are you at climbing overhangs?"

Drexel borrows Gagnon's scope and scans the huge slab. "Better yet, I'll just launch a cable over the top and zip up. I should be able to negotiate the overhang, then winch the rest of you up and over."

"What about the sledges?" you ask.

Drexel shakes his head. "No way are we going to get the sledges over this, they'll just jam at the top."

Drexel's suggestion is the sensible option. The ground is getting steeper with every step and drilling through the ridge is out of the question.

"Piver!" you call out. "Get a launcher set up and shoot a cable over the top. The rest of you, get packing. Take only what you can carry. Enough for two days."

With excitement, everyone starts sorting gear and equipment. By the time Dagma has finished, her pack is bulging with energy bars.

With a swoosh of compressed air, Piver sends a grapple flying over the pressure ridge. Then he reels it in tight, making sure it's well snagged on the other side. Drexel is quick to attach his harness and pull the trigger on his zipper. Everyone watches as he rises up the line. Once at the top, he swings a leg onto the lip and pulls himself up and over the overhang.

"Okay let's get the lightweight winch hooked up," Piver says.

Once Drexel has hauled the winch up and attached it safely to the rock above, the expedition members are lifted, one by one, up and over the obstruction.

After overseeing the operation from below, you are last to clip on to the cable. The ride up gives you a great view of the surrounding area. When you reach the top, strong hands help you over the lip.

On solid rock again, you pull out your scope and search the slopes of Kakona for any signs of old lava tubes. They are hard to pick out on the smooth black surface as shadows tend to look just like the rock.

But when you see a faint glow coming from a spot about half a mile up the mountain, you wonder if what you're seeing is the light from a moon moth colony or something else. Moths always nest underground, in the mouths of caves, tunnels, or hopefully in this case, the entrance to a tyranium filled lava tube.

"Okay, I see something," you say. "Rope up everyone and keep your hooks ready."

Climbing even a gentle slope would be impossible without the diamond studs on the heels of your boots and your guide stick. But steep ground is made slowly, and anchor bolts need to be put in every twenty yards or so for protection. A few of the Lowlanders, unused to traveling on black glass, have minor slips, but your Highland sliders are quick to arrest their fall.

After a hard climb you finally reach the source of the light. It isn't moon moths, but something much stranger. What you first thought might be light coming from a moth colony, is actually sunlight reflecting off a robot, the likes of which you've never seen.

"What the heck is that?" you say, looking at the snake-like contraption.

Piver slide over for a look. "I think it's a self propelled drill. See, this hole is far too smooth to be a lava tube."

"Okay, but who built it? Trodie, is this something you Lowlanders have built?"

Trodie shakes his head. You can tell by the confusion on Trodie's face that he's telling the truth.

"Looks like it's broken down," Piver says. "The teeth on the front are all twisted out of shape and it's starting to deteriorate in the weather."

Gagnon slides over and looks into the tunnel the machine has drilled. "Maybe we should go in and have a look? There could be crystals down there."

You shrug. "But who would abandon something of such value? Did they find crystals, is that why this machine is still here?" You climb up a few steps to get a better look at the abandoned machine.

Then, as you are about to send a couple sliders down the tunnel to check it out, a waft of something rank hits you. At first you think Piver has farted again, but then you hear a familiar slurping sound, like suction cups being pushed on and off a slightly damp surface and the clacking of sharp teeth.

"Morph rats!" Shoola yells. "Directly uphill!"

Up the slope, about a hundred yards away, you see a wave of the hairless horrors, their teeth gnawing at the air, the slime on their wrinkled bodies reeking of fart.

"Sliders, to me! Emergency wedge formation!" you yell. "Lowlander get in behind."

The six sliders on the mission quickly climb to your position and form themselves into a wedge, each with the hook end of their guide stick pointing forwards towards the threat. Dagma, being the strongest, positions herself at the pointy end of the wedge.

As the plague of rats rolls down the slope toward your position, your troop braces itself and gets ready to sweep the rats left and right as they move like an unstoppable wave down the mountain.

"What are they doing up so high?" Gagnon says. "This can't be happening."

But happening it is. The wave of slimy rats is moving down the hill, their teeth clacking, the stench growing. And they're coming right at you.

"There are too many!" Dagma yell. "We'll never sweep this many aside!"

Your brain throbs as you work on a solution. There must be something you can do! Then you remember the hole drilled in the slope by the strange machine. Anything is better than getting eaten by morph rats.

"Quick, to the hole," you say.

Everyone breaks formation and slides back to the hole. It is dark inside and you don't know where it leads, but the rats are nearly upon you. You either go down the hole now, or get eaten alive.

"Woot woot!" you yell as you slide into the hole. "Follow me!"

After a quick look at the approaching rats, the others don't hesitate.

Once in the hole, the ground slants steeply and keeping your feet isn't an option. In seconds you find yourself on your backside sliding faster and faster into the darkness. You hear a few woot woots behind you, but your main focus is staring at the blackness and hoping you don't run into anything unexpected. Then you remember your headlamp and reach for the switch.

"Geebus!" you hear Piver yell behind you. "This is freaky!"

The little engineer isn't wrong. This is the scariest thing you've ever done. You think of your family and wonder if you'll ever see them again. As you slide deeper into the mountainside, you feel the heat increase. Will this hole end up in a pool of lava somewhere? Was it the heat that twisted the teeth on the strange drilling machine?

When the tunnel makes a sharp turn to the right you nearly lose your lunch. Someone screams behind you. Or was that your hook dragging? Then the slope steepens again and you're in freefall. You headlamp barely shows you ten yards ahead. Seeing almost makes the experience scarier. You close your eyes for a moment. After what seems like ages, the tunnel's angle lessens, and then, finally, you pop out into the light.

You've come to rest on a flat section of rock that overlooks a lake. Around the lake are domed structures made from triangular pieces of black glass, beyond these are orchards and fields.

"Where are we?" Piver asks as he comes to rest beside you. "And what are those strange constructions?"

"That is a very good question," you say, admiring the beautiful buildings.

There are gasps from the others as they slide to a stop. Gagnon is one of the first to his feet. "Look, someone's coming!"

He's right. A girl about your age is walking towards your group. She is wide eyed and staring at your group. But her expression is one of curiosity not fear.

"Hello," the girl says. "You must be the ones from the other side of the cliffs."

You step forwards. "So you know about us?"

The girl laughs. "Of course we do. Our robots have had you under observation for ages."

A tiny robotic bird flies near the girl's shoulder. Its lens of an eye zooming in and out as it observes your group.

"Wow!" Piver says. "You make robotic birds too?"

The girl nods. "We make lots of interesting things."

You look up at the high mountains behind you. "So what now?" you ask. "How do we get home?"

"First you need to come and rest. The settlement is preparing a feast to celebrate your arrival."

"A feast?" Dagma says.

"Yes. For our cousins from over the mountains. We're all related you know."

You hesitate. "But…"

"Hey, she said a feast," Dagma is quick to interject. "Let's not disappoint our new friends." For once, Dagma is right.

The girl smiles. "Once you've eaten and rested, and told us your stories, we'll get you back to your sledges with the tyranium you seek."

"You know about that too?" you ask. "But how?"

The little bird flies to your shoulder, its eye scans you closely, then it flies back to the girl.

"Our tiny friends miss very little," the girl says.

And then as the sun drops below the ridge and you start to feel a dampness in the air, you hear a long blast from a whistle.

"Come, dinner's ready," the girl says. "I hope you brought an appetite with you."

You look over at a grinning Dagma. "Oh yeah. We never travel without one of those."

Congratulations, this part of your story is over. You've discovered a new settlement, been promised the tyranium you seek and are about to enjoy a feast in your honor. Well done.

But have you tried all the paths this story can take?

It is time to make a decision. Do you:

Go back to the beginning of the story and try a different path?
P163

Or

Go to the list of choices and read a different chapter? **P308**

You have decided to make camp on the plateau.

"Okay let's fire up the burners and get some broth heating," you say. "Piver, would you please get the hammocks and tarps up."

Everyone works together and before long you're sitting around a warm burner with a hot cup of broth in your hands. After getting some food in their bellies your troop is starting to tell stories and joke with each other. Some even sing songs.

As the sun goes down, a light dew falls across the slopes, making it dangerous to move out of camp. Damp rock is way too slippery, even for sliders with guide sticks and diamond-studded boots.

Still, with the anti-slip mats down, and your hammocks and tarps up, there is no need to go anywhere. But then just as you're starting to relax, you feel the ground shake and the crash of rocks landing on the slopes around you.

"Eruption!" Gagnon yells as everyone leaps to their feet.

The next big shake knocks you back to the ground and rocks smack into the ground only yards away.

"We're sitting pangos here," Piver says. "We've got to get to the caves or we're going to get flattened."

But how are you going to get to the caves? Dew has fallen and the rock is too slick.

Then, a huge rock smashes one of the sledges into a million fragments. Your protective tarps and a row of hammocks are taken with it, turning your camp into a disaster zone.

More rocks fall, hitting members of your troop.

As you crawl to your knees, wondering what to do, it is Piver that makes a move.

"Quick, clip on to this," he says picking up a length of cable. Piver fires a couple anchor bolts into the rock and quickly attaches the end of the cable to it.

As another shake shudders through the slope and more rocks crash into your camp, only six of you manage to clip on to Piver's lifeline.

Piver runs the cable through a ring on his harness and then grabs your arm, pulling you to the far right hand side of the camp's safety mats. "Everyone over here, we need to run and throw ourselves off the left side of the mat far as we can. Ready?"

"I hope you know what you're doing," you say.

"Got another plan?" Piver yells. He gives you a stern look. "No I didn't think so. Right on three, two, one go!"

And with that the six of you run as fast as you can and throw yourself onto the slippery rock.

"Woot woot!" you yell.

At first, as you slide in a straight line, Piver pays out cable. But then, as gravity takes hold and it starts dragging you down, you and the others become the pendulum on the end of a long piece of cable. Suddenly you reach the end of the cable you change direction and start swinging back below the camp and over towards the entrances to the caves in the old lava flow.

You and the others are really moving now, sliding across the rock in a perfect arc. Piver grabs a handheld launcher from his utility belt and points it at the lava flow as your reach the end of your swing. Just as you're group starts to slow, he pulls the trigger and the bolt streaks out and lodges in the rock of the old lava.

"Got it!" Piver says.

After unclipping from the long cable the six of you pull yourselves over to the cave's entrance and duck inside. And not a moment too soon

Another eruption and rocks are landing all over your abandoned camp.

You and the other survivors work your way deeper into the cave, helped by the faint glow of a moon moth colony nesting near the entrance. Once you're well out of the firing line, you sit and shake your head at your mistakes.

You should have realized those rocks on the plateau had been thrown from the volcano. Why didn't you make camp in the safety of the cave from the very beginning? Then you wouldn't have lost half of the members of your expedition and 95 percent of your supplies.

Unfortunately this part of your story is over. You will be doing well just to get back to the Pillars of Haramon, let alone bring any tyranium crystals with you.

However you still have a decision to make.

There are three choices. Do you:

Change your mind and go check out the caves? **P268**

Or

Go to the beginning of the story and try another path? **P163**

Or

Go to the list of choices and start reading from another part of the story? **P308**

You have decided to check out the caves.

"Let's head towards the caves," you tell your group. "There are too many rocks being ejected from Kakona for us to camp out in the open."

As if to illustrate your point, a rock about the size of a fully grown pango slams into the slope not more than 100 yards away.

"Geebus!" Piver says. "Let's get a move on. That was a bit close."

Without wasting any more time, you slide towards the old lava flow. The first couple of caves you find are quite small and don't go into the rock very far. But then you find one that looks more suitable. It has a flat section near its opening for setting up the burners, plenty of room for the sledges, and good spots to hang hammocks. A little way in, the cave meets up with a much larger tunnel that runs up and down the mountain.

"I wonder how far this lava tube goes?" says Gagnon. "It's huge. Who knows, there might even be crystals in it."

You agree with your navigator. "Let's have a bite to eat and a good sleep. We can get some extra lights and go exploring in the morning."

Most of the troop is only interested in food. Unpacking the burners and getting some broth on the heat is always high on the Slider Corps priority list.

You notice that Trodie is particularly interested in the cave. "So, you think this is an old lava tube eh?"

"It's a lava tube alright. See those ridges along the walls? They mark the level of different flows that have come through here."

Trodie runs his hand along one of the distinctive lines in the rock. "So how do you know if it's still active or not?"

You shrug. "That's the problem. You don't. That's why we'll camp in the smaller offshoot near the entrance and not in the main tunnel."

Trodie shakes his head. "I don't know how you Highlanders survive up here. It's so much safer in the Lowlands."

You laugh. "You've got a point. But then life is what you're used to.

I can't imagine what living on the flat would be like. It would seem strange without the views, the howling wind and the slick black rock."

Trodie is quiet as he looks off into the darkness. You suspect he's thinking about his home far below. You doubt he's the only one.

Piver breaks Trodie's trance by handing him a steaming cup of broth. "Here you go LoLa, wrap your lips around this."

"Thanks, HiLa," Trodie says in reply, giving the little engineer a wink.

You chuckle under your breath at how well Trodie's handled Piver's slight insult and wonder if he's made up HiLa on the spot, or if it's a term in common usage down in the Lowlands.

Language, and slang in particular, is an interesting topic, but a sharp twinge in your stomach reminds you how hungry you are. It's been a long hard slide and your nerves have taken a beating today. What you really want is a nice steaming bowl of hydro and a good night's sleep.

Thankfully, the night passes uneventfully, despite being woken by a major rock shower just after climbing into your hammock. It's just as well you chose to camp in the cave, otherwise your group would have been in serious trouble.

The next morning you wake up early. The air outside is fresh and clear. The volcano has taken a nap and has stopped throwing rocks all over the slopes around you. While the rest of the troop sleeps, you decide to strap on a headlamp and check out the main lava tube.

After a quick slide down, and zipping back up, you see that there hasn't been enough pressure for crystals to form. By the time you get back up to the others, Dagma has got the burner going and the troop is sitting around it stuffing their faces.

Grabbing some food, you sit with the others. "Okay everyone, the volcano's taking a break, so let's eat fast and get moving. Who know how long it will be before Kakona blows its top again."

Gagnon looks up. "Don't you want to check out the lava tube?"

"I've just had a look. This tube is too fresh for crystals."

Gagnon looks disappointed, but being the slider he is, he takes the news with his normal calm. "Time to climb a volcano then."

"We'll leave the sledges and free climb from this point," you say. "Pack just enough for two days, nothing more. The terrain is going to get steep and we'll need to move fast."

Within twenty minutes everyone is packed and ready to go. But as you stand in the caves entrance, a massive boom blasts the top fifty feet of Kakona into a million pieces, sending a great plume of steam and rock into the air.

The shock wave from the explosion, hits you a few seconds later, knocking everyone but Dagma and Shoola off their feet.

"Holy moly!" Piver says, dusting himself off.

Then the rain of rocks begins.

"Get back!" you yell.

Rocks and boulders start landing all over the slope. Some are so large they shake the ground when they slam into the slope. Hundreds of thousands of cubic yards of material fall in a wide arc around the mountain creating havoc. Boulders roll like wrecking balls down the slope, crushing everything in their path. Everyone moves deeper into the cave.

As the rocks continued to fall, your group cowers in the main lava tube, hands over heads and thankful for the solid protection over your heads. A few rocks bounce into the cave, but are stopped by the sledges which suffer minor damage.

Finally, when the rocks stopped falling, you and the others move toward the cave's entrance, not quite knowing what you'll find.

When you reach the cave's mouth and look outside, dust fills the air, blocking out the sun's rays. But after a few minutes, the breeze clears the dust away.

Many rocks cover the plateau outside. Only they aren't just rocks. Amongst the basalt and black glass are chunks of tyranium the size of your head. Hundreds of them.

Piver's grin is so wide, he's in danger of splitting his head in two. He runs out and picks up a huge crystal. "It's raining gems, holy moly, it's raining gems," he says as he does a funny little jiggle.

"You're crazy, Piver," you say to the little engineer.

As you exit the cave and walk amongst the material the volcano spat out, you see more tyranium lying on the ground than your troop could carry back with a dozen sledges. It's only the rocks that have landed on flat ground that haven't slid off into the crevasse field further down the mountain. But that's still quite a lot.

But it's when you look up at the mountain, that you realize the magnitude of what just happened. Kakona's once majestic cone is now a row of broken teeth.

It is a time of awe and gratitude. Imagine what would have happened if your troop had been out on the plateau. Not one would have survived. And by the look on everyone's faces, they are well aware of this.

After making some quick repairs, the sledges are loaded with as many crystals as they'll carry, aftershocks rumble under your feet. Everyone works hard in their desire to leave this place as quickly as possible.

"We can't take it all. Leave some for next time people," You say as you inspect the strapping on the sledges yourself. "The last thing we want is an unstable load causing an accident on the way home."

Sliding downhill is always more dangerous. Once a heavy sledge gets moving, it's a hard thing to stop.

Within an hour you've ordered everyone to get ready to move out. They don't need to be told twice. The ground is trembling and lava still flows down the flanks of Kakona.

"That's it, we're ready," Piver says. "Let's go home."

The trip back is slow. Maneuvering the heavy sledges over the bridges takes twice the time. When the Tyron Cliffs appear in the distance everyone's spirits are raised.

"Woot, woot!" the Highlanders call out. "Woot, woot!"

When your group reaches the cliffs, you call a halt. "We'll stay here tonight."

"As least its mainly downhill from here," Trodie says. "I can't say how pleased I'll be to get back to the Pillars."

"And then home eh?" you say. "Back to your family."

Trodie nods. "Yeah, and some flat ground for a change. Up here I feel I'm always on a lean."

After slinging your hammock, you're pleased to take the weight off your sore feet. The slide back to the Pillars of Haramon should be routine, assuming the weather holds.

As you lie back, you wonder if you'll get a star for your efforts. You have no doubt your expedition has exceeded the council's wildest dreams. You also feel you've forged a strong bond with Trodie and the other Lowlanders. This is a real bonus, especially with the Lowlanders and Highlanders struggling to maintain a truce.

The next morning, as you move out, all you can think about is getting everyone home safe. But it isn't until your group reaches the top of Long Gully, for the long slide down to the Pillars of Haramon, that you finally start to relax.

"The Pillars!" Gagnon yells out. "I can see them!"

And then, you can see them too. Never before have the two shimmering black monoliths looked so beautiful. As you sweep down the gulley in a series of S-turns the whole of Petron opens out before you. Past the Pillars, off in the distance, the Lowlands stretch out towards the sea. Petron's smallest moon has risen and sits just above the horizon. The sun in low. Dewfall will be soon. If you hurry, you'll have just enough time to get home.

But despite your rush, for a moment, the expedition slows down and comes to a stop. For almost a minute, the only sound is the faint screeching of a distant pango colony. Then you hear movement beside you. It's Piver.

"Geebus," the engineer says. "Isn't that just the most beautiful site you've ever seen?"

Congratulations, this part of your story is over. You've made it back from the Volcano of Fire and brought a big load of tyranium needle crystals back with you. You've also helped cement friendly relations with the Lowlanders. Well done!

But it is time to make another decision. Do you:

Go back to the beginning of the story and try another path? **P163**

Or

Go to the list of choices and start reading from another part of the story? **P308**

You have decided to go up and around the Tyron Cliffs.

"Well if we've got to climb, we may as well do it while we're fresh," you say.

Gagnon nods. "Righto, it's uphill then. I'll start planning. At least the maps we've got of this side of the mountain aren't too bad."

You nod. "But who knows what we'll find on the other side eh?"

Gagnon smiles. "Well, as the old saying goes, you've got to break open a pango's egg to find out if it's rotten."

Suddenly you hear Piver break out in laughter.

You stab him a look. "What now?"

"That saying is sillier than brain dead pango," Piver says. "Any engineer knows rotten eggs float."

"It's a metaphor, Piver," Gagnon says. "No need to take things so literally."

After the loading has finished, everyone starts the long climb.

Dagma and Shoola lead the charge by climbing a hundred yards, using toe studs and then putting in an anchor bolt. Then the sledges are winched by hand up the slope. Then another slider takes their turn climbing and the others repeat the process.

By mid afternoon you realize you've made a mistake. This is taking far too long. The terrain is too steep for sledges, and even if you did find a load of tyranium, you'd never get a sledge load of the crystal back down the mountain without someone getting injured or worse.

You drop your hook and come to a stop. "Stop everyone, this is crazy. We're going to have to come up with another solution."

Drexel see his opportunity. "Let me try to climb over. It will save us so much time."

You look at Drexel and then up at the sheer wall of black glass. "But it's straight up!"

"It's steep alright, but I reckon it's possible."

"I'm willing to give it a go," Trodie says. "Us Lowlanders can climb too you know."

"Race!" Dagma yells. "Woot! Woot!"

The others on the expedition like the idea too. Everyone likes a race, especially when it means that they can stop climbing for a while and rest their weary legs.

"High, high, high, high!" the Highlanders chant.

"Low, low, low, low!" The Lowlanders reply.

You look at the smiling faces around you. "Okay, looks like we have two contestants who want to be the first to climb the Tyron Cliffs."

Then you think about safety. A race on such a treacherous cliff might tempt one of the climbers into taking one chance too many. You're determined to get home without losing anyone. But what can you do?

You climb onto a sledge and point up. "This is a dangerous climb and racing is risky. Just getting up this monster cliff will be an amazing effort. But we risk our lives every day on the Black Slopes and it's important that someone manages to climb it. So I'll open the challenge up to anyone who wants to try it."

Trodie and Drexel start sorting out the gear they'll need for the climb. Then you see that Piver is also sorting gear out.

"What the heck do you think you're doing, Piver?" you ask.

Piver looks up from his task. "You did say anyone could climb didn't you?"

"Sure but…"

Then Piver pulls out a couple of his hand launchers, and tucks them into his utility belt. Another couple he stuffs into his jacket. "I have a plan," he says, a big grin on his face. "I may not be the best climber, but I can zip faster than anyone because I'm light."

"You're crazy, Piver," you say. "But I like the way you think."

"High, high, high, high!" the Highlanders chant.

"Low, low, low, low!" the Lowlanders reply.

As the three climbers approach the wall, everyone else gathers around.

Trodie and Drexel are kitted out with the more traditional climbing gear of needle crystal picks, anchor bolts, and lightweight cables. In addition, they each have an extra spike strapped onto the front of their boots.

Piver, despite having nowhere near as much gear as the others, looks relaxed with only a few anchors and some light-weight cable in his pack.

"We'll start the climb when I say go," you say. "I know this is a race, but please be careful. You don't win if you're a messy splat on the rock."

The excitement builds. Everyone is jostling for the best positions to watch the action.

You lift your arm. "On my mark! Three … two … one … Go!"

And with that, Trodie and Drexel start kicking their toe spikes into the rock and swinging their picks. For every two kicks and two chops, the climbers gain a little bit of altitude.

"I said go, Piver!"

"Yeah, I know." Piver turns and walks away from the wall, until he's about 10 yards back. Then he pulls one of his hand launcher out of his jacket and takes aim.

With a hiss of air, a tiny bolt rockets out of the launcher and embeds itself into the rock fifteen meters up. Then to the shock of the other two climbers, Piver pulls the trigger, runs towards the wall, and the hand-launcher zips him up and past them.

"Woot! Woot!" the Highlanders yell."

"Hey!" Drexel says. "That's cheating!"

Piver looks down and giggles. "Show me that in the rule book, Pango brain!"

While Drexel argues the point, Trodie keeps climbing and moves into second place.

Then Piver's real plan is revealed. He starts pushing himself away from the wall, swinging on the cable. As he come back to the cliff face each time, his short muscular legs act like a coiled spring. The fourth time he springs back, he fires another bolt up the cliff. Then, after removing the first bolt, he zips up. As he repeats the process, he gains altitude and quickly and leaves the other climbers behind.

It doesn't take long before Drexel and Trodie realize that Piver is going to win the climbing race by a huge margin. Not because he's the best climber, but because he had the best plan.

"High, high, high, high!" the Highlanders cheer as Piver nears the top.

Trodie and Drexel decide to save their strength and rappel back down. They leave Piver to continue on to the win.

"Geebus!" Piver cheers as he reaches the top. "I win! Bow before me, lowly Petronians."

"Well done Piver, but cut the boasting. Nobody likes a braggart," you yell up to him. "Now send a line down so the rest of us can get over these cliffs!"

Piver giggles and sends a thin line down to where you are waiting. You tie a stronger cable on to this and he pulls it up and feeds it through a pulley he's anchored to the rock.

"We'll just take one sledge with us from here," you say to your troop. "It will take too much time and energy to haul both of them up."

Just over an hour later your troop is on top of the Tyron Cliffs. On this side of the obstacle, the ground slopes gently down to a reasonably flat plateau. Beyond the plateau, the volcano sweeps up to a mighty cone shrouded in purple mist, and oozing lava.

With only one sledge, you've got plenty of muscle for pulling once your troop has negotiated the slope down to the plateau. A quick change of rig and you've four pullers harnessed up for the ten mile slide to the foot of Kakona.

The only thing that gives you concern are the rocks you see scattered about the otherwise featureless landscape.

"These rocks must have been thrown out of Kakona at some stage," you say to Gagnon, pointing to a shiny black beast the size of the sledge not more than a few hundred yards away. "I'm feeling a little exposed out here. What about you?"

"I was thinking that too," Gagnon says. "Let's just hope Kakona doesn't need to sneeze today."

Half way across the plateau Piver yells for you all to stop. "That boulder over there looks interesting. I want to check it out."

You call for a break while Piver slides over to the rock that's caught his eye.

"I've never see red crystals like this before," he says, inspecting a streak down one side of the boulder. He takes his small blue diamond pick out of his utility belt. "I'll just test how hard it is."

Piver raises the pick and swings it onto the red rock. "Geebus!" Piver says as the pick bounces off the rock and flies out his hand. "It's harder than blue diamond!"

"But that's impossible," you hear one of the others mumble. "Blue diamonds are the hardest thing on the planet."

"Not anymore," Piver says looking for a dent or some other indication of where he hit the rock with his pick. "Not a scratch!"

You walk to the sledge and grab a larger pick. "Here you go Dagma, take a swing and see what you can do."

Dagma is always happy to show off her strength. She unhooks her harness and slides over to the rock with the big pick in her hands. She braces herself, feet wide, heel studs jammed into the black rock at her feet. Then with a roundhouse swing, she takes aim at the red section of rock.

Twang! Clatter, clatter goes the pick as it bounces off the rock and skitters away from where Dagma is standing.

Again Piver checks for a mark. "Nothing!"

"Wow," Trodie says.

"Wow," Shoola says.

"Holy moly," you say. "So what now, Piver? This boulder is too big to fit on the sledge."

"No worries," Piver says. "We'll chop all the basalt off and just load the crystal. Nobody at home is going to believe what we've found."

"So what will we use it for?" you ask.

Piver giggles. "Are you kidding me? We'll be able to drill into black glass twice as fast. We can make tunnels we never dreamed of, make tools to cut steps and form tracks … Geebus, all sorts of stuff."

"But it's not tyranium," you say. "That's what we've been sent to find."

This time Piver's booming laugh echoes across the plateau. "It's better. Believe me, the council are going to think this is the best expedition of all time. Look at the size of it."

Gagnon slides over. "Piver's right you know. It wouldn't surprise me if they give you a promotion for this."

Everyone is in good spirits as they work, chipping the basalt off the boulder. In the end, you are left with a red diamond that takes four sliders to lift.

After strapping the diamond carefully onto the sledge and covering it with a tarp, you start the trip back the way you came. With the sledge being overloaded, it takes you twice the length of time to get back past the Tryon Cliffs and along the tracks to the top of Long Gully.

It takes a couple days to retrace your slide, but the closer you get to home, the more animated your troop becomes. Everyone is laughing and telling jokes. Some sing songs. Dagma, knowing that more food is close to hand, has no hesitation in eating her last two energy bars.

Finally, after camping out for two more nights, the shimmering Pillars of Haramon appear in the distance. It is only then that you truly feel your mission has been a success.

Crew from the base are outside the loading bay when your sledges pull up. You can even see they've put a burner on for broth.

"How did it go?" one of the crew asks. "Find anything?"

"No nothing," Piver says trying to keep a straight face. "Except a great big red diamond! Geebus, you should see the size of it!"

Congratulations you've finished this part of the story. You've led a successful mission and found red diamonds that will help in your community's efforts to build the much needed trade routes between the Highlands and the Lowlands.

But have you followed all the different paths the story takes?

It is time for you to make another decision. Do you:

Go to the beginning of the story and try a different path? **P163**

Or

Go to the list of choices and start reading from a different part of the story? **P308**

You have decided to go down and around the Tyron Cliffs.

You point at the contour marks on Gagnon's map. "I don't think the Lowlanders will be able to handle the steep terrain if we go up. I'm not even sure that we can. We'd better go down and around."

Gagnon nods. "Let's just hope everyone's legs hold out on the climb back up."

It is a risk, but what else can you do? You're convinced there will be accidents if you try to push a route up. Previous volcanic activity has left the upper slope littered with obstacles. And then there's the matter of the thin air. Less oxygen means tired muscles.

"Okay everyone," you say. "Three brakes in the back, one up front steering. And keep your speed down. These sledges are heavy. If they get away on you, you'll be going to the bottom and not in a good way."

Gagnon and Shoola move to the back of their respective sledges and organize the extra sliders. You and Gagnon, being the most experienced sliders, take control of the steering runners at attach yourselves to the front. Trodie and Piver free-slide while the others climb aboard the sledges.

You let Gagnon, the better navigator, lead off. "We'll keep the cliffs in sight," he says. "But be ready to stop in a hurry, this area isn't fully mapped and who knows what we'll find."

With that said, he leads off with a slight push of his stick. Gravity does the rest.

The screech of hooks is a constant companion as your group works its way down the mountain. Dagma, Shoola and the other sliders are working hard to keep the sledges from gaining too much momentum during the turns.

Gagnon takes a zigzag route. A quarter mile away from the cliffs and then a quarter mile back, keeping the sledges side on the slopes as much as possible.

You're just beginning to think the day is going to go by without incident when you hear a yell from the front sledge.

It's Gagnon, calling for an emergency stop.

"What is it?" you call. "Why are we stopping?"

"Take your light and shine it on the ground at your feet," he says.

"Why?"

"Just do it. You'll see what I mean."

Confused, you detach the headlamp from your helmet and point it towards the ground. As the bright light nears the surface, you see the beam penetrate the black glass and go right through to the other side. "What the—"

Then you realize what Gagnon's trying to say. You're not on solid ground at all. Your troop is traveling across a glass bridge suspended over a massive crevasse. Sure, black glass is tough stuff, but here it can't be more than a six inches thick.

"Holy moly," you say under your breath. "I wonder how deep the crevasse is."

"Stay where you are," Gagnon say. "Best if we move one at a time."

"What's going on?" Dagma asks

"We're sliding on a glassed-over crevasse," you say, trying to keep the fear out of your voice. "I don't suggest you stomp around at the moment, otherwise you might break through."

"Geebus," Piver says, having overheard. "I'm glad I'm not riding on a sledge."

You give Piver a sharp glance for scaring the Lowlanders. "The weight's spread evenly over the runners," you say. "Don't worry, everyone will be fine."

Or at least you hope they'll be fine.

With a wave you signal Gagnon to move out. "We'll stay here until you get on to solid rock. Signal us when you're clear."

The first sledge slides slowly downhill. Gagnon has his headlamp strapped to his right thigh so the light shines down on the ground in front of him. He slides another twenty yards before the glass no longer allows the light to penetrate and he screeches to a stop and waves.

"Okay everyone, it's our turn. Slow and easy now," you say with a slight push. "No sudden movements."

Your shoulders tighten as the sledge slides towards Gagnon. Faint tinking sounds vibrate through the ground as the crystalline structure of the glass fractures as the weighty sledge passes over it.

It isn't until you've reached Gagnon that you breathe easy. "I don't want to do that again in a hurry," you say. "That was way too freaky."

"Unfortunately, these bridges look just like the ground until you're on them," Gagnon says. "We can only cross our fingers and hope there aren't many more."

Then you have a thought. "Hey, Gagnon. I want you to disconnect and scout out front. We'll put Drexel on the front of your sledge."

Gagnon nods. "Good idea. If I see a glass bridge, we can head closer to the cliffs where the ground will be more solid."

As you look out over the landscape you see the Tyron Cliffs stretch off in the distance. Another day of this is going to test your nerve. The air is cool as you suck it into your lungs. You try to admire the beauty around you rather than think of the possible dangers. Worrying about something you can't change is pointless. You've been given a job and all you can do is your best. But before you have time to move out again. Piver breaks the silence.

"Hey," the little engineer says. "I've got an idea."

Please to hear any idea that might make your expedition a success, you look towards Piver. "Okay I'm listening."

"Well," Piver says. "This huge crevasse we've just slid over…"

"Yes?"

"I wonder how far it goes?"

You don't quite understand what Piver is trying to get at. "Why does that matter?"

"Well what if it cuts under the cliffs? What if we can break through the glass surface of the bridge and use the crevasse as a tunnel under the cliffs?"

You have a think for a moment. "Gagnon? What do you think?"

You can see that the navigator is thinking hard about Piver's theory. "It's worth checking out I suppose," Gagnon says.

You nod, "My thoughts exactly."

"Okay, Piver, let's do it. Just be careful, I don't want you falling in."

Piver giggles nervously. "You're not the only one."

Piver searches through the gear on the sledges and finds a bright chemical light and a couple of extra anchor-bolt guns. He puts in one anchor and hooks a line to his harness. Then he slowly walks back out looking for the edge of the crevasse.

About ten yards out, he stops. "Okay, this is where the solid rock ends. Time to find out how hard this glass really is."

You know that black glass is very strong in some ways, but not so strong in others. It can withstand huge pressure, but is not very shock resistant. Bridges have been known to hold a weighty sledge and then shatter when someone drops a cup of broth.

Piver points an anchor-bolt gun at the glassy surface, lowers his visor, and pulls the trigger. *Bang!* The anchor-bolt slams into the surface. At first nothing happens. Then you hear a faint tinkling sound and you know that a shock wave is running through the glass weakening it.

Bang! In goes the second bolt.

This time the ground at Piver's feet cracks into a thousand pieces and crashes down into the crevasse. Piver only just manages to jump back in time.

"Wow!" he cries. "Did you see that!"

You move a little closer and look through the gaping hole Piver's created. The crevasse is deep, but there is a narrow ledge running along its side about twenty feet down.

"Looks like a series of earthquakes have caused this," you say, looking down. "I wonder if this ledge runs all the way under the cliffs?"

"I could check it out," Piver says.

You admire Piver's courage. "Let's both check it out eh?" You turn towards the others. "Hey, Dagma, would you please get some cable and lower us down?"

As your feet touch the ledge a few minutes later, you're pleased it slopes towards the wall and not the other way. At least you won't need to worry about slipping off into the void. You switch on your headlamp and push off. "Stay close, Piver."

As you and Piver slide along the narrow ledge, it doesn't take long before the light coming through the hole in the surface fades. The light from your headlamp begins to show up tiny specks of blue and red in the shiny black walls of the crevasse.

"It's like looking into the sky on a clear night," Piver says behind you.

The further you go, the bigger the flecks becomes. The scene is mesmerizing. You slide on in a semi-trance admiring the beauty before you.

"We must be under the cliffs," Piver says. "The added pressure has formed crystals."

Within another fifty yards, the wall has gone from having flecks to having wide veins of blue and red crystals.

"Wow, it's like another world down here," you say. "Like a dream."

"You do realize this wall is full of tyranium and diamonds don't you?" Piver says. "I'm not sure what the red is, but it looks like diamond with a faint trace of something else in it."

"Can we mine it?" you ask.

"Geebus yes! We've struck the jackpot."

The place you've discovered is so beautiful you don't want to leave. "I suppose we'd better get back and tell the others."

Piver sits on the ledge, his legs dangling over the edge. "Maybe we could just sit and enjoy it for a while?"

You sit down beside the little engineer and breathe a sigh of relief. "What a good idea, Piver. We'll never have the opportunity to see this for the first time again. We should enjoy the moment."

In a few minutes you'll let the other know what you've found, but for now you just want to take it all in.

"This has got to be the biggest find in history," Piver says. "We're gonna be famous. Our grandchildren will talk of this find."

"I suppose they will. I just hope it doesn't change us too much," you say. "I like my life at the moment. All I ever wanted to be was a member of the Highland Slider Corps."

Piver sneaks you a glance and grins. "Geebus, you'll always be one of those. Didn't they tell you when you signed up? It's a lifetime contract!"

Congratulations. This part of your story is over. You've lead a successful mission and found a rich source of tyranium and diamonds. Your community will be very pleased. But have you tried all the paths? Have you been to the interior? Or the volcano?

It is time to make one of these three decisions. Do you.

Go back to the beginning and try a different path? **P163**

Or

Go to the list of choices and start reading from another part of the story? **P308**

Or

Go read about the history of Petron. **P305**

You have decided to go check out the spaceship.

"Let go check it out," you say. "If they've come all this way to find us the least we can do is say hello."

Gagnon frowns. "But what if they're unfriendly?"

"If they're smart enough to build a craft that can travel though space, surely they must be smart enough to realize that fighting is just a waste of time and resources."

Gagnon doesn't seem convinced by your argument so you give him a choice, "Well I'm going to check them out. I'll leave it up to the rest of you if you want to join me."

The two of you slide back down to camp and explain to the others what you've found. Everybody but Villum is excited and wants to come along.

"Okay Villum, you stay here and guard the sledge. We'll see you in a while."

"Pango head," Piver mumbles under his breath. "What sort of idiot doesn't want to check out a space ship?"

As you slide towards the ship, more of its detail becomes visible. The outer covering is made from tiny metallic feathers of gold and silver. Ports in the ship's side have covers that open and close like the iris of your eyes.

"Geebus!" Piver says. "It's a beautiful piece of engineering."

When your group is twenty yards away. A port opens and a set of steps swing out. A person, in uniform, walks out onto the top step and waves.

"Ahoy there!"

"Wow," you say. "They speak our language."

After sliding a little closer you see that the young person is a female about your age. Her long dark hair is braided and coiled on top of her head.

"Gre—Greetings." you say.

"Thanks," she says with a smile. "Are you the leader of this group?"

"Yes."

"Would you like to step aboard so we can talk? I mean you no harm."

You look over at Piver and then at Gagnon. Both are nodding their heads. The girl seems friendly. "Well um … okay."

She takes you to a small control room and offers you a seat. "This must be a shock for you."

"It is a bit. What brings you here?"

"My name is Helena. I'm commander of this landing pod from the *Victoria II* which is currently in orbit. Long ago, our ancestors discovered this planet while looking for a new home. On their travels between the stars, they sent three landing craft full of settlers and equipment down to this planet's surface in the hopes that they would establish colonies here and prosper."

You look at Helena. "You seem so young to be a commander. How do you know how to fly this thing?"

"I'm not much younger than you. But to answer your question, while we sleep in our cryo-chambers, we learn all sorts of things, we just don't age much. I've been trained in communications, languages, navigation and I'm a fully qualified pilot. I've been woken up to come down and see how our cousins on Petron are doing."

"So we're related, your people and mine?" you ask, still trying to get your head around what the girl is saying.

"Yes. Distantly. The results of our survey show that descendants of all three groups have survived."

"Three groups?"

"Yes, three. The Highlanders, those you call Lowlanders and descendents of Eve, whose family settled in the jungle of the interior."

"There are people in the interior?"

"Yes, you've been heading in their direction for the last couple days. Once you reach the eastern end of this mountain range you will start finding their settlements."

Your head is spinning with all this new information. So the crazy miner who found tyranium in the interior has already met these people?" you ask.

"He was one of our scouts gathering information."

"Are these people in the interior dangerous?" you ask.

The girl laughs. "No not at all as long as you're honest with them. And they're keen to start trading now that the Highlanders and the Lowlanders have settled your differences and have called a truce. They have plenty of tyranium crystals to trade. They have advanced mining machines and other technology you Highlanders haven't developed yet. Trade will be good for all three settlements."

This news sounds great. "But what do they want in return?" you ask.

The girl smiles. "It seems our inland cousins have grown rather fond of roast pango. Something I believe you Highlanders have in great abundance."

You can't help but laugh. "Tyranium for pangos? Sounds like a good deal to me."

Helena stands and calls out some instructions to her crew. "Would you like to take a quick trip with me to set up a meeting? It will only take a few minutes to get to their settlement in our ship and will save you a few days slide."

"Fly in your machine? Really?"

"Sure, we have room for you and one other if you like."

You know exactly who to take along on the trip. From the top of the step you look down at the rest of your troop. "Gagnon, can you take charge for a few hours, I'm going to go find us some tyranium."

Gagnon nods.

"Piver, would you like to come for a ride?"

Piver's eyes pop with excitement. "Really? Me?"

"Yes you. Now hurry up and climb aboard."

The little engineer wastes no time getting up the steps. He caresses the hull of the ship as he enters through the portal. "Geebus!" Piver say. "This thing is amazing."

Piver's excitement is contagious. Soon both of you have wide grins on your faces.

"Okay, buckle up for takeoff," the young commander says pointing you to a couple of seats.

The door closes and you feel a low vibration run through the hull of the ship. Then, you feel the ship lift off.

"I'll leave the viewport open so you can see the sights," the young commander says.

Then, as if by magic, the craft streaks off around the last of the mountains before turning northwest towards a large lake in the distance.

"Oh, there's one thing I forgot to tell you. Although all Petronians have some plant DNA spliced into them so they can breathe the carbon dioxide rich atmosphere here on this planet, those of the interior are almost as much plant as they are human. So don't be surprised if they grow a tendril and wrap it around your hand. It's just their way of being friendly."

"Geebus!" Piver says, having the time of his life. "This should be interesting!"

Congratulations. This part of your story is over. You're off to set up a meeting with the people of the interior to exchange pangos for the tyranium your communities need. You've also made contact with the *Victoria II* and learned some interesting facts about your planet's history But have you tried all the different paths this story can take? Have you been to Crater Canyon, or the volcano, Kakona? Have you fought off the morph rats or discovered giant crystals?

It is now time to make another decision. Do you:

Go back to the beginning of the story and try another path? **P163**

Or

Go to the list of choices and read a different chapter? **P308**

You have decided to observe the spaceship from a distance.

You look through your scope at the ship again. "I don't see any movement over there. Maybe whoever's in that thing hasn't seen us yet."

Gagnon instinctively crouches down as you continue to study the craft.

"So what do you think?" Gagnon asks. "Should we get the heck out of here?"

You shake your head. "No let's get back to the others and tell them to keep hidden. I want to hang around and find out what this thing is up to."

The troop is in the process of packing up when you and Gagnon slide back into camp. "Quiet everyone. There's been a development."

As you explain what you've seen, there are a variety of reactions. Dagma wants to slide right over to the ship and demand to know what they're doing on the Black Slopes. Piver wants to go over too, but so that he can study the craft from an engineering perspective.

A nervous Villum wants to slide home as fast as possible and then come back in force, while Trodie is interested in the newcomers but cautious.

You pull Trodie aside. "What we do now could have big consequences. Any suggestions?"

Trodie scratches the back of his neck as he thinks. "This could be a good thing. I mean why would they come all this way just to hurt us? There are billions of planets out there. What are the chances of them finding ours unless they knew we were here to begin with?"

"You think they've been here before?"

Trodie shrugs. "It's possible. And isn't that what the *Book of Myths* says?"

"But those stories aren't real." And then you realize how silly what you just said was. "Or are they?"

"Maybe we should go check it out. Find out once and for all."

You are about to agree with Trodie when you feel a low vibration in your chest. When you look across the slope, you see that the disk is off the ground and a strange blue light is radiating from it. Once it's a hundred feet or so off the ground, the ship takes off like a bolt of lightning into the sky.

"Geebus, look at it go!" Piver says, twisting his neck so he can follow the ship's path.

Within seconds, all you can see is a blue speck high overhead.

"Look," Piver says, pointing upwards. "There's another one!"

A larger ship has come over the horizon and is heading towards the disk that has just taken off.

"It's going back to the mother ship." Trodie says. "That's written about in the book too."

"… *and children of the mother ship were sent to seed the planet,*" you quote from the *Book of Myths*, remembering the stories you've read ever since you were a child.

Trodie shrugs. "I'm not normally one to believe in fairytales, but I'm willing to change my mind when presented with solid evidence."

"So do we carry on in our mission, or do we go back and report this?" Gagnon says.

"I want to see the spot where it landed," Piver pipes up. "They could have left something behind."

What Piver says makes sense.

"Okay, let's go check it out," you say. "The rest of you, finish the loading and get ready to move out."

It's a quick slide to the spot where the ship was standing and at first, apart from a few scorch marks and some strange dust, the black rock looks the same as everywhere else. But as you are about to suggest a return to the troop, Piver notices a small yellow disk imbedded in the slope.

"What is it?" you ask.

Piver pulls a probe out of his utility belt. He gets onto his knees and wedges it under the edge of the disk.

"It won't budge," the little engineer says. "I think it's fused into the rock." Piver raps the disk a few times with the probe's handle and then stands. "It sounds hollow."

A faint tremor runs though the rock beneath your feet.

"Geebus! Do you feel that? The ground's vibrating."

You point at the disk. "Is that thing causing it?"

Then with a crackling buzz a beam of light, brighter than the strongest torch, shoots out of the disk and up towards the stratosphere.

"What's going on?" you ask Piver. "And why would they leave a light?"

Piver looks nervous. He looks up in the sky, back at the disk, then back at the sky again. His hands are shaking. He knows something that he's not telling you.

"What is it, Piver?"

"I think it's a landing beacon."

"But the only reason they'd need a landing beacon is if they…"

"Were coming back!"

This news is a shock. What do you do?

It is time to make a decision. Do you:

Wait for the ship to return? **P294**

Or

Go back to the Pillars and report the ship? **P300**

You have decided to wait for the ship to return.

Suddenly the light goes off.

"I must have triggered it somehow," Piver says. "What should we do?"

"I think we should wait for the ship to return," you say. "We need to find out what they are up to and if our communities are in danger."

Piver agrees. The two of you slide back over to your troop. When you tell them your plan, most of the sliders nod their heads in agreement. But you see doubt in Gagnon's face.

"What's the matter, Gagnon? You disagree?"

"But how do we know how long they will be?" he says. "It could take years for them to return."

You look up. The mother ship is still visible near the horizon. "Okay, you've got a point. If they don't come back by tomorrow morning, we'll go back to the Pillars and make a report. In the meantime let's move closer to the landing zone. I want a better look at them if they come back down."

Gagnon has his scope out and has spotted a fissure in the slope just above the landing spot. He points towards it. "We can hide in that crack while we wait."

"Good idea, Gagnon," Dagma says. "That way we'll be above them if we need to attack."

You spin and face Dagma. "Take it easy, who said anything about attacking?"

"But…"

"If this ship has come across the galaxy, do you really think its occupants would have any problem dealing with half a dozen sliders with guide sticks and catapults?"

Dagma kicks the ground with her boot. "But I…"

You give the big slider a friendly smile. "Look, I know you meant well. Now, put on your happy face and let's climb up and get settled in that crevasse."

With that, your troop gets ready to move off. The spot Gagnon's located is about 200 yards above the landing beacon.

Once you're all hunkered down, a black tarp, normally used to cover the sledge, is rigged up to hide your position from above. Dagma lights a burner and gets some broth heating.

"We'll take turns on watch," you tell your troop. "An hour each."

As the others nap and tell stories, a lookout watches the ship for signs of activity. An hour later Shoola shouts a warning.

"It's moving west!" she yells

Everyone leaps to their feet and watches as the mother ship moves slowly westward, towards the Pillars of Haramon and disappears beyond the horizon.

"What are they doing?" Piver asks. "Are they going to attack the Pillars?"

"I don't know," you say. "But we can't hang around here any longer. Get loaded everyone. We're sliding top speed to the Pillars."

"Geebus, top speed?"

You nod. "That's right. We'll leave the sledge here and take only what we can carry."

Trodie is concerned. "I don't think Villum and I can slide as quickly as you Highlanders."

Trodie's right of course. They are Lowlanders after all.

"Okay, Drexel can stay with you two. Just slide at a pace that keeps you safe. The rest of us are going to go for it. The Pillars might need all the help they can get."

Sliders are well trained to pack and move quickly. In less than five minutes you, Gagnon, Dagma, Piver and Shoola are ready to move out. Drexel looks a little anxious. He's not that keen about being left behind with Trodie and Villum but he also knows why you've done it and will carry out his instructions to the best of his ability.

"Okay, Sliders on my mark!"

And away you slide, crouching low, your arms tucked to your side to reduce drag, with toes pointed downhill just that little bit more, letting gravity speed you across the slope.

The first run is done in ultra-quick time. When you've lost all the altitude you can afford, Piver sets up a portable launcher and fires a bolt into a pinnacle up the slope. You clamp on your zipper and let it pull you up the fine cable. After removing the bolt, Piver repeats the process until your group has regained enough altitude to start another high-speed traverse.

The speed is exciting. You love traversing as fast as you can. It's a skill you've learned well.

After sliding most of the day your leg muscles burn and sweat drips down your back. Because of the speed you're traveling, you've nearly fallen a few times. Thankfully a quick tap with your guide stick stops you from plummeting to the bottom.

Dagma urges everyone on. Her endurance is only exceeded by her need for competition. The slide to the Pillars soon turns into a race, with each slider determined to be first to the next waypoint.

Piver slides well. His low centre of gravity keeps him balanced. And he's smart. At one point you see him hook onto Dagma's backpack without her realizing it and get a free ride in her slipstream. When she screeches into the waypoint ready for the next zip uphill, her jaw nearly hits the ground when she turns around and discovers Piver standing there giggling with barely a drop of sweat on his brow.

The sun is low and it's nearly dewfall before you see the Pillars of Haramon. Your muscles ache and you back is stiff from the headlong slide back to Long Gully.

You take out your scope and scan the terrain below, not wanting to slide into a trap should the strange flying craft be in control of the base. It isn't until your lens moves up towards the command pod on the northernmost pillar that you see the silver disk sitting on top of the tower.

Gagnon has his scope trained on the pillars too.

"Do you see what I see, Gagnon?" you ask.

"I don't see any fighting going on," he replies. "Everything looks normal."

The navigator is right. You can see sliders going about their normal business. Being near dewfall, sledges are being move into their storage pods and the cableway between the two pillars is moving workers from the command pillar to the accommodation pods in the smaller pillar further down Long Gully.

"It's getting late. Let's go," you say, pointing you foot downhill and pushing off with your stick.

Piver rockets past you. "Last one home's a pango's bum!"

And with that the race is back on. Dagma pushes hard with her stick and drops into a slider's crouch. Her extra weight gives her an advantage over the much lighter Piver. But Piver cuts a clean turn and it isn't easy for Dagma to catch him until he is nearly outside the command pillar. She reaches out with her guide stick and hooks Piver's backpack, pulling the little engineer back.

"That's not fair!" Piver yells as they screech to a halt on the loading platform. "You hooked me!"

The two are still arguing when you and the others slide up. "Piver! Just let it go."

Piver gives you a smile. "Geebus okay. Don't get your boots in a tangle."

"Besides," you say. "I seem to recall you doing something similar not that long ago?"

Piver giggles and turns to Dagma. "Good race. Let's call it a tie."

With your troop happy again, you waste no time entering the pillar and jumping a cable lift up to the command pod. When you step off the lift, members of the council are sitting around the table talking to a young woman dressed in a uniform you don't recognize.

"Ah," the chief says when he sees you. "Come … join us. You look like you've had a long slide." As you walk towards the table, the chief stands. "Let me introduce you to our guest."

"Hello," you say, bumping elbows with the visitor. "We saw you further east and decided to—"

"Make sure we weren't attacking your outpost?" the visitor says.

You can feel your face redden.

"Don't worry. I would have done the same," she says.

"Sit," the chief says. "We've been learning lots of interesting things this afternoon. Commander Helena is from a planet in another solar system. Seems we're related."

"Really?" you say.

"Distantly," the young commander says. "Our ancestors settled this planet many generations ago while traveling between the stars to their new home."

The chief smiles. "She's come back to do a survey to see how we're doing."

You're not quite sure what to say. You've often wondered, while sliding around the Black Slopes, how life began on Petron and why you were here. But you never thought it was a question you'd get the answer to.

"Seems we have more relatives in the interior. Relatives with more tyranium than they know what to do with. Helena's offered to take us to them to talk trade."

"Wow," you say. "We're going to go of course?"

The chief stands. "That's what I want to speak to you about."

You cross your fingers and hope the chief is going to say what you think he is.

"I'd like you to go meet these people of the interior as our representative. You young people are the future of this planet. I think it's only right that you learn as much as possible from our guests in the short time they are here."

You find yourself smiling and nodding eagerly at the chief's suggestion.

"And," he says, "you're young enough, so that in 80 years time, you will still remember this day and be able to say to the others that you saw Helena's ship with your own eyes."

The visitor rests her hand on your shoulder. "I have room in my ship for you to bring a friend along if you'd like. We'll leave first thing tomorrow morning."

"Now I'm sure you're tired after your slide," the chief says. "Go get some rest at report here at sunrise."

You head back down to where your troop is drinking broth and chatting in one of the storage bays. After explaining what you've discovered you have one last piece of news to impart.

"Hey Piver, the commander of the landing ship says I can take a friend along tomorrow when we go to visit the interior. Would you like to come?"

Piver's eye widen, his hands clasp in front of his chest and he does a little jiggle as he looks up at you. "You mean fly in the ship? Geebus! Would I ever!"

Congratulations, this part of your story is over. But have you tried all the different paths this story can take? Have you been to Crater Canyon, or the volcano?

It is time to make a decision. Do you:

Go back to the beginning and take a different path? **P163**

Or

Go to the table of contents and start reading from another part of the story? **P308**

You have decided to go back to the Pillars and report the ship.

"We need to let Command know about this," you say.

You and Piver race back to your troop.

"Dagma, Shoola, Gagnon, get loaded. We're sliding top speed to the Pillars."

"Geebus, top speed?" Piver says.

You nod. "That's right. We'll leave the sledge here and take only what we can carry."

Trodie seems concerned. "What about us? You can't just leave us here."

Trodie's right of course. They are Lowlanders after all.

"Drexel, I need you to escort the Lowlanders back to the Pillars. Just slide at a pace that keeps them safe."

Drexel doesn't look happy, but you know he'll follow orders.

It takes less than five minutes before you and your reduced troop are ready to move out.

"Okay, on my mark! Sticks tight and knees bent."

Piver locks his boots together, ready for the high-speed slide. "Geebus! This should be interesting."

And away you slide, with feet pointed downhill just that little bit more, letting gravity speed you across the slippery black rock.

Despite the urgency of your slide and the wind whistling past your visor, you still have a chance to sneak a glance at the view from time to time. This is the part of being a slider that you love most. Far below, the high meadows are covered in green. Beyond the meadows patterned fields of the Lowland crops stretch all the way to the sea. It is a view you never tire of.

The first run of eight miles is done in record time.

"Set up a launcher and lets gain some more altitude, Piver."

The engineer works quickly. He fires a bolt into a pinnacle further up the slope and everyone clamps on and lets their zippers pull them up the fine cable. After removing the bolt, Piver repeats the process until your group has regained enough altitude to start sliding again.

Dagma races past you. "Come on, we're never going to get home if you slide like my grandmother."

Shoola crouches down lower and pushes hard with her stick in an effort to keep up with her arch rival.

Neither of them see the patch of morph rat slime in their path until it's too late.

Dagma hits the patch of slippery goo and immediately loses her feet. Without the grip her glide boots provide, she immediately veers off down the mountain.

Shoola has enough time to drop her hooks, but she still hits the slime at speed and falls.

Thankfully you and the others are fifty yards back. "Stop!" you yell, dropping your hook just in time to avoid the stinky mess.

You hear the screech of hooks on the mountain below you. Dagma and Shoola are both putting their full weight on their hooks in an attempt to stop.

From your position, you watch the drama unfold. Further down the hill is a pinnacle. Maybe Dagma or Shoola will be able to get an anchor into that. It may be their only chance.

You pull out your scope to follow the action. Dagma has her anchor gun out. "Come on Dagma! You can do it!" you yell in encouragement.

Dagma licks her lips and pulls the trigger. The bolt shoots out of her anchor gun and hits the pinnacle. Now it just needs to hold.

As the cable tightens, Dagma's line down the mountain is altered and she begins to swing in the direction of pinnacle.

Then you see Shoola pull out her anchor gun. But the pinnacle is too far away for her to hit it. None the less she is taking aim at something.

With a pop, Shoola's anchor bolt rockets towards Dagma.

"Ouch!" Dagma yells. "You shot me in the bum!"

Dagma stabs a glance at Shoola then grabs the fine line protruding

from her buttock, and wraps it around her wrist so the anchor doesn't
pull out and Shoola doesn't fall.. "Just you wait Shoola!"

"They're stopping!" you tell the others. "Dagma's line is holding."

Piver is already moving. He has a portable winch set up and is
lowering a line to the two sliders.

It takes about half an hour to winch Dagma and Shoola back up to
safety. Dagma is limping and in pain from the wound in her backside.
Shoola supports her. Once they are both out of danger, Gagnon puts a
medical dressing on Dagma's injury and gives her a squirt of moth
mist to deaden the pain.

"You owe me, Shoola," Dagma says.

Shoola laughs, "Just as well I had a big target to aim at, otherwise
I'd be heading for the bottom."

Then she pulls out a couple energy bars and hands them to Dagma.
"Here eat these, that'll take your mind off things."

"Okay everyone, we need to get moving," you say. "Can you slide
Dagma?"

Dagma nods. "As long as that pango headed Shoola doesn't shoot
in the bum again I'll be fine."

"Right then. Let's get around this patch of slime and get moving."

After another two hour's sliding, your leg muscles ache and your
forehead is covered in sweat. It is nearly dewfall before you see the
Pillars of Haramon.

You take out your scope and scan the terrain below. "Looks
peaceful enough."

Gagnon has his scope out too. "The ship is on top of the command
pillar, but I don't see any panic."

The navigator is right. Sliders going about their normal business.

"It must be okay. Dewfall's not far away. Let's go," you say as you
point you toe downhill.

Once you arrive, you waste no time jumping a cable lift up to the
command pod. When you step off the lift, you see that the council is
sitting around the table talking to a young woman dressed in uniform.

The Lowland general is here too.

"Ah," the chief says when he sees you. "Come … join us. You look like you've had a long day." As you walk towards the table, the chief stands. "Let me introduce you to our guest. This is Helena, commander of the landing craft and representative of Earth II."

You smile at the visitor.

"Sit," the chief says, pulling out a chair. "We've been learning lots of interesting things this afternoon. Our guest here is from a planet in a nearby solar system. Seems we're related."

"Really?" you say.

"Distantly," the young woman says. "Our ancestors settled this planet long ago while traveling between the stars to their new home."

You're not quite sure what to say. It's all a bit of a shock.

"Seems we have more relatives in the interior," the chief says. "Relatives with more tyranium than they know what to do with."

'Wow," you say. "Are they friendly?"

Helena smiles. "As long are you are honest with them, you'll have no problems. But that isn't the reason I'm here."

The chief stands and comes around to where you are sitting. "Now that's what I want to speak to you about." The chief pats you on the shoulder. "I'd like you to go with Helena and be our ambassador to their planet. The time has come to start trading. We have minerals on this planet they need. And they have technology we need. It will be very beneficial for us both. Young people are the future of both planets. That's why I think it's only right that you become our representative ."

You find yourself smiling at the chief's suggestion. What an adventure it will be.

Helena comes to stand beside you. "I have room in my ship for you to bring a friend along if you'd like."

After Helena has answered all your questions, you head back down to where your troop is drinking broth and chatting in one of the storage bays. You can't quite believe how excited you are. After explaining what you've discovered you have one last piece of news to impart.

"Hey, Piver. The commander of the landing ship says I can take a friend along. Are you interested in a trip between the stars?"

Piver's eyes widen and his hands clasp in front of his chest as he looks up at you. "You mean all the way to another planet, in their spaceship?" Piver does a funny little jiggle. "Geebus! Would I ever!"

Congratulations, this part of your story is over. But have you tried all the different paths this story can take? Have you been to Crater Canyon, or to the volcano? Have you fought off the morph rats or discovered giant crystals?

It is time to make a decision. Do you:

Go back to the beginning and try a different path? **P163**

Or

Go to the table of contents and start reading from another part of the story? **P308**

History of Petron.

The Black Slopes are the mountainous region of Petron, the fourth planet circling a yellow-dwarf sun 12,000 light years from the centre of a galaxy, known by some as Andromeda.

The Black Slopes are made from volcanic glass that erupted from Petron's core not long after its formation some 13 billion years ago. As it cooled and hardened, this magma formed razor sharp ridges, half pipes, steep valleys, near vertical cliffs and towering pinnacles. It is a landscape that is beautiful and dangerous.

Petron was colonized long, long ago, by people from another galaxy.

There are three groups living on Petron. The Lowlanders, who farm and fish, the Highlanders who live high on the Black Slopes, and the Others on the far side of the mountains. The Others are the descendents of Eva and her family. Some of this family are part plant and animal. You'll meet them, as well as space pirates, game playing monkeys, and other characters if you read BETWEEN THE STARS.

You are a Highlander, of that you and your family are very proud.

The Highland Sliders are not only a defense force, they are also expert guides, equipped to escort others along a system of tracks the Highlanders have constructed between the various communities, hydro growing centers, and mining operations over the generations. Without a highly trained Slider escort, traveling around the slopes would be near impossible.

But even highly trained Sliders with their tyranium needle-crystal boots and diamond tipped guide sticks know to watch their step on the Black Slopes when it rains.

Although currently at peace, the Lowlanders and Highlanders of Petron haven't always been friendly. For many generations the Lowlanders tried to conquer the Highlands so they could gain access to the Highland's rich mineral deposits and the huge colonies of red-beaked pangos, a bird that provides one of the planet's most valuable and tasty sources of protein. For generations the Highland Slider Corps repelled these invasions.

It is time to make a decision. Do you:

Go back to the beginning of the story and read a different path? **P163**

Go to the list of choices and start reading from another place? (This is also a good place to make sure you haven't missed parts of the story.) **P307**

Or

Check out some more 'You Say Which Way' adventures. **P310**

List of Choices

More 'You Say Which Way' Adventures .

Between The Stars

Pirate Island

Lost in Lion Country

Once Upon An Island

In the Magician's House

Secrets of Glass Mountain

Danger on Dolphin Island

Volcano of Fire

The Sorcerer's Maze Adventure Quiz

The Sorcerer's Maze Jungle Trek

The Creepy House

Dragons Realm

Dinosaur Canyon

YouSayWhichWay.com

Printed in Great Britain
by Amazon